LAURENCE DONAGHY is Belf
for approximately 32.5 per ce
the Falls Road, where he curr
young children. A geek before
follower and writer of sci-fi and ⸗ ⸗ ⸗ ⸗ his life. The first
novel in the *Folk'd* trilogy was published by Blackstaff in 2013, and
the sequel, *Folk'd Up*, was published in 2014.

G000091410

Completely Folk'd

LAURENCE DONAGHY

BLACKSTAFF PRESS

First published by Last Passage

This edition published in 2015 by Blackstaff Press
4D Weavers Court
Linfield Road
Belfast BT12 5GH

With the assistance of
The Arts Council of Northern Ireland

Supported by
The National Lottery®
through the Arts Council of Northern Ireland

arts
council
of Northern Ireland

Typeset by KT Designs, St Helens, England

Printed and bound by CPI Group UK (Ltd), Croydon CRO 4YY

A CIP catalogue for this book is available from the British Library

ISBN 978 0 85640 927 1

www.blackstaffpress.com

*This book is dedicated to anyone who has ever taken
a chance on an unknown author.
And to everyone who enjoyed Folk'd
and told others about it.*

The Future

'Look,' the man on the judging panel sighed, 'you're not bad looking, certainly, but please. The spontaneous human combustion – tired. Juggling cars – yawn. Dancing sharks – seen it. The Britney cover – tuneless. All a bit cruise ship, isn't it?'

A chorus of boos erupted from the audience behind him. The man passing judgment rolled his eyes theatrically and ignored the flashing neon 'TWAT' sign that had appeared above his head. There was a ripple of a cheer, before the sign popped into nothingness once more.

Watching this unfold from the comfort of his living room settee, the father frowned as a silent summons came from upstairs, nudging its way into his mind, a subtle little notification on the taskbar of his cerebral cortex. Getting up, he silenced the viewer and let his wife know that he was on his way.

'You're watching *Britain's Got That X Factor Talent* aren't you?' she asked as he came into the room.

'Um, a bit, yeah,' he said guiltily. 'Lost track of time.'

'Explain how that's possible,' his wife said, projecting a giant image of Big Ben into his mind. She had a point. Nobody in the country had overslept in almost a decade – unless they'd wanted to. You had to be pretty fucking creative with an excuse to your boss these days.

'Thought you'd be done ages ago,' he said. 'What's going on up here? She okay?'

He looked over his wife's shoulder into their daughter's bedroom. The child's sleeping form was visible on the bed, which was unusual in itself. 'She's still here?' he said. 'Why hasn't she flipped?'

'Didn't you get my permission slip a while back?'

He frowned. Come to think of it, there *had* been a tug, right about the time Ant and Dec had been quietly taking the piss out of Buster the Dematerialising Dog. 'Sorry love,' he said, 'I just accepted it, I didn't *oh*.'

She nodded, knowing he had finally bothered to look at what he was giving permission for. 'Oh.'

'She's so young.'

'I know.'

He licked his lips, which were suddenly dry. 'Has she ...' he began, trying to think how he was even going to frame the question without scaring himself. 'Has she recognised any of it?'

'I don't think so.'

Another successful postponement of *that* particular conversation, then. He couldn't help but feel relieved.

She tugged his hand, pulling him into the child's room. 'Come on in. You know what it's like, it's a long oul tale. I've had to break it into segments, and I think she's about to come round from the second. She might want to see us both.'

His nerves jangled. Seeing his daughter's peaceful form, he felt

2

a bit daft for being so nervous. Like every child since the dawn of time, her sleeping form belied none of the mischief going on beneath the surface. If every kid was as angelic as they looked when they slept …

'For God's sake,' his wife clucked, popping the halo he'd unconsciously conjured above his daughter's head. 'What're you like? Ya soppy eejit.'

'You're just jealous cos you didn't get one.'

'A halo wasn't exactly what I wanted to conjure between us tonight,' was the retort. If it was designed to sting more than any cheap comeback, it succeeded.

He watched as his wife curled her fingers around the child's clasped hands and felt her gently bring their daughter out of the embrace of sleep. It was more than sleep, of course; but then everything was *more* these days. His head hurt just thinking about it. There were days he missed the simpler times, when the world got dark all by itself.

'Mummy?'

'Hey, princess. Look who's here too.'

'Right, smelly head?' he winked.

'Daddy,' she smiled, still woozy. 'Is it morning?'

Some older part of him, sensing the glorious light outside, wanted to reply *yes*, but of course it was the wee hours of the night. 'Not yet, sweetheart,' he replied. 'You've not even finished your bedtime story sure. What one'd you pick?'

His wife glanced over at him, surprised at the feigned ignorance. Honestly, he wasn't even sure why he had done so himself, but some daddy radar sense had steered him down that path – correctly, as it turned out.

She threw off the covers and sat bolt upright, vibrating with energy, all wooziness forgotten. 'I'm gettin' the Origin, Daddy! No one else in my whole entire class has heard it yet! Not even big Suzy Robinson and sure she looks about thirteen!'

'Ach away,' he sneered theatrically, turning to his wife. 'Sure she's far too young for that. Can she not have that one about the annoying wee lion who finds out Darth Vader's his da? Or the one about the frigid princess?'

'About the *what* princess?' his wife choked.

''The one that turned stuff to ice. What?' he said, assuming an innocent manner under his wife's suspicious glare.

'Daddy!' his daughter howled. 'I'm not too young for it! I understood every bit of it. Mummy's even letting me hear the version with all the really bad curs–'

Mummy chose that precise second to clear her throat very loudly.

'Cursing, eh?' he asked his wife.

'Frigid?' she replied.

The child sighed, sensing a Mummy-Daddy moment. 'Anyway,' she said meaningfully, 'I've already seen all the start bits: Danny being miserable cos he's got Ellie and Luke and he thinks he should have a great life and a big important job.'

'But he very definitely did have a big important job, didn't he,' her daddy said gravely. 'Looking after his wee chicken Luke, which is The Most Important Job In The World.'

There was an embarrassed silence. Mother and daughter exchanged a look of mutual empathy – the sort of look women have been swapping for eons while in the presence of a man who has just proven to be a disappointment.

'Daddy, d'you think some of them candles on my birthday cake were for decoration?' the child asked, layering enough genuine curiosity into her voice that her mother let out a startled bark of laughter.

Chastened, he remained silent as she laid out the Origin she had heard to date: Danny Morrigan and his trip down the parallel-world rabbit hole into the seemingly perfect, responsibility-free life he had craved. A life he ultimately rejected, before setting out on a quest to find his girlfriend and his wee son.

'So that's where we're up to?' he asked a tad doubtfully, checking the time. 'Cos there's still a lot more.'

'Ach I'm away past that now,' she scoffed. 'Danny's met the Morrigan in the Otherworld and –' the child suddenly shivered. 'Mummy I'm gonna get back under the covers. It's cold.'

Now it was Mummy and Daddy's turn to exchange a look. He grimaced. 'Sure, love.'

Sub-duvet, the girl continued breathlessly. 'But the Morrigan's still trapped as a crow but she's helping Danny by showing him where she came from and all that, it's really good because he realises he was silly and then Carman – the evil oul witch who's kidnapped wee baby Luke – had him killed and put into the Cauldron, but he realised it was a test and managed to pull himself back together and realised his da didn't leave him cos he didn't love him, and now he can use his powers really good,' she paused to service her pressing need for oxygen, 'the bit where Danny got killed was *brilliant* it was all

5

gory an' everything like.'

Somehow he managed to follow the 100mph child-speak. 'Okay.'

'And then Ellie and Steve went to see Ellie's uncle Dermot to see if he could help find wee Luke cos they realised the wee baby Ellie had was a changething–'

'Changeling,' her mother corrected her gently. What did they teach her in that school? She'd have to have a word with Headmistress Greene next time she saw her. 'So is the story magical enough for you now?' she asked.

'Ach yeah, Mummy it's really magical now. There's spells and creatures and it's *class*.'

'And that's what magic is, love?'

The child frowned. 'What else would it be?'

Her mother stifled a smile. 'Nothing. Go on, love, your daddy needs to know where we finished if he's gonna help me create the story bubble and make it even better.'

The child continued, words tumbling out in a rush as she retold the tale of Ellie and Steve's capture by Carman's evil son Dother; of Ellie's father slaying Sarah, the monstrous spider and of Dother killing him in retaliation.

'Oh so *that's* where you got to,' the child's father interrupted. 'Ellie taunted Dother until he grabbed the Sword and all of Ireland vanished?'

'Yes!' she exclaimed, practically bursting with excitement.

He glanced at his wife. 'You left her at that bit? I am impressed at your cruelty, milady. Okay well,' and there it was again, that twinge of nervousness.

Everything in this new world was something more. This wasn't just a bedtime story, it was the Origin. The problem was, it wasn't just the Origin of this world …

'Ready?' he asked his wife, and she knew exactly what he was asking.

'She is, even if we're not,' his wife replied.

The bubble came together under their delicate gestures and ministrations, swirling from their skin, pooling from their pores – a little coloured sphere which caught the light that the blackout curtains couldn't quite shield and threw it off in a myriad of dazzling, beautiful, complex patterns. It was easier to create with two people; the bubble pulsed with vigour, a universe of memory and sensory experience, craving a host –

– and finding one.

Unlike the previous bubbles, this one did not drop gently into an outstretched palm. This one shot like a bullet, a forehead-seeking missile striking their daughter squarely in the temple. She did not cry out or make a sound; she had time for neither.

Both parents eased their now unconscious daughter back onto the bed. The silence inside the room screamed at them. The father's nerves, just as they had before, flared into existence, dropping the ambient temperature by a good ten degrees; their daughter's deep breaths now formed little wisps of condensed air above her mouth. The mother reached over and placed a calming hand on his shoulder to arrest the snap-freeze.

'This is it,' he said. 'There's no going back. When she comes out of this, there's a chance she could know.'

'She already knows what matters,' his wife whispered, transferring her hand from his shoulder to the child's cheek. 'She's our daughter.'

The Change

THE SKIES ABOVE BELFAST, NOW

The 9.15 from Newark, poised to touch its wheels onto the tarmac of the Belfast International Airport, found itself gliding over nothingness.

Captain Lansing, the pilot, was a trained and seasoned professional. Only two years before he had single-handedly landed a plane with two engines out of commission, an action that had earned him a modest amount of media attention.

He panicked.

The co-pilot, Peters, was a novice, not long out of training. He had endured Lansing's arrogance all the way across the Atlantic, listening to umpteen speeches about how he still had a long way to go and a lot of things to learn – he dimly suspected the man was a big fan of the movie *Training Day* – so for the last hour he'd taken to glumly staring at the instruments.

Now, on seeing the pilot panic, Peters indulged in a quarter-second of vicious glee before his flight school training kicked in and he remembered the emergency protocols for landing in poor visibility with inaccurate altitude readings.

He aborted the landing procedure, trying desperately to hail a ground control that was no longer present (impossible) and tell the plane's computers that contrary to readings the plane was *not* taxiing down a runway but still descending into empty space (even more impossible).

Dimly he heard himself scream at Lansing to pull himself to-fucking-gether, then at one of the flight attendants to get the passengers to brace for impact, brace for an emergency landing, brace for *something*–

The plane fought him, but the most impossible thing about all of this, the complete and utter lack of terra firma below, was the thing that was saving them – there was no ground to crash into. The plane continued to descend. According to their instrumentation, they were now at minus 400 feet. Minus 500. Minus 600.

'Where is the fucking ground?' he heard Lansing gibber beside him. 'Where the fuck has the fucking ground gone? What the fuck is going on?'

Peters nudged the nose up, got the plane stabilised. The windows showed only blackness outside. All kinds of half-assed theories were going through his mind. He found himself fervently wishing he hadn't read Stephen King's 'The Langoliers' as a teenager: he half-expected to see nightmarish creatures assembling outside the cockpit window, gobbling up pieces of reality ...

Keep it together, he told himself sternly, feeling his entire body convulse in fear. He didn't want to crumble like the oh-so-heroic Captain Lansing alongside him.

He swallowed, hard. 'I'm taking us back up,' he said, his voice level.

'We need to find the ground!' Lansing insisted. 'It's gotta fucking be there! It can't just vanish, Peters! A whole fucking city can't just up and vanish!'

'Captain, we're already six hundred feet below the surface!' Peters returned. 'The ground is gone. Do you hear me?'

'So why are we going up? Why go up?' Lansing whined.

Peters spared a second to stare directly at Lansing. 'Do you want to be six hundred feet below if it comes *back?*' was all he said.

He'd been afraid that this would push the captain over the edge altogether, but it seemed to do the opposite. Lansing exhaled, straightened his shoulders, and, with a nod at Peters, grabbed the controls. Together they angled the plane upwards and the altimeter began to climb towards zero. When it span into positive numbers both men exhaled as one.

'What the *hell* is going on?' the inflight supervisor demanded from behind them. 'I've got a hundred and fifty people scared out of their fuckin' minds back there … hundred and fifty-one if you include me.'

'We–' Peters began.

'Tell them there's been a power cut,' Lansing broke in. He was all smoothness again. 'We need to go back up, circle awhile, make sure they're ready to have us come in. Nothing to worry about, have a drink on us, sorry for the inconvenience.'

The inflight supervisor was a career woman, with the airline twenty-seven years. Frankly she scared the hell out of Peters – his first flight, she'd given him a look that could have withered Jack's beanstalk.

'Fine,' she said, fairly vibrating with indignation. 'But you tell me right fucking now what's *really* going on.'

The plane banked left. Peters started in surprise; he hadn't initiated the manoeuvre.

'That,' Lansing said, taking one hand off the controls to point. His finger shook. His voice was little more than a whisper. 'That is what's *really* going on.'

The Irish Sea had been halted, as if by the hand of God, in an irregular line. The waters swirled and rebounded off an invisible wall, preventing tens of millions of gallons of seawater from rushing in and filling a great nothingness – a vast void where the island of Ireland had been.

Ireland was gone. Lock, stock and barrel, it was gone.

'Get me Heathrow. Get me Glasgow. Get me *anyone*,' Lansing said softly.

Screams sounded from behind them.

'That'll be the passengers,' the Inflight Supervisor said calmly, as though in a dream. She stared directly at Peters, all traces of her former fearsomeness wiped away. 'I better give them those drinks …'

'Don't let them up here,' Peters told her retreating back. He hated himself for saying it, but it was necessary. Panicking passengers storming the cockpit wasn't going to solve anything, unless you counted the question 'What's the quickest way to get us all killed?'

The door closed. He fumbled for the radio to raise Heathrow, feeling a cavernous pit open in his stomach that threatened to dwarf the Ireland-shaped one hundreds of feet below. What if no one was out there? What if this plane was all that was left, doomed to fly the empty skies looking down at nothing but ocean and former landmasses now removed as simply and effectively as a child might pluck a jigsaw piece from a completed puzzle, until their fuel ran dry and they were forced to pitch into the raging sea …

Fuck you, Stephen King, he thought, and made the call.

DUBLIN HARBOUR, NOW

We're packed in like bloody sardines, Tom Beckett thought, glaring daggers at the rear spoiler of the people carrier in front of him and trying to ignore the the six-year-old brat in the back seat who was pulling the most ludicrously annoying face Tom had ever seen. This was the same kid who'd spent 90 per cent of the voyage over running pell-fucking-mell across the fucking ship while his useless fat parents had sat struggling to breathe as they choked down burgers and fries.

Still. Another few minutes and the ship would be fully unloaded and he could leave that people carrier behind and start winding his way to Mullingar, where even now (according to the last text he'd received, anyway) his fiancée Suzie was browsing her extensive selection of Ann Summers lingerie, choosing the outfit she'd be wearing to greet him when he arrived at her door.

His hands tightened on the wheel. Somehow, that thought wasn't doing much to relieve his impatience with the unloading process …

Ah! The cars were moving! He thanked God and edged

forward, moving slowly from the massive ferry's interior and into the Dublin night, greeted immediately by a spray of water from the wind whipping up the waters below.

That little *bastard* ahead of him flicked him the V-sign. Tom debated whether to return the favour.

It was then that the cars started moving faster. For a whole second, perhaps two, Tom thought that his ship had quite literally come in. He actually smiled.

And then the screaming began.

The people carrier in front of him vanished, allowing Tom to see what lay ahead.

There was nothing beyond the exit ramp.

He slammed on the brakes and the car stopped, briefly, but the untethered exit ramp, no longer anchored securely to the Dublin harbour, was swinging freely and he was unable to stop the vehicle's forward momentum for long. As if to underline this, the white van behind him slammed into his back bumper, forcing him forward. He screamed as his car was pushed over the edge.

He fell into the abyss.

THE LIMELIGHT NIGHTCLUB, BELFAST, NOW

'Decent music!'

'What?'

'I said, decent music!'

She shook her head happily and pointed to her ears. 'Sorry! It's just really loud!'

'I SAID, THE MUSIC IS DECENT IN HERE!'

'The music? Aye! Fuckin' shit, isn't it!'

Cal considered his options for a moment before replying. 'Aye! Shit!'

As the wall of noise continued to pound around them, Alice leaned into him until she was practically nuzzling his ear. Cal felt a bolt of electricity go through him, and wondered at the strangeness of it – he'd had his share of experiences with the fairer sex, and yet the merest hint of a touch from Alice was making him tingly.

'Do you want to get out of here?' Alice bellowed into his ear.

He paused to consider this for as long as would not seem desperately grateful, and then shrug-nodded in a nonchalant, *if you fancy it* fashion. She smiled and slipped her hand into his.

She led him through the mass of bodies toward the exit doors and his mind raced. *Oh my God. It's going to happen. All those Lircom office rumours aren't just going to be just rumours any more. And to think they were offering overtime at Lircom Tower tonight, and I was this close to taking them up on it …*

They were at the club exit doors now. It was early enough that most of the traffic was going the other way, so they had to wait for an opening to pass through. They smiled at each other, and Cal – he of the Withnail fixation and the perfect student-house setup and the friends who had sworn to one another that to get involved with anyone in a serious way would be stupidity on an epic scale – leaned in, turned Alice's face towards his and saw the *yes* in her eyes. He kissed her –

– and the world *changed*.

They broke the kiss, and he saw the *wow* reflected on her face. *She felt it too*, he thought. *Jesus Christ. I've never felt a kiss like that in my entire life.* And then, inevitably, hard on the heels of that thought and panting excitedly like a Tex Avery cartoon wolf, *if that's what a kiss with her feels like …*

There was an opening in the oncoming crowd and they both charged through, hand in hand, neither one noticing that the stomach-dropping sensation they had experienced during the kiss had not been exclusive to them and had, in fact, been shared by everyone.

As they left the nightclub, so enraptured were Cal and Alice by one another that they completely failed to notice the groups of people standing around – some slightly dazed and holding onto walls or one another for support, some looking to the skies above.

Had they looked up, they would have seen that the sky – clear when they had entered the club – was now streaked with thin clouds that crossed the horizon like a thousand skeletal fingers, and which only partially blocked out the moon.

Not a normal moon. Not a pale circle of milky white light, a shining coin in the celestial wishing well. This was a moon not seen on Earth for thousands of years. It was too big, too close.

And it was red. Red as blood.

OTHERWORLD, NOW

The hill playing host to the huge pack of oversized, unearthly wolves began to shift. For a moment it looked as though someone had crudely superimposed a picture of a building onto the skyline – a picture sketched on a balloon that was still expanding, causing the ghostly outline of the building to explode outward in all directions.

The centre of this expansion was not the hill upon which the wolves were gathered, but a circle of astoundingly massive standing stones about four miles away that made Stonehenge look like something from *Spinal Tap*.

As the wolves watched, the mighty monoliths seemed to liquefy into one another, solidifying into the image of a huge skyscraper – one that any resident of Belfast would immediately have recognised as Lircom Tower – before morphing partway back to the standing stones. The oscillation began again, a symphony of topographical mutation, ebbing and flowing, enough to make more fragile mortal minds creak under the strain. The grass beneath the wolves' feet hardened and grew cold and gray.

Like the 9.45 express from Reality, the human world was colliding with the Otherworld.

'Prepare yourselves for the hunt,' the largest wolf, only recently named Wily, called to his fellow pack members. Howls of excitement rang out from all around him. These were the soldiers of the Otherworld, the standing army of Queen Carman's faerie realm. They had gone nameless for millennia until the passing through their lands of a single man.

Danny Morrigan. One of *the* Morrigans. The ancient enemy. Yet he had entered these lands, talked Wily out of eating him, ridden the great wolf over their hills. More than any of this, he had given Wily his name, and the capacity to name others. Like a flame, the desire to claim an identity had spread among their number.

They were the Named now.

The world had changed and it was time to demonstrate exactly how much.

'Show no mercy,' Wily said, as the pack spread throughout the streets of Belfast.

NOWHERE

Even in the formless ether, the between-space he was by now almost accustomed to that signalled his transition between times and places, Danny Morrigan sensed it. A change had been made, like the change he'd performed himself at his father's cottage twelve years in the past, but on an unimaginably bigger scale.

For what seemed like centuries now – and fuck knew, he *had* been a formless body drifting in a blank slate proto-universe where time didn't even exist, so perhaps it *had* been centuries – he had journeyed. To an ancient Ireland he'd thought only existed in legends, to an Otherworld he'd thought was nothing more than myth. To his own recent past to make the kind of peace with his father he'd never considered possible.

Everything he thought he knew about his father, about his life, had been shot to shit. He was part of an ancient bloodline, charged with protecting Ireland from being overrun by a race of beings who had come to be known as – ha! – faeries. Wee green tunic-wearing girls pissing about with Peter Pan? If fuckin' only.

He'd seen first hand the size of some of those faeries – giant wolves so big he'd been able to ride one like a horse; things that looked like enormous wasps, all wings and mandibles, poison dripping from stingers; creatures that oozed along the ground like massive slugs – it was as though Carman, from her throne in Otherworld HQ, had taken everything that walked or scuttled or slimed and had *twisted* them to resemble the stuff of nightmares. They were huge, merciless, and worst of all, intelligent.

The feeling refused to go away. The world had changed.

Something, he thought. *Something ... is different.*

Yes, the Morrigan confirmed, now just an incorporeal voice in his head. She had been there with him, curled up in his mind since this insane vision quest had begun, but back in the Otherworld she was currently trapped in the form of a crow; a mere shadow of her former glory as the Celtic Goddess of War. He had yet to discover what had diminished her powers so. *Time's running out, Danny.*

Where are we going? he asked her.

One last thing you need to see.

Images and sounds sped past him, a movie so accelerated that he would have once found it impossible to follow. Now, he knew how to use his synaesthesia to look with more than his eyes, to hear with more than his ears. In a sense, he had been doing so his whole life; he just hadn't done anything with the data.

He saw the Morrigan returning to the halls of the Tuatha Dé Danann with Glon and Gaim, her two sons. Separated from their human father and exposed to their Tuatha heritage, the two boys grew quickly. In only a few short years, they were as full-grown as human men and mighty warriors, revelling in their demi-god status, fighting alongside their mother with gusto and courage.

And fight they had to. Bres had slowly been granting his Formorian kin more and more powers to lord themselves over their former Tuatha masters. Before long, all-out war erupted between the Tuatha and the Formorians. Danny watched one battle as the massed lines on each side came together with the unmistakable *crunch* of armour on armour, sword on sword.

I recognise this place, he realised. *I know this battlefield.*

It was more than a sense of physical place. When magical beings battled each other on this scale, they distorted such mundane concepts as mere geography. *We've been here before*, she confirmed. *This is Mag Tuired.*

Unlike his first visit here, when the assembled Tuatha Dé Danann – prior to their foolish decision to crown Bres as their King – had massacred the Formorian hordes, he was not standing amongst the fighting. The outcome of the battle, however, was much the same as before. With the Morrigan returned to their ranks, the Tuatha turned on the Formorians and secured their freedom. Bres was deposed as King and Nuada reinstated, his severed hand first replaced with silver and then, through magic, with flesh.

A happy ending? Danny dared to guess.

The Morrigan's voice was there, as ever. *No. Bres lived. And in his rage at defeat, his humiliation at being beaten and stripped of his rule, he reached out beyond the borders of Ireland. He made a call for help across the world and there was one who heeded it.*

Carman, witch-queen of Athens, had answered Bres' call.

To cross the seas between Greece and Ireland, Carman and her sons had turned their attentions to the skies above. Dub had blackened them. Dian had given them violence. Dother had granted them a dark purpose. On ships made of thunder, Carman and her sons made landfall on Irish shores.

Carman's first step onto Irish soil had caused every piece of fruit, every vegetable pulled from the earth to perish, and those remaining under the soil to shrivel. On her second step, all of Ireland's livestock sickened and died, their carcasses swarming with maggots.

On her third step, she'd stepped on a truly *massive* cowpat. The legends were largely silent on this bit.

Her three sons accompanyed her on this journey – Dub, the warrior, a massive and unstoppable force of darkness; Dother, the strategist and the very essence of malevolence, was able to outmanoeuvre the cleverest of the Tuatha, turning overwhelming odds against him into stunning victories on the battlefield; and the youngest son, Dian, the enigma. Where he went, previously harmonious villages erupted into orgies of violence and hatred. Neighbour turned on neighbour, husband on wife, mother on children.

Faced with no food, attacked from all sides by enemies they could not yet comprehend, the Tuatha had converged en masse at the Hill of Tara where the treasures of the Tuatha were kept – the Lia Fáil, the throne of kings which would cry out beneath Ireland's rightful ruler; the Claíomh Solais, the Sword of Light; and the Dagda's Cauldron, which was now the only source of food for the Tuatha. It alone prevented them from succumbing to starvation.

It could not produce enough. We were too many.

Carman had come to the Hill of Tara under a flag of truce and presented her ransom demand – Ireland's food supply would be restored, and she and her sons would leave the island ... in return for the Dagda's Cauldron.

They had faced each other for the first time then, the Morrigan and Carman. Despite her starring role in the second battle of Mag Tuired, the Tuatha were not to be ruled by a woman. So the Morrigan was relegated to an advisory capacity behind her king, Nuada, as he considered the offer.

As a gesture of good faith, Carman produced a gift for the assembled Tuatha, rolling Bres' head to a stop at the Morrigan's feet. His dead eyes stared up into the face of his old nemesis.

For what seemed like centuries, the Morrigan and Carman had stared one another down. Bres had, indirectly but no less deliberately, caused the dissolution of the Morrigan's happy existence amongst humans when he had ordered Formorians to attack the human settlement she had lived in with her husband Caderyn and her sons.

Almost the entire village – all except her own family – had been killed that day. Not at the hands of the Formorians or the Tuatha. When, in the aftermath of the Formorian attack, Glon, her oldest boy was fatally injured by one of the human villagers, the Morrigan had slaughtered every man, woman and child herself.

Afterward, having witnessed his wife's true self, and horrified at her brutality, Caderyn's love for her had been the final casualty.

Bres had caused all of it. He had been hers to kill. Carman

had taken that from her.

Nuada accepted the terms and our food supply did return, so Carman and her sons were allowed to proceed back to their ships.

Contrary to her promise, Carman and her sons did not leave Ireland. She had not taken possession of an artefact as powerful as the Dagda's Cauldron for anything so mundane as producing food or drink.

Instead, she perverted its magic to create an army of twisted beings. The remains of the Formorians; Ireland's native fauna, its wolves, spiders and wasps; shadows of the dark powers she and her own sons possessed – all of these things went into the Dagda's Cauldron. Out came her creations in their thousands – mindless, evil and utterly devoted to her. They were the legions of faerie.

LIRCOM TOWER, BELFAST, NOW

Her son and partner were missing. She'd just left an alternate reality where she was with someone she normally couldn't stand and mother to a baby who had turned out to be a changeling. She'd watched that horrible little monster save her life from a wolf the size of a pony. She'd been a passenger in a car which had been thrown through the front of a house – she was pretty sure a few ribs were broken, her breathing was too wet and, even now, when she brought her hand to her mouth, it came away bloody. A giant spider had tried to kill her and her father – *her father!* – had fought it off and slain it with, of all things, a golf club before he had been run through with a glowing silver sword, dead almost as soon as he hit the ground.

And then Steve ...

Steven Anderson, Danny's best friend and her Bizarro-world beau. She had made a life with him, if only for a few confusing days. Had even shared a bed with him. When they (both) came to their senses, they had shared their first real moment of understanding – veiled through guilt, of course – about what made the other tick.

But Steve was dead now too. Already nursing serious injuries from the car crash earlier, he had been callously tossed from a moving limo on the way to Lircom Tower. 'Unnecessary baggage' Dother had deemed him, laughing. How long before she gained the same status? What made her and Danny's father Tony and her own uncle Dermot essential enough that they had been kidnapped and brought here, to Dother's lair?

She had lost so much over the past few days that she could have just given in to the grief that was threatening to swallow her whole ... instead Ellie Quinn chose strength.

She had taunted Dother over the death of his minion, Sarah, the spider-girl, remembering the anger with which he had run her father – *no don't think of it* – through with the sword. And it had worked; Dother had blustered about plans and last-minute rescues before activating a hidden panel in the wall which opened to reveal the same silver sword that had killed her father.

'I think,' Dother said softly, as they shielded their eyes from the majesty of the Sword of Nuada. 'To hell with the way the story's supposed to go. Let's do this right *now*, shall we?'

He reached out and grasped the sword.

Ellie felt as though she were in a lift that had plunged down a floor or two before stopping itself. The building around them did not so much as tremble but every single human present in the office gasped and clutched at their stomachs at the sensation.

'What did you do?' Tony Morrigan wheezed.

'I'll tell you what he did,' a new voice sounded from behind them. 'Started without me, is what he did.'

As one, they turned and beheld the figure standing between the two guards at the office's entrance.

'Mother,' said Dother.

'*Mother?*' Ellie choked, staring at the figure before her in disbelief. 'But ... but you can't be!'

HILL OF TARA, 46 AD

The scale of the battle was almost beyond his comprehension.

In approaching the circle of standing stones in the Otherworld, he had passed through what seemed like untold throngs of faeries. Five times that number now swarmed all over the Hill of Tara and the surrounding countryside – too many shapes and sizes to catalogue, not all of which even had an easily identifiable analogue in the animal kingdom.

Some, the worst, seemed to spring straight from nightmares – the ones we do not remember clearly; the formless shapes we cannot quite re-coalesce into a cogent shape when we emerge from sleep. They are the creatures that are without form, without purpose. They are the things we *should not* remember; if we did, they would begin to consume our every thought.

Horrors like these had sprung from the same cauldron his own dismembered corpse had been tossed into. The Morrigan's words came back to him – she had spoken of earning the right to return from death unscathed by the Ordeal. Fail to do so ... and this is what emerged.

The odds were stacked, steep, unforgiving. For every ten faeries, one Tuatha. Danny saw more than a few Formorians in there too, fighting alongside the Tuatha. As monstrous as the Formorians had been, he saw clearly the distinction between them and the faeries. The Formorians may have been murdering bastards, but they were a people, a race. The faeries were nothing more than the instruments of their Queen's will. Living weapons. An ancient form of genetic experimentation, with dark magic taking the place of high science. Teeth and claws and fangs to be pointed and expended as necessary.

Expended they were, in their thousands. The Tuatha and Formorians were hopelessly outnumbered, but they were by far the superior warriors. The majority of the faerie gains were made through sheer weight of bodies. He saw two Tuatha surrounded by about fifteen wolf-faeries and watched as the two dispensed faerie after faerie with their massive broadswords. With each swing they grew slower, more fatigued, until the final five wolf-shapes leapt, knocking their swords to the earth. Their screams turned to gurgles as the grass ran red.

Danny was, quite literally, now knee-deep in the dead. Everywhere he looked, corpses were piled high. He couldn't see a single blade of grass from one horizon to the other that wasn't occupied by the dead, those locked in mortal combat, or stained crimson from the slaughter. The stench was overpowering.

Through it all, there she was. The Morrigan – so far from the washerwoman in the human village as to be unrecognisable. Gaim on her left side and Glon on her right, the three formed a triangle of whirling iron that cut through the faerie ranks, felling them with scarcely a pause or flicker of effort, a tornado of death making directly for the centre of the faerie army and the witch at its heart.

Straight for Carman.

At some unwitnessed signal, the crowds of faeries parted to allow the Morrigan and her sons unopposed access. Whether this was Carman's attempt to spare the lives of her troops or a way to hasten the inevitable confrontation, Danny didn't know, although he suspected the latter.

It took little effort for him, insubstantial as a ghost, to move through the armies and follow the Morrigan. He was there when the final few faeries either fell upon her sword or fell away altogether and the Morrigan and her elder sons faced their enemy.

Danny had his first good look at Carman then. Back in the Otherworld, just trying to glance at her face had almost caused his brain to leak out his ears, but here, either due to his partially-there status or to his developing grasp of his powers, Carman projected no such field of confusion around her features.

Without much fuss, Danny's legs went from under him. He fell on his spectral arse, unable to comprehend the implications of what he was seeing.

Who he was seeing.

*

They said it was a black dog. A big, black dog with eyes full of fire and gleaming white teeth, like a shark's mouth. That was the conclusion drawn by the chittering girls in her class at school, the rhyme they chanted as they played skip-rope.

> *Skip skip jump skip! Down St. John's by night*
> *Jump jump skip skip! You'll get an awful fright*
> *Big black hound, come to play*
> *You can't skip or jump away*

They were fools. This was no hound. She knew a wolf when she saw one.

> *Run back home, fast as you dare*
> *Makes no odds, you won't get there*
> *For your every step, the hound takes four*
> *You won't be going home no more*

Entirely unafraid, she sat cross-legged on the cool grass as it padded toward her. It wasn't going to chase her; no, she was certain of that. It wasn't going to eat her.

'You are a very special little girl, aren't you,' the wolf said, in a lady's voice.

'I dreamed of you,' said the girl.

'I heard you crying.'

'I want him to go away.'

The wolf stopped, as though considering its options. She wanted to giggle, but she knew the wolf would not like this, no, not at all. 'I will take his years from him and give them to you,' it said eventually.

The girl considered this. 'I don't understand,' she said.

'He is seven and you are nine. I will remove his years and he will … go away. You will have his years. You will be sixteen.'

Her heart leapt. 'I will be … grown up?' she repeated. She would be old enough to escape the morons in her class, old enough to escape her parents' home. She would have to pretend to be interested in some boy or other to do so. *I can do that*, she thought.

'Is this desirable to you?'

'Yes.'

'I will want something from you in return, little one,' the wolf said, now no more than three feet from her. They had been right about the eyes, if nothing else. She ached to stroke the wolf's muzzle, but some tiny sense of self-preservation prevented her from acting on this urge.

'What do you want?' she asked it.

The wolf cocked its head to the side. 'When you are old and tired, I will come for you. I will eat you all up.'

'I don't want you to eat me all up.'

She expected the wolf to growl or to pounce on her, but instead it almost smiled. 'Child,' it said, 'I promise you this – I will not eat you until you are willing to be eaten. How does that sound?'

The child mulled it over. She could never imagine a time when she would want the big black wolf with the voice of a lady to eat her, so it seemed like a very good deal indeed. Seeing her nod, the wolf did growl, but the little girl somehow knew it was from satisfaction and not anger.

'Bring your little brother to the circle. Bring me little Colm and I will take him away.'

'Will it hurt him?'

The wolf was silent a moment. 'Do you want it to?'

She thought of him, little Colm, the long-awaited son and heir her da had rejoiced to hold, and how he would smile and stamp and get what he wanted, and how ever since he could walk he had been nothing but cruel and spiteful to her without hint of reproach from her ma and da. Seven days ago, tired of him, she had pushed him and, clumsy and fat little thing that he was, he had fallen and broken his arm.

How he'd howled. In the split-second before the cries erupted from him, however, his eyes had met hers and, even as they filled with tears and pain, there had been a glimmer of satisfaction evident, some small nugget of certainty in his countenance. *You hurt me, and how you're going to pay, big sister.*

She bore the bruises from the beating her da had given her, a beating Colm had worn a broad, fat-faced smile of satisfaction to witness.

The wolf licked the big bruise on her leg, and it vanished.

'Yes,' the girl said. 'Yes, make it hurt.'

COUNTY ARMAGH, 1975 AD

'Tell me,' Dother asked Sarah, still in her monstrous spider form. 'How are your typing skills?'

He did not get to hear her reply; the silver Sword of Nuada blazed with light in his hands, illuminating the hilltop on which they stood and the unconscious body of Tony Morrigan at their feet.

'It seems your mother is *very* pleased,' Sarah observed.

But Dother's good humour had gone as even he was forced to shield his eyes from the Sword's light.

'So soon?' he spluttered, as though to thin air. The light flickered in response, pulsing rhythmically – Morse code between the planes of existence itself. 'But you have no-one up here to …' and he trailed off as the Sword beat out a tattoo of light.

'I see,' he said. Beckoning to Sarah, he indicated Tony Morrigan's body. 'Grab him and get out of direct line of sight. Quickly.'

'We're saving him?' Sarah asked disbelievingly. 'He's the Morr–'

'Now!' was the snapped response.

His most trusted lieutenant did not question him further. She effortlessly wrapped Tony Morrigan's body in spun silken thread and in barely ten heartbeats, Dother stood alone.

'This will drain you,' he warned the night. 'Maintaining a physical presence here won't be easy, even for you.'

It was useless to argue. He held the Sword aloft. It flared like a small nuclear blast, one line of plasma arcing itself deep within the earth, the other searing up to the heavens. Dother screamed soundlessly, his flesh burning and bubbling, even as he felt his mother's presence emerge from every blade of grass, every shrivelling insect and dying earthworm for three square miles around him, sucking down the thousands of little deaths like a banquet.

The light died. Dother's body fell, a blackened mockery of a shape, a rasher of bacon cooked at gas mark supernova. Sarah would find him like that, and she would carry him back home as gently as a mother carrying her young. It would take Dother many weeks of agonising regeneration to recover.

His real mother, meanwhile, was long gone. She had an appointment to keep.

REGENT STREET, BELFAST, 1975 AD

Blood spattered the sink below as she coughed, the spasms wracking her entire body. She could do nothing but wait and let them run their course, before wearily beginning to swab and clean the blood. It was the same routine.

A flicker of movement from the plughole caught her attention. A spider leg was emerging. Now a second. The rest of the little beastie heaved itself into her sink, having somehow survived the deluge of water, blood and Christ knew what else she was hacking up these days. It would probably outlive her, at this rate.

It scuttled towards her. She had no great fear of spiders, but she pulled her hand away and ran the taps all the same, watching as it was caught up and washed back down from where it had emerged.

'Sorry,' she wheezed. 'You don't want to be near me, little thing.'

She turned–

The walls of her bathroom were black with them. A seething mass of spiders, emerging from every nook and crevice, every tiny pinhole gap. The ceiling above was the same – a black carpet of spiders, many now dangling from delicate threads to suspend themselves before her face, their legs pulsing. On every surface, they clambered over one another, some losing their grip and falling in that gentle lazy way spiders fall, as though caught by some caring hand. Those who reached the floor oriented themselves and made for her bare and uncovered feet.

She did not scream, or run. The spiders reached her feet and seemed to pause. Then, at some unseen signal, they parted like the Red Sea, creating an arachnid-free channel for her to walk through. There must have been hundreds of thousands of them now, all shapes and sizes – some she swore were not native to Ireland, or perhaps even to this world. The bigger ones trampled over their tinier cousins. One gloriously impossible specimen, with a carapace as black as night, was the size of a small dog.

Passing through her kitchen on her way to her favourite chair for what she was sure was the last time, she was confronted by the smell. The spiders had avoided the fruit in her bowl, and for good reason. It had been fine mere moments ago; now, it had spoiled worse than anything she had ever seen. Strange blue-purple growths had taken hold and the stench was indescribably bad, but she had no more disgust left to give.

'Let me sit,' she said, quietly, and the creatures covering her chair obliged. She lowered herself carefully, wincing at the pain that blossomed, but she forced herself to sit up as alertly as she could manage.

'Knew you'd come,' she said into the swarm.

It is time.

It wasn't the spiders who spoke, because that would have been impossible. And yet, in every way that mattered, the words came from them. She could sense it now; a presence, hovering in the air, nourished by the mass of eight-legged life infesting her house.

'Why did you let me remember?'

Suspended before her, in the tiny stinking little room she called home, the presence with the lady's voice did not answer.

'My da …' she wheezed. 'Without Colm, he was different.'

He did not beat you.

'He did worse,' she said, hugging herself tightly. 'I was sixteen, I always had been sixteen, to everyone else, but in my head I was still just a child!'

I promised you your brother's years. Nothing more, nothing less.

'The pain,' the woman coughed, and kept on coughing. She was just thirty-seven years old, but looked twice that, at least. 'You did this to me?'

I did not make you sick.

'Cancer!' the little figure in the chair managed to say, between the spasms that plagued her.

I do not know this word.

'I don't believe you,' the woman spat, trying to stand, and failing. She pointed a quaking finger at the presence all around her, circling her in a decreasing spiral, a spider circling the plughole. 'How can a fish not know the word for water?'

Little girl, it is time.

'I'm not even forty–'

You are old, and you are tired. It is time for me to eat you all up. Is it not?

The woman thought of the days and nights of pain, and of the dreams that plagued her every time she slept. 'Yes,' she sobbed. 'Yes, it's time.'

Good.

'Will it hurt me?'

Do you want it to?

'Yes,' Bea O'Malley managed. 'Yes, make it hurt.'

With that, the order was given, the dam was released, and the last thing she ever felt was the sensation of millions of spiders climbing her body, biting, biting, biting as they went. They were on her legs and her breasts and on her face and now they were biting her eyes and going into her mouth …

Consider it granted, Carman said, over her screams.

LIRCOM TOWER, BELFAST, NOW

'*Bea?*' Ellie managed.

Bea smiled. As she did so, the image she projected, of the frail little old woman who had lived a few doors down from Ellie and Danny with no life to speak of beyond tea drinking and curtain twitching, that image rippled, as if someone had skimmed a stone across its surface, distorting it for fractions of a second, allowing them to glimpse beneath.

Below that projection lurked something ancient, and immeasurably dangerous.

HILL OF TARA, 46 AD

Carman raised a hand. As one, the faerie army ceased to fight.

'It *can't* be,' Danny kept spluttering, as if the words themselves would rewrite reality and make everything all right again. *Bea? Bea was Carman? BEA?*

A pulse of quiet descended over the battlefield. Carman's orders extended only to her faerie kin, but so thrown by this sudden ceasefire (and, he couldn't help but notice, so grateful for it) were the combined ranks of the Tuatha and Formorians that they, too, stopped whatever duels they were engaged in.

Feeling faintly ridiculous, Danny got to his feet on legs that were still slightly unsteady. All of the confidence that had been building in him was draining away, and quickly. How could this be? How could Carman – Carman the witch, Carman the unstoppable force – how could she be the little old woman from a few doors up the street? The same little old woman who had ... first mentioned faeries, and the supernatural ... had a bowl on her kitchen table with fruit that had rotted away to filth ... been unaffected by the changes the Sword had made to the world ... brought him to the gateway to the Otherworld ... *Satan probably has his da check under the bed to make sure she isn't under there ...*

'She wanted me in the Otherworld,' he said softly, feeling like the world's biggest dickhead. 'She wanted me there all along.'

'Hear me!' Carman was saying, her hand still held aloft, her words carrying across the massive battlefield. Now that he was over his initial shock, he could begin to take in the rest of her appearance. She was Bea, there was no doubt about it, but she looked a good twenty to twenty-five years younger than the tea-obsessed version of herself she'd used to masquerade as a geriatric Regent Street resident.

Yet, as in the circle of standing stones in which he'd first laid eyes on her, Carman's features suddenly flowed and rippled, and the likeness of Bea retreated like the tide to be replaced by one, ten, a hundred other visages.

Danny realised the truth. Yes, Carman was Bea, or at least had been possessing the body of a woman who called herself Bea, but that no more forced Carman to resemble that woman than water poured into a jug would forever retain the shape of the jug itself. His newly-sharpened synaesthetic abilities had merely illuminated the truth and, now that he no longer needed the revelation, Carman's features flowed once more, never truly settling.

Regardless of her mobile features, she looked every inch the queen – proud, fierce, tough as nails. With Dub looming behind her, however, it perhaps wasn't surprising she looked confident. That fucker was so big he practically had snow on his shoulders.

'Be silent, witch.'

As imposing as Carman looked, the Morrigan was every bit her equal. The energies of battle had not wearied her as they had, fatally, some of her kin – instead, it was as if she'd been feeding from the carnage on all sides. Power seemed to crackle from her skin, earthing itself into the grass around her feet. Her words, like Carman's, easily carried across the distances to be heard by the assembled combatants.

'You call for respite because you realise this battle is not the foregone conclusion you assumed it would be. Your creatures are no match for true warriors. Go back to Athens and resume begging the gods of Greece to notice you.'

When the words *true warriors* had passed her lips she had nodded, almost imperceptibly, to indicate her own sons. Glon and Gaim, realising they were being cited in their mother's speech, straightened their backs and hefted their axes, faces encrusted with faerie blood.

Yet Danny still saw in them the two messy little urchins that had jumped with abandon onto their mother's back in that washing-pool. It had been a different lifetime, a different existence, but buried under the Tuatha lineage, under all the myth and the pomp, some part of those two little boys in the muddy pool remained.

Danny was surprised to find himself suddenly angry. Was this really any life for two wee fellas? War and death? He thought back to Caderyn, the Morrigan's human husband, and his insistence that she would not take their youngest son, little Coscar, too. The man had been right.

Carman regarded her battlefield rival and smiled the slowest, cruellest smile Danny had ever witnessed. 'Ah,' she said. 'The mighty Goddess of War lectures me on begging. Does your expertise come from your desperate pleas for your human husband to take you back?'

As one, tens of thousands of hardened Tuatha warriors and faerie monstrosities retreated a step. Danny had been around his own ma long enough to recognise the look on the Morrigan's face. 'Ohhhhh *fuck*,' he said softly.

'I *will* possess this lovely island,' Carman went on as if the

Morrigan were unworthy of further discourse. 'Every blade of grass, every fortress, every stream. Just as you took it from the Formorians, so I shall take it from you,' again, there was that smile. 'You have simply met your superior.'

'Then,' the Morrigan hissed, 'we have nothing further to discuss.'

Her body tensed as if to spring and Danny could sense the *moment* in the battlefield around him. Hands tightened on weapons, claws were readied, muscles tensed as if some great finger was about to press 'play' again and unpause the panorama of butchery.

'Wait!' Carman said. 'I tire of slaughter. There is a more civilised option. Nominate a champion and I will fight them, to the death. Winner take all.'

Of course. This battle – this entire war, immense in scale though it was – was, essentially, a sideshow. It was always going to come down to this.

The Morrigan did not reply right away. Silence descended, and to fill the time Danny found himself wandering closer to where his sometime companion, sometime tormentor stood, unblinking, before Carman. The old 'if looks could kill' adage was so insufficient to describe the intensity of the staredown between the two women it was laughable.

'She's going to cheat,' he said.

'No shit,' the Morrigan murmured right back.

He recovered from this particular shock rather quickly. The surprises had been coming so thick and fast just recently that he was becoming practised at it.

'You can see me?'

'My memories. My rules.'

So someone *had* pressed pause. It made sense now. He looked back at Carman, awaiting the response, and then back at the Morrigan. 'You accepted, didn't you? It's what you were hoping for anyway, right? Back to your warrior days. Back to the Goddess of War, with your sons at your side, and now a free crack at the bitch-queen fuckin' about with the entire island? You must've been ecstatic.'

He was surprised to see her shoulders sag, before reminding himself that this was, after all, a simulation, and not how the real event had unfolded.

'At this point,' she admitted, 'all I was thinking about was my husband. The night before this battle, Nuada had expected me to come into his tent. To lie with him.'

'Lie with–?'

She fixed him with a glare. 'Do you need me to draw you a picture?'

He coloured. Fair enough. 'But why?'

'It's linked to my powers. At the moment of,' and she paused, 'clarity, I am able to divine a plan of battle that ensures victory to the side I favour. It becomes prophecy.'

'Part of the whole Goddess of War thing?'

'Yes,' she said sardonically. 'Part of that whole thing, yes.'

'But not this time.'

'Not this time. Not since my return.'

'Because of Caderyn.'

'Yes.'

'That's …' he floundered, at a loss for what was expected of him. 'That's good?' he hazarded.

'*Good?*' the Morrigan bit back. '*Good?* Look around you. Look at the dead. My role, my *duty*, was to my people. Because of me, we had no battle plan beyond pointing and charging, and look where *that* got us.'

'But,' he said, confused now, 'you did it out of love.'

'Love?' she spat. 'Let me show you, Danny, what *love* is responsible for.'

With that, she seemed to jerk out of her director's commentary role and back into the feature presentation.

'I accept,' she snarled at Carman. 'Name your time and place. It is,' she looked physically ill, 'your right.'

'Tonight, at dusk. On the summit,' Carman replied. If she was pleased that her plan to lure the Morrigan into single combat had worked, she betrayed no outward sign of pleasure.

'Weapons?'

Now Carman did smile. Danny rather preferred it when she didn't.

'Only what we take with us,' she said.

LIRCOM TOWER, BELFAST, NOW

'You? You're not Carman.'

Bea swung her attention to Tony. 'Oh no?' she said.

Tony didn't so much as flinch. 'Not a fuckin' chance,' he said. 'Carman's trapped down there. That's the whole reason for all of this, isn't it?'

Bea laughed. 'Down there?' she repeated mockingly, moving towards the floor-to-ceiling windows of Dother's office. She gestured to the night sky outside. 'Look.'

Unable to help himself, Tony stepped towards the window, Ellie and Dermot following suit. Only later would he wonder if it really was his own curiosity that drove him forward or whether his body had no option but to comply with Bea's order.

'What are we supposed to be–' Tony began, and then his voice caught in his throat, for he saw it. They all did.

The moon had emerged from behind the clouds, huge and red. Bathed in its crimson light, Belfast looked like a city during wartime, besieged and aflame. The rippling waters of the harbour, themselves ruby-lit, only added to the hellish appearance; as though the Irish Sea had become the River Styx.

Bea placed her hand against the glass and suddenly they could hear the sounds on the streets below. The screams.

'What's happening down there?' Ellie was the first to speak.

Bea smiled. She met Dother's eyes and her smile was reflected in his own expression. Her gaze moved to Tony, just long enough to confirm that at least one human observer knew *exactly* what was going on.

'Sport,' she said.

BELFAST CITY CENTRE, NOW

'Keep running!' Cal said. 'Alice, we have to keep running!'

'I can't!' Alice sobbed. 'I can't!'

Her breath was coming in ragged gasps. She was pulling more

and more on his hand now, tugging him back. He could either cut her loose or stay with her, but there was no decision to be made – he stopped, pushed her into a doorway and placed his hand over her mouth as he tried to get his own ragged breathing under control, tried to stay quiet.

They hadn't moved fifty feet from the nightclub when it had become abundantly clear that something was very, very wrong.

The first clue had been the screams. One had rung out, a few streets away and was upsetting to hear, but not exactly completely uncommon in Belfast in the wee hours. Cal's hand had tightened around Alice's and he had drawn her closer to him.

The second scream caused them to stop walking. It was coming from directly ahead, around the next corner in fact. The third, forth, and fifth screams – at least two of which sounded as if they had come from men – came from behind them. They turned, still able to see the entrance to the nightclub, and saw a group of *somethings* move in a way that people couldn't towards the nightclub entrance. The doormen there, to give them credit, stood their ground.

It did them no good.

Something carried across the chill evening air. Not a scream this time, a growl. Low, animalistic, guttural. Hungry.

The young couple had been paralysed for a moment, not knowing what to do, what to think, where to run to … and then the moon had emerged from behind the clouds, and the world had been painted in scarlet hues, and from around the next corner a dark pool had begun to seep.

They had run. How far they had moved before something had begun to give chase Cal wasn't sure. He knew only that they'd been joined in their flight by other refugees of the chaos. He had met the eyes of one young guy, a few years younger than he, and seen the terror there as something had sailed through the air from behind him as he'd passed the mouth of an alleyway. He'd gone down screaming and been pulled backwards into the darkness, crying out for someone, anyone, *please* to stop and help him–

Cal ran without looking back.

Now, sandwiched in the doorway with Alice, screams punctuating the night air every few seconds, peppered in-between times with the occasional low growl that signified the endless movement of the things that were out there, hunting.

A growl sounded. Close. Alice's chest, which had only just stopped heaving from the exertion of the sprinting they'd done, began to rise and fall rapidly again next to him. Not so long ago, he would have been thrilled to have felt that. Now, all he could think about was survival.

He bent down, picked up a piece of loose masonry from his feet. It was little more than a pebble. Against these things, it would be less than useless. Another growl sounded, this one closer. It was toying with them.

He leaned in close, just as she had done in the nightclub. 'When I say run, you run,' he hissed.

Something in his face, his voice, negated the possibility of argument. She nodded.

He emerged from the doorway and faced the thing that was stalking them.

At first, it seemed almost human-shaped. Cal blinked, and like one of those old lady / young woman optical illusions, now it was anything but. It was a massive bug, segmented, with a head that could pivot in a full circle, and eyes that took up half of its head – compound eyes in which he could see his own terrified face reflected. The bug-thing opened its mouth and issued a rapid series of *clak-hiss* noises, even as viscous goop slavered from its fang-laden mouth.

It was going to attack. Cal hefted his rock and bellowed to Alice to run, run, *RUN*! The thing leapt, and as time stretched some small part of Cal's brain registered that aside from this thing's *clak-hiss* noises; he could hear an animalistic growling.

The wolf came out of nowhere.

One perfectly timed leap, one precise snap of its jaws, and it was all over.

LIRCOM TOWER, BELFAST, NOW

Bea removed her hand from the glass and, like a curtain falling, the silence descended once more, the screams from below cut off abruptly.

On Dother's desk, his phone rang. It was such a domestic, everyday occurrence that it seemed jarringly out of place with the events unfolding. As such, it attracted all of their attention.

'The phones still work?' Bea said, surprised.

'Lircom *have* won several customer service awards, Mother,' Dother said, wounded by the query. 'Besides,' he added, perhaps seeing his mother's expression darken, 'how do you think we're harvesting the fear of the humans? The first thing they do now when presented with an event of any kind is to reach for their smartphones.'

'To call for help,' Bea nodded, smiling with understanding. 'Perfect.'

'*Call?* Oh good God no,' Dother replied, aghast. 'The older ones maybe, but anyone under the age of thirty will be social media-ing like a maniac right now. Update to Facebook: *Argh! I'm being mauled alive by a giant wasp!* he chuckled. 'Lircom, of course, will Like this immediately.'

'My son, you've been up here too long,' Bea observed.

Dother shrugged. 'After a few hundred years, it grows on you.'

'So long as it hasn't made you soft.'

Dother's phone rang again. Bea glanced up in obvious annoyance. Dother shrugged in a *What am I supposed to do?* way. He reached down and with one casual yank ripped the phone out of its wall socket.

'You're right,' Bea turned her attention to Tony. 'My power was trapped down there, in that prison. The safeguards placed against me escaping were fiendishly clever. But thanks to my clever boy,' she nodded to Dother, who accepted the accolade with a slight incline of his head, 'I was able to extend my influence …' she sighed, '… on the surface …' she sighed again, louder, '… and live in your world … Fuck's *sake* will someone answer that fucking phone?'

Dother, by now extremely puzzled, reached down to the freshly-disconnected phone which was indeed ringing once more.

He lifted it to his ear, raised an eyebrow, shrugged, and replaced the handset.

'Wrong number?' Bea asked, barely keeping her voice under control.

'Dead line,' Dother replied.

'As I was saying,' Bea went on, sending one final look at her son, 'to borrow a human phrase: if you cannot go to the mountain, then merge two dimensions together at a metaphysical crossroads. I could not leave the Otherworld – at least not completely – so I had your world brought to me.'

'You lived in my street. You wanted to do my tea leaves,' Ellie said. She sounded as if she were speaking in slow motion. 'Last week you gave me a recipe for soda bread.'

Bea paused in her monologuing. 'Ach, so I did. Did you get a chance to make any?'

'No,' Ellie said, still sounding like a robot. 'I didn't have any buttermilk.'

'Ach, you should have said. I'd a carton of it in the fridge. Doesn't go off til next Tuesday.'

Dother coughed significantly. Bea glanced at him.

'Soft?' was all he said.

Bea's face darkened. 'Be careful how you speak to m–'

To his last breath, Tony Morrigan swore he never saw Ellie move. One minute she had been standing dumbly with the rest of them talking about her bitterly disappointing lack of buttermilk, and the next, she had crossed the room and, fist moving like the wrath of God, had laid one right on the old lady.

The body of Beatrice O'Malley rocketed backwards from the

blow and her head hit the window with a wet *crack* before she slid down to crumpled heap on the floor.

The whole world, blood-red moon and all, seemed to take a sharp intake of breath.

Ellie Quinn, fist still clenched, looked at the haphazardly sprawled body of the old-age-pensioner-slash-demonic-witch-entity she had just laid out. She was trembling like a leaf, her cheeks flushed, her eyes narrowed, focused on the seemingly-frail figure. When she spoke, it was not a shout, it was not a screech. It was a simple statement of how things were going to be.

'You will give me my baby. I don't care who you are. I don't care what you are. I don't care where we are, why we're here, or how many centuries this has been foretold. Give me my little boy. And if so much as an eyelash has been nicked, I will kiss him and I will put him somewhere safe, and then I will come for you. I will come for Every. Single. Fucking. One of you. And it won't matter what's been foretold in what prophecy, what grand plans you've made, what magic you've performed, none of it will matter because nothing will keep me from you. You killed Steve. You killed my daddy. You took Danny from me, you took Luke from me. It stops, now. It ends, now. *Give me my baby.*'

Tony felt like punching the air, or punching one of the hulking guards, or punching Dother in his smug face. Right then he felt like he could have taken on the lot of them. *Danny you lucky bastard.*

'Lovely speech,' Dother commented. 'Just one problem,' and he walked to where Bea lay crumpled against the glass. He lifted her head from her chest in a move that Tony first imagined was intended to rouse her from the impact but when Dother let go, Bea's head lolled to the side, eyes wide and staring in a final snapshot of surprise. 'She's dead.'

'Oh,' was all Ellie said.

The huge, hulking guards began to close in on the group. Dother straightened up, homicidal intent on his face. There was nowhere to run, nothing to fight with. Tony searched desperately for a weapon – anything. He tried to lift the chair he'd been standing beside. It was bolted to the floor. Though, even if he had lifted it, it looked as if nothing short of an RPG round would dent the huge fuckers approaching them. If they were amazed at the death of their Queen, their anger had quickly covered that up.

'Yip, we're pretty fucked,' Tony said.

Ellie glanced at him. She knew it too. 'I'm sorry,' she said.

'Sorry? Ellie, love, don't you dare be sorry,' Tony was grinning from ear to ear. 'I have never been more proud of anyone in my entire life.'

She found the time to smile weakly back at him before, with a bestial snarl that belied his respectable businessman veneer, Dother launched himself forward. Tony tried to defend himself, tried to push Ellie behind him, but it was irrelevant.

When the killings came, mere seconds later, they were swift and efficient.

HILL OF TARA, 46 AD

Dusk had fallen on the Hill of Tara. From the eastern and western edge of the summit's crest, their amassed armies grouped behind them, the Morrigan and Carman walked toward one another.

'What's going to happen?' Danny couldn't help but ask the question.

What always happens, in life, the Goddess of War whispered in his mind. *Nothing you expect.*

BELFAST CITY CENTRE, NOW

Cal stared down, open-mouthed, at the remains of the creature that had threatened him, even as the giant wolf released the carcass from its mouth.

'You're welcome,' the wolf grunted, glancing at the humans before it with what looked like bemusement at their paralyzing fear.

A second wolf appeared at its shoulder, sniffing the air. 'How goes the hunt?'

'Prey is plentiful. Protect the humans. Serve the Morrigan. Honoured are the Named.'

'Honoured are the Named,' the second wolf responded, and leapt, gone in an instant.

'What the fuck *are* you?' Cal managed to say.

The great wolf examined him, and despite the fact that it had just saved his life, Cal couldn't quell the fear shaking through every part of his body.

'My name,' the massive creature said, with evident pride, 'is Wily. And I am not a *what*.'

*

Tom couldn't quite process the fact that he was still alive. He was quite pleased about it, you know. All things considered it was one of the better things that had happened to him tonight, this whole 'not being dead' thing. Though, seeing as how his car plunged off a ferry exit ramp into an endless abyss tonight, it wasn't up against particularly stiff competition. It was, quite frankly, a proper fuckin' puzzler.

He had come to only moments ago, his head resting against the steering wheel. The car was sitting motionless on a dark, flat surface. He could see lights though the windscreen and, turning on the car's headlights, he made out the shape of several other vehicles, also with their lights on, including an Ulsterbus tour bus and the people carrier which had plunged into the nothingness seconds before he had.

As his senses sharpened into focus, he caught a whiff of something unpleasant and reached down to his lap. 'Aw, fuck's sake ...'

Strangely, his mental ship began to right itself after that. He had a case full of clothes in the boot and a toiletries bag so he got out of the car and stepped onto the table-flat surface. He wondered if he should call out – or would that bring some sort of messy death upon him? If this was Hell, would his cries attract creatures or demons or something?

Besides, he smelt of piss. Get a pair of clean trunks on first, then exploration.

As he opened the boot of the car he heard the unmistakable sound of a car door shutting somewhere off in the distance. So others had survived too then. Well, it was reasonable to assume they had – if his car could plummet for what seemed like about a week before coming to a gentle stop on all four wheels with no outward signs of damage, why couldn't theirs?

Ha ha ha, some part of Tom's mind was giggling throughout all this. *Ha ha ha.*

He was vaguely worried by this, as it seemed like a classic sign that he was losing his shit. He decided, as he found a plastic bag with tie handles and piled his pissy clothes into it, that he would worry about the *ha ha ha* later on.

'Hello?' he called out. He needed a torch; the only light down here was coming from headlights. He looked up, and for a wonder, saw stars, but only on about half of the sky. The other half was pure inky blackness, and … and …

… moving. The sky was moving. More accurately, the sky was rippling.

Ha ha ha. Ha ha ha.

His phone! Of course. It had one of those torch apps on it. He fished it from the glove compartment and, before he found the correct app, realised he had full bars.

Forty-two missed calls. It had been on silent.

The phone started flashing again and his mother's picture appeared on the – *ha ha ha* – screen of the – *ha ha ha* – phone. She was phoning him right now – *ha ha ha.*

'Mu-Mummy?' said the thirty-four-year-old man as he answered the call.

She shouted and screamed and rejoiced for a full five minutes while he stood dumbly and listened and waited for her to stop. He was alive! Alive, her little boy! Did he realise what had happened to the entire fucking *island* of Ireland? Did he have any *clue* what had happened? And yet here he was, her precious son and *he was alive!*

Another driver must have regained consciousness then, because a new set of headlights flicked into life close to where he was standing. This car was facing the other way.

As his mother raved her delight, Tom walked forward, slowly and deliberately, into the path of light. Others were there too, he saw. Others had already seen what they were close to and had approached it also.

He was barely feet from it now.

Towering above all of their heads, stretching high towards the heavens, was a great wall, a towering immensity which had blocked half the stars from view.

Well, okay, it wasn't a wall, per se. Walls were solid and not, for example, made out of water, because that would – *ha ha ha* – be crazy! You couldn't form a small bucket of water into a wee tiny wall, let alone get what looked like tens of millions – *ha ha ha* – of gallons of water to act as a fucking massive wall! Except that presumably you could. Because here it was.

The blackness that he now knew to be water seemed to stretch on as far as the eye could see. Kneeling down, he ran his fingers along the ground. It was impossibly smooth, impossibly featureless. There was not a grain or a pebble. Something had buzz-sawed Ireland down to its bedrock and spirited it away. Something held the seas in place around where its borders once lay.

'Thomas!' his mother was screaming down the phone. 'Thomas

speak to me! Where are you? What's going on?'

He was already running back to the car. It roared into life first go, thank God, thank God. Others around him were doing the same. The driver was piling passengers back into the Ulsterbus as fast as he could shove them. Sightseeing was over.

'Can't talk now, Ma,' he said, ending the call, setting off across the great plains of the former Irish landmass. Everyone standing before that great wall had had the same thought, all at once – if an entire sea could be held back at a whim, it could be let go just as easily.

LIRCOM TOWER, BELFAST, NOW

Dother's opponents hadn't stood a chance. They'd barely had time to register his attack before he had cut them down, one after the other, with barely a pause between kills.

He stood in the midst of the carnage, surveying the corpses strewn at his feet.

Scarcely daring to breathe, completely unscathed, Tony, Ellie and Dermot tried to process the last few moments.

Dother had cut clean through his own guards. As they had been poised to take revenge on the humans who had caused Carman's death, her own son had eviscerated them without even breaking a sweat.

Dother had saved their lives.

'Right,' their saviour said briskly, wiping blood and entrails from his previously-immaculate Savile Row suit with a faint look of distaste. 'Questions?'

If there were indeed questions to be asked, they never got a chance to voice them, for, in the centre of Dother's office, an object had popped into existence and a creature emerged from its depths.

Ellie's first instinct was to scream.

The Rescue

Danny didn't know what kind of battle to expect. He'd half-anticipated some sort of all-out gymnastic extravaganza, with Carman pulling off triple somersaults, blades flying, like something from *Star Wars*.

It wasn't like that at all. Oh, it wasn't dull, or amateurish – both of the fighters were obviously immensely skilled. The Morrigan wielded Nuada's Sword while Carman had a pair of daggers which, if Danny was honest, didn't seem very magical at all. At least if you didn't count the skill with which she manoeuvred them through the air, fending off her opponent's attacks.

They circled each other, probing, waiting for some sign that the other wasn't quite as ready as they should be. If such a sign was given, then the other would immediately close in and blades would whirl and clang, almost too fast to follow, yet there was no hint of showiness. This wasn't about pretty choreography – it was about finding an opening and using it to press the advantage. It was about trying to take the other woman's head clean off her shoulders.

Throughout this the two armies had gathered on either side to watch. The only beings within the circle of combat were the two opponents, Carman's three sons, and the Morrigan's sons Gaim and Glon.

Hatred crackled in the air. The periods of calm between the short exchanges of metal on metal were, he found, much more intense than the actual fighting. Neither woman taunted the other. No words were spoken, but plenty was communicated in that silence. It was mostly of the *I'm gonna kill you slowly and painfully* variety, admittedly, but there was plenty of it.

The Morrigan lunged, swinging the Sword in a wide arc. Carman leapt, slashing with the daggers, forcing the Morrigan to throw herself to the left. Even as she fell the Sword came up, fending off the daggers as Carman attempted to slash her throat. The Morrigan sprang to her feet, kicking out, catching Carman off-balance and toppling her over.

Carman turned her forward momentum into a roll, and the Morrigan's downswing found earth instead of flesh, the Sword biting deep into the hilltop. She tried to pull it free and realised that, in the time it would take to do so, Carman's daggers would run her through. Instantly she abandoned the attempt to free her weapon, leaving it half-buried, and brought up her arms to grab Carman's wrists and lock on.

They stood together, toe to toe, almost nose to nose, their arms straining. The two points of Carman's daggers glittered in the sunlight as the witch tried to force them downward, into the Morrigan's breast.

Only now was the silence broken.

'Is this it?' the Morrigan said. If the tug of war she was engaged in was causing her any physical stress, her voice did not betray it. 'This is the mighty Carman of Athens? Little wonder Olympus rejected you.'

Carman roared in anger at this, but could not move her daggers any further. Danny could see the strain etched on her face, she was no match for the Morrigan's strength. Her wrists were being forced back on themselves, and those glittering points began to turn accordingly, to point back at their owner.

'Fool,' was all Carman said. 'Now!'

At this signal, her sons moved. Dub's physical form imploded and then expanded as he morphed from oversized human into a cloud of darkness in a fraction of a second. The darkness shot across the combat circle, but did not go anywhere near his mother or the Morrigan.

It went straight for Glon and Gaim.

A howl of anguish escaped from Carman's lips as the Morrigan's hands clamped around her wrists. The daggers were lost from her suddenly-numb fingers and in the Morrigan's control in a heartbeat. She swept Carman's feet from beneath her and in a flash was kneeling over her prone adversary, a dagger poised at each ear.

Meanwhile, Dub's ethereal form had barrelled full-on into the two younger Tuatha. Confused, they had tried to fight it, but how exactly were you supposed to fight something almost entirely without substance? As Danny watched, horrified and fascinated in equal measure, he could see solid shapes in the dark cloud; onyx fists, blue-black against the blackness, that lashed out with lightning speed and effortlessly incapacitated the

Morrigan's sons. As they slumped, Dub's form re-solidified back to human.

'Go ahead,' Carman rasped. There was no fear in her voice, only triumph.

Poised to deliver the killing blow, the Morrigan could not help but turn her head to take in the sight of her sons, semi-conscious, their arms pinned securely behind their back. Glon was held by Dub, Gaim by Dian. Both of Carman's sons held daggers against the throats of their hostages.

Dother, Danny couldn't help but notice, hadn't moved a muscle. He stood stock still at the far end of the combat circle amongst the various bits of equipment and apparel Carman had brought.

'You have broken the covenant,' the Morrigan said heavily. She beckoned for her fellow Tuatha to come to assist. They tried to enter the combat circle, but were stopped by some intangible force at the perimeter.

'I have broken nothing,' Carman replied from beneath her. 'We agreed on choice of weapons. Have you forgotten?'

'Whatever we take with us,' Danny murmured. Which, for both women, had included their sons. He could see realisation dawn on the Morrigan too, as her eyes moved from the helpless opponent lying at her feet, to her sons, similarly helpless, now coming back to consciousness and realising the predicament they were in.

'Do it, Ma,' Glon urged her, refusing to be cowed. Danny could see in him the little boy who had jumped onto his mother's back in an effort to save Gaim from another ducking in the washing-pool. 'Kill the witch and be done with it.'

As for Gaim, he said nothing. He met his mother's eyes and Danny could see that the younger boy – *man* – didn't trust himself to speak, couldn't be sure that his words would be as brave and self-sacrificing as those of his big brother. So he said nothing, just looked at his mother with one corner of his mouth twitched upward in a brave attempt to smile.

Horns blew, long and loud.

Danny looked for their source, Tuatha or faerie, and soon realised neither was the cause of the blast. The thousands peppering the Hill of Tara from both sides were belatedly realising that they were not alone any more.

From all sides, from everywhere it seemed, humans were approaching, encircling the amassed ranks of Tuatha and faerie alike.

The horns blew again. As the approaching army – as surely it was – grew closer, Danny could see standard-bearers. He didn't recognise the colours, but something about the cut and cloth of the humans seemed familiar.

Within the combat circle, no-one had so much as blinked. They were not ignorant of the new arrivals, but no outward acknowledgment had yet been made. Most likely each side knew that the slightest drop in guard could lead to the beginning of swift carnage.

Still the humans came, more and more, pouring from every direction. As impressive as the numbers of faerie and Tuatha had seemed, they were nothing compared to the force of arms being demonstrated here. As far as the eye could see, heavily-armed men stood shoulder to shoulder, arranged in neat rows. They looked well drilled, professional – this wasn't some small incursion, this was an invasion.

The advance stopped at the foot of the hill, just shy of the Tuatha on one side and the faeries on the other. A few of the faeries snapped and circled menacingly, but there were no outbreaks of violence. He wondered if Carman, even prone and with daggers at either side of her face, was exerting some sort of invisible control over her monstrous creations.

Horns blew again. The ranks of men parted at the bottom of the hill, and a small party emerged from within. He heard distant voices, saw the Tuatha who had earlier attempted to come to the Morrigan's aid conversing urgently amongst themselves. Some sort of decision was made.

A party of men began to advance up the hill, the Tuatha parting ranks to allow them to proceed. He couldn't help but notice that the hole the Tuatha had created in their numbers swallowed up again as soon as was practicable. Whoever these men were in the advance party, they had been quickly and effectively cut off from the remainder of their numbers. It was a hell of a risk.

The stalemate within the combat circle remained intact. The Morrigan and Carman clearly knew the game had changed and Danny imagined they were awaiting to see exactly by how much – there would be little point in hasty bloodshed given the overwhelming size of the invasion force that had just shown up in their midst.

The Tuatha nearest the circle parted and Danny got his first look at the advance party. If *he* was surprised by what he saw there, it was nothing compared to the reaction from the Morrigan, or from her sons.

'Da!' Gaim said, Dian's dagger still pressed against his throat.

Caderyn it was. He looked much older than the last time Danny had seen him, after the harrowing events in the village. What was the saying? It's not the years, it's the mileage.

Caderyn was flanked by what looked like three noblemen, all dressed in fineries, but with the unmistakable bearing of men who knew full well how to handle themselves in a scrap.

The Tuatha were the first to break the silence. The Dagda stepped forward and inclined his head. 'We welcome the Milesians to our shores,' he said formally. 'How was your crossing?'

'Hellish,' the central figure spoke. 'The storms were the worst we have ever seen. Three of every ten of us perished in the time between shores, including five of my own brothers.'

'Almost as though you were being told to stay away,' the Dagda said calmly.

The one who had spoken glanced at Caderyn, whose attention throughout this whole exchange had been fixed on his former wife. 'We have been told enough,' he said. 'We have been informed of the chaos that exists here. How men are subjugated to the whims of beings like you. Human lives are forfeit in your games. The very land cries out to be rid of you. Even now,' he continued, gesturing towards the frozen inhabitants of the combat circle, 'your cycle of death plays out.'

'You speak well,' the Dagda said, genuine admiration in his voice.

'I am Amergin, ruler of the Milesians. These are my *remaining* brothers, Eber Finn and Eremon,' he indicated the remaining two noblemen, who did not bow to the Tuatha. They looked, in fact, as if they rather expected it to be the other way around. 'And this is …' he began, turning to Caderyn.

'Caderyn is … known to us,' the Dagda broke in with no small measure of understatement, glancing at the Morrigan.

'I knew you would come back, Da,' Gaim said. Though he had the body of a young man, Danny could see the childlike wonder in his eyes, the unquestioning hero worship. 'I told Glon-'

'Shush now, Gaim,' Glon said harshly. He regarded his father for a long moment.

'You've grown, son,' Caderyn said. Danny could tell the man was calling on every ounce of strength he had to stay calm, to ignore the daggers with which Dub and Dian were holding his sons hostage. Danny saw him try to step forward, to break the circle's perimeter, and be pushed back by whatever invisible barrier had been erected.

'This ends now,' Amergin said. 'We will discuss the terms of our occupation.'

'Occupation?' Carman snarled. It was the first word she had spoken since the humans had arrived on the scene. 'Humans? Occupy my island? Not while I draw bre-'

'I *beg* you to finish that thought,' the Morrigan snarled back, still crouched over her, twin daggers poised, each ready to deliver the killing thrust.

'Release her, Regan,' Caderyn called to his former wife.

'I can't,' the Morrigan replied. She did not shout, did not need to. 'You don't understand, Caderyn. If she's allowed to live, none of us will ever be safe. Tuatha and human alike. You don't know what she's done. You don't understand–'

'What *she's* done?' Cadeyrn said bitterly. '*You* broke your promise, wife. How do you think I felt when you took my sons from me, to this life? Look at them, by the gods – what have you done to my little boys?'

'Me? How dare you blame me,' the Morrigan shot back. 'Your kind killed my son! Humans butchered my little boy! Was I supposed to let that happen?'

'My kind?' Caderyn echoed sadly. 'Is that why you took him from me, Regan? You were unable to leave him with "my kind" any longer?'

The weight of Caderyn's words pressed down on her, and the Morrigan's grip on her daggers faltered, only for an instant, but it was long enough for Carman to move and to twist herself free. With a kick, she sent the daggers flying to the soil, diving after them as the Morrigan spun and, with one mighty heave, ripped the Sword of Nuada from the earth.

Battle was resumed, with twice the ferocity of anything that had gone before it, and now all attempts at subtlety or mind games were out the window and it was just weapon against weapon as the two combatants threw themselves into the fight with every ounce of hatred they possessed for the other – a seemingly inexhaustible fuel source.

Caderyn was living every blow, Danny saw. He couldn't take his eyes off the fight, but there was none of the rapt awe in his expression that the others standing by him – the Dagda and the Milesian nobles – demonstrated. He wasn't excited by the battle, he was simply terrified for the woman he once loved.

'Die!' the Morrigan cried out and, ducking under a flurry of blows, she lashed out with the flat end of the blade, disarming Carman's right hand and opening up her flank for a savage swing of the Sword that would bisect the witch from hip to shoulder.

'No!' The horrified cry had come from Caderyn, but it hadn't been directed at his wife.

Gaim fell heavily to his knees. His hands went to his throat, blood pumping through his fingers as he tried desperately to stem the flow from the slash wound Dian had just inflicted. Gaim's warrior tunic, so resplendent, so pristine, was soaked in red. He looked from the frozen expression of his mother to the hollow, grief-stricken face of his father, and he tried to smile.

'You came back,' he gasped, and pitched forward.

'GAIM!' Caderyn screamed, anguish and anger consuming him utterly as he threw himself against the combat circle. He rebounded fruitlessly from its intangible borders, hitting the ground, weeping and hollering.

The Morrigan's momentary advantage had been derailed completely by the sight of her son's murder. Carman struck, planting a foot high into the Morrigan's chest and sending her sprawling backwards. She swooped to grab the displaced dagger and threw herself up and forward, raising the daggers high above her head as she leapt, meaning to impale the Morrigan when she landed.

At the last second the Morrigan rolled out of the way and Carman, having missed her target, roared in frustration and lashed out wildly. There was no finesse in her strikes but their ferocity drove the Morrigan back – with one well-timed blow she cut a deep gash across the Morrigan's left thigh. Carman, sensing victory, pressed on once more, trusting that a combination of grief and pain would serve to ensure a swift end to the battle.

Her mistake.

The Morrigan came out of her half-crouch, her sword-free left hand bunched into a fist that connected so solidly with Carman's jaw that the crack of hand on bone was heard around the Hill of Tara.

Carman landed flat on her back, the jarring impact knocking her daggers from her grip. Not bothering to attack straight away, the Morrigan instead picked up the daggers in one hand and, without even looking, threw them back over her left shoulder and right into Dian's chest.

Dian gasped in shock, took a long step backward, and brought a shaking hand to the hilt of one of his mother's daggers, protruding from his chest. His mouth was filling with blood. He looked from his mother to his murderer. 'Thank you,' he said, before slumping, dead before his body hit the ground.

His lifeless corpse had fallen beyond the invisible borderline at perimeter of the combat circle, moving the daggers outside the reach of anyone within. No one went to him.

The Morrigan, silver Sword in hand, moved to stand over the prone body of her opponent.

'Glon, no, please no. Not Glon too, please gods no,' Caderyn sobbed helplessly, pale as a ghost, knowing what he was about to witness.

The Morrigan, looked then at her firstborn son, eyes wide in desperation.

'Do it,' Glon nodded. 'Put me in the Cauldron afterward. I can come back to you.'

'Try it,' Carman hissed. 'I beg you. Try it.'

'Let her go, Regan' Caderyn whispered, on his knees at the edge of the circle. 'Please. Let her go.'

She shook her head, eyes brimming with tears, and raised the Sword.

Dub's hand moved, once. That was all it took.

From behind her she heard the sound of choking and gagging and she knew was hearing the life leave her eldest son. Glon slumped to the ground, exactly as his younger brother had done only minutes before. There was no time for final words or a last goodbye.

Caderyn tried to call Glon's name, but he was too out of his mind with grief to make any coherent noise. What came from his throat was not a word. It was the sound of a man's heart breaking.

'I have nothing left to lose,' the Morrigan sobbed, as she stood ready to deliver the final blow. 'So now, you die.'

But before the Sword could descend, the final cruel twist in Carman's plan unfolded. Dother, until now nothing more than a bystander, finally moved. He reached down amongst the bags Carman had brought into the circle with her and unwrapped, untied and removed the gag from something previously hidden amidst it all, something red, shaking, and terrified.

The child's hysterical cries rent the air. The Sword froze in the Morrigan's grasp.

Dother held a dagger to the little boy's throat. 'Say hello to Mummy and Daddy, Coscar,' he said pleasantly.

Danny started forward as if to mount a rescue attempt before realising that anything he did would be futile. The same could have been said for Caderyn, who must have known, based on previous attempts, that any effort he made to enter the circle of combat was doomed to failure. Nonetheless, the sight of his youngest child in mortal peril was enough to make him throw himself against the invisible wall once again–

– and pass right through.

Danny felt sure the man should have paused for a second, taken stock, been surprised or even thrown off-balance by his unexpected success. If he had, Dother might have had time to react, might have done something quite horrible. Caderyn didn't so much as slow down.

With a primal roar he launched himself at Dother, bounding in a way that put the most acrobatic of the wolf-faeries to shame. He knocked Dother off his feet so quickly and so completely that little Coscar was thrown free, unscathed, and suddenly there was a sword in his hand and Dother hadn't even the time to cry out before Caderyn buried it deep in his heart, right up to the hilt.

Caderyn looked over at his wife, and nodded, once.

'No–' Carman said, or started to say, but got no further before the silver Sword was plunged down–

'Stop. This is bullshit. Stop this now,' Danny said, anger bubbling inside him. The silver Sword, paused in mid-impale of the witch queen, was released by the one delivering the killing stroke. The Morrigan, now back in director's commentary mode, glanced coolly at Danny who did nothing to disguise his annoyance.

'This is all lies. This isn't what really happened,' he said.

'No,' she admitted.

'So why?'

'Because!' she shouted at him, anger overtaking her at long last, 'It's what should have happened! Caderyn's love should have been powerful enough to break that barrier and allow him inside. He should have been able to knock Dother away. He and I should have ended it right here! Love. Love *should* have been enough to save us!'

'But it wasn't.'

Her lip curled. 'Watch.'

Time rewound several moments. Once again, Dother held a dagger to the little boy's throat. 'Say hello to Mummy and Daddy, Coscar,' he said pleasantly.

Caderyn threw himself against the barrier … only to be thrown back.

'Here's what's going to happen,' Dother went right on talking. 'You're going to release my mother. You're going to declare her the victor of this fight. In return, I will spare Coscar. My mother won't exercise her right as victor to kill you–'

'*What?*' Carman choked in disbelief.

'Face facts, Mother,' Dother went on. 'The Tuatha are a significant force in themselves, and now they've been joined by five times their number of humans. Humans who have made it clear they want to see the back of us. Violently, I would imagine. If we want to avoid wholesale extermination, we're going to need to show a willingness for compromise here. Plus' – and he ruffled the howling little boy's hair in what he probably imagined was a passable imitation of paternal affection – 'isn't he *cute*? Look at his widda nose!'

'He speaks wisely,' Amergin said.

'That witch murdered my sons! You have no right!' Caderyn said.

'Enough, Caderyn,' Amergin said warningly. 'I hold you in high esteem, but you do not rule our people. I do. We have already paid a heavy price for agreeing to come to your aid in reclaiming your son.'

'You thought I took him,' the Morrigan said, looking to Caderyn.

'What was I supposed to think?' he demanded. 'You made it clear the day you left that you considered us beneath you. I woke up one morning to find my son gone and I tasted the same magic in the air as I did the day you slaughtered every man, woman and child–'

He trailed off, but too late.

'What did you say?' Amergin said, disbelievingly. He drew his sword. His brothers followed suit. '*She* is the one responsible for the village massacre?'

The Tuatha around him likewise drew their weapons. Danny couldn't believe what he was seeing. Everything was falling apart.

'Shall I tell you what will happen now?' Amergin went on harshly. 'You will call an end to this madness, as he has already suggested,' and he nodded towards Dother, who pulled off a mock salute, 'to spare further bloodshed. When this has been accomplished, you – *all* of you, faerie and Tuatha alike – will surrender to us. Unconditionally. Or we will repay you a hundredfold for every human death you have caused.'

He raised his voice, so that as many as possible of the assembled Tuatha and faerie could hear his words. 'The age of magic is over,' he said. 'Now begins the Age of Man. Accept that, and we may choose to be merciful. Resist, and we will annihilate you. Your choice.'

'Idiots!' the Morrigan raged. She glared death at Amergin, at Eber Finn, Eremon and Caderyn. 'Mercy? Sparing this thing,' and she kicked savagely at Carman, who took her blows without flinching, 'would be mercy? She won't rest until she finds some way to kill us all!'

'Is her death worth that of your people and your son?' asked Dother.

The Sword was still suspended above Carman. The Morrigan had held it aloft all this time. To have done so, Danny knew, took almost incomprehensible strength – no human could have possibly held a sword so heavy in such a position for so long. Her muscles, the muscles of a goddess, glistened with sweat. At her feet, Carman stared up balefully. One downward stroke would put an end to her once and for all.

She lowered the Sword. It clattered to the ground.

'I concede,' she said, so softly that Danny barely heard it.

Carman's eyes sparkled with triumph. She backed away on her hands and knees, watching the Morrigan for any sign of movement, and only when she was a few feet away did she get to her feet and move to stand beside Dother. Dub had joined them now also, carrying Dian's body in his massive arms.

'One last parting gift,' Carman said, and reached for the dagger in Dother's hand–

'No,' the word came from Dother.

Carman's eyes widened in outrage. 'No?' she echoed.

'No,' Dother said again. He threw the dagger aside and pushed Coscar free, into the waiting embrace of his mother. Caderyn, at long last free of the barrier around the combat circle, was there a moment later.

Carman, betrayed, stared at Dother for several heartbeats too long. 'I won't soon forget this,' she said.

Dother only smiled, and there was an element of weariness in the gesture. 'Dear Mother, I'd expect nothing less.'

Coscar struggled free of his mother and threw himself into his father's arms, great whooping sobs shaking the little boy's body.

The Morrigan was now empty-handed, the Sword of Nuada discarded at her feet. She left Coscar and Caderyn to their reunion and went to the bodies of her elder children. She fell to her knees when she reached them, placing a hand on each of their heads and closing their eyes for the final time.

The grief overtook her then. Her howls, terrible and empty filled the air.

*

The fate of Ireland was decided on the Hill of Tara that day.

Above ground, the physical, mortal realm that humans called their own, was to be the sole property of the Milesians, their kin and descendants. No magical creature was to be permitted residence there.

In return, the Milesians swore to stay away from the world beneath the surface – the Otherworld, as some called it. It was to become the sole property of the magical beings. The two worlds, human and magical, were to be split from one another, and all entrances and exits between the surface and the Otherworld were to be sealed off.

The most prominent of the Tuatha divinities promised to perform the necessary magics, swore individual oaths that when the time came they would, without protest, lead their people down into the Otherworld. Once there, at a secret location, they would, en masse, enter a voluntary period of sleep – a species-wide hibernation.

They did not specify when, if ever, they would awaken from this hibernation – only that, as a minimum, it would last many centuries. Knowing a good deal when they heard it, and having seen the Tuatha in action, Amergin and his brothers knew that, while their superior force of numbers likely gave them the advantage, many would perish if they forced the Tuatha into violent revolt.

Carman was not so accommodating. Only with much persuasion from Dother – mocked for his cowardice by his brother Dub for his troubles – did she come to see the wisdom in not taking on the humans. She agreed to lead her people into the Otherworld, but made no promise about hibernation, and went so far as to hint heavily that once locked away she would not rest until she found a way back for her and her spawn and Ireland could be reclaimed.

'Do not concern yourselves,' the Dagda reassured Amergin and his brothers, even as Carman and her hordes were swallowed by the gateway that now existed at the foot of the Hill of Tara. 'We will use deep magic to keep her imprisoned down there. Humanity will not see her kind for many scores of years, if ever again. In the meantime, tell your descendants the stories. Keep the fear alive. Be vigilant.'

Only one of the Tuatha refused to co-operate in the migration, or enter hibernation. The Morrigan was appalled by her people's plan to sleep for centuries and not to actively fight the faeries, and she had no particular faith in the humans to keep the stories alive. 'Give them a century, they'll probably come to believe faeries are pretty things that grant wishes', she was heard to remark.

And then there was the matter of her remaining son.

'He is a magical creature,' Amergin had said, from his makeshift throne on the summit of the Hill of Tara, for what seemed like the hundredth time. 'And I will not permit magical creatures, half-breeds or no, within this kingdom.'

'This *creature* is my son!' Cadeyrn protested.

Amergin looked warningly at his subject. 'Much has been sacrificed in his name already.'

'You have a new kingdom to divide,' Caderyn shot back.

'Spoils beyond reason. All I want is my son, my little boy. Let me go with him. I want no riches. No estate. Just my son and the chance to live a normal life with him.'

'Show mercy,' the Morrigan said. She stood beside her husband, their son between them, uncomprehending, while his fate was being decided. 'As a half-blood he will be unable to enter sleep with the rest of the Tuatha. He will be alone, in the Otherworld, with Carman and her hordes.'

'He will have you,' Amergin pointed out.

The Morrigan's face flushed with anger. 'My people have made it known that any who refuse the call to sleep once within the Otherworld will be stripped of their human form and of their powers.'

The crow. Another piece of the puzzle fell into place in Danny's head. So that was why the Morrigan was trapped as a bird, powerless.

Amergin paused. He was not without mercy. 'Is there any way the magical lineage within him could be taken?' he inquired. 'If he were fully human like his father, I would welcome him into our society.'

The Morrigan hesitated. 'Perhaps,' was all she said.

Back with her people, the notion did not sit well.

'Magic cannot be destroyed!' the Dagda raged. 'What you're proposing is monstrous! It has never been done!'

'What option do I have?' the Morrigan returned. 'He is not of one world, nor the other. The humans will not accept him unless he is one of them. Please. He is just a child!'

The Dagda considered this. He was also not without mercy.

'We will try,' he said. 'But destroying a child's birthright is an act of destruction. Dark magic. It may be beyond us.'

'But not,' a new voice sounded, 'beyond me.'

Dother.

Danny felt his head spin. 'What's that cunt doing here? Why would he help?'

'The Dagda is correct,' Dother said smoothly, unaffected by Danny's interruption. 'Magic cannot be destroyed. The Morrigan's human line cannot be purged of magic. Not entirely. But the full bearing of the boy's gift from his Tuatha lineage can be moved, through time itself. Think of it as a hibernation. Certainly enough to satisfy the Milesians, and to allow the child to live amongst them.'

'Why would you, of all people, do this for us?' the Morrigan asked him, asking Danny's question for him.

'Simple,' he said easily. 'If I perform the necessary ritual, all of the potential magic in your descendants – *all* of it – will be dumped into one body. And that will be tainted by us, by our mark. Think of the destiny that person will have, Morrigan. Think of what he could accomplish. He will be greater than any of us. He will bestride our worlds. He will hold the key to reuniting them. And it will be for him to choose which one to embrace.'

Throughout all of this, Danny felt as if his body were being lowered into liquid nitrogen. Cold fingers grabbed at his heart. It had once seemed so simple – the Morrigan represented the good and the faeries the bad. But in reality, the Morrigan – and, centuries later, his own father – had conspired with their enemies to bring about every bit of the misery he'd undergone.

They had created him.

'Now,' her voice whispered in his ear, 'you understand. You have everything you need. The Ordeal is over.'

The world around him fragmented. He felt his grip on himself, on the fragile unreality around him, slip.

'Remember,' she went on, 'remember what love brings. Strength, yes. But it also brings weakness, Danny. You will have your own choice to make. Make it wisely.'

Before he could ask what the hell she meant by that, the pain hit him, like nothing he'd ever experienced, and considering he'd recently been ripped limb from limb and tossed into a cauldron, that in itself was quite the achievement. Pressure built in his body, his mind, as if everything he was and ever had been was being compressed, his soul ground down to a paste to be passed through the cosmic toothpaste tube …

Jesus Christ, he realised, with the one small corner of his brain that wasn't begging for death to come and come swiftly. *I'm being born …*

The pinprick of light up ahead became a dot, became a tear –

Danny Morrigan, whole and reborn, shot out of the Dagda's Cauldron. Sights and sounds and sensations overloaded him, as if he were experiencing each of his senses for the first time – as if he were a newborn infant overwhelmed by the intensity of existence outside the womb.

He hit the ground and curled up into a foetal position until the roaring in his ears subsided and he was able, nursing his head and blinking furiously, to slowly get to his feet. The white and dark blobs around him resolved themselves into shapes. Some sort of howling noise was echoing through his ears. Something was approaching him, fast. He could feel it.

He expected, not unreasonably in his opinion, to see the circle of standing stones; to see the place he'd entered the Cauldron in the first place.

Instead, he found himself in Dother's penthouse office in Lircom Tower. Before he could adjust, however, he was knocked off his feet by the creature emitting the howling noise he'd heard earlier. It was not, as he'd imagined, the feral growls of some faerie monstrosity, it was Ellie, and she was crying out in joy.

Ellie Quinn, in the flesh. Her eyes were wide, streaming with tears, full of knowledge. This was not the Ellie Quinn of the other reality who had known him only as a friend.

This was *his* Ellie.

'Danny!' she cried, wrapping her arms around him.

He drew her closer. It seemed a lifetime ago since he'd stolen a kiss from her in the impossible little domestic setup she'd had with Steve. He thought then of the Cauldron and he realised in a very literal way that it *had* been a lifetime ago. He kissed her again, not a stolen kiss this time, a full and hungry kiss that felt like fuel to his impoverished body.

When she broke from him, her body began to shake with uncontrollable sobs. She looked at him with a face full of sorrow and he knew in that horrible, bottomless moment that something terrible had happened.

Only much, much later would Ellie realise that after that kiss, the injuries she had carried since the car crash had faded away as though sustained in a dream.

'My daddy,' she whispered hoarsely. 'Danny, he's–' and she could go no further.

He drew her closer and let her cry. His synaesthesia – his magical ability, whatever it was – blended the sadness, proximity and strength of her grief together until it came close to overpowering him. He was carried along by the wave of her bereavement. Michael Quinn, her father, had been no friend to Danny – the older man had hated him with such awful intensity that it had stunned him – but he was Ellie's father all the same.

When he and Ellie finally broke apart, Danny saw his own father. He reacted purely on instinct.

'Son, I … *ooffff*,' was all Tony Morrigan was able to say before his son enveloped him in a hug that took his breath away.

'I know!' Danny said, babbling like an excited little boy. 'I was there with you in the cottage, Da! I know everything!'

'Cottage?' Tony returned, his mind whirling. 'Son, what–'

As though it were the most natural thing in the world, Danny released his embrace enough to touch his fingers to his father's forehead. There was no visible evidence of what he was doing, no spark jumping from fingers to head, nothing so showy – at least not in the visual spectrum the assembled humans could perceive – but the effect was immediate.

'Jesus,' Tony gasped, losing his equilibrium so suddenly and so completely that Danny had to catch and steady him. 'So that's where that big fuckin' TV came from.'

They remained in a half-embrace for a moment longer, and a

look was exchanged between father and son, the sort of look that hadn't been passed – at least not both ways – from one to the other since Danny was ten years old.

There was something else in his father's demeanour. Some piece of bad news that he had to impart. Danny could see it as clearly as if it were written on the his father's face in flaming letters.

'Steve,' he said. 'It's Steve, isn't it? Where is he? What happened?'

BELFAST CITY CENTRE, NOW

None of this was going according to plan.

When the mortal world had collided with their own, the Queen had instructed them to have their fun, had set them loose to engage in the sort of sport they had been denied for hundreds of years. Humans had grown weak. Oh, they had developed better weapons, that was certain, but the majority of the human population had allowed themselves to grow soft. More than half were now fat. The arts of swordsmanship and combat were long forgotten.

At first the hunt had indeed been easy and he had enjoyed skittering from rooftop to rooftop, watching the humans below him scatter in panic and fear as his faerie brothers and sisters herded them like cattle, picking off little groups and doomed individuals here and there. He had chosen three targets and descended upon them in a flurry of excitement, beating the stubby little wings he possessed – wings, which if they followed the laws of science the humans held so dear, could never have allowed him to get off the ground.

That had been before the wolves – his *brothers!* – had appeared. He had welcomed them initially. They were the most efficient warriors they had, devastating and disciplined. Evidently they still were; but it was not against the humans that those skills were being employed. He had watched, from the safety of a rooftop, as they encircled the humans and, rather than devouring them, had protected them, turning their fury on the attacking faeries and taking them apart with surgical precision.

How dare they! His proboscis vibrated with anger. He considered flying to the circle of the standing stones, imparting the news of the betrayal personally to the Queen. Perhaps she would look favourably on him for doing so.

He hesitated. That was an awfully big *perhaps*. She was equally likely to take out her anger on him and tear him apart. Stories of his Queen's temper were, in every sense of the word, legendary.

No. She would know by now anyway. Nothing escaped her notice for very long, in his experience. She would know and she would exact a terrible vengeance on the wolves for their rebellion, and that would be that. In the meantime, all that was left for him to do was to stay out of their way and–

His compound eyes spotted a human moving slowly, painfully, in the street below. Wounded prey. His wings spasmed with excitement. The wolves were close – he could smell them, taste their scent in the air – and he knew he would risk detection if he left the rooftop, but he couldn't resist the lure of wounded prey.

Yes. Yes, he would swoop, and pick up the miserable thing, and be back at some secluded place in a matter of seconds, and there he could feast over this one at his leisure, drawing out the death of the human for as long as possible to keep the meat fresh.

He launched himself from the roof and realised, with some degree of puzzlement, that the human below him had his hands and feet bound together – by whom, he could not guess, but it was an incredible stroke of fortune. Wounded prey that had no chance of fighting back? Oh, this was going to be such *fun*!

His six legs unfurled from his segmented body and spread out, ready to envelop the human in their embrace and lift–

Suddenly there was movement to his left, a growl, and a sensation of *pressure*.

Then nothing.

*

Wide-eyed, Steve took in the sight of the giant wolf that had just caught the oversized wasp in mid-air with its massive jaws. With a wet and horrible *crunch*, the wolf brought its jaws together once, shook its massive head, and casually tossed the wasp-thing's broken body thirty feet or so to land in the middle of the dual carriageway. There, it was promptly ground to a pulp by several speeding vehicles, their drivers terrified out of their wits at the madness unfolding all around them.

'Mmmmfffff …' Steve whimpered weakly through his gag, panicking as the wolf dipped its enormous head towards him, teeth bearing down.

With a delicacy that Steve would not have believed possible, the wolf bit through the bonds holding his ankles and wrists together. He wriggled free, pain still coursing through him and tugged at the gag around his mouth.

'You are injured,' the wolf said, looking at Steve as it spoke. It had the most remarkable set of eyes he had ever seen – soulful, gentle, and strong. Absurdly, he thought of Maggie.

'You talk,' Steve returned faintly. It was, in his view, a fair riposte.

'It is not safe.'

He looked over at the pulverised remains of the man-sized wasp that, thirty seconds ago, had been poised to snatch him away to Christ-knew-where. Cars roared by, tyres screeched and he could see more of the wasps hovering around. Screams rang out in the Belfast night. He could see flames erupting from various points in the city. He heard the sounds of crashes, of breaking glass. Unearthly shrieks followed by very human ones. And the howls of wolves, first one, then another and another – a chain of them ringing through the city.

'Might be onto somethin' there,' Steve said.

The wolf got down on its belly and bowed its head. 'Onto my back,' it said. 'I will take you to safety.'

''Kay,' he said, putting up no resistance. Trusting a hugely oversized talking wolf now seemed like the thing to do.

He was badly injured, he knew. He was coughing blood, and imagined he could feel some of the crushed glass rolling around inside him like trainers in a washing machine. Yet almost as soon as he clambered onto the giant wolf's back he thought he could feel a slight easing of the pain. Fearsome and nightmarish though it was, somehow this beast was healing him with its very proximity. He couldn't explain it but he was grateful nonetheless.

'Where do you need to go?' the wolf asked, turning its head around to look at him. Steve scanned the Belfast skyline around him, searching for a particular shape … there. City Hospital, the great squat box.

He pointed. 'Big cube,' he managed.

'Hold on,' the wolf replied, and it leapt forward, bounding along at an incredible rate, travelling through a city gone insane. He wondered what had happened to Ellie and Tony, if they were even still alive. If Danny had …

We don't need this one. He's of no value.

Dother's words burned in him. He'd been thrown from that limo, cast aside and left to die. He was not important enough even to bother kidnapping. Why he'd been spared, how he was still alive, he had no idea, but he knew one thing; he was tired of being discarded.

'Change of plan,' he said, his voice hitching in rhythm with the impact of the wolf's paws on the ground below. 'Place to the right. Medicine inside.'

It was a chemist. Closed, naturally, at this time of the night, but that didn't bother his mount one little bit. Stopping just shy of the glass-fronted façade, the wolf reared up to protect its passenger and with one sweeping motion of its front right paw reduced the reinforced glass window to shards. Ordinarily the noise would have drawn a lot of attention; tonight, it was just one more chaotic noise in a symphony.

Searching inside, Steve found painkillers and swallowed a handful. Bandages were applied to the cuts still oozing blood. While he was doing this three creatures defying description – he had made out claws and teeth and drool – had attempted to force their way past the wolf guarding the entrance, only to be summarily executed. One of them, however, had managed to lash out with a barbed tail and gash a channel in the wolf's underside.

'Hold still,' Steve said, as the pills began to take hold and the worst of the pain ebbed. He did the best he could with what he had to close the wound and stop the wolf's bleeding. When he was done, it regarded him with those impossibly intelligent eyes.

'I am Larka,' it said, and Steve realised that, although the voice could not exactly be said to be female – at least not in any human sense of the word – the wolf itself was. 'Thank you.'

'Steve,' he replied, feeling wonderfully fuzzy-headed and that everything was beginning to make sense. 'And I fuckin' *loooooove* drugs.'

Larka cocked her head at this. 'Steve,' she said, 'there will be others who need my help.'

'I know,' he replied.

The creature that had wounded Larka still lay on the pavement beside them, and seeing it there gave Steve an idea. He dropped to his haunches beside the thing and ripped out its barbed tail, swinging it through the air and liking very much the *zzzzip* sound it made as he did so.

Before Larka could react, or protest, he had swung himself up on her broad back once more.

'Well, what we waitin' for?' he asked. 'Let's fuckin' *get* these ugly cunts.'

Larka grinned and launched them forward into the night.

LIRCOM TOWER, BELFAST, NOW

No. No, it couldn't be true. Steve was … Steve had always been there. Would always be there. Even through all this madness, he'd imagined Steve drifting along with his usual laidback approach to life and, when it was all sorted, there he'd be, pushing for a KFC, making some quip. His best friend, tossed out of a moving car.

'Danny, I'm so sorry,' Ellie said.

'I know.'

'He …' she hesitated, 'I was wrong about him, Danny. I just wanted you to know that.'

Danny nodded. The grief for his friend was hot and raw but as horrific as it was to contemplate, there wasn't time to feel the loss right now. He forced his attention onto the figure standing a little way away from the rest of them.

It looked like Dother, sounded like him, but it wasn't him. Danny concentrated, called upon the things he'd learned, and looked through the filter of his other senses. The sixth sense people called telepathy wasn't really a sixth sense at all; it was a combination of the other five working in perfect synchronicity. Get it right and it was like pulling back a veil, enabling you to see the truth of things.

'Dian?' he said.

'At your service,' Dian replied, bowing slightly. 'Apologies for the temporary meat-coat, but long-range possession isn't the easiest of feats to accomplish, never mind having to transport yourself down a telephone line to do it. Thankfully,' and he grunted at the irony, 'my dear brother was considerate enough to upgrade his network, or it might never have worked at all.'

'Dian?' Ellie asked. 'Who's Dian?'

THE OTHERWORLD, 47 AD

'Brother?' Dother called into the void. A note of impatience entered his voice. 'Brother, I know you're in here. This is getting ridiculous. You've already stayed in here too long to come back in your own body. Mother is *not* pleased.'

The formless nothingness around him ignored his pleas.

Carman was in a foul mood when Dother emerged from the pocket dimension within the Dagda's Cauldron. Not that he was surprised. Greece had been an awful lot bigger than Ireland, and it had stifled her. Trapped here in an Otherworld which was smaller still had done nothing to improve her claustrophobia.

'He doesn't want to come out,' he told her.

'Perhaps you do not want to find him,' rumbled Dub.

'Oh, go hide underneath somebody's bed,' Dother spat.

Dub exploded into a black cloud of wrath at the insult. Dother rolled his eyes. 'Go ahead,' he said, 'annihilate me. Pulling myself back together will pass the time for a few days. If I can remember what *days* are, that is.'

Carman flung them both thirty feet apart with nothing more than a glance in their direction. The wind knocked from him from the impact, Dother could do nothing but glower impotently in his mother's direction as she drew herself up, sucking power from the world they inhabited, rearing up like a cobra before funnelling her entire monstrous form into the throat of the Cauldron.

Silence descended on the Otherworld in the wake of her departure. Dother and Dian moved cautiously towards the Cauldron.

'What are you smiling at?' Dub demanded.

'Wondering where I could get a really *big* cork,' Dother replied.

Dub's forehead creased. Given a few decades, he may even have come up with a response, but he never got the chance. From the Cauldron came more than a scream, more than a howl. It was the sound of raw bleeding pain, of an unwilling foetus ripped from a comfortable womb.

A shockwave rippled out over the crimson-hued hills of the Otherworld, causing the various creatures that inhabited this wretched prison to slink to their knees and clasp what mangled excuses for hands, paws, claws (or whatever else they possessed) over their heads.

Carman shot from the Cauldron at such speed that it was sent spinning end-over-end. She got to her feet, her arm outstretched, seemingly trying to throttle thin air.

'I don't *care*,' she hissed, 'if you don't want to come back. You're my son, and you'll do your duty, understand? Your stubbornness has cost you a permanent form. Fine, roam this world as a restless spirit – just get the hell out of my sight!'

A presence that was unmistakably their younger brother rocketed past Dub and Dother and out into the hills, gone in an instant.

The two brothers very slowly turned to look at their mother, busy now retracting her extra limbs so as to appear relatively human once more.

'Needy little shit,' she said.

HILL OF TARA, 1798 AD

Free.

Lurching away from the United Irishmen battlefield in the body of one of the fallen, Dian could barely contain his excitement.

Centuries. Millennia. What meaning did years have, when you couldn't really die? As a boy in Greece, he had lived in a land where magic had sloshed in abundance. Beginning as a human shaman, his mother had used her keen knowledge of herbs to heal the sick. Credited with magical powers in the minds of her peers, this belief had shaped reality and she had crossed the line from human to something more than human. Over time, this effect had extended to her sons.

As their worshippers grew in number, however, they began to detract from the adoration of the ruling pantheon, the gods of Olympus. Only by a few hundred really, but it was enough for those powerful eyes to turn in their direction, and the gods were as creative as they were omnipotent. They sent tsunamis, diseases, terrible storms with spectacularly accurate lightning bolts – all designed to terrify the followers of any rival semi-deity.

Under the weight of such an onslaught, Carman's worshippers soon turned back to the big players – to Zeus and Hera, Poseidon and Ares. Abandoned by her followers, her powers began to wither and she had raged against the slopes of Olympus. She stamped her feet and screamed and cried to be accepted – to ascend to those stratospheric heights and take her place amongst the elite. The gates had remained firmly shut. The gods had not even done her the courtesy of saying no, they had simply ignored her.

Hearing the call for aid from Bres, hearing of a new land with a ruling pantheon in turmoil and a power vacuum at the top, his mother had not hesitated, and he and his brothers were forced to follow.

They had had many names, Dian and his brothers. Dother had been called Olc for a time. The name still meant 'Evil' so you had to admire him for sticking with a theme, at least. It was the same with Dub – or Dubh – whatever way you wanted to spell it, the name still meant 'Black'.

For a time, in an isolated part of their new home, where he had pretended that his mother could not see him, Dian too had gone by another name – Calma. Unlike his brothers though, he had chosen a completely new theme. He had spent too many years as Dian – as 'Violence'. Now, as Calma, he would be 'Valiant'.

In that place, which was no more than a few towns and pathetic little settlements, he had changed his appearance. He had helped the crops to grow, instead of sowing dissent and violence. He had blessed the union of couples, rather than being the whispering voice of jealousy in a husband's ear. He had not sought worship from those uncomplicated little handful of humans. He had craved *appreciation*.

He had become someone else to find himself.

When Carman had finally tired of feigning ignorance over his little experiment, the things she had done to that little group of people ...

No. He forced himself to pull away from those memories.

Ever since his mother had dragged his essence from the afterlife within the Dagda's Cauldron, he had played the dutiful son – a task arduous beyond anything he had ever endured, but it was the only way to regain his mother's trust. Ensuring it was he, and not Dub, who had been picked to accompany Dother to the surface had been the greatest trick he had ever pulled.

And now he was free.

The body he was occupying would not last much longer, but it would make it to the nearest human settlement. When it fell, so too would Dian, this he swore. He would be Calma once again.

LIRCOM TOWER, BELFAST, NOW

'You possessed Dother when the phone rang?' Tony guessed.

'I'm a little surprised you didn't recognise me, Tony,' Dian replied.

'Recognise you?'

'We don't have time,' Dian waved a hand. 'Yes, possession is one of my particular skills. Not so famous as my party trick of creating war out of peace, turning pacifists into berserkers. But I think, Danny excepted,' and he gestured towards Ellie, 'we've *all* seen that ability in action.'

Everyone but Danny turned to look at Ellie who, feeling all eyes upon her, flushed red and cast a look over at something slumped by the windows. Something that looked an awful lot like a broken body.

'I miss somethin'?' Danny asked.

THE OTHERWORLD, NOW

In the midst of the standing stones, doubled over in pain, Carman roared in outrage and betrayal. Her elite creatures, the ones permitted access to the inner sanctum, shrank back and trembled in fear as her anger rolled over them.

'Mother?' Dub asked, for the tenth time it seemed. Save for one other, he was the only being within that inner circle brave or foolhardy enough to be within striking distance of the Queen. The other was immune to her rages. Dub had no such guarantee. Yet there was no fear in him – only concern, written all over his huge, uncomplicated features.

'My host,' she said. 'Destroyed.'

The old woman's body had been her shell in the human world for almost forty years and it had been destroyed by something as mundane, something as miserable, as a punch from a human girl (well, a *mostly* human girl). Granted, that host body held only a fraction of the abilities that Carman possessed but the girl would pay for that.

'The Morrigan?' Dub asked, his massive hands folding into fists. 'He survived the Cauldron?'

'Of course he did,' Carman said dismissively, wishing once again that Dub was blessed with a tenth of the cunning of his younger brothers. She got to her feet, having tumbled off her throne when her human host had perished. 'He was not the one who destroyed the host.'

'Then who?' and Dub scowled. It was a terrible thing to behold. Darkness crackled around his humanoid form. Parts of him dissolved into mist, became insubstantial, and then phased back again. 'Dother?'

The two brothers had despised each other all of their nigh-eternal lives. Carman saw the anger in her eldest son and wheels began to turn in her mind, wheels greased with centuries of lies.

Ah, Dother – he was by far and away the most brilliant of her three children. Dian was shrewd all right and Dub was just a powerhouse – an all but invincible formless cloud of malevolence, so vacant that if you stood too close to him you could hear the ocean. But Dother had served her tirelessly and brilliantly. Without his scheming and planning, she knew she would not be standing here now, so close to the Merging, so close to her final victory. If anyone was going to take over her empire one day, it was Dother. He was her natural heir.

There was only one slight problem with that, of course. Carman was eternal. Carman was forever. She was her *own* heir. Plus, there was the small matter of his denying her revenge against the Morrigan all those years ago. She had promised him she would not forget that and the debt was now due.

'Yes,' she said. 'Dother has betrayed me. Destroy him, Dub. Go forth. I cannot leave the circle until the Merging completes.'

She glanced around the standing stone prison – for such it was – and what she saw lifted her mood slightly; the Merging was happening faster than she dared hope. The red-lit hilltops and valleys of the Otherworld were being overlaid with something decidedly more metropolitan as modern-day Belfast phased into being. Within the circle, the massive outline of a glass-and-concrete behemoth – what the humans called, with their typical sense of grandeur, a skyscraper – was forming itself from the ether.

The Tuatha had congratulated themselves on the totality of the protective spells they had woven into her prison, but they had failed to foresee that she was quite happy to remain in the Otherworld … so long as the mortal land, *her* land, could be quite literally brought down to her level.

Soon enough, the Merging would be complete, and her confinement within these standing stones would be over. Carman would be free to walk the lands once more, and her many thousands of faerie children would have more humans than they ever could have dreamt of to entertain themselves with.

Until then …

'I will find him,' Dub promised.

'Bring the Morrigan to me,' she ordered him. 'Alive.'

He imploded into darkness and dissipated in an instant. He knew exactly where to find his brother, and the phasing of realities around him would prove no barrier. He was darkness itself, and darkness can lurk everywhere.

'Alive?' came a voice from beside her.

She looked in surprise at the speaker. 'So quickly you grow. Before long you'll be a man.'

'And then I'll be ready?' the voice was eager now.

'Yes. And then? Will you do what's necessary? Will you do it for me, little one?'

'I will, *Mitéra*,' the child responded, using the Greek word for mama.

She reached across and ruffled the child's hair, ostensibly a loving gesture, but in actuality a way to gauge the power radiating from within him. Yes, he was almost ready, and when the time came, he would prove to be the ultimate weapon.

'You're my good boy, Luke,' she said. 'You make your *Mitéra* proud.'

LIRCOM TOWER, BELFAST, NOW

Danny looked from Ellie, to the dead body, back to Ellie again. This wasn't how heroic showdowns went in the movies, he reflected. John McClane didn't storm the top of Nakatomi Plaza to find Holly had done in Hans Gruber with her stiletto heel. At the same time, though – *wow*.

'But how?' he asked out loud. 'How did you …?'

Dian, still in Dother's body, was the one to answer. 'The old woman was just a host body. Probably died years ago. Carman has been reanimating her ever since.'

Danny looked at Ellie triumphantly. 'Fuckin' told ye she smelt like death, didn't I!' he said.

'I thought Carman was trapped? Down below?' Tony spoke up.

'She is. Most of her. This,' and Dian indicated the body, 'this was a puppet she used to pull your strings. That's why Xena Warrior Princess here was able to lay her out. Well,' he amended, looking at Ellie and, oddly, at Dermot Scully with what seemed like an expression of sadness, '… mostly.'

'Something's coming.'

As one, everyone turned to look at Tony. He was standing by the windows, pointing out at the city.

'How can you tell?' Danny asked him, suddenly wondering if there was anything his father was hiding from him, any other big secrets lurking in his past.

You could just take it from him. Whatever the secret is. Just reach in and pluck it out.

He pushed away the thought with a shudder, astonished that it had even surfaced. No longer in the Otherworld, no longer surfing the celestial planes, being back in reality – or at least, as close as this particular version of Ireland got to it – was akin to spending all night drinking in a bar and imagining himself fairly sober until walking outside. He felt intoxicated. Connected.

Amending his father's memories in the cottage had taken considerable effort. Restoring them here had been accomplished almost before he'd even realised what he was doing. He would need that power, of course; would likely need every last joule of it if he had any hope of doing whatever the hell he needed to do in order to…

To what? Get Luke back? Obviously that was the first priority, yes – but what if getting Luke back solved nothing else? He had bigger responsibilities now, didn't he? Wasn't that what his extended whistle-stop tour of pocket dimensions and ancient Ireland was intended to teach him?

'Look,' Tony said. He pointed out at the Lagan. At first, Danny didn't see it.

'In the water,' Ellie said softly.

'What am I looking for?' Danny asked, frustrated.

'The lights,' his father said, the pitch of his voice going up another octave. 'Look at the fuckin' lights!'

He looked. Lircom Tower cast a long reflection in the river – it was a twenty-four-hour workplace and so was always illuminated. For motorists driving into the city it was the first visible sign that they had arrived in the heart of Belfast. But, floor by floor, the lights of Lircom Tower were going out.

'What is it?' Tony asked Danny, as if expecting him to have all the answers.

Unfortunately, he was right. Danny knew exactly what was coming for them. He remembered the Morrigan–Carman face-off on the Hill of Tara and the flowing, encompassing darkness that had attacked the Morrigan's warrior sons.

'Dub,' he said.

'My big brother,' Dian explained, for the benefit of a baffled Ellie. 'A cloud of living darkness.'

'A fuckin' cloud of fuckin' living darkness?' Ellie said.

'Seriously? Your family's fuckin' *shite*, you know that?'

''Think so?' Dian replied with evident amusement. 'We have another problem. Dub loathes Dother. He always has.'

'But you're in Dother's body–' Danny began.

'Not for much longer.'

'Why?' Danny asked.

Dian looked pained. 'Because,' he said, clutching his chest and staggering. 'Possession of a dead human is one thing. Possession of a live faerie princeling is another. Dother wants his body back.'

'So,' said Danny. 'We're trapped at the top of a skyscraper in the middle of a city overrun with monsters, we've got a cloud of unstoppable living darkness rising to meet us from below, and a mighty fucked-off faerie prince about to reclaim his body and discover one of us has killed his ma. That about sum it up, aye?'

'Not quite,' Tony said. 'We've got you.'

The quiet pride in Tony's voice startled Danny. His father had complete and utter faith in him.

'We've got two Morrigans, not just one,' Danny returned.

Tony nodded. 'Dub's about to get his hole handed to him.'

'You also have this …' Dian said, activating the secret panel behind Dother's desk and extracting the silver Sword of Nuada from its compartment. Suddenly, he clutched his hands to his head and emitted a short howl of pain, before waving away Danny's offer to assist. For a moment, just a moment, his eyes flashed red and his expression changed–

''Take it!' he gasped at Danny. 'Use it!'

With that Dian fell to his knees, using the last of his strength to toss the Sword to Danny. As it left his hand, the silver light it was emitting faded; the glow only seemed to exist when the Sword was in someone's grasp.

As one, every single source of light in the office died, plunging them into darkness as the final floor of Lircom Tower succumbed to the encroaching shadow.

Every source save one.

The silver Sword, caught securely in Danny's grasp, was now shining with a glow so incandescent it caused all save Danny to shield their eyes against the glare.

'*Morrigan …*' a voice in the shadows rumbled.

'Dub,' Danny returned, hefting the Sword in his hand experimentally. It was heavy and unwieldy and his half-baked assumption that somehow his heritage would grant him instant Jedi-like abilities was proving to be optimistic to say the least.

Dother stood up, Dian no longer.

'Danny?' Dother said, taking in the scene around him. His gaze fell on the crumpled shape of Carman's human host.

'What have you done?' he demanded, his human features rippling and revealing the demonic countenance beneath, his teeth elongating into fangs, his ears growing to points, his stance changing to that of a beast ready to pounce.

It was then that a huge fist made of pure darkness materialised from the shadow all around them and smashed him straight out of the twenty-fourth floor window.

Danny's air-swordplay wilted mid-stroke.

Tony Morrigan, still standing nearest the window, fancied he saw from somewhere far, far below in the gloom, a small fountain of water erupt from the Lagan's surface.

'*Never liked that little shit,*' Dub's voice boomed from the shadows.

No one spoke for a long moment – at least, no one except Dermot Scully, who had seemingly had enough excitement for several lifetimes and had taken to convulsing quietly and emitting small *bub-bub* noises.

'Um …' Danny whispered to his companions. 'Ideas?'

'Hand him his arse,' Ellie began.

'*Sssh,*' Danny and his father spoke simultaneously.

'Bub-bub,' Dermot agreed.

'*You will all come with me. Carman will see you.*'

'I want my son,' Danny said, gathering himself. Huge fists of darkness or not, he wasn't going to be shaken.

'*You will see him,*' the voice responded, laced with amusement. '*He is with Carman. You can both go to him, if you wish. We have no further desire to keep him against his will.*'

Ellie was suddenly in front of Danny, her hands on his shoulders. The glowing Sword cast her features in silver relief and made her look like some sort of glorious sculpture. There were tears in her eyes, of relief or disbelief he didn't know.

'Too good to be true,' he said, softly enough for only her to hear.

'And?' was all she said. Looking at her then, he knew that, so long as the bait was her little boy, there was no trap that Ellie Quinn wasn't prepared to face.

He squeezed her arm with his free hand. She was right. At this point they didn't have a choice – it had been too long, too much had happened. If this had been an eighties' action movie, right now would be the montage scene where he and Ellie weaponed up for the final showdown.

'Murdering bastard!'

The cry came from somewhere to his left, followed by a soft, fleshy noise, and a sharp inhalation of breath.

As if on slow castors, Danny's eyes were dragged across the office. To his father, then to Dermot Scully. Dermot held Dother's executive letter opener in his hand, now stained in red. Tony was sucking in great whooping breaths of air as he took an involuntary step backward to rest across the great ornate desk. He brought his right hand up to his left breast and when it came away, it did so plastered in blood.

Tony didn't say a word, didn't have time to. With an almost apologetic look at his son, he sagged to the office floor.

Tony Morrigan was dead.

In the silence that descended upon the room, Dermot turned from his act of sudden homicide to face Danny and Ellie. He dropped the letter opener from his shaking hands as though it was scaldingly hot.

'My father,' Dermot croaked. 'My father!'

As the reality of Tony's murder hit him, Danny's scream of outrage and pain seemed to ignite the Sword in his hand. The glow it emitted increased in intensity, so far beyond blinding that Ellie could see her veins and arteries, red and blue, through her own skin.

A mega-tsunami of light roiled out in waves, with Danny at

its epicentre, When the front hit Dermot Scully, the man simply *popped* out of existence, as substantial as a soap bubble.

As it passed over Ellie, she screamed – not in pain, but in empathy. She was feeling Danny's very soul, pure and unfiltered, and right now it was howling in agony with the pain of watching his father die.

The power being thrown out by the Sword amplified the wail of anguish, fusing a wall of sound to the blast of light. Every drop of Danny's grief and shock and rage, enhanced by his synaesthesia, amplified through the Sword, was boiling out.

Lircom Tower, until that moment shrouded in Dub's darkness, went from a black silhouette to blinding silver beacon as the light from the Sword and the sound of Danny's scream tumbled outward, bathing Belfast in sound and fury.

The Sting

'Ready for this, son?'

Tony Morrigan, sixteen years old and frightened out of his wits, managed to nod. His father squeezed his shoulder reassuringly, even as the Triumph Herald spluttered to a halt at the appointed door. It was 3 a.m. and theirs was the only car on the street. Tony was amazed every single bedroom curtain in the street wasn't twitching like crazy.

''Mon,' his da said, and turned to open the driver's side door.

'Da, wait. Please. Are you sure about this?' Tony asked. He was pale as a ghost.

'I'm sure.' James regarded his son keenly. 'Son, you've been begging me to let you get more involved for the last couple of years. This is it. It's time.'

James reached inside his coat and produced something that glinted in the streetlight's glow. It was a dagger, simple enough in design, but its edge, even in the dimly lit vehicle interior, looked sharp enough to have its own satirical column in a society magazine. Tony was transfixed by that razor-thin edge, that gleaming point.

'Take it.'

Numbly, he reached out and it was placed into his hand. He felt its weight. The reality of what it was, what it meant, what they were about to do, threatened to short out what was left of his reason. He felt as though he were simply a vessel to be steered.

'Is …' Tony swallowed as they walked to the front door. 'Is he on his own in there?'

'He's waiting for us.'

'But–'

He got no further before the front door opened. A man stood in the doorway. He looked human. Tony had hoped he'd have pointed ears, or horns, or a big cardboard sign around his neck with *I Eat Babies* written on it or somesuch.

Nothing like that. He was overweight, approaching middle-age and he looked tired – when he saw Tony and James on his doorstep, he didn't react in fear or anger, but with a sense of weariness.

'In you come,' he said, and opened the door fully, stepping back to let them pass.

'You heard him,' James said, and made as if to step into the house. Tony tugged anxiously at his father's sleeve, the dagger hidden inside his overcoat seeming to weigh a thousand tons and getting heavier.

'What are you doing, Da? We can't just walk in!'

'Yes we can,' his father said firmly, and brokering no further discussion on the subject, entered the house, nodding curtly to the occupant as he stepped inside. Tony followed, sticking as close to his father as he could, heart thudding in his chest like a jackhammer, mind racing, mouth dry, fingers white-knuckled around the dagger. Like a zombie on autopilot he found himself mirroring his father as he sat on an armchair in the living room. The middle-aged man sat on a kitchen chair he'd pulled in from the other room. Obviously the house only had two comfy chairs, and they had been reserved for guests. Or murderers.

Murderers. MURDERERS!

The word began to bounce off the walls of Tony's brain like Steve McQueen's rubber ball in *The Great Escape*. He felt like cupping his hands over his ears in an effort to drown it out, except of course that would mean letting go of the dagger inside his coat–

MURDERER!

'He new to all this?' the man asked.

'Learning the trade,' James said.

The man grunted. He steepled his fingers and regarded James. 'So,' he said eventually. 'Let's get it out in the open. Ask.'

'You human?'

'Not completely.'

James shrugged. 'That'll do me.'

'That'll do? You're not curious as to why I invited you into my home when I noticed you following me?'

'No,' James admitted. 'I've heard of some of you – the infiltrators – who get bored with being stuck in this world and just want it to end. Go back home. So you seek us out.'

'*That's* what you think this is? Suicide by Morrigan?'

'Isn't it?'

Genuine emotion entered the man's voice for the first time since he'd invited them inside. 'No it isn't,' he said, leaning forward.

'I invited you here because I wanted the chance to talk to you.'

'Talk? Ah right. About how humankind will one day fall back under your faerie heel?' James guessed. 'Spare me. I could act a part in that speech, mate.'

'No! I'm not some fuckin' wolf or wasp getting kicks off of eating wee girls!'

'Da,' Tony spoke up. 'Maybe we should hear him out.'

'Don't make me regret bringing you, son,' his father snapped.

'Listen to him!' the man urged.

'All my son sees is your shell,' James retorted. 'I've seen what you do, those of you who can pass for human. You think it's funny, don't you? To pretend. Sometimes you even stretch it out for days, or weeks, or maybe even months. But never for good. Eventually, you get bored. My da took me along to get one of you in Tralee in '51. Living as a postmaster for six months. First the pets went missing, then the kids. The things I saw inside that house,' and to Tony's amazement, his father's voice wavered with emotion. 'You can't hide what you are.'

The man's face fell. 'And that is?' he asked, as if wanting to confirm the answer he already knew was coming.

'Monsters.'

With that, James reached into his coat and pulled out a dagger – the companion to the one he had given his son. Tony saw the determination on his father's face and his stomach lurched, flopping as if kicked – he thought he would throw up then and there at the inevitability of what was about to occur.

'Da?'

Both men and Tony started at the unexpected voice. A boy

of five or so stood at the bottom of the stairs, wearing a pair of tattered blue pyjamas that looked as if they'd been made from scrap wallpaper. From the corner of his eye Tony saw his father hide the blade back inside his coat. The movement was almost too fast to follow.

'Da?' the little boy said again, sleepily, as he registered the two strangers sitting in his living room. 'Heard you talkin', Da.'

Tony hid his face behind his coat. He couldn't meet that little boy's eyes.

'Back to bed, son. You've school in the morning. Don't waken your big brother getting back in, there's a good boy.'

'Daddy, who–'

'Dermot,' the man said in a warning tone of voice so paternal, so familiar, that Tony felt tears begin to flood his cheeks, much to his horror. He watched through blurred vision as the little boy took a final doubtful look around and then padded softly back upstairs.

'How long you been pretendin' to be his da?' James asked, furious.

The man's shoulders slumped. 'It doesn't matter what I say to you, does it?' he said, all the life gone from his voice once more. 'Six months.'

He was lying. Tony knew it. Since they'd entered his house, all of the things the man had said had rung true, except this. He had not been pretending to be that little boy's father for only six months. Bile rose in Tony's stomach. They couldn't do this! They were supposed to be the fuckin' *good* guys!

'Da, please!' Tony tried again.

'Don't wanna hear it,' came the response. 'As for you. Don't really think here is the best place, do you? Considering.'

The man just sighed. 'No. I suppose not. Considering.'

He went and got his coat. He put on a pair of slippers, retrieved a packet of cigarettes and lit one as they exited the house. He locked the door, softly. He cast a look up at the upstairs bedroom window and to the curtain that moved there, ever so slightly.

He got into the front passenger seat of the Herald and sat without a word as they drove through the deserted city. The first rays of dawn were beginning to break free of the bonds of night when they pulled over at the end of a deserted country lane, a few miles from the city boundaries.

'Get out,' James said. The man complied. 'Walk to the ditch.'

Tony wanted to scream. He wished the man would run, but instead he continued to do as he was told, going calmly to the ditch at the side of the road. Tony and his father kept pace with him.

Before James could stop him, the man reached out and touched Tony on the chin, gently moving the boy's face up to look at him. Whatever remained of Tony's childhood evaporated in that touch, boiled away by the look in the man's eyes.

'Will you remember this?' he asked. Tony could only nod, dumbly. The man smiled, and for the first time, Tony could see something dangerous lurking beneath the surface. 'Good. Because I will.'

James Morrigan's arm moved, once, twice. There was a soft sigh and the hollow noise of a body hitting the earth.

'Go back to the car,' James said, discarding the dagger and

picking up the spade they had brought along – a spade that had seen use many times. 'Wait for me there. We'll be home soon, son. You did good, I'm proud of you. I know how you feel now, but you should be proud.'

Tony never fully forgave his father for that last lie.

*

Maria Scully sighed as the small presence at her hips tugged at her skirt for the fourteenth time this hour. The stew did not make itself, no matter what those under the age of ten seemed to think, and much as she was the envy of most of the women in the street for only having the two wains, she was willing to wager that the younger of the two at this precise moment was proving all by himself to be more trouble than any five of the street's little terrors you'd care to name.

'Dermot,' she said warningly. '*What* have I told ye? Do you want nothing for your dinner, is that it? Do ye want to be sittin there with only a slice of bread and nothin in the bowl to dip it into?'

'It was a car Mammy,' Dermot insisted. 'He went away in a big oul car so he did. Him an' two fellas.'

'I'm sure he did,' she sighed. 'And I'm sure the Lone Ranger was riding right alongside them on Trigger. Now go on. Get!'

'Mammy s'not Trigger! It's *Silver!*' Dermot said, aghast.

'Get!'

Off he huffed, leaving his mother behind. He moved into the street, a little man on a mission. It was a Saturday afternoon and the place was one heaving mass of children. A game of football was moving up and down the street, winding its way around the little pockets of girls playing a series of complicated throw-and-catch games.

Into this tableau of youth went little Dermot Scully, a big-brother seeking missile. 'Our Michael! Our Michael!'

Some of the girls took up the cry – he was still young enough to be considered adorable. 'Michael Scully! Michael Scully! Your Dermot wants ye!'

The football game was put on pause for the briefest of moments as a skinny, bony, dirty-kneed urchin strode towards his moppet-headed, runny-nosed little brother.

'What's it?' Michael said impatiently. 'We're gettin' beat eleven six!'

'Our da still hasn't come home,' Dermot said.

'Jesus, Dermot, not this again– '

This was all the leverage Dermot needed. 'I'm tellin on ye!' he said immediately. 'You said a bad word, I'm tellin on ye!'

He turned to go and felt himself tugged back by his big brother. There was not much brotherly affection being radiated toward him at that precise moment.

'You're not tellin' nothin', right?'

'He was taken away,' Dermot insisted. 'By two bad guys. I knew they were bad guys cos I could tell our Da was ascared of them.'

'Bad guys,' Michael scoffed. 'That's all them Westerns you watch. An' who'd wanna take our da away, like? He's only our da.'

'We'll look for him. Me an' you! If he's in trouble, we'll be able to help him!'

Michael sighed, but he was beaten and Dermot knew it. 'Right.

If I help ye until dinner's ready and our ma calls us, will you not say about me sayin' …'

'Aye, aye, aye,' Dermot nodded vigorously. 'Swear.'

''Mon,' Michael said, and trotted off, shrugging his shoulders and gesturing towards Dermot in response to the questioning looks of his football mates. Dermot jogged to catch up with him, fairly bursting with excitement. It wasn't often that his big brother allowed him to hang around with him, and they were off on a proper rescue mission as well!

They turned the corner at the top of the street–

Michael laughed. 'Well,' he said, already turning on his heel. 'Easiest rescue mission ever. Over here, JP! On the head! On the head!'

Thirty feet or so away, coming down from the main road, was their da.

It was something of a ritual for Dermot to drift, seemingly by accident, to the entrance of the street around the time his da usually came home from work. Upon seeing his Daddy, the wee fella would completely lose his mind and charge towards him, arms and legs flailing, ready to launch himself into his arms.

Today he didn't move a muscle. Something kept him rooted to the spot until his da reached him – only then did he slowly lift his head so he could look at his father's face.

'There's my wee man,' his da said. His voice was slower than normal, as if it was an effort to speak. He was dirty. He smelt. There was soil on him.

Dermot stared up at him, mouth frozen and unable to reply – a car with its front wheels accelerating and its back wheels reversing.

His father crouched down on his haunches so that he was level with the boy. He smelt strongly of earth, which was strange, but there was another scent surrounding him, one Dermot couldn't place at all. He looked at his father's hands, which were blackened with soil, the fingers raw and torn, like sausage meat.

'You're hurt,' Dermot said. 'Was it them men, da?'

His da smiled, weakly, reaching out with those ruined fingers and brushing Dermot's cheek. The boy recoiled instinctively at the coldness of the touch.

'Son I need to speak to your ma in the house for a wee while. Find Michael. Don't come in 'til I say so.'

Dermot should have been terrified, but the only thing radiating from him was confusion and sadness. 'Da, you're gonna be all right,' he said.

The reanimated corpse in front of him said nothing for a moment. Eventually, it nodded. 'Yes, son. It's all gonna be grand. Now please, do that for me.'

In a rush, Dermot came forward and hugged him, though the coldness of his father's skin must have been hard to take. 'I'm your wee man, am'pten I?' he said, in a small voice.

'Always.'

Then Dermot was gone, vanishing into the crowd of children like a fish re-entering the shoal.

Too quickly, the man stood before the place that had been his home. He closed the front door behind him, such an unusual act in the communal Belfast streets that the click of the latch caused his wife to come from the kitchen to investigate. Her face lit up when she saw him, until she took in his appearance.

'Holy Mary, Mother of God!' she cried. 'Dermot was right! What in God's name'd they do to you?' She threw her arms around him to embrace him–

And froze. When she pulled back, pulled away, he could see that her concern had been replaced by all-out alarm.

'You're so cold,' she said.

'Sit down, please,' he told her.

She grabbed his hand in hers as if to test its temperature. 'Your hands!' she babbled.

He moved her to the nearest armchair. She was turning his hands over in hers and her skin felt so warm, so incredibly warm and inviting and full of life. Every time she touched him it was as if she was bringing him back to life, but briefly, much too briefly.

'Maria,' he said, gathering every scrap of strength he had. 'You have to listen to me. You have to listen to everything.'

'I'm gettin' Dr Blackwell,' she said, as if she hadn't heard. 'Did they lock you in a freezer? Why you? You're not involved in anythin'? You've never said. Oh *Jesus God* look at your fingers. Maybe we should go straight to the hospital – yes, yes, I'll go and rap wee Mrs Bradley and ask her to feed the boys at her house and we'll go to the Royal and get you sorted.'

He closed his fingers – what remained of them, anyway – around her wrist, not tightly enough to cause pain, but enough to get her attention. Slowly, he brought her hand up to his chest, placed her palm directly over his heart.

'What?'

'Sssh.'

For a few moments they sat there, her hand on his chest. He

watched her expression cycle from puzzled to alarmed to terrified to uncomprehending, until it was all she could do to stare at him.

Looking at her, at how beautiful she was, he couldn't help but remember the very first time he'd seen her, back when she was Maria Quinn. He'd known he wanted her.

This was it. This was his one chance. His last chance.

'Maria, I'm dead,' he said. 'I'm not human. In truth, I never was. The men who came here last night, they knew that. Do you understand? I'm not a man, Maria. Not completely, at any rate. I lost my permanent body a very, very long time ago. Ever since I have had to move from one body to another. Possessing, I suppose you'd call it. I did that for centuries.

'Then, forty years ago, I possessed a doctor working in the Royal. One day they brought in a wee boy who'd fallen on his head. His brain was gone, and his body was shutting down. He was empty, Maria, do you see?'

She was so warm, so beautiful. He almost felt as though his heart would beat again, sitting so close to her. He paused. 'I took him, Maria and I've lived his life ever since – a human life. I've grown old, I've lived, I fell in love – so in love – with you. I've had children.'

She said nothing, she didn't move. He pressed on. What did he have to lose?

'This body is dead now. It'll start to decay. It's already started. I want to go to the hospital, with you, now, as you suggested. To the coma ward. Find someone there my age, someone brain-dead like the wee boy was, and take him. This body will die, but I'll live on, and maybe' – he sighed, knowing how unlikely this was – 'I know it'll take time, months, a few years, I don't know, maybe with enough time, we can be together again, you and me. Our kids. They mean so much to me, Maria. More than you can imagine. They'll need me to guide them when they grow up. Someday we can tell them the truth about their lineage. We'll be …'

He stopped. His wife still hadn't moved. Hadn't even blinked.

'… a family,' he finished, the words empty.

He released her hand from his chest. She began to shiver at once, as though dipped into liquid nitrogen. Her arms and legs jerked spasmodically. Her lips were blue.

'Maria, no!' he cried.

In his chest, his heart beat. Just once. Enough for him to cough up blood and catch it in his hand. The warmth he'd been feeling, it hadn't been his imagination. He'd been leeching life from his wife's body, transferring it to his, like some grotesque vampire, like–

A monster.

Desperately, not daring to touch her, he sought out blankets and wrapped them around her. He stoked the living-room fire drawing on the remnants of his powers to feed it. The room temperature increased. He checked on Maria. The blue tinge to her lips had receded, but she was still staring blankly ahead.

He waved a hand in front of her eyes. No reaction.

For a while – maybe minutes, perhaps as long as half an hour – he sat there with his wife, knowing that it was going to be the last time he ever did so and not wanting it to end, not ever.

He had to go, had to leave her. He stood up, moved into the hallway and opened the front door. Dermot rushed in seconds later, ravenous as a wolf, rushing straight to the kitchen table. He leapt out of the little boy's way, afraid to touch his own son.

He stepped out into the street.

'Da? You goin'?' It was Michael speaking now. There was strength in the boy, ambition unbounded. He probably got that from his grandmother. The man just hoped there would be compassion too. He had been determined to see that there would be.

'Yeah,' he told the boy.

Michael frowned, taking in his da's odd appearance and voice. 'Where you away?'

'Look after them.'

'What?'

'*Look after them*,' he repeated harshly.

Michael recoiled back as if stung. 'Da?' he said, the pitch of his voice now significantly higher, betraying his confusion. He reached out as though to grab his father's arm and pull him back–

'Go back to the house,' Dian said, pulling away from the boy's outstretched fingers. 'Wait for me there, I'll be home soon, son.'

Michael never forgave his father for that last lie.

LIRCOM TOWER, BELFAST, NOW

'We've got two Morrigans, not just one,' Danny said.

His father smiled. 'Dub's about to get his hole handed to him.'

Dermot Scully only wished he felt as confident in pat little sound bites. At least when Dother's minions had held them under siege earlier that night he'd been on home territory, able to fashion some form of mystical defence, no matter how improvised.

He thought of his brother's surprise victory against the spider-thing that had attacked them during that siege – he'd been so proud of Michael at that moment. His whole life, it seemed, his big brother had viewed him as a burden, as a badge of shame. Dermot had watched his brother's grip on empathy, always tenuous, ebb away as the years progressed. But there, in the basement, wielding that golf club in defence of his daughter and brother, he had found redemption.

All too briefly.

Michael was dead. The very people he had died trying to protect had been taken anyway. His big brother had died for nothing.

A creature from nightmares was on its way to finish them off and the only weapon they had was a sword – granted it was the Sword of Nuada, but Dermot wasn't convinced that it would be enough. Even Dian, their unexpected saviour, was losing his grip on Dother's body. He had fallen to the ground, eyes flashing red just before every single source of light died in the office, plunging them all into darkness.

It was at that point, just as the lights went out, that Dermot Scully's head exploded. Agonising waves of pain smashed into his conscious mind. He fell to his knees as the darkness around them was banished by the Sword in Danny's hand.

He wasn't alone in his head.

Desperately, he tried to cry out for help. The noises died in his throat, strangled by a competing series of instructions being sent to his body, as if he had grown a second consciousness that had a veto over anything his body performed. All he was able to do was to half-sit, half-slump on the office floor, convulsing quietly. They were all ignoring him anyway.

He saw Dub's giant fist smash Dother out of the window and knew that Dian was no longer resident in the latter's body, because it was Dian who now had a timeshare in his cerebrum. He didn't know where his own mind ended and Dian's began – his memories pooled. He had a human life, his own, and *another* life which had lasted centuries, and he could access every memory simultaneously.

Dermot was there the night his father had begged, in vain, for his life.

He was there on the car journey as his father was driven to his place of execution.

There with his father as, having waited for James Morrigan to finish filling the grave dug for him, he began the slow and agonising process of clawing his way back to the surface.

A million miles away, Danny and Ellie were having a conversation.

'Bub,' Dermot managed to say. 'Bub …'

Rage boiled within him. Rage like he'd never felt. After his father's disappearance, his mother had become little more than a zombie and little Dermot had been utterly convinced something supernatural was going on. He had been mocked by his peers, by his own brother, for this belief, but with his eyes and ears open, he had begun to notice other strange things.

Two years later, Tony Morrigan had tracked him down. He'd claimed to have heard about this little boy who saw things. So their lifelong partnership had begun. Except it had been a lie. Tony had known all along who Dermot was, how he'd lost his father, and had never had the balls to admit it.

All these years he'd been working with these bastards. He'd risked his fucking *life* to help Tony Morrigan have the son he never should have had, the son that had brought about all of this madness in the first fucking place. He'd watched his brother die because of it.

Just like that, he had control of his body once more. He staggered forward, his eyes trained on Tony Morrigan. The letter opener was in his hands. It felt solid, heavy. It felt *right*.

Tony saw him coming. He even saw the blade of the letter opener glinting in the silver light cast by the Sword. Realisation dawned on his face at what was about to befall him.

'Murdering bastard!' Dermot spat out as he thrust the sharp end of the letter opener into Tony's chest. His aim was straight and true.

As the light went out of his former best friend's eyes, Dermot felt the presence in his mind recede and vanish, a snake uncurling itself from his cerebral cortex. He stared down at his blood-covered hands. At the corpse of Tony Morrigan, and at the expression on Danny's face as, silver Sword in hand, he beheld the man who had just murdered his father. The weight of what he'd just done pressed down on Dermot. All of the righteous fire was gone from him. The letter opener – the murder weapon – clattered from his numb fingers to the floor. He had to explain.

'My father,' he managed to croak. 'My father …'

He got no further. A supernova of silver light, fuelled by Danny's scream of grief, struck him full-on, tearing at every molecule of his body. He bore its impact for a fraction of a second before it overwhelmed him completely.

When the tsunami of energy finally subsided, after it had lit the penthouse office suite of Lircom Tower like a lighthouse beacon, visible for miles all around, Dermot Scully was nowhere to be seen.

REGENT STREET, BELFAST, TWO DAYS AGO

Beatrice O'Malley let the curtains fall back into place, and pondered the man standing at her front door. She hobbled to answer the insistent knocking, apologising profusely for being old and weak and slow and God love ye and blah blah blah …

The door opened.

'You can cut that oul shit out, for a start,' Dian said, through the mouth of a terrified Jehovah's Witness.

Bea reached forward, hooked her fingers around the man's collar and, with superhuman strength, yanked him inside the house. The door slammed shut so hard behind him that it caused a painting in wee Mr Whitaker's house next door to fall down.

'Son,' she said.

'Ma,' Dian returned, and produced a knife from his pocket.

She raised an eyebrow. 'Free gift with subscriptions to *Watchtower?*'

'Took it from his kitchen this morning,' he said.

She made a disappointed face. 'Please tell me you're not playing house again.'

Pain etched across his face. 'Don't,' he said warningly. 'Don't you ever talk about them!'

'If you're gonna stab me, stab me,' Carman clucked, letting the

Bea identity fall back over her like a shroud. 'I'm away to stick a wee pot of tea on. I could murder a cup. Want one?'

'Go fuck yourself,' he said, following her into the kitchen.

She tutted as she rummaged for the cups. 'I do love it when you make time to visit your wee mummy,' she said with a hint of rebuke.

'I spoke to Dother last night. He asked me for help.'

'And so you thought you'd come and stab me?' she shrugged. 'He must have been more direct than normal.'

'He didn't ask me to stab you.'

She fixed him with the sort of crestfallen look only a mother can perfect. 'Would it kill any of you to show some initiative?' she said.

'You sick, twisted old hag!' Dian exploded, putting his fist through the nearest wall. He winced and held his head to the side. 'Oh will you shut up?' he hissed. 'I know it's broken. I'll drop you off at the hospital.'

'Trouble with the passenger, love?' Bea said, leading him back in to the living room, a tray with two steaming cups and a plate of biscuits in her hands. 'Sorry I've only a mint Kit-Kat. I know you like a jammy Wagon Wheel. You should just kill your host now. I'm hardly likely to let him walk out of here, am I, him being a witness to this wee conversation. Are you sure you won't have the wee mint Kit-Kat?'

Dian simply looked at her.

'Too late, the flies are on it,' she said, and began dipping it into the tea and sucking the melting chocolate with a noise that would have made Hercules wet himself. 'Sit down, would ye, for God's sake, you're making me tired looking up at you.'

'Stop the cutesy old woman *bullshit!*' Dian exploded, kicking over the table and the spare cup. Bea had seemingly anticipated this outburst and had retracted her legs to safety, her own beverage and snack safely in her grasp. She watched impassively as Dian continued to rage and scream, dunking her chocolate biscuit into the tea.

'Ach,' was all she said after a few moments. 'See what you done – wee Mr Whitaker's his listening glass pressed to the wall.'

She snapped her fingers. There was the faintest of thuds, undetectable to the human ear, but both she and Dian heard it clearly.

'And him only over the last stroke,' she said. 'That's him blind now, God love him. I must say to his wee Home Help. Lovely wee girl. Very big hands. Think she's a lesbian.'

Dian sat down. His legs were trembling. 'Stop,' he said hoarsely. 'Stop it.'

'You first,' she said mildly.

It was at this point that Dian began to cry. Thankfully he was too engrossed in this to see the truly epic eye-roll that this induced in his mother. She passed the time waiting for the sobs to subside by telephoning the ambulance for wee Mr Whitaker, telling the operator that she'd heard him calling for help. Which was true, in a way – his mind was rather screaming at the moment. She reached into his head to silence him and muddy the waters of his short-term memories. She had done this so often down the years that it was little wonder the oul fella could barely remember how to tie his shoes.

'Now,' she said cheerfully, setting *Emmerdale* to record. 'What can your wee mummy do for her baby boy?'

He looked at the knife, still grasped in his hand. 'You could die,' he said softly. 'But I know that's not going to happen.'

'No, no it's really not,' she smiled. 'But this is makin' progress, son! We're talking again. Now, how about it. Tell me what you're after and we'll see what we can do. Eh?'

He sighed. 'What I'm "after", *Mitéra*? I want a life, or at least a semblance of one. I want to be able to leave this fucking hateful little island. You're the one who put up the wall stopping me from possessing anyone who leaves; don't bother denying it. I want to go to the other side of the world and live my days in peace, to have children again, a wife. I want free from all this bullshit – yours, my brothers', the fucking Morrigans'. I want to be Calma again.'

She smiled. 'Done.'

He studied her. He knew how this worked. 'And in return?' he asked warily. 'What do you want from me?'

'Only what I've always wanted,' she said. 'I want you to make me proud.'

THE OTHERWORLD, NOW

From her stone circle prison, Carman could sense the oncoming tsunami of light rippling outward from Lircom Tower.

'To me, Luke! Quickly now!' she said, holding out her hands. Without a flicker of hesitation the child ran into her arms. 'Here it comes. Are you ready, my son?'

This was the moment she had been waiting for.

The light washed over them, over the circle. The power of a Morrigan's rage, unleashed in full and amplified through the ancestral weapon of the Tuatha. Properly directed, it could have destroyed her, but there was nothing focussed about it – it was the frenzied thrashing of a baby crying, ripe for her to use as she saw fit. She felt it pulse through her body and she redirected every joule of power at the landscape around them.

The Otherworld, which until now had continued to pendulum from modern-day Ireland and back, anchored. The arrhythmia of a magical world and a human world was dispelled. Millennia of separation was no more. Thanks to Danny Morrigan, and to her own baby boy, the Merging was complete.

She lowered the child to the ground and watched as he flowered and grew once more, now imbued with the power she had channelled through herself. More years fell upon him like leaves. His frame broadened, his shoulders filled out. He screamed in agony as his body went through hyper-accelerated ageing – bones cracking and muscles knotting.

'Mitéra,' he moaned, reaching for her, but she had already turned her back. It was as she hoped – the barriers holding her in place within the standing stones were no more. She was free to roam, to explore her new domain.

But there was no need to travel just yet. Everything she wanted would be coming to her soon enough. She sat down on her throne and glanced at the youth doubled-over in pain on the ground at her feet.

The trap was set.

*

Like petrol on a flame, Carman's use of Danny's powers caused the Merging to spread far beyond the confines of Belfast, the Otherworld expanding to encompass the whole island of Ireland.

In rural areas, places that legends and tittle-tattle had spoken of for generations as 'fairy rings' or suchlike crossed the line from harmless local curiosity to something much more deadly. As the Otherworld and the human world blended in a way they had not done in thousands of years, such places became doorways.

Through these doorways, Carman's children streamed. Hideous, terrible things – some animal shaped, some without shape at all. They ran, they flew, they crawled, they oozed from those doorways toward the nearest signs of human life.

Urban areas, possessed of less in the way of ancient sites, fared better than their rural counterparts. The same Lircom network that had, unknown to the populace of course, powered the melding of worlds had also kept the telecommunication lines alive. So long as the call began and ended in Ireland, the phones worked perfectly. Emergency services were swamped within minutes, hopelessly deluged with more calls and cries for help than a force a thousand times their number could have dealt with.

Families called one another. People were terrified, under attack and under siege – children called parents and begged for help. The lines stayed open. Terror flowed down the Lircom network like blood through a circulatory system and, in her circle of standing stones, where all of the leylines crossed, Carman sat and drank and drank.

In parts of Belfast, however, things were a little different. The orgy of faerie triumph and human death was not going completely to plan.

The Named were hunting.

They moved from street to street, systematically targeting all other faerie life-forms and ripping them apart with an efficiency that only terrified the humans they were rescuing a little bit more.

One wolf amongst the multitude had a rider. Veins coursing with adrenalin, terror-deadened due to determination and no small measure of painkillers, the rider was proving himself to be every bit a terror to the monsters stalking the city's streets as the wolves themselves.

Whipping the barbed stinger above his head, Steve brought it down hard on the head of what looked like the bastard child of a slug and a cockroach.

'Smell that fer a hairy doot, Cunty McBallix!' Steve whooped. Beneath him, Larka had pinned another formless nightmare to the pavement and was severing its head from where it would have had shoulders. Judging from the thing's choked-off screams, its particular species found decapitation no less fatal than more terrestrial life-forms.

Rider and mount took a moment to survey their surroundings. They were on Royal Avenue, the main shopping thoroughfare in Belfast city centre. The nearby Castle Court shopping centre's upper levels were thronged with humans, herded successfully there by the Named. The three entrances to the centre were under constant attack from faeries but thanks, in no small part to the efforts of Steve and Larka, this particular entrance was currently clear.

There were people in a nearby doorway, lying with their backs up against the glass, trembling. Steve felt he should say something to them, little realising that, a bloodstained bedraggled figure holding a disembodied spiked tail and sitting atop a giant wolf was unlikely to provide much comfort at this point in time.

'And I'd give up forever to touch you …'

He started. Larka turned her head around to look at him with a remarkably quizzical expression.

'Cos I know that you feel me somehow…'

He reached inside what remained of his jacket, and pulled out a mobile phone. The world had gone to hell, had been invaded by monsters, but he was still getting full signal. Hooray. Maybe when he had a quiet minute from dealing death on top of this talking wolf he'd be able to check the Champions League scores.

That ringtone … he'd set it in a moment of romantic foolishness, in what seemed like a lifetime ago now. As he flipped the phone open to take the call, he felt his mouth dry up.

'Maggie?' he said.

He listened for a few minutes. Larka padded this way and that, checking the perimeter. She had time to communicate to a few of her fellows that this was their station now. They acknowledged the command. Nothing save the Named and the humans they were herding would get past.

Steve closed the phone. Larka fancied that her new friend, ill though he already was, had grown a shade or two paler in the time it had taken for him to speak. She tensed her muscles for fast travel, anticipating what was coming next.

'We need to go,' he said. 'We need to go *now*.'

BELFAST CITY CENTRE, NOW

A few hundred yards from where Steve and Larka had just made a fast exit, fresh from herding a group of humans into a secured building, a single crow landed in the midst of a group of the Named.

'Honoured are the Named,' the bird said.

'Morrigan,' Wily said in greeting, emerging from the midst of the group.

The bird and the wolf faced one another. 'You're going a little off-script, aren't you?' the Morrigan observed. 'Protecting humans?'

'We owe your descendent a debt. We protect the humans as part of that debt, and also,' Wily added, giving the crow a long look, 'because we now know it is the right thing to do.'

The crow's head darted this way and that, taking in the ranks of the wolves assembled around her, clearly liking what she saw. 'Had quite an effect on you, didn't he?'

'He shared his humanity with us. In a way, he is our father and our creator,' Wily replied.

'I don't believe he meant to create you. But then,' she added drily, 'he *does* have a history with that type of thing. So what do you think of your god?'

Wily took a second to ponder this. 'He swears a lot,' he said.

It was then that the blinding flash of white light flared across the city. Wily and his wolves turned away from it, but the crow did not. It fluttered in that ungainly way crows have, hopped up into the air as the wave of light broke across them. For a moment the bird was silhouetted, a tiny black speck against a silent blast wave of white.

When the wolves had regained their sight in the aftermath of the flash, they saw that the crow was gone. In its place was a woman, resplendent and shining, clad from head to toe in green battledress and with flowing black hair cascading down her shoulders.

The Goddess of War had returned. She was magnificent. She was glorious. She stood proudly and held up her arms aloft in trium–

'Oww-oww-oww! My bastard *neck*,' she complained, aborting the triumphant stance to wince and rub at the offending part of her body. The wolves watched as the goddess stretched every inch of her imposing frame, as if working out some long-standing kinks. 'I've spent nearly two thousand years as a bird. Cramp is a bitch,' she offered by way of explanation.

Thirty feet away, right in front of the main gates of Belfast City Hall, another, smaller flash of light signalled the appearance of a small stone statue. A second appeared only a few feet away from the first, and a third an equal distance to the opposite side. With a succession of flashes, stone statues had soon formed an orderly perimeter around the grand old building, ringing it in a perfect rectangle of mini monoliths.

'The payment,' the Morrigan whispered, her eyes shining with tears.

*

Carman raised her head, as if listening. Her entire body pulsed with power. The world outside the circle was solidified now, a perfect fusion of old and new, ancient and modern. Only Lircom Tower was holding on to its dual identities; phasing in and out of existence, perfectly within the boundaries of the stone circle as though the building had been designed with this eventual destiny in mind.

'Ah yes, the payment,' she echoed, laughing as she looked across the city. 'Old friend, consider it paid in full.'

LIRCOM TOWER, BELFAST, NOW

Cradling his father's body in his arms, Danny didn't even notice the first tremors that shook Lircom Tower. A second tremor was hard on its heels, this one stronger than the first, and coming from the opposite corner of the building. An incredible rumbling began, like a freight train coming at them from the floors below. A portion of the office ceiling crashed down around them. Cracks fractured jaggedly across the windows, the floor.

'What's happening?' Ellie shouted desperately. She hung onto Dother's desk for support. Only Danny seemed unaffected by the quakes. He remained stock still, holding his father's body, his eyes closed. He hardly seemed to be breathing.

'The Merging is complete. All save this building.' It was Dub's voice. No longer disembodied. He stood in the centre of the office, huge and clad in the robes of an ancient King.

Ellie noted the surprise in his expression, as if he were still trying to figure out how he'd transformed from dark mist to physical being.

A third quake, and then a fourth. The roaring became so loud it was hard to think, and now the building began rocking from side to side. The ceiling above them dropped by about a foot, the pressure blowing out the floor-to-ceiling windows all around them with a huge report of smashing glass.

Ellie, having moved closer to the windows in order to see what was happening outside, threw herself backwards to avoid the fragments, but thankfully most of the glass had shot outwards into the Belfast night. She crawled over to Danny as the floor below them began to sag.

'Danny,' she gasped, blood trickling down her face from where a few shards of glass had caught her. 'There are four stone pillars. They're coming up straight through the building!'

At the rear of the office, a section of the floor fell away to nothingness below, cascading downward and smashing through the lower floors like dominos. The roof above their heads slipped once more, and she shook Danny by the shoulders, trying to get through to him.

'Danny!' she said. 'Danny, we have to go!'

He opened his eyes. He was close to losing it, she could see that. 'He's dead,' he said.

'I know,' she replied, tears streaming down her cheeks – she had gone through the exact same ordeal only hours ago. 'I *know*, remember? But we're still here, Danny.'

He blinked, seemingly oblivious to the danger they were in. Nothing mattered to him except the body in his arms. 'Dermot was meant to be his friend ...'

Ellie looked wretched beyond belief. 'I know,' was all she said.

A huge shadow fell across them. Danny looked up, and up, and up.

'Not enough time to leave,' Dub said, knowing every word counted. 'The Sword – use it. Now. Or we die.'

'Use it how?' Danny said.

The roof above them finally collapsed. Ellie had time to scream and raise her arms above her head in what was sure to be a futile gesture before being crushed.

Dub grunted, every massive sinew in his gargantuan neck standing out like ropes as he supported the weight of tons of concrete above his head, stopping it crushing every single one of them.

'Make … something … up,' he managed.

The building was history. It was a miracle that the thin strip of floor they had gathered on was still mostly intact. Ellie watched in horrified fascination as the four great stone pillars moved inexorably upward, pulverising the modern steel and concrete of Lircom Tower as though it was nothing. She felt the entire superstructure lurch to the right, and then back, as if the whole thing was a giant Jenga construct and some idiot had removed the wrong brick.

'We're going over,' Dub said. 'This is it.'

Silver light washed over them.

The tower collapsed in a matter of seconds.

Those who saw it from miles away braced themselves for the rumble underfoot. Those who were within its enormous shadow, sheltering in adjoining buildings or running for their lives along the city centre streets, covered their heads with their arms, or stood, helpless, watching the gargantuan behemoth of concrete and steel topple over – flies ready to be swatted into nothingness by a monstrous hand.

It was not to be.

Somewhere between vertical and horizontal, the tower lost any semblance of physical presence. By the time it would have impacted the surface, it was no more than a ghost, a whisper. Those in its path could only cower and bear witness as phantom walls and floors, many thousands of tons of them, swept through them where they stood.

Lircom Tower was no more. Its destruction and fall, an act that should have spawned a crater a hundred feet wide, caused neighbouring buildings to collapse, created a disastrous surge in the Lagan that would have swept over the riverbank, instead caused none of these things.

In the tower's place, four enormous stone monoliths had risen into the Belfast night, each one taller than the building they had chewed through in their violent birth. And just outside these four giant pillars, a small group had phased into existence sometime between the tower crumbling and fading. Anyone looking closely enough at the two events would have observed that the moment the group appeared, the tower lost its physical presence.

It was safe to say none of the available witnesses were looking that closely. Mostly, they were finishing the process of thoroughly shitting themselves.

'You did it,' Dub said, looking at Danny with unabashed relief.

Danny ignored him. Only he, Dub, and Ellie were present.

Tony's body was not with them. 'My da,' he said. 'Where'd he go?'

Ellie hadn't quite recovered from the eleventh hour reprieve. 'I don't know, Danny,' she said, steadying herself by reaching out and holding onto his free arm, the one not holding the Sword.

'Where'd he *go*?' Danny demanded, holding the Sword against Dub's Adam's apple, which in Dub's case made an actual apple look about the size of a grape.

'He was dead,' he offered. 'Perhaps that is why he was not transported.'

Danny pressed harder with the Sword and a line of blood appeared on Dub's throat.

'My mother may know more,' he added.

'What happened to big shadow-cloud unstoppable darkness guy, by the way?' Danny asked him, not retracting the Sword by so much as a millimetre. 'One minute you're the smoke monster from *Lost* and knocking your brother out a top storey window, and the next you're Mr Agreeable, begging *me* to save you?'

Dub's eyes were wide with alarm. He said nothing.

Danny went back over the events in the penthouse office. Dub had been an insubstantial cloud of darkness until ... *of course!*

'The light.'

Rather than reply, Dub pointed with an arm like a gunboat to the interior of the stone pillars, the message behind the gesture clear. *Answers in there.*

Carman lay within. Once Danny went inside, he knew there was no going back. He wished the thought of this journey ending was more reassuring. He still had no idea what to expect in there. Only that Carman had his son and for that reason, if no other, he knew he would have to go inside. He had lost so much already, too much to think about. Steve. His father. He would *not* lose his son.

The loss of his father ate away at him, threatened to consume him. Every time he tried to focus on the task ahead, the awful memory of Scully striking him down reared its head. It was all he could do not to curl into a foetal ball.

He'd skipped through time and space, through death and rebirth, and had finally understood why his father had done what he'd done. Had finally grasped what it truly meant to be a Morrigan. Only for his father to be taken from him moments after he'd been able to return those crucial memories.

Ellie's hand found his, and squeezed. He looked into her eyes and felt ashamed – he was not the only one going through the searing pain of seeing a parent die. Michael Quinn had died to protect his daughter and no matter what his role in all of this had been, that deserved respect. He had made the ultimate sacrifice–

Wait. Wait a fucking minute. What was he *thinking?* This wasn't the human world. A quick glance at the huge blood-red moon hanging overhead would readily confirm that, if the unearthly creatures flapping and buzzing through the night weren't enough of a clue.

This was a world of magic now. A world where magic cauldrons could return the dead to life, and where a sword – a fucking *magic fucking sword* – could spare a city from the catastrophic collapse of its tallest building. The world had gone to shit. Every notion of what was normal or right had been swept away. Christ, he himself had been torn apart, ripped limb from limb, and now here he stood, alive and well.

'Ellie, I'm going to get them back,' he promised, foolishly, stupidly, but not caring. 'I don't know how, but I will. Your father. My father. Steve. Everyone.'

She just nodded. He wasn't sure whether she actually believed him, or whether she was humouring him because he needed her to do so, but at some level he realised it didn't matter.

Dub had used Danny's distraction in order to take a long step backward, out of range of the silver blade. 'The invitation was for you only, Morrigan.'

Danny turned his back on the hulking prince. He had more important things to do. He took Ellie's hand in his, wondering if he should reach out, use the powers he'd honed on his journeys to instantly convey what he wanted to tell via touch, as he'd done with his father. But no, that didn't seem right somehow. If he couldn't find the words, if he stumbled over them, he'd have to trust, as every man did when trying to say something important, that the emotions behind them would let her know what he wanted to say to her.

'Ellie,' he began, 'I've seen things, I've been to places you wouldn't believe.'

Ellie raised an eyebrow and indicated the world around them. 'I wouldn't believe? Seriously? Are you takin' the fuckin' piss?' she said.

She had a point. 'Okay, maybe you would,' Danny admitted. 'I'm talking about the first place we found ourselves. The world where we weren't together.'

'Oh,' she said, biting her lip.

'Yeah. My time was my own. I had the job I'd always wanted. Well paid, big car, all that shit, and' – he figured in for a penny, in for a pound – 'the sorta life I always dreamed about having when I was with you.'

She didn't slap him, as he had somewhat expected. She just nodded. 'Yeah,' she said, and seeing the look on his face, gave a thin laugh. 'What? I'm meant to be surprised, Danny? This may astonish you but you're not exactly Russell fuckin' Crowe in terms of acting ability. Now, no harm, but I think we've bigger fish to–'

'Wait,' he said, holding up a hand. 'I'm trying to tell you that having everything I wanted wasn't enough. Not cos I knew it wasn't real, but because it wasn't *right*.'

She said nothing. He could see his words weren't being lost on her, though. He pressed on.

'There's probably a million lovely poetic ways to say what I'm trying to say,' he said. 'But what it boils down to is – I got everything I thought I wanted, and I didn't want it. I wanted my life back. My life with you, and with Luke – shitty nappies, kids' TV, fuck-all money, late nights. All the rest of it. I know I didn't choose how it began. I know you didn't either. But I know now that it doesn't fuckin' matter how something begins. It's why we choose to keep going that matters.'

She looked about to say something so he pressed on quickly before she could. This needed saying, before anything else happened. Before he lost anything more.

'Ellie Quinn, I love you,' he said. 'Maybe I didn't always. Maybe I didn't when Luke was born, even. But by fuck, I love you right here, right now, today. When I think of how close I came to never having you, it scares the hell out of me. So I'm standing here now asking you to forgive me for ever not knowing that.'

He paused, trying to decide if he'd said all the things he wanted to say in case he never got another chance to. 'I want to–' he began, but whatever he was about to say, it was rudely interrupted by a deluge of blood. It spattered over him, over Ellie, over everything. His first horrified thought was that something had happened to her but, thankfully, it didn't take long for him to realise she was fine. His second thought was that something had happened to *him*, and his mind had yet to catch up.

He turned to find the source of the blood to see Dub, all ten feet of him, holding his own innards with nothing but stunned amazement on his face. Beside him, soaking wet, was Dother. His face was elongated into something wolfish and his hands were claws – his right hand, a particularly vicious-looking curved claw that was now covered in blood and flesh. He had just eviscerated his older brother.

Dub's mighty form keeled over, a Lircom Tower collapse in miniature, except this time there was no last-minute reprieve. His massive body hit the deck with a thump that Danny and Ellie could feel in their bones. Watching with satisfaction, Dother shifted his face and body back to fully human.

'I never liked you either, fuckface,' he spat at his brother's corpse. His gimlet eyes burned hot as coals as he turned to take in the two humans before him – his face a terrifying thing to behold … then, with a broad smile, he began to applaud. 'Danny, lovely speech. Sorry to interrupt.'

Danny raised the Sword in one smooth move, taking a step backward to better put himself between Ellie and Dother.

Dother snorted and rolled his eyes derisively. 'Please,' he said. 'You're safe. It would be the understatement of the century to say that I can't be arsed with you. I just had a score to settle with this big bastard … going back a *very* long time. My thanks for weakening him, by the way. It's hard to spill someone's guts when they're intangible. Believe me, I've tried.'

'Some fuckin' family,' Danny commented. 'What went right with Dian? How come he's the only decent one among yous?'

Dother's smile only grew. 'Ah yes. Blessed Dian,' he said. 'Amazing what you learn when you're struggling to repossess your own body.'

He sat himself down on his brother's corpse like it was a park bench. His body language was one cigarette away from post-coital. 'Y'know,' he said, sighing, 'it's not easy being the middle child. I did what my mother wanted for two thousand years and where did it get me? She thought higher of this brainless lump and that other sap than she did me. So fine. I'm done with it. Go in there and do what you need to do. But before you do, and seeing as you gave me the window I needed to settle my score, you deserve to know the truth.'

'I wouldn't believe you if you told me–'

'Oh, shut the fuck *up*, will you?' Dother hissed, with a ferocity that caused Danny and Ellie both to take a step back. 'What's happened to you, Danny? You used to be the one cutting through all the story time bullshit, didn't you? Now look at you. Think you have this all figured out, don't you? Big epic hero? Last minute speech to your beloved? March in there magic weapon in tow, and get your baby boy back, right? You couldn't be more wrong.'

Danny glanced at Ellie, and saw that she too was thrown by this. If Dother was lying, he was doing a truly spectacular job of it.

'Okay,' Danny said. 'Tell me. There can't be many fuckin' surprises left anyway.'

THE OTHERWORLD, 1980 AD

'Whoever would have guessed,' Carman said, boredom dripping from every word.

'I know.'

'Months of waiting around, and for that?'

'Was it months? I remember months. They were like longer days, weren't they?'

'Kristin?' Carman said, ignoring this. 'Kristin?'

'Mmm. Should've been Bobby.'

'Pfffff,' Carman blew out a breath. 'Bobby! That wimp! Sue Ellen, now – *that's* a woman!'

The Morrigan flapped her wings and hopped up and down, a gesture Carman had long since learned to interpret as tacit disagreement. 'She's weak,' the crow replied dismissively. 'Finds her solace in a bottle rather than taking a blade to the miserable bastard as she should have done.'

With a gesture of annoyance, Carman swept her hand across the surface of the Dagda's cauldron, abruptly curtailing the *Dallas* closing credits. Her eternal nemesis was perched peacefully on the rim of the Cauldron, tucking her beak under a wing to preen a few feathers that had been caught up during flight.

'How did it come to this?' Carman asked, as she always did.

The Morrigan's little bird head reappeared, a beady eye focused on the woman responsible for the death of two of her children, the exile of her people, the loss of her home and way of life.

'Don't start that again,' she said. 'At least you have representatives up there.'

'Yes,' Carman agreed. 'A scheming, backstabbing bastard who constantly plots my downfall and lusts for my throne, and Casper the Friendly Faerie. *Mitéra's* special boys.'

'I had sons once,' the Morrigan spoke quietly. 'Remember?'

'Oh bitch, bitch, *bitch*.'

They remained in contemplative silence for a few moments. The rolling landscape of the Otherworld stretched out in all directions around them. Walk in a straight line for a few days in any direction away from the circle of the standing stones and lo and behold, it would reappear on the far horizon once more.

'Won't be long now,' Carman spoke up, unable to keep the anticipation from her voice.

'Thirty-odd years, give or take. It's amazing,' the Morrigan said quietly.

'Amazing?'

'Us. Working together, wanting the same thing. What does that say about us?'

'That we've grown older and wiser,' Carman replied.

'Or that we aren't as wise as we should be,' the Morrigan said softly. 'I hate being a crow. Have I mentioned that?'

'Soon,' Carman promised her companion. 'A few decades, give or take, and when the Merging is complete, my first act will be to restore you to your former glory. So long as you play your part, of course. Which you will, I trust?'

The crow couldn't meet her eyes. 'Yes.'

They looked at the vista spread out before them. The Tuatha Dé Danann, hopelessly nostalgic to the last, had chosen to style the Otherworld after the scene of their two greatest victories. They had recreated Mag Tuired's landscape on a massive scale. Whether it was intended as a tribute to the warrior woman who had secured them victory on both occasions, the Morrigan did not dare to speculate.

'I'll bring them back,' the crow said, and with a flurry of wings it took off over the plains, leaving Carman standing alone.

Not long now, the Morrigan promised herself as she flew. One more generation in human terms, and then ... then she would once again stand amongst her people. Be a part of something again. Her people would live. Ireland would be their home once more.

That was worth a few human lives, wasn't it?

BELGRAVIA AVENUE, BELFAST, NOW

Larka tossed a slug-faerie into a lamppost. 'Steve, behind you!' she bellowed.

Steve turned and through sheer chance, managed to use the barbed flail he carried to shatter the skull of a half-human, half-millipede being that had, on hundreds of miniscule little legs, been sweeping down the nearest wall with the intention of tearing his head off.

A Humfipede, he thought. *That's a new one. Has to be worth seventy points, surely.*

Larka used her massive jaws to finish the job. Steve had to hand it to her – she'd have been great in a zombie movie. She always made sure of the kill.

Their immediate perimeter was clear. He ran to the door and began to pound on it. Not entirely to his surprise, no-one answered.

'Maggie! Maggie, open up! It's Steve!' he shouted, as loudly as he could, hoping fervently there wasn't a squad of wasp-faeries overhead that would zero in on his cries. There were more varieties of these disgusting fuckers than he could keep track of. Someone, sometime, was going to have to document all of this. It wouldn't be him, though – with his limited literary capabilities it would be a pop-up book with pull-tabs. *Look Daddy, when I yank on this, the fucker's head comes right off! I can see into his brains! COOL!*

The possibility existed, he reflected, that he might have taken a shade too many drugs.

'We need to get inside,' he told Larka. 'Door's locked and bolted to fuck and back and no one's answering the door or the phone.'

'Stand aside,' she replied calmly.

Crash.

'Will that suffice as an opening?'

He picked a particularly large splinter of wood out of his right nostril and brushed pulverised brick off the top of his head, peering through the sudden dust cloud to see a gap you could have jack-knifed a Humvee through.

'Do rightly,' he said, stepping into the house. 'Maggie! *Maggie!*' he called. There was no answer. He felt his stomach drop another foot or so.

'I can smell something,' Larka observed, stepping cautiously into what remained of the entranceway, sniffing the air around her.

'Yeah,' he replied.

'I apologise, Steve. I know you fear for your mate.'

'She's not my mate. She's not even my friend at this point.'

'I don't wish to alarm you,' Larka continued, ignoring the interruption. 'But what I smell has the unmistakable aroma of ...'

He knew where this was going. 'Death?' he guessed.

She hung her head in sadness. 'I fear so.'

'This is Belgravia Avenue,' he said dismissively. 'Three fellas live here. *Student* fellas. What you're smelling now is boxer shorts so old that if you handed them into the Antiques Road show, the presenters'd piss themselves with excitement.'

'It's strange,' Larka commented. 'I thought I grasped the fundamentals of English, but clearly I have more to learn–' She stopped, abruptly, and changed her stance from the deceptively languid investigative gait she'd adopted since entering the house to something more rigid and battle-ready. Her head swung to the closed door of the room they were approaching on the right, the downstairs front bedroom.

'There is movement inside,' she said softly. 'Coming toward the door. Be ready.'

He tightened his grip on the flail. It had tasted blood tonight and he was ready to give it more if it meant protecting Maggie.

Maggie. Jesus. That he should be here, now, braving the unknown horrors of the apocalypse to defend her of all people. That, incredible as it now seemed, they'd been in the same room together mere hours ago – she was apparently with Danny just as he'd been with Ellie. Memories of that almost-verse still lingered. What did it mean? What did any of this craziness mean?

Right now, it didn't matter. Hearing her terrified voice on the phone begging him to come to help her had cut through a lot of baggage, both real and semi-real, that had built up between them.

Larka tensed her body, ready to spring the moment anything hostile poked its head, heads, or lack of head through that doorway.

The door opened and Steve's first act was to reach out his hand and stay Larka's leap with a gesture.

'Christ,' Flan said. His spindly, dishevelled form was clad in a tartan dressing-gown with a hairstyle that suggested every single strand of hair on his head had a pathological hatred of every other strand of his hair and had decided to stay as far apart from them as possible. On his head he sported a pair of headphones so ludicrously big you half expected him to be ordering around a squad of Cybermen.

'Flan!' Steve said. 'You're alive! Where's Maggie? She okay?'

Flan blinked. It took him a few goes, but he managed it.

'Is he injured?' Larka inquired.

'I don't think "injured" is the right word, no,' Steve said carefully.

'OH MAN ...' Flan shouted, rubbing his eyes. 'SORRY, YOU KNOCKIN WERE YE? I THINK I, UM, I THINK I

FUCKIN' FELL ASLEEP OR SOMETHIN' ... TIME'S IT?'

'Flan, will ya take them headphones off, fer fucks sake!'

'WHY'VE YA BROUGHT A *DOG*? LOOK'T SIZE OF THE CUNT! IF IT CURLS ONE ON THE CARPET, LANDLORD'S GONNA SHIT A BRICK.'

Flan tailed off. He had just spotted the splintered, ruined remains of the front door.

'Is he an idiot?' Larka inquired.

'Give him a minute ...' Steve began, and then reconsidered. He reached forward and ripped the massive headphones from his friend's head, causing Flan to yelp in pain and give him a wounded look.

'Somethin' happened or what?' Flan asked in a small voice.

'You might say that,' Larka told him.

'Flan ... *where* is Maggie?' Steve asked again, feeling his patience ebb.

Flan didn't answer. He was staring at Larka, seemingly wondering if he'd really heard the huge dog in front of him speak. He reached forward with his hand and, as Steve looked on, amazed, and as Larka narrowed her eyes but remained still ... he petted the great she-wolf's head, slowly and carefully, as if he were MacGyver choosing to cut the red or blue wire with four seconds left on the doomsday clock.

'Who's a nice doggie?' he said.

'In centuries past these people wore bells,' Larka observed. 'That made them easier to identif– *oooh*' and her tail wagged as Flan's fingers found a particular spot behind her left ear. '*Oooh* that's good ...'

'Flan! Maggie! Where the fuck's Maggie?' Steve tried once more in despair.

Flan turned his head. 'Aye, Maggie. She turned up earlier,' he said in a singsong, please-leave-a-message-after-the-tone sort of voice. 'Lookin for you, funny enough. After that I went to bed. Tell you what, her voice gives me a sore fuckin' head, lad.'

They heard it then.

'The roof,' Larka said.

Steve took the winding staircases three steps at a time, turning the corners inside the three-storey house like an Olympian. At the top of the final staircase, the ladders leading to the attic had been pulled down. He scaled them like a monkey, finding himself in the ancient mustiness of the Belgravia Avenue vintage attic, a place that made the rest of the house smell like a rose garden in comparison. Someone had placed a box under the open skylight – no doubt to stand on and get a better look out into the night.

Zzzzzztttt.

That was all the warning he got.

The wasp-faerie smashed into him from behind, descending from the attic's ceiling where it had curled all six of its segmented legs flat against the wooden beams, subsuming itself into the darkness until he passed by below. Claws lanced into his back, ripping into his flesh.

The barbed flail went skidding across the attic floor, hopelessly out of reach. He felt hot, rancid breath on his neck as the thing brought its snapping jaws down. Larka had been behind him on the stairs, but how would a wolf her size climb a ladder and squeeze her enormous body into this confined attic?

He was alone up here. Alone, and doomed, and about to feel those teeth rip into the soft flesh of the back of his neck …

'Leave him *alone!*'

He felt the weight of the wasp-faerie lift off his back, heard it hiss in pain and outrage as, from a set of decades-old decomposing boxes, a newcomer wielding the flail recently knocked from his grasp managed to land a glancing blow at his attacker.

A hand found his. He was pulled to his feet. His back felt wet and warm and he heard the spatter of his blood hitting the floorboards. He was dimly aware that wasn't good.

'You came,' Maggie sobbed.

He wanted to reply, to hold her, to do more than that perhaps, but there wasn't time. The wasp-faerie was only winded, knocked off-balance and, if anything, enraged by the unexpected setback. Steve took the flail from Maggie's unresisting fingers and swung it meaningfully in the air, forcing his adversary to back up a few feet, darting back and forth, awaiting its chance to strike. Drool fell from its mouth in copious quantities as it eyed them hungrily.

'What is it?' Maggie wailed. 'They're *everywhere*, Steve … what is it, what is it, *what is it?*'

Steve didn't reply. He took a long step to his left and brandished the flail threateningly, causing the wasp-faerie to move few feet to the right. Right over the attic trapdoor.

Larka's massive head surged from below like the shark on the *Jaws* poster, swallowing the oversized insect as far as its thorax before clamping down, neatly severing the wasp-faerie in two. It had time for one, final surprised *zzzzzztttt?* before its upper half thudded to the attic floor, thin wings flapping uselessly in death.

Seeing this, Steve resisted the urge to gather Maggie in his arms, instead crossing to the skylight and closing it firmly, drawing the curtains back. Only when this was done did he walk towards her and embrace her, kissing her hair, her forehead, her lips over and over, telling her it was all right, it was dead now, it was dead and everything was going to be all right.

'I was driving away from Ellie's house,' she said, when she had finally composed herself, 'And I don't know, Steve, something happened. All these memories washed up on me. I was with Danny for the last two days, as if we were a couple? As if we'd always been a couple. And you – you were with Ellie – you had a *baby* with Ellie – how's that even possible?'

'I don't know,' he said.

'I went back to Ellie's house, but you'd gone. So I came here. I wanted to talk to you. I needed to see you. Flanagan let me in then went back to his room. There was this light from somewhere over there ...' she pointed to the blocked-up skylight window, indicating the city centre., 'A few minutes later, I started hearing all these screams. I was scared. And the TV, most of the stations went out except the local ones. Have you seen what's happening, Steve? They're saying everything beyond Ireland, has gone. *Gone.* How can that happen?'

'I don't know,' he said.

'And I–'

'Maggie?' he said gently. When she was upset like this, there was a special key you had to talk in to get her attention. He slipped into it without a second thought.

She focussed on him then, seeing him, properly, for the first time. Her mouth made an O of horror.

'Steve?' she said. No sooner did his name tumble from her mouth than he felt whatever strength was holding him upright give way. He slumped, but didn't fall – she supported his weight against her.

'Is he injured?' Larka called from below. 'Bring him down. I can tend to him.'

'Larka,' Steve croaked. His strength was failing fast. The drugs, the adrenalin, all of it was wearing off.

Through the concern, Maggie had time to look puzzled. The unseen voice that had wafted up from below sounded feminine, if a touch deep. Thus far, all she'd seen down there was a massive wolf that had just eaten an oversized wasp hell-bent on murdering them both.

'Larka? Friend of yours?' she asked.

Steve was smiling as he slipped into unconsciousness.

OUTSIDE LIRCOM TOWER, BELFAST, NOW

'My hole,' said Danny, summing up.

Dother looked at him almost pityingly. 'You think I'm making this up? Yes, you're right, I am. Dian didn't possess the body of Ellie's grandfather in a pathetically misguided attempt to become human. Because if he *did*, of course, that would mean that not only is your son the latest in the looooooooooong line of Morrigans, he's also …'

'Directly descended from Carman.'

'And I am too,' Ellie said.

'You got it, niece,' Dother said brightly, seeming to revel in their numb horror. 'Never mind, Danny. Gives you some justification for how you used to think of her ones.'

Ellie's hands bunched into fists. Dother saw this, but merely laughed and stepped backwards, waving his arms in a placatory gesture. 'Cheap shot,' he admitted. 'But hey, if your mother Christens you "Evil", let's see how fuckin' good *you* turn out. Now, I'm not so keen on sticking around for the bloodbath to come, so I think I'll be off. I'd say best of luck, but of course, I despise you utterly! Say hello to my great-nephew though, won't you? Such a cute widda nose on him. *Slán!*'

He crouched, and his form rippled slightly, his back legs elongating to lupine proportions. In only a few bounds, he was fifty yards away and accelerating fast.

If Dother's revelation was a shock to him, he could only imagine how Ellie must be feeling. Her family was descended from the monsters that had caused all of this misery. Her son – *their* son – had Carman's blood in his veins. The Sword felt heavy, his hands huge and clumsy. His grandfather and father had forced Dian from his human host. For whatever reasons, however rightly or wrongly, they had robbed two young boys of the only father they'd ever known.

That, then, was why Dermot had done what he'd done. Danny wasn't sure if the motive made him feel any better. He had hoped that his father's old partner had been bewitched somehow, hadn't been in his right mind. But maybe he had – maybe Dian had influenced him, turned his anger up by a few million degrees. It was his superpower after all.

Fuck Dermot, Danny thought suddenly. What must *Ellie* be going through? She was staring after Dother, her back turned to Danny. He reached out toward her, unsure of what he was going to say to try and make sense of all of this madness–

'Right,' she said abruptly, turning on her heel. There was no ocean of pain in her eyes, no soul-searching. Nothing but determination that could have cracked rocks. 'Mon, let's go.'

'Go?'

She gestured to the interior of the circle. 'In. It's time, Danny. We're gettin' our son back, me and you.'

'But–'

'I know,' she cut him off. 'I heard him and I believed him, which amazes me. So I'm descended from' – and her voice wavered slightly, almost with embarrassment – 'from an evil Greek witch-goddess. So my – *our* – son is too. So what?'

'But–'

'But *what*?'

Danny stopped to consider his options – enter Carman's arena for the final showdown with the most powerful witch in this or any other realm; or stay out here and try to explain to his girlfriend how her family background in any way made the slightest bit of difference to how he felt about her. How he felt about his son.

Especially when, quite simply, it hadn't changed a thing.

'But nothing,' he replied, hands tightening around the Sword once more as he felt the heaviness drop from his shoulders. As they walked under the great arches of stone, he found himself wishing that he had more than just one weapon at his disposal, no matter how formidable the Sword might prove.

When her hand found his, and their fingers interlaced, he was grateful that someone, somewhere, was still in the wish-granting business.

*

'He's coming,' Carman said.

'I'm ready,' Luke replied. Fully-grown, every inch the perfect warrior, he held aloft a black sword that was a twin for the one his father carried in all but hue. 'I'm ready, *Mitéra*. I want to see him. I wish to see the look on his face as I end his life.'

Carman smiled. 'Consider it granted.'

The Battle

The room smelled into focus. For a moment, Steve baulked at this: after years of sneering at Danny's 'gift' of synaesthesia, was it pleasing whatever passed for the gods out there to make it contagious?

No. He wasn't suddenly seeing through his nostrils or smelling through his arse – God forbid – or whatever the fuck it was Danny did. It was simply that, upon returning from consciousness, his senses had reactivated out of sequence – smell first. That could only mean one thing. He opened his eyes and his suspicions were confirmed.

'All right?' Flan said.

He was in Flan's bedroom.

'Steve? You're awake?' Maggie's voice came from outside the room.

'Maggie?' he called. 'Maggie, you're all right?'

'I'm fine.'

'Let me see you.'

'Erm,' Maggie responded. She stuck her head round the door and gave him a meaningful look, trying to look at her own nose as she did so, which unfortunately only made her look bog eyed. 'Now that you're all right again, could you come out?' she suggested.

He got to his feet and squeezed past Flan who, to Steve's surprise, was booting up the Playstation. 'Lad?' he said. 'You comin' with us, like?'

'Nah.'

'What?' Steve exploded. 'The world's gone to fuck! There's *things* roaming about the streets! People are dyin' all over the fuckin' place! You're just gonna sit here and play fuckin' *Grand Theft Auto* are ya, aye?'

'Aye,' Flan nodded. 'All that shit outside sounds fuckin' trunks, no harm. I'll give it a miss. You knock yerself out with Maggie there but, see if you can get her to show you the oul beard again, sure.'

'Show me the—' Steve repeated in astonishment. Flan took his reaction for puzzlement.

'Aye,' he said. 'The oul whale's ear, you know what I mean. She's still up for it, I think, and there's plenty of rooms up the stairs, like. Stick the sheets in the wee washbasket afterwards will ye?'

There was no real response to this. Steve settled for exiting the room and closing the door behind him, shaking his head in wonder as he did so, because some part of him knew that, not so very long ago, he'd have been doing the same as his friend and burying his head in the sand. Sticking to the familiar. Now, look at him – charging about a city turned into a warzone. What had happened? What had changed?

'Hey,' Maggie whispered in his ear. She'd been waiting for him in the doorway to the sitting room and as he passed, she grabbed him and snogged him, a proper full-on tongue-melter that left him breathless. It was only out of a desire for oxygen that he reluctantly broke the kiss.

'You came when I asked,' she said.

'You came looking for me first,' he pointed out.

Behind Maggie lurked a welcome shape. Maggie beamed, 'Larka fixed you.'

'A pleasure,' Larka rumbled.

'How?' Steve asked, patting himself. He was moving without pain, and the fogginess of the painkillers was also gone. In fact, he felt better than he had in years. 'How did you do it? And um, not to sound ungrateful, but why didn't you do it before? When we first met? Why let me go and drug myself to fuck if you could have just magicked me well again?'

'It is complicated,' she replied. Steve was far from an expert on the body language of sentient wolves, but even he could sense that Larka was troubled. He felt a sudden chill down his spine. Healing of the sort she'd performed on him was nothing short of miraculous. Left to their own devices, the accumulated wounds – both internal and external – would probably have left him in serious danger. It had only been the cocktail of painkillers he'd consumed in the chemist that had allowed him to ignore the effects for as long as he had.

Was there to be a price for the miracles she'd performed? And if there was, what was it?

'Larka's been telling me what's going on,' Maggie continued. It seemed she hadn't registered the potentially ominous reason for Larka's reluctance to elaborate. Steve didn't press it. Perhaps now wasn't the time.

'Has she, aye?' he said, surprised. He looked at Larka. 'Wouldn't tell me an' all, would ye?'

'It's the Merging,' Larka said. 'For thousands of years our world and yours have been separated. That is ending, tonight.'

'What does all of this have to do with Danny?' he asked.

'He is the Morrigan,' she replied, as if it were the most obvious thing in the world. 'Carman, our que– ... *former* queen,' Larka amended, 'knows that for the Merging to be complete, the Morrigan's line must be destroyed.'

'She's going to kill him?'

Larka hesitated. 'Protections exist on the line,' was all she would say in return. 'Deep magic. It would be best – for her – if the line destroyed itself. If she was able to influence others to do the job for her.'

'Others? Like who?'

'Most likely, those of his own line. That way, blood magic is strongest.'

Steve's mouth worked silently. 'His own line?' he repeated. 'You mean his ma or his da?'

'No.'

'But you said–'

'Of *his* line. His mother and father are not of his line. He is of theirs.'

'That makes fuck-all sense. If he's of their line and he's their son, then someone of his line would have to be–'

'Yes.'

'You can't mean Luke?'

'Yes.'

'He's *eight months old!*' Steve exploded. 'How's he gonna kill Danny? Combat dummy? Knife-Me Elmo?'

'Magic affects time. Think of time as water. If you know how, you can stem the flow of the river, store it up. Build a dam of time and release it in controlled bursts. Carman knows this.'

Steve remembered the times he'd spent with Luke. Every time he'd looked at the gloriously fat little monster, with his googly eyes, elastic neck and the single terrifying tooth with which he took great delight in chomping down on Uncle Steve's soft and yielding arm flesh, he couldn't help but think, *I wonder what mine would have looked like.*

He thought back to the day after Luke had gone missing. Danny had tried desperately to convince him that the little boy had even existed – had even punched Steve in the jaw in his frustration. Steve had been convinced his friend was going mad and, recollecting that now, the guilt was almost too much to bear. He was staggered at what they'd done to Danny. They'd taken everything from him. His baby. His girlfriend. His whole world.

'I've got to help him, Larka,' he said. 'He's my best friend.'

She dipped her head in simple assent. 'I understand. I will take you to him.'

'Wait!' Maggie said. 'Steve, you can't! Them things are everywhere! People–'

'–are dying,' he finished for her. 'Yeah, I know. Don't you think I want to pick up the phone? Call my ma and da? Call my sister? But what if I call and it's too late, Maggie? What if they're gone?

You heard Larka. If Danny goes, this is the way it's gonna stay. But if I can help him, there's a chance this all goes away?' and he looked to Larka. 'Right?'

Lie, he implored the she-wolf, little suspecting that across town Danny was trying to wrap the exact same comfort blanket around himself. *For the love of God, even if it's not true, just fucking lie to me. Tell me this might all reverse itself. That there's a big cosmic 'undo' button that'll make the world all right, make everything make sense again.*

'There's a chance,' Larka replied. She had the same look in her eyes as before, when she'd refused to elaborate on the method of Steve's healing.

'Besides,' Steve said. 'Have these cockheads forgot what country it is they're trying to fuck about with? This isn't Switzerland, this is Northern Ireland! We've got guns comin' out of our holes!'

'You mean the police?' Maggie said.

Steve looked surprised. 'Fuck aye. Forgot about them,' he admitted. 'Surprised we haven't heard shots already come to think of it, but we haven't time to wait. I have to get to Danny.'

'I'm coming with you.'

'Maggie–'

To his surprise she pushed him back against the wall. Larka emitted a low growl – whether out of protective concern or amusement, he wasn't quite sure.

'Don't you fucking "Maggie" me, Steven Anderson,' she whispered fiercely. 'I'm coming with you. Not to give you a big head, but where do you think I'm gonna feel safer, out there with you and the Big Good Wolf or in here with Flan? What's he gonna fight monsters off with? Achievement Points?'

'The girl makes a valid point,' Larka admitted readily. 'The idiot boy would be an inadequate protector.'

'Plus,' Maggie added, looking away, 'I don't want anything to happen to Danny's wee boy.'

When she met his gaze, her face was carefully composed, with an expression that seemed to dare him to make anything more of what she'd just said.

'Room for one more?' he asked Larka instead.

As they left Belgravia Avenue, the momentary shroud of invincibility fell away slightly. Shouts and shrieks, some human and some not, could still be heard across the city. Maggie drew closer to him. He helped her onto Larka's back, showed her how to hang on, then swung himself up to sit in front of her.

Maybe it was that the comforting shroud of fuzziness the painkillers had thrown over him had dissipated, maybe it was the fact that Maggie was with them, but Steve felt a sight more nervous about what unknowns lay ahead than he had done earlier.

'Ready to take 'em all on?' he asked, as much to steady himself as anything.

Larka had cocked her head, listening to something on the night winds, something undetectable to human ears – or human minds, perhaps.

'Maybe we won't have to,' she said, and leapt forward.

BELFAST CITY CENTRE, NOW

He'd been in here many times before, of course. He'd seen the place packed out a few times, on a Saturday afternoon or during some city centre event. Never quite to this extent, though. Hundreds of people had already been squeezed inside by the time he and Alice were shoved in to join them. Thankfully someone had smashed out the upper part of the windows in order to allow some air inside, otherwise oxygen would have already become an issue.

'It's all right,' Cal told her for what seemed the millionth time.

She looked up at him with an expression that said *Give me a break.* The platitudes died in his throat.

'It's funny,' she said hoarsely. 'I was in here last week. Had a Flame Grilled Whopper.'

He glanced at the sweaty and morose crowd, all trying to avoid one another's eyes. Before being shepherded inside by the enormous wolves that had appeared on the streets, most of those present had seen horrors none could have previously imagined were possible. Looking at each other, seeing that reflected on someone else's face, would have only made this bad dream seem too real. No-one seemed quite ready for that yet.

'Fancy something?' he asked her.

It was a weak joke, even by his standards. She offered him a smile for it anyway, seeming to prefer the attempt at humour to the attempt at meaningless comfort. But then, she had always laughed at his jokes – it was what had first tipped him off that she might have been interested in him.

'Where the fuck are all the peelers?' Alice wondered aloud.

'I don't know,' Cal admitted. That had been gnawing at him too. Thousands of armed police in the country and so far, not a one to be seen.

Moans of fear came from those closest to the large window at the front of the building. The crowd pressed back against him, and he remembered a programme he'd watched once, where scientists had calculated that humans plus terror plus a crowd equalled drastically reduced IQ. Right now he'd have bet on a sheep solving a crossword puzzle before this terrified mob could.

'*Owwww!*' Alice gasped, as she too was pushed back. She was holding his hand and he felt, slowly, terribly, their grip begin to separate.

He was looking frantically around, desperate to get them both to safety, when he saw it. Like many fast food restaurants there were a series of booths on the ground floor, each divided by a partition wall of about four or five feet. One of these partitions was just to his left. He tightened his grip on Alice's hand, knowing he was probably only to get one good, proper shot at this and hardly daring to think of what might happen if he didn't get it right. He *pulled* with everything he had, dragging her toward him through several fellow crowd members, while at the same time bracing himself against the nearest booth. She was now crying out in pain but he kept pulling and bracing.

She came free of the crowd in a sudden rush. He scrambled up onto one of the seats then onto the partition itself.

'Come on!' he told her. 'Climb!'

She followed him, pain still written on her face. Now with a vantage point, he could begin to see what was causing the crush. The attacks outside had stopped a while ago, right around the time the wolves – it hardly seemed appropriate to call them wolves, the size of the fuckers, but even so – had finished herding them inside.

A few had remained outside to guard the doors; a few of the panicked humans inside had tried to bolt past them and been firmly made to U-turn. One wolf had been forced to land a blow to the side of a terrified teenage boy's head in order to knock him out – he'd been insensate with horror, screaming that he had to get home, he'd heard his sister screaming on the phone and he had to get home ...

Cal had thought of his own family then. His phone was out of credit. Alice had tried to phone home with her own mobile, but no sooner had she taken it from her pocket than it had been snatched away by someone in the crowd, gibbering that he had to make a call. He'd vanished into the refugee masses and been swallowed up. Since then neither of them had tried to think too much about what might be happening to their loved ones. Naturally, both had failed.

Now, it seemed the cessation of hostilities outside had come to an end. Their guards were gone. Where, he didn't know, couldn't see. He saw a wolf retreating slowly, as if it were backing away from something. Anything that could make those huge fuckers think twice was something he didn't want to think about. Those people nearest the doors, those with a clear view of whatever was going down outside, were backing up as far as they could, little caring for the chain reaction behind them.

They couldn't stay here. Climbing the partition wall had given them a temporary respite, but it wouldn't last. Already, others had seen what they'd done. Hands were reaching up, grabbing, pleading for him to reach down and pull them up. He knew if he did that he'd be pulled down amongst them, and once that happened–

The doors were only about twenty feet away. They may as well have been twenty miles. The sea of faces below him, all pressed far too close together ... the hands raised above heads ... he'd seen nothing like it since the last concert he'd been to.

Concert ...

He looked at Alice. 'D'you trust me?' he asked her, feeling her hand in his, making sure his grip on her was tight.

She looked at him with not a little incredulity. 'You're asking me this *now?*' she replied.

'Yes. I'm asking now! Yes or no, do you trust me?'

'Yes,' she said.

'Good,' he replied, and Alice's scream rose briefly above the frantic hubbub of the crowd as he threw them both forward, into the panicked mass below.

OTHERWORLD, 1992 AD

She watched the crow fly away. Sometimes it would be days before it returned, but it would always, always come back to her. Loneliness was a condition against which even hatred eventually foundered. Carman knew this. In this place, she could control the very fabric of existence. She had control of its space, and time. The latter she had used against her ancient enemy. Even an immortal could be made to feel the crushing futility of aeons passing with no sense of change or progress, or hope.

The crow was gone now. Gone back to watch over the hibernating Tuatha Dé Danann – now hundreds and hundreds of stone statues, spaced with supernaturally perfect evenness about a great plain. The Morrigan would watch over her stone fellows: a vigil kept when the loneliness had ebbed. When it returned, she would fly back to Carman and they would talk and argue and watch the humans in the world above.

Meanwhile, Carman's children were busy. Always busy.

When the Morrigan was here, they worked at her place of vigil.

In the beginning, Carman knew, when their imprisonment here was still fresh, her adversary would have noticed the smallest changes to her silent charges. But now …

'It's here,' Dub said.

They brought it in. Set it before her. She descended from her throne and walked around it, running her fingers lightly over its surface.

'You're sure?' she said. 'It's him?'

'Yes.'

'You've been wrong before,' she said.

Dub winced as the memories flitted across his mind. Memories of wrath and screams. His mother and failure did not see eye to eye. 'This time we're sure,' he said firmly.

Seemingly satisfied by this, she inhaled deeply, drawing on parts of herself that she called upon only rarely. Stepping forward, placing both hands flat on the stone pillar, she exhaled and shuddered. Her brow creased with effort. This was not easy, despite the long centuries of practice with many hundreds of seemingly identical monoliths.

Carman removed her hands from the pillar. The imprints of her palms burned briefly, and then were absorbed into the rock. The stone began to dissolve, from the top down. As it did, the figure inside was revealed. At first it seemed like no more than a corpse, but after a few moments the figure's limbs began to twitch. A minute or so later, and its eyes had opened to take in its surroundings, and the one responsible for its awakening.

'Dagda,' Carman said in cordial greeting.

The ancient god regarded her. A glance at his surroundings informed him how utterly alone and completely outnumbered he presently was.

'I seem to have awoken early,' he observed.

'My fault, I'm afraid,' Carman admitted. 'What can I say? It's been too long. *Thousands of years too long.* A girl gets bored of waiting.'

'The Morrigan–'

'She's around,' Carman said airily. 'Flapping this way and that. Not quite the girl she used to be, though. Thanks to you.'

His attention fell on the cauldron that lay before her throne. 'You still have it.'

'Call it an extended loan.'

'What do you want?'

There was no point in lies. No time for them. 'Revenge.'

He didn't seem surprised. He cocked his head up and to the side, as if listening to something. 'They have moved on,' he said. 'The humans. They are beyond us now, Carman. You must see that.'

'I'm not asking for the world,' Carman smiled. 'Just my piece of it, Dagda. My way of life.'

'She will stop you. She always does. Kill me if you like. I'll simply return. The same goes for the rest of us. This is futile, Carman. Sleep. Sleep like us. One day, perhaps, the world will be ready for our return. Humans won't last forever.'

'You're right,' Carman said. She gave a signal. Several of her larger and more monstrous children moved until they loomed over the Dagda from all sides. 'Killing you will only bring you back. Sooner or later, you *will* return ...'

She pointed. The Dagda had time for one scream, curtailed abruptly as Carman's elite minions each grabbed an arm, a leg, a head, and literally tore him apart. The pieces of him they threw into the Cauldron that he had created.

'I'm counting on it,' she said.

THE OTHERWORLD, 1994 AD

'You were always the pretty one. I hated you for that.'

Ériu said nothing.

'You scampered about with your flowing dresses and your luscious hair and your big come-hither eyelashes. Goddess of Sovereignty. Huh! What's that even mean? Well I'll tell you what it means. Goddess of cliques! If our canoes had landed in America instead of Antrim, you'd have invented shoulder pads two thousand years early. And they go and name the place after you, even after you hook up with that complete dickhead Elatha and give birth to that wanker Bres who, last I looked, tried to grind our entire race under his heel because he didn't have the stones to admit he wasn't kingly material! And you Goddess of Kings! So on top of everything else you're guilty of staggering levels of job-related negligence!'

Ériu never said a word.

'Don't look at me like that,' the Morrigan snapped. 'Don't think I can't see that look you're giving me.'

The crow hopped up and down a few times on its perch, a few feet from the stone pillar that had once been Ériu. It was Ériu's pillar, she was sure of it. She had known who each and every pillar had once been ever since her people had led themselves down here and petrified themselves. She had flown amongst them. Perched on them. Talked, as she was doing now, at great length to those she had known; to Nuada and to the Dagda, of course. From time to time, though, she came down and talked to those she visited less often – those like Ériu.

Tactfully, when speaking to Ériu she failed to mention the small, grey-white stains that pockmarked her pillar. When a crow had to go, it had to go.

'Anyway,' she carried on, because the sound of her voice was the only sound here and any sound was better than nothing at all, 'I'm going to bring you all back. Yes, even you. You wait and see, sister of mine.'

She trailed off. Try as she might, she couldn't think of anything else to say. Nothing new. Her voice faded and there was only silence, as there always was in this place.

'I'll bring you all back,' the Morrigan said, over and over, into the silence around her.

*

'Impossible,' the Morrigan said, over and over.

Her people had come back. One by one the stone pillars had dissolved into the Tuatha they had once been, flashes of white light illuminated the Belfast night as the magic rolled back the confinement spell placed so many centuries ago.

After only a few, she had known something was wrong, terribly wrong. As the first of her people had awoken, she had rushed to their side, embraced them and, throwing her arms around them, the people she had waited an eternity to see, the people she had sacrificed so much to bring back, they had felt wrong. Looked wrong. *Smelled* wrong.

And when they had opened their mouths to speak ...

Impossible. Impossible. Impossible. *Impossible*!

'Happy to see me, sister?'

She spun. Her stomach felt knotted. Were she human, she might have thrown up on the well-kept lawn in front of the great Portland stone building that was City Hall.

'Ériu?' she said weakly.

It looked like her long-lost sister, that much was true. You could imagine, perhaps, that once it had been Ériu, renowned for her beauty. When the moonlight caught her now, at a certain angle, you would have been close to swearing it was her. The effect was strongest when she stood still. But when she *moved* ...

She had, in her years of observing the human world and its obsessions, seen their fascination with the end of things, with imagining their own demise. She had watched their projections of what might happen if they unleashed their atomic weapons en masse, of what terrible once-human creatures might emerge from the ruins. Mutants, they called them. Once people, now transformed, degraded into something horrible.

That was how her sister appeared to her now. A shambling, degraded, disgusting perversion of a Tuatha.

'*You spoke to me. You spoke to me often.*'

Despair was rising within her, complete despair. All that she'd done, all that she'd betrayed, was for this, for the reclamation of her people who were shambling toward her now from all sides, no life in their eyes, their faces a twisted mockery of their former visages. All of them had, somehow, been transformed. Into this.

'I,' her voice was dry in her throat. Her feet felt like lead. She knew they were all around her, scores of them now. A mutant multitude. 'I wanted to bring you back.'

'*You did,*' Ériu replied with a stiff, rictus smile. '*But you were not the first to do so.*'

The Morrigan felt a hand on her shoulder. She turned, and for the first time in many hundreds of years, she screamed – a cry of rage and loss and sorrow. By the time it faded, she had already sunk to her knees in front of the figure before her.

'*Morrigan,*' slavered the Dagda.

'No,' she sobbed helplessly. 'No, you can't be like this. I brought you back! I saved you all!'

With jerky, unnatural movements, what had once been the Dagda moved his great head to look down at her. '*She woke us first, one by one. Killed us while you slept. Put us into the Cauldron and tainted us with her own filth.*'

Tears burned her eyes. 'Why? All she talked about, all she wanted, was to go back to how it was. Us against them. That was our agreement.'

'She lied. To you. To us. To the humans. To herself. She wants to be noticed, Morrigan. She wants the whole human world, every Pantheon, to sit in awe of her.'

'Kill her!' Ériu hissed.

The Dagda shook his head. 'No! I cannot–'

He tried to fight it, that much was clear. He even managed to turn, make a half-hearted swipe against one of his former warrior caste. Some of the faerie mutation seemed to fall away, and for a moment she glimpsed the Dagda of old, come to her aid, come to help save the day.

The Tuatha ripped him apart.

A hand with fingers like claws grabbed a fistful of her hair. She was picked up like a rag doll, spun and forced to face the snarling, too-wide mouth of Ériu. Shimmers ran over the once-beautiful face of the woman she'd always envied, revealing the monster racing to the surface.

'Don't worry, sister,' Ériu growled, as she brought her free talons to bear on the Morrigan's exposed neck, 'when we're finished with the humans, I will name this masssacre in tribute to you.'

Her human body freshly restored to her, the Morrigan could have tried to stop her sister. In her prime, she could have snapped Ériu's pretty little neck like a twig for daring to lay a hand on her, faerie-monster or not. Now, she found that she simply didn't have the strength of will to resist.

Luckily, she didn't have to. From all around her, with a sound like the world ending, the ranks of the Named leapt upon the Tuatha. Battle was joined.

*

Steve swung himself off Larka's back, taking in the battle before him. Her fellow wolves were locked in mortal combat with scores of what seemed, at first glance, to be humans.

Only at first glance.

Maggie nudged his shoulder. 'Steve, look. Those people, they're trapped.'

He tore his gaze away from the carnage directly ahead with some difficulty. To his left, the nearby branch of Burger King was heaving with people. Faces were pressed up against the windows which were starting to crack under the pressure. Though, judging from the crush that must have been going on inside, that was probably no bad thing … if you discounted the semicircle of inhuman figures advancing on the front doors.

'Larka!' he said urgently.

'I see it.'

'Maggie, go. Somewhere,' he added, anticipating her next question. 'Anywhere but here. I'll find you.'

Her hand tightened around his wrist in response and making a snap judgement, Steve turned, kissed her and shoved her away all in one smooth movement. She half-fell into the doorway of a shop, sheltered for now.

He hefted the flail and, with Larka at his side, he charged.

Crowd-surfing over a crush. Not the most orthodox method for avoiding a particularly painful death but, under the circumstances, Cal was pretty sure the poor bastards beneath him and Alice weren't going to part sufficiently for them to slip between the cracks.

Between the terrors of the unknown in the street outside or being crushed to death, Cal would have chosen the unknown any day.

He was thrown unceremoniously onto the pavement outside, landing on his arse – hardly surprising given the circumstances – and immediately gloried in the ability to move. Alice, still surfing the crowd, cried out for help and he scrambled back to help her down.

In the chaos a middle-aged man, who had clearly lost it, punched him in the face. Cal fell back, his hand in Alice's, and managed to pull her free with his backward momentum. She landed with a thump on top of him. They finally had a few feet of space in which to breathe, which would have seemed unthinkable only moments ago. He breathed a sigh of relief. Maybe they could actually make it out of this.

On his back, facing the wrong way, the first hint of the danger behind came from Alice. She screamed.

Cal got to his feet and forced himself to face what was coming. On first sight, he was almost relieved – they looked like people. Okay, oddly dressed, menacingly-advancing people, but people. Compared to large wolves and nightmarish insect-things, surely a step up?

The streetlights, flickering on and off intermittently, came on again, and his initial cautious optimism withered and died. Something was deeply, deeply wrong with the figures coming toward them. Oh, they were people all right. Or at least they had been.

His brain sensed their wrongness as much as his eyes saw it. Meanwhile, the awful certainty that a painful death loomed in his near future bypassed the brain entirely and went straight for the soul.

Somehow, though, by some fluke of evolution or chance, Calvin McDermott was one of those people who finds hitherto unknown reserves of courage in the face of a crisis – the meek little cubicle dweller who blinks dazedly into the camera lens as he tries to fathom how he pulled those people from the rubble.

'Come on,' he turned to the panicking hordes behind him, waving his arms like a maniacal orchestra conductor. 'There's fuckin' hundreds of us! There's only a few of these cunts! Let's fuckin' *NAIL* 'em!'

His words rang out across the penned-in humans and, for a wonder, the crowd ceased its relentless retreat. Looks were exchanged. A ripple of almost-intent passed through them as they looked to their new, unlikely trailblazer.

Cal knew he almost had them. He needed something more: A symbol, a battle cry.

Alice pressed something into his palm. A piece of the doorframe. Large, blunt and heavy. The approaching horde was only ten feet or so from the doors now. He could see a long silver string of drool escaping from one creature's mouth as it regarded the humans trapped inside with nothing but murderous hunger.

Cal lifted the club and unleashed his call to arms, a cry that rent the night sky asunder and ignited the fires of courage in his makeshift army. It was his Gettysburg Address, his Million Man speech, his 'One giant leap'.

'STATE O' YER FUCKIN' BALLIX!' he roared lustily, and charged.

With an answering Belfast-born howl of approval, the crowd surged forward, streaming out through the doors. Humans being humans, those who were in danger of being crushed in the retreat soon stood at serious risk of being crushed in the advance. The danger soon abated when, after one too many impacts, the main front windows smashed outward and the crowd was released.

The former Tuatha, freshly awakened and confused by this turn of events, and now unsettled by the sudden drop in delicious fear their human quarry were exhibiting, hesitated for a moment.

A moment in which, from behind them, Steve and Larka attacked.

To the side, a fresh wave of the Named crashed into the former Tuatha. Huge jaws snapped, Steve swung the flail this way and that with deadly intent, and humans, with far less finesse but making up for it in sheer weight of numbers, served to distract the ex-Tuatha long enough for their more powerful four-legged allies to bite and swipe.

Humans in the adjoining buildings, until now hiding in terror, saw what was happening. A Mexican wave of violence began to spread as shop-fronts burst open and the refugees inside flowed back onto the streets. The former Tuatha and the various faerie abominations found themselves under sustained attack for the first time.

Larka was gone, launched into the fray. There were people, creatures and the Named surrounding Steve. He saw a hellish shape detach itself from the eaves of one building and engulf a luckless woman below. Raising the flail, he moved towards the creature, wondering how to aim for a vital organ in something that seemed to lack structure or definition.

Slam. He was thrown to the right and a spiked tail missed his head by inches – the impact had saved his life. Blood spattered over his face. Not his own. He wiped it away and, without time to do anything else, brought the flail down into the head of a misshapen being trying to pull apart a middle-aged man. The head partially exploded with the impact, and he was forced to wipe more goo, and who knew what else, from his eyes.

Something grabbed his right leg, knocking him to the ground, and he was dragged along the pavement. He felt a breath on his leg, as if a huge mouth was about to close …

He swung desperately with the flail. There was a choking, guttering gurgle and he was able to stand. To his relief, he had not in fact brained his Named rescuer but the amorphous horror he had set out to tackle in the first place. Rather than having the good grace to fuck off and die, it seemed to turn itself inside out before emitting a rasping, slurping noise.

Something like a tongue lashed out of the thing and wrapped itself around Steve's arm, dislodging the flail and yanking him forward. Instinctively – and truthfully, out of sheer dumb luck – Steve's other hand managed to snag the flail even as it tumbled and he brought it up, over his shoulder and down–

This time, the creature stayed still.

A shapeless mass landed at his feet. He stiffened his flail arm, relaxing only when he saw that it was a former Tuatha's mangled corpse, dropped carefully from Larka's jaws. She looked at him with the faint air of a cat expecting praise for bringing its master a mouse. He didn't get a chance to oblige; within seconds more assailants had set upon them and it was time to dodge and swing once more.

He could never quite piece together the order of what happened next. He knew they moved further away from City Hall, shop by shop, retaking the centre of the city as they went. Reinforcements from both sides were forthcoming at several points, renewing the battle and threatening to tip the balance, but the momentum was with the humans and the Named from the start and they were not about to let it go.

At some point the human army must have raided an outdoor goods store and a sports store because he started seeing people swinging camping axes and hurley sticks. His arms ached beyond reason, but even through the fog of adrenalin he remembered thinking they didn't hurt as much as they *should*. He wasn't this fit. He wasn't this good at fighting. Yet here they all stood, these motley humans, engaged in pitched battle with creatures out of nightmares. Anything less than full slaughter would have been a miracle, and yet they seemed to be *winning* …

Who knew how much later, he was finally able to stop swinging the flail. He looked for a target or for someone to assist, but all he could see was the fluid shapes of the Named and other exhausted humans looking back at him, some bent double, some bleeding.

Many were not moving at all.

*

'Alice …?' Cal said, unsteadily, walking toward her. His face was deathly pale. Blood dripped from his fingertips onto the asphalt below.

She smiled back at him, and tried to respond, tried to say his name, but found that she could make only a grating noise with her throat. Touching her hand to her neck, her fingers came away dark and wet.

The crowd melted away to let him pass as he half-ran, half-staggered to her. She collapsed before he could get to her, impacting hard. He gathered her up, put her head in the crook of his arm. Blood was everywhere. Something had slashed her from collarbone to chin. She opened her eyes.

A shadow fell across him. He heard a wolf's heavy breathing and a young, male human voice.

'Please,' Cal sobbed. 'Help us.'

'Larka?' Steve asked.

Larka swung her head to look at Steve. There was sadness in her huge eyes. 'Perhaps,' was all she would say.

'You can bring her back?' Cal croaked.

'Yes, but–'

'Do it! Just do it, please!'

Larka's head dipped to the wounded girl in Cal's arms. She opened her mouth and for one heart-stopping moment Steve worried that helping this girl meant consuming her, but no. Something, some spark, some hint of life, passed from Larka's mouth to Alice beneath her, entering the girl's mouth and causing her to dissolve into a fit of violent coughing. As Steve watched in disbelief, the huge wound in her throat shimmered and began to close – the blood covering the boy holding her started to pool and return in little rivulets to the wound.

With a shriek, Alice regained consciousness, her arms and legs jerking spasmodically. Cal held her tightly, reassuring her through his tears that she was all right.

'What are you doing?'

The voice belonged to another wolf, another of the Named. He was huge, easily the biggest Steve had seen. The way he carried himself instantly marked him out as the pack leader. Upon his entrance, Larka instantly adopted a posture of subservience, which, strangely, rankled with Steve a little bit.

'I am sorry. I saw no other choice.'

'Sorry?' Steve said. He faced down the new wolf with as much courage as he could muster – not easy, given the sheer size of the fucker. 'Why should she apologise for saving lives?'

Wily merely turned to look at Larka. She could not meet his eyes.

'My wife,' someone called from nearby. 'My wife is dying too. Please, help her.'

The call was taken up by many. There was a carpet of the dead around them, no shortage of corpses or almost-corpses. Larka growled and whined simultaneously, and Wily made a noise that neither Steve nor anyone else present had a hope of comprehending or translating.

Finally, Wily's head seemed to dip. He looked defeated. 'The Named will assist,' he said quietly, and without another word, many of his fellow wolves spread themselves out among the human casualties. Steve watched as the process that he had witnessed with Alice was repeated over and over. Death was chased away. The humans rose again, blinking, disbelieving. There were embraces, tears and expressions of thanks toward the Named, but Steve didn't take his eyes off Wily and he grew only more troubled by what he saw.

'We must move the humans,' Wily rumbled, looking to where, not so long ago, Lircom Tower had stood, growling softly even as he spoke. 'The Tuatha are gone, but there are other dangers.'

'Wait,' Steve said. More than anything he wanted to ask what they were hiding about this miraculous process of resurrection, but he forced himself to wait. 'We have to help Danny.'

'Danny?' That got Wily's attention all right. 'You know the Morrigan?'

'I'm his best friend.'

Wily gave him an appraising glance, taking in the flail, the bloodstains, the dead Tuatha-creatures at his feet. 'Yes,' he said approvingly. 'Yes, I can see that.'

Absurdly, Steve flushed. He'd anticipated being eviscerated by one of these fairytale creatures tonight, not validated. He took a moment, though, to glance down at himself and to take in what had happened over the last few hours. He'd gone from being thrown out of a moving car as a piece of excess baggage, to a knight on wolfback, to an impromptu battlefield commander.

All of the self-doubt that had plagued him, made worse by the head-fuck of the trip into parallel-land where his 'son' had turned out to be a monster and his parenting skills had been found sorely wanting, seemed a long time ago now.

Wily issued orders. Steve made sure one of the strongest of the Named was assigned to look after Maggie, and then he, Larka and Wily split from the group, making straight for the four immense stone pillars that occupied the space previously taken up by Lircom Tower.

BELFAST / OTHERWORLD, NOW

The last time Danny had been here, the area had been filled with the worst of Carman's creations. He had been terrified almost out of his mind, barely able to perceive her. He'd been ripped apart at a single gesture from Dub, unable to do so much as squawk in protest before they'd dismembered him and begun his journey back to life through the Cauldron.

Passing through the stone arch, he sensed immediately that no matter what the rest of Belfast looked like, inside those four great pillars was still old-world Otherworld. Not a sign of technological progress. Grass underfoot. Even the clouds above looked different, as though they belonged to a different sky to the rest of the city.

The Belfast skyline should have been easily visible through the stone arches. It wasn't. If you squinted, if you strained, you could, perhaps, hazard a guess that outside the standing stones lay a city. It was as though when you left the perimeter you entered a different place altogether.

He felt the transition as they moved inside. Ellie must have done so too – her hand tightened around his at the exact moment the sensation washed over him. He squeezed back. She looked at him and he realised that, with Dother's revelations, she hadn't responded to his clumsy declaration of love. Somehow, this didn't seem quite the time either.

Things were different inside now. The elite creatures that had thronged the innerspace were gone. Sent out to enjoy themselves, perhaps. And Dub ... well, Dub wasn't going to be there, for obvious reasons. That left only Carman, and–

'Oh my God,' Ellie said softly.

She'd instantly recognised the young man before them. Of course she had. Danny had seen this man once before, over a decade ago in a tiny cottage in the arsehole of nowhere. Then, he had been a visage adopted by one of Carman's faeries, designed to destabilise Danny and draw him to his death.

This was no vision. The man before them was flesh and blood. He was dressed in armour and fineries, as the Tuatha Dé Danann had been dressed in ancient times, as Glon and Gaim had been dressed.

Behind him, sitting on her throne, Carman waited and watched. The queen on her throne. He took a moment to stare directly at her, ensuring that she saw him focus on her. Whether she had dropped her previous senses-scrambling defences or whether he had simply evolved beyond her ability to deflect him he couldn't be sure. He hoped fervently it was the latter.

'*Luke?*' Ellie said, shaken to her core but somehow, through her astonishment and despite all that she'd been through, still thrilled beyond words. 'Luke, it's … it's you, isn't it? My baby?'

The man before her did not move a muscle or say a word. If his chest hadn't been gently rising and falling and the sword he was holding wasn't twirling gently in his grasp, it would not have been hard to think of him as a statue.

'Luke, it's me. It's your mummy.'

Danny purposefully came to a halt about ten feet from his son. Ellie clearly wanted to keep walking. He gently but firmly kept his fingers interlaced with hers until she was forced to stop a pace in front of him. She looked back at him, need and anguish and confusion and love raging across her face. He ached to see it. He felt the same things, just as strongly. In strictly chronological terms it had been only a few days since he last held his baby in his arms. It had also been a lifetime.

Hard as it was, he spoke not to Luke, but to Carman.

'I have lived the Ordeal,' he said. 'Gone into the Cauldron and emerged from it.'

'Yes,' she said. Nothing more.

'I … *we*,' he amended, 'have come for our son.'

He saw Luke narrow his eyes when he said that. He ignored it. Whatever process the child had gone through to make him a man in a matter of days was clearly magical in nature. That meant it could be reversed. It *had* to.

'So you have,' Carman said. She seemed quite calm.

'So don't try and stop us!' Ellie burst out, clearly unable to hold herself even a second longer. 'I've killed you once tonight, you oul bastard. I'll kill ye again!'

Danny's held his breath. He half-expected all hell to break loose; hordes of hitherto invisible horrifying monsters to burst upwards from the soil and attack them from all sides; Carman to stand up and unleash blue lightning at them, Emperor Palpatine style. He shot Ellie a look that was meant to be slightly rebuking, but when he met her eyes he saw only defiance, determination and love. Strangely, rather than frustrating him, that cheered him.

'You've changed since we last met here,' Carman said. 'Stronger. Fiercer. Your family's heritage running strongly within you.'

'A wee bit,' Danny said modestly.

'I wasn't talking to you,' Carman snapped.

The colour drained from Ellie's face. 'What?' she said. 'I wasn't—'

'Oh but you *were*,' Carman purred. 'You and your little boy, guests of mine. Only a few days ago.'

Ellie staggered. Danny was there to catch her; the strength seemed to have fled from her limbs. She was breathing heavily, eyes wide. She looked at him with barely-concealed panic. 'Danny,' she whispered. 'She's in my head.'

'I know,' Danny said. He could feel it too; that pressure he'd felt in the Otherworld that had accompanied the senses-scrambling effect. The effect itself was gone, but the pressure remained. It was as though his mind were a web and Carman had just scuttled into the centre of it to sit, squatting, the way a spider could stay still for days at a time if it needed to.

He reached out and touched Ellie's face—

The mobile. She had just wound it and Luke was lying gurgling up at it. The bottles were on the counter, the bath was running. Danny was coming home and she was going to tell him he needed to make a choice. She was tired of the way the pressure would build and build and then he would blow up and she would spend the day worrying that today was the last day. She needed to know.

It was then that she had noticed Luke's stuffed hippo, his precious Gar-gah. With trembling fingers she had reached out over her son's cot and touched Gar-gah and sent the toy spinning end-over-end, for Gar-gah was floating in mid-air, gravity no longer applying. She felt light-headed, the world a closing iris, an inverted telescope and she was falling down into it. She saw Luke rising from his cot on a cushion of nothingness and reached out for him, closed her fingers around his little arm, just as on the verge of her hearing the front door opened.

She was here, in this place, between the stones. She was here with the monsters. But that was impossible because monsters didn't exist. She would not let the baby go, she would not, no matter how the monsters pushed and prodded, she would not let go because she would protect him until they both woke up, her little child that she was hugging so tightly that—

They were laughing at her, all of them laughing, the queen and her court of monsters. The queen held a little baby in her arms and pointed to the baby's mummy and coochie-coo'd and Ellie thought, That's a nice baby, but it's not as nice as my Lu– ... Aaron. I really should get back to Dan– ... Steve, and she blinked because the thoughts felt minty-fresh in her head. The thoughts had new car smell on them and the queen was making the little crying baby wave goodbye at her and wasn't that nice, the baby was waving goodbye, she must tell little Aaron about all this—

Ellie uttered a shuddering, gasping cry and fell, breaking

Danny's touch. He caught her before she hit the ground. All of the images he had accessed had been passed between them, he knew. So this place, this was where Ellie had come to, when she had vanished that first day and night, before the world had reset and taken them both along with it for the ride.

'Ellie?' he said. Her eyes were closed. 'Ellie?'

She stiffened in his arms as control of her muscles came back to her and she was able to support herself again. When she opened her eyes, he had to fight the urge to take a step backward, for there was a deep and real hatred revealed by the blocked-off memories; not directed toward him, but at the woman on the throne.

'You brought me here,' Ellie said.

'I did,' Carman said. 'The price your father paid for my services to him. I returned you to the world when I had rebuilt it into something more to both of your liking.'

'You stole my son.'

'Stole him?' Carman laughed. 'You couldn't *wait* to leave him behind.'

'You lying BITCH!'

Danny managed to hold her back – for about a half a second. He grabbed her again, but this time she broke away even more quickly, causing him to fall, unceremoniously, onto his arse. Ellie's move toward Carman, or more accurately the movement of her hands, nails and teeth toward Carman's waiting throat, seemed utterly inevitable. Carman didn't seem inclined to stop it, either. Danny saw a hunger on her face.

He held out a hand and called upon his new abilities, and Ellie's legs froze in place where she stood.

'Ellie, stop! She'll kill you!' he said desperately.

She turned her upper body and glared at him accusingly. '*You're* doing this?' she said.

He placed his hands on her shoulders – with all the appropriate caution of someone belling a Bengal Tiger – and tried to quell that murderous intent in her eyes. 'We're here for Luke. Her time will come, Ellie. I promise you that. If you rush her now, she will kill you, I know it. Please.'

Some of the fire died, but only some. He risked letting her go. She took a half-step forward and stopped.

'Don't you *ever* do that to me again,' she hissed at him.

'I won't,' he lied.

'And you, Danny!' Carman continued merrily, as though the drama of the last few seconds meant nothing to her. 'We can't forget about your little adventures. Finding peace with your father. Finding purpose. Becoming a true heir of the Morrigan line!'

'You,' he said quietly. 'Don't talk about my da.'

'Yes, I saw,' she waved a hand at the Cauldron sitting at the base of the steps to her throne, at its shimmering liquid surface. 'A shame. Still, he was able to accomplish what he set out to do. Continue the line. Bring about the' – and she waggled her fingers in the air to create quotation marks – '"Chosen One".'

'He sacrificed everything for me,' Danny said, unsure why he was even saying this, especially to her. Maybe it just needed saying, no matter the appropriateness of the audience. He needed to hear it himself. 'I won't let him die for nothing.'

'And here he stands, before me,' Carman went on, savouring every word. 'The Chosen One. The Morrigan the prophecies spoke of. Mightiest of the line. Oh, a shame about the separation from his father part, but a necessary evil, wouldn't you say? What's worth gaining without sacrifice, after all?'

'Nothing,' said Luke. It was the first word he had spoken.

With that single word, Danny finally understood. The great puzzle that had been assembling all this time before him, the final piece had finally slotted in, and only now was it clear that he'd been looking at the whole fucking thing arse about face.

'It's not me.'

'You?' Carman said, and indulged herself in a good laugh. 'You? It was *never* you.'

Luke stood up straighter and, though Danny hadn't previously thought it was possible, his adult son grew even more physically imposing. While not obviously oversized as Dub had been, Luke was an incredibly powerful-looking young man. His arms were thick. His eyes were steady. His breathing calm.

'It's Luke,' Danny said. 'He's the one.'

'Yes. A child of both lines,' Carman said. 'The Tuatha, you see, were *so* in love with their own cleverness. When the time came to imprison me and my children down here, they devised spells within spells, rules within rules. Magic is a funny thing, Danny. It's limited only by the imagination. Fiendish imagination, fiendish rules.'

'But the Network …? I thought that was all you needed. Isn't that how you were able to merge the worlds? Bring Ireland to you?'

'It got the engine running,' Carman admitted. 'But what I really needed, Danny, was you.'

That brought him up short. 'What?'

'That little light show you put on earlier, when Daddy ...' and she pantomimed getting stabbed in the chest, and made a sad face, causing the roles to reverse and Ellie had to grab Danny to stop him from advancing.

'Ah yes, I see you remember. That sealed the deal. Your rage, your power, all of it surging through the Network, through the Sword. Right here. Ground Zero. Merging complete. We couldn't have done it without you, Danny. All of this – all of your training, all of your little vision quests and detours, putting you into the Cauldron. All of it was to train you, make you aware of your power. All we needed then was a catalyst for you to blow your stack. Exit Tony, stage left. Honestly, bravo. Now, Luke and I have some big plans for this brave new world, and you've more or less fulfilled your usefulness so, Luke? Kill Mummy and Daddy like a good boy.'

Luke charged.

Danny had only seconds to shove Ellie clear. There was no time for finesse; his one priority was getting plenty of distance between her and the fight in which he was about to be embroiled. He'd been foolish enough to allow the Sword to drop to an off-guard position during the latest round of revelations, but now he held it high and it met his son's with an echoing *clannngggg*.

He had parried the blade. The charge, however, he could do nothing about. Luke's bulk was considerable, his musculature far superior to Danny's own. Immediately after the swords met, Danny was knocked clean off his feet and sent sprawling to the grass. He rolled and kept rolling, his danger senses screaming at him to keep moving. He sensed rather than saw or heard his son's blade bite into the earth inches behind his rolling body.

Gathering his legs beneath him and pushing off his feet, he sprang from his vulnerable horizontal position into a passable crouch, bringing the Sword up over his head in a defensive stroke to prevent Luke's blade from cleaving his head clean off his shoulders. He pushed back against the stroke this time, managing to negate some of the immense physical strength behind each of his son's blows and stopping himself from being knocked back on his arse once again.

Momentarily thrown, Luke took a half-second to recover, a pause that gave Danny time to get to his feet. He couldn't afford to be so unprepared for another charge, he knew. Luke wouldn't fail to finish him off if he managed to get him on his back once more. Staying on his feet was critical to staying alive. He feinted to the right and left, letting Luke know he was ready and able to dodge out of the way of another brute-force assault.

Luke got the message. He dropped out of his head-down stance and began instead to whirl his sword through the night air in extraordinarily complicated strokes as he moved forward step by step, closing the gap between himself and his father, hoping that Danny would be so dazzled in trying to follow the path of the blade that he would leave himself open for a quick debilitating stroke to the sword hand or to the neck.

Danny heard Ellie screaming from somewhere to his right, and with a part of his mind currently not concentrating on staying alive, hoped that she would stay out of range.

Anyone watching Danny with the sword, at least anyone who

had witnessed Tony Morrigan in combat, would have commented how similarly the two wielded a blade. This was more than genetics; Danny knew that when he had reached inside his father's mind, both in the cottage and in the office shortly before he died, he had exchanged more than memories. He had absorbed Tony's skill with a blade. It was lucky for him that he had, or Luke would have been able to cut him in two with that initial lunge.

Luke went for his father's throat in a sudden burst. Danny took a long step back and to the left, ducking under the swipe and, adjusting the Sword in his hands, was able to lean forward and connect the flat of the blade with Luke's behind.

It made a *thwack* sound that echoed long and loud. Luke recoiled and issued a gasp of pain, whipping his sword around, but Danny was ready and the two blades met evenly. Looking into Luke's shocked, outraged expression, Danny decided to try something that might just be suicide.

'Bad boy!' he said, in a tone of voice he'd have used a week, and a lifetime, ago.

Luke blinked. For just a second, some of that arrogance, that invincibility he exuded, seemed to crack, but soon the warrior was back and Danny was again fighting for his life, parrying and retreating and jumping out of the way of a series of increasingly angry strokes.

He couldn't do this forever. Luke was better; there was no doubt about it. Younger and fitter and stronger and, from all available evidence on show, quite willing to kill his opponent which Danny most certainly wasn't. Luke held all the cards, but for now, the memory of that unexpected spank with the flat of the Sword was still burning brightly and the anger it had generated was making him rash enough to be clumsy, even predictable.

That wouldn't last forever. And when Luke regained his composure, when he cooled down and started planning his attacks properly, Danny had no clue what he was going to do.

Well, strictly speaking, that wasn't true. He was pretty sure he was going to die.

Think, he urged himself. No matter what age he looked, Luke simply *couldn't* be an adult. He had the body of one – given his build, more like the body of one and a half – but where, how, *when* had he grown up? Here. In this twisted place, under some time-accelerated conditions. Danny burned with a deep and terrible anger at that. If he died trying, he'd make that witch responsible for perverting his son's childhood, make her pay for what she'd done.

Right now, however, he had to take control. If this was to stay a physical fight, he was going to lose. It had to be more than that.

'You're my son,' he said, timing the words so they were audible between sword-clashes. It was difficult enough staying out of the range of Luke's blade. Doing so while trying to come up with a verbal angle of attack was only going to make things worse, but he had no choice. He *had* to try and get Luke to talk. Only then could he assess what damage had been done to his son's mind.

'I know,' Luke replied, lashing out with a foot and striking Danny a glancing blow on the left knee. Pain exploded from the impact. Danny half-staggered, forced to abandon all attempts at a graceful defence and simply duck and run to gain some breathing space. What strength did his son have if that was how painful a glancing blow could be?

'Luke, *stop* this!' Ellie pleaded, coming as close as she dared to. 'We love you! We came here to save you!'

'*Love* me? *Save* me? Neither of you ever wanted me!' Luke snarled. 'I *watched* you!'

'Watched?' Ellie was confused. Danny wished he was. His own trips through time and space with the Morrigan for company had been harrowing enough, but he had at least been an adult when he underwent them. It was suddenly clear from the look on his son's face exactly what Carman had done. How she had turned him.

For the time being, Luke had stopped his relentless assault. He didn't even look out of breath. Danny looked, and felt, like he'd gone twelve rounds with a Kodiak bear.

'Show them,' Carman commanded.

Luke planted his sword in the earth. Raising his hands, he swept them forward. In that instant, the area inside the standing stone circle contracted and shifted. Ellie and Danny found themselves somewhere neither of them had ever expected to see again.

THE ROYAL VICTORIA HOSPITAL, BELFAST,
8 MONTHS AGO

'Are you all right?' Ellie was asking, as she lay on the hospital bed, wearing a flimsy hospital issue nightie, not a drop of makeup on her, forehead covered in sweat, and a large midwife between her legs.

'It's me,' the second Ellie, the one Luke had just spirited here from inside the standing stone circle, said in astonishment. She turned a full circle, her mouth agape as she took in their surroundings.

'Uh ... yeah, not too bad,' Past Danny was saying numbly.

Danny reached out for Ellie. He was finding this a little disconcerting himself. It was one thing to be flung Scrooge-like to the ancient past or even to the 1980s. It was another to be three feet from yourself and marvel at how pale and shit-scared you once looked. His younger self would have needed a blood transfusion to pass as a corpse.

'They can't see or hear us,' he told Ellie, finding her hand. In a strange moment of symmetry, he squeezed it just as his younger self squeezed Past Ellie's hand.

She turned to him. Now over the initial shock and awe of seeing herself in a position in which no woman should ever have to behold herself, Ellie was struggling to cope with the enormity of what she was re-experiencing. Her eyes shone with tears.

'Danny,' she said softly. 'This is *incredible*.'

'I know,' he said softly. What with ancient battles and creating universes and time travel, he'd almost been desensitised to miracles. He was glad she was there to remind him. He was just glad she was there.

'Right, when I tell you to push, you push!' the midwife ordered.

Past Ellie looked up at Past Danny. 'I,' she said in a reasonable tone, 'am going to murder her.'

'I don't remember saying that,' her future self said, flushing

194

hotly, then flinching as Past Ellie gave a *yeowl* of agony that echoed throughout the delivery suite. 'I remember that, but,' she said ruefully.

'Push! Push, Ellie!'

They noticed Luke – warrior Luke – for the first time. He was leaning casually against the far wall, watching the proceedings with a detached air. He had the look of someone who had seen this particular film many times before and could have acted a part in it. Which, of course, he was about to.

'I can see hair!' the midwife exclaimed.

As Past Ellie asked his younger self to go and see what colour it was, her future self, unable to contain herself any longer, moved a few steps closer. Taking a *very* deep breath, she leaned forward on her tiptoes to see past the midwife. Danny had to wonder at the sight of his past self and Ellie's future self each craning their heads to look, in perfect symmetry over Past Ellie's akimbo legs.

'Mmmm …' Past Danny said, clearly trying to give himself time to form coherent speech so it wouldn't be unexpectedly replaced with puke, 'Black.'

Ellie, meanwhile, merely rocked back on her heels. She very slowly and very carefully walked back to stand beside Danny. She pointed at his crotch with one finger and, with her face utterly composed and calm, warned, 'Come *near* me with that thing– '

'Aye, aye, I know,' he cut her off. He couldn't help but smile. Luke, seeing this exchange, curled his lip in disgust and slammed his palm against the wall of the maternity suite. The real and solid wall of the hospital room stayed intact, but the ethereal, *Quantum Leap* wall of the projection rippled, bending slightly at Luke's touch.

As the ripple spread, it dislodged the clock from the wall behind Ellie's delivery bed. It clattered to the floor below with a resounding *crash*. Danny – both versions of him – seemed to be the only one startled by the impact, but for two entirely different reasons.

This isn't just a vision, Danny realised. *This actually happened. Luke was always meant to be here. Always watching this moment.*

Which means Ellie and I were always here too …

With this racing around in his mind, he watched as their younger versions went through the final, astonishing moments of labour. Watched as Luke, tiny and red and screaming, emerged from Ellie and was placed in Danny's grasp.

Danny's attention wavered from the birth to the young man standing at the opposite side of the room, watching it all with a cold expression.

'Why bring us here?' he asked Luke, moving forward, walking through the midwife as he did so. 'What does this prove? How can you say we didn't love you? Look. *Look* at us.'

He stopped in front of his younger self, barely a foot from him. Past Danny was cradling his newborn son in his arms, even as the midwife told him it was a boy. Luke moved from his position against the wall. He had no sword here in this place, but then neither did Danny. Thankfully, the weapons hadn't made the journey. As Luke moved toward him, rather than electing to walk around or through the stool Past Danny had been sitting on, he shoved it casually aside. Again, despite their insubstantial nature, he succeeded in knocking it over.

Luke reached out and touched Past Danny on the forehead – he was performing the trick Danny had first accomplished on his father in the cottage in Wexford, reaching *inside* his head with his fingers to directly sample the memories that lay inside.

Danny remembered that exact moment in the delivery room – an immense coldness and sense of panic had gone through him. He'd put it down to finally realising that he'd become a parent and that his life had changed. Perhaps in a large way that remained true. But he also remembered what had happened next.

He took a moment to recall the necessary skills he'd learned during his Ordeal, then his hand joined his son's in probing the mind of his younger self.

Entering his father's mind had been, undoubtedly, one of the stranger experiences of his life, even by the rather skewed standards of the last few days. It was nothing, however, compared to the unmitigated oddness of plunging headfirst into the raging, turbulent rapids of a mindscape that was his and yet not his. Memories overlaid on memories, experiences on experiences. He slipped under those waters.

Panic … not good enough as a father … Dad gone … out of the blue … no-one knows … don't talk, never show it … glad you did, glad you left … life is better … no responsibility … better off gone … weakness … so small in my arms … I'm going to let him down …

It took everything he had to fight his way back up to the surface and deliver the message he had already delivered.

No. No you're not. It's going to be all right.

Luke retracted his fingers as if burned. His eyes flashed with anger. 'Stop it! You're changing everything! This isn't how it's supposed to go!' he protested, sounding so childlike that it physically pained Danny not to be able to reach out and reassure his son.

'I saw what you were thinking – I was an accident! Neither of you wanted me born. You!' and he rounded on Ellie, pointing a shaking finger at his mother. '*You* hated me because getting pregnant ruined the way your father looked at you. Steady Ellie, gone!'

To Danny's astonishment, Ellie nodded at this. 'I get it,' she said. 'You've looked inside our heads. She's shown you a compilation DVD of our worst bits.'

As if at some invisible command, the maternity scene around them melted away, and reformed itself into a tiny little living area. Danny recognised it instantly – Ellie and Maggie's apartment in the Queen's University Halls of Residence. At first he thought it was empty, but after a few seconds, he was able to make out a soft sound coming from the tiny little bathroom.

He walked toward it, past his son, past Ellie, who made no move to follow him. She seemed to know what he would see there and had no desire to witness it herself.

It was Ellie. Slumped in a foetal position, her back to the toilet, legs folded up against her. A home pregnancy test lay beside her. Another was in the sink above her. She was sobbing. Defeated.

'The happy news,' Luke said.

Danny took it like a shot to the stomach. He'd gone over the moment he'd received that text from Ellie a thousand times in his mind. It had never really occurred to him to think how she had felt when she'd realised she was pregnant – on some level he had assumed that she had simply dealt with it.

'What did you expect?' Ellie said. There was no trace of shame in her voice. 'I was twenty years old. Halfway through a degree. Single. Broke. I wasn't thinking beyond the next weekend and I liked it that way. Then I'm late by a day, then two, then four. Next thing I'm going to be a mother? What'd you expect me to do?' she asked again, looking at her son with mounting anger. 'I knew the second that blue line appeared that my whole life was going to change. I didn't underestimate that. I was saying goodbye to how I had lived every single fucking day of my life up until that moment. And, yeah, I was terrified of how my da was going to react when I told him.'

'I was a mistake,' Luke said.

'No,' she replied quietly. 'An accident, yes. Not a mistake. *Never* a mistake. And if you're showing me this,' she gestured to her younger self, 'to make me feel guilty … well, sorry, but I don't. I was giving up a lot and I was fucking well entitled to be scared and to grieve a little for what I was going to leave behind. But I fuckin' did it, Luke. I didn't choose when you came, but I chose *you*. Don't tell me that the Queen of the Damned didn't give you a quick tutorial on the other options open to people who think getting pregnant is a mistake?'

'I'm supposed to be grateful you didn't have me aborted?' Luke returned.

Ellie looked around the apartment. 'You think you've seen

everything you need to see?' she snapped back. 'Why not skip us ahead a few hours?'

To Danny's surprise, the apartment around them darkened. Night had fallen outside and Ellie was now sitting with her mother on the sofa. Christina looked as if she were trying very hard to make as little contact with the furniture around her as she possibly could.

Danny watched Luke; studied him intently. The man (child? all of the above?) before him didn't seem quite as sure of himself as he had before. Perhaps it was the reality of seeing his mother and father in the flesh, really there this time, and have them react to what he was saying, able to answer him back.

How lonely, how crazy-making must it have been to have witnessed your mother and father arguing over your baby self, unable to touch, or do anything but influence the environment in the most minute ways?

'You're *what*?' Christina was saying.

'Mummy, don't start, please. I don't think I could handle the lecture now.'

'Well you'd better *start* getting ready to handle the lecture!' Christina declared. 'When your father hears about this, he'll … oh! It's just going to break his heart. You're his Steady Ellie! Your degree, your career – all ruined!'

This outburst finished, and with no reply from Ellie, Christina composed herself with some difficulty and exhaled. 'Who's the father?'

'Danny.'

'Oh for fuck's sake!' Christina said. It was the first curse word

Danny had ever heard the woman use. He muttered something distinctly uncomplimentary, not exactly under his breath.

'He doesn't know yet. No one does. Just you.'

Christina was silent for a few seconds after her daughter said this. An awful suspicion began to form in the pit of Danny's stomach. By the look on her face, Ellie's mother was working up to something, something that didn't take a massive leap of imagination to anticipate.

'No-one ever has to.'

Both versions of Ellie stiffened when Christina said this. Danny looked at Past Ellie and had to admit that, as bad as she'd looked in the delivery suite, she now looked even worse.

Luke's expression had changed. He wasn't watching this with the same air of sullen detachment that he had previously adopted. He seemed involved.

'You've so much to lose,' Christina said. She moved closer to her daughter and, after a momentary hesitation, put an arm around her daughter. Ellie gratefully sank into her mother's embrace. Danny ached to hold her. 'To give up everything you want to do, for the sake of one silly mistake.'

'If you call my child a mistake one more time I will never speak to you again,' Ellie said softly. Danny saw Luke flinch as if the words had physically struck him.

'Ellie,' her mother said, putting just a touch more steel into her voice. 'Think about this. This isn't an option you can dismiss without at least giving it some thought.'

'I can't,' Ellie said.

'Medically it's safe. Is it religion? I never thought–'

'It's not that,' and Ellie sat up and took a shuddering breath. 'Mummy, Granda Quinn left Dad and Uncle Dermot. Just upped and left them. He couldn't handle being a parent, so he decided to cut and run.'

Listening to this, Danny felt cold fingers grip at his heart. 'Granda Quinn' had done no such thing, at least not of his own volition. He thought back to Dermot and the moment the little downtrodden man had taken Tony Morrigan's life. Danny was no closer to forgiveness for that horrific act, and he doubted he ever would be, but it was an uncomfortable reminder all the same that any notions he'd once held of there being a clear-cut good vs evil split in all of this had been unceremoniously pissed on from a great height.

As for Luke, he remained rapt, hanging off his mother's every word.

Christina continued. 'I don't see what that has to do with any—'

'It has everything to do with it,' said Ellie. 'It wasn't Dad's fault that his father couldn't handle being a parent. And it's not my child's fault that I still feel like too much of a child myself to handle the news that I'm pregnant with anything but terror.'

Luke's never seen this memory before. That had to be it. This was new information for Luke, and he was drinking it down greedily, struggling to process what it meant.

'And what if Danny doesn't want to know?' Christina said. 'What then? You'll be a single parent. You'll have to drop out of university. Lord knows when you'll be fit to resume your studies. Is that what you wanted, Ellie?'

'No,' Ellie said. 'No, Mummy, it's not what I wanted. But it's what I've got, and I'm taking responsibility for it.'

Mother and daughter froze in place.

'You see?' Luke said in bitter triumph. 'From your own lips! I wasn't what you wanted!'

'Haven't you been listening this whole time?' Ellie asked him. 'Getting pregnant now, at this time? Of course it wasn't what I wanted. I wanted to be in a good job. I wanted to be in a stable relationship. I wanted a written fucking guarantee from the Archangel Gabriel that labour would last four seconds and feel like eating a fucking jumbo Fruit & Nut bar! What does it *matter* what I wanted? When you came along, none of it mattered. I had you. I had Danny. And we tried. We tried the best we could.'

'Yes,' Luke said. 'I saw.'

The scene changed once more, this time refusing to settle on merely one vignette from the past and instead moving fluidly between several: the night Ellie had broken down after being unable to produce sufficient quantities of breast milk; early morning feeds where Danny had been reduced to tears in trying to diagnose why Luke was refusing to take the bottle he had been screaming for; snatches of conversations, some so recent Danny flinched upon witnessing them.

'*It's not my fault you didn't finish it. I didn't finish my degree either, in case you didn't fuckin' notice. I had to get that wanker of a job. There's not a lot of applications out there that say we'll let ya in with half a degree.*'

'*You had to get that job. You didn't have to do anything.*'

'*Yeah? Well you didn't have to get fuckin' pregnant, did ye?*'

Danny saw himself pulling away from Ellie's touch on the morning they'd been taken from him, the day his life had gone straight to hell. He hated himself for pulling away from her, wanted to reach out and throttle himself for doing it, especially when he heard his arrogant younger self proclaim, '*I don't know if I can do this.*'

Remarkably, as they watched the grim scenes unfold, he and Ellie had drawn closer together. Though it was far from easy to witness, somehow it felt like watching someone else's life.

Ellie began to move her arms this way and that, conducting the orchestra of space and time around them. He doubted if she was even conscious of the easy expertise she had already shown, but he wasn't about to bring it to her attention in case it broke the spell.

'Okay, mister,' she told Luke, her voice now reeking of that particular maternal brand of don't-fuck-me-about. 'Let me show you how we tried.'

It was Regent Street, again. Baby Luke was sitting up in the midst of his blankets, gumming mightily on some unidentified object, watching television with wide eyes. Something on the screen scared him; his face crumpled and he began to wail, and within seconds, there was Ellie, scooping him up and twirling him around and *sssssshing* him, cuddling him to her chest and rocking him. She sat with him and still he cried, upset by whatever it was he had seen, until she talked and tickled and teased and *peekaboo'd* him. Within moments she was using his tiny little hands to stroke down her face, singing some nonsensical song or other …

It was night-time, and he was being sick, throwing up great milky curds of bottle and baby rice, tears streaming down his little face, and Ellie was there wiping and cleaning and *sssssshing* like some sort of mummy-slash-Hindu-goddess; arms seemingly sprouting from nowhere ...

They were playing with a toy mat with shitloads of buttons and the cow was going 'moo moo moo' and Luke giggled furiously every time his mummy went 'moo moo moo' ...

He was sitting in the front of a supermarket trolley and, when she was sure none of the other mothers were around to look at her funny, she was racing him down the aisles making him squeal with laughter ...

They were together, all three of them, and mummy and daddy were fighting sleep because it was after midnight, but sitting between them, right in the middle of the sofa, was wee fat Luke, absolutely full of life. When daddy's eyes dared to close, those little chubby fingers would poke and prod and touch daddy on the face and mummy would half-laugh, half-sigh ...

BELFAST / OTHERWORLD, NOW
'Enough!'

The standing stone circle was reasserting itself around them. The silver Sword returned to Danny's right hand and he knew that Luke would now be similarly armed.

Carman was back too. She had lost control over the propaganda visions, Danny knew. The later vignettes had all come from Ellie. Was she able to do that because of her faerie heritage?

Or was it just because, quite frankly, she was fuckin' awesome?

'You tried,' Carman said, with a voice that could have been

applied to squeaky hinges. 'But deep down both of you wished that you could go back to how it was before your son came along. Your wish was granted.'

'Why are you doing this to us?' Ellie demanded, obviously deciding to change tack. 'You've won. You've got your hell on earth going on out there. Why do you need my son?'

Carman seemed offended. 'It's Luke who needs me. He has power. He has a great future ahead of him. I can help him with that. I can be the mother he needs.'

Uh-fucking-oh, Danny thought. Absurdly, but before he could stop himself, he took a long step away from Ellie. If she wanted to rush Carman, he doubted anything short of an anchor the size of the Andromeda Galaxy could have slowed her.

'You are *not* his mother you evil, hateful ugly fucking oul bitch!' Ellie exploded. 'I am his mother, and if you so much as *look* at him again I'll fuckin' kill you! Stick to your own sons!'

'Mine are disappointments to me. But Luke … Luke can be my true heir.'

'Oh aye, mother of the fuckin' year, you are!' Ellie spat. 'Your kids disappoint you so away they go and let's go steal somebody else's, eh? You couldn't mother your way out of a fuckin' wet paper bag you oul cunt!'

Luke was watching the two women battle it out. One was a queen – glowing and glorious on her throne, every inch the model of fairytale perfection. The other was dishevelled, sweating and currently throwing out a word-speed of roughly thirty cunts a minute, which even Danny had to tip his hat to.

Luke was lost, torn. He looked wretched. The sword was no

longer gripped tightly in his hand. His warrior's stance had been abandoned. Everything he'd been brought up to believe – no matter how magical or how accelerated that bringing-up process had been – was being challenged. Everything he thought he knew about his family was collapsing around him.

'Son,' Danny said, getting Luke's attention.

There was no rage, no murderous coldness on his son's face now, only great swathes of confusion and loneliness. His childhood may have taken only days in human terms, but in looking at him now, Danny knew that Luke had lived every single day of those time-warped years alone and contained in this Petri dish of weirdness, trapped with only an insane megalomaniacal witch, her cadre of pet monsters, and a collection of bad memories swirling around him. Cold ghosts of days long past that he was doomed to walk amongst and powerless to interact with; a childhood exposed to visions that had ultimately created an enormously bitter, hugely confused young man, like *A Christmas Carol* run in reverse.

'Luke,' Danny said, extending a hand. 'I love you, son. You're my little boy, and you always will be. Come home.'

Carman was standing now. 'It's a trick!' she thundered. 'I warned you, Luke, that if you delayed too long over the kill they would do this! Strike! Strike *now!*'

Luke's hands tightened around the sword once more. He raised it off the ground by a foot or so. Danny didn't back away. He took a few steps towards his son, not to gain an advantage in another round of fighting, but simply to be closer to him. He dropped the silver Sword onto the grass with a soft thump. Weaponless, defenceless, Danny paused at arm's length from Luke, and extended his hand once more.

'I was your first word,' he said.

Luke raised his sword hand. Carman moved like a cobra from her raised throne dais, skimming across the surface of the grass more than actually running. Her entire body was tense with hungry anticipation.

'You will do as I tell you!' she screamed.

Luke's sword fell to earth. 'No.'

Carman's expression changed. His back to her, Danny didn't see it happen, but his son and Ellie must have witnessed it firsthand, for he saw and heard their reactions. Ellie screamed while Luke's eyes widened in fear. Danny *felt* Carman approaching and knew she'd be upon him before he would even get the chance to turn around.

There was no time. He had thought – guessed, hoped – that she was sitting on that damn throne because the effort of merging the two worlds together was draining her to a greater degree than she had been prepared to show.

Seemingly not. And now he was about to pay for that mistake with his life. The last thing he would ever see would be his son's horrified face as the woman he'd come to think of as his mother revealed her true visage. He hoped Luke would at least have time to retrieve his dropped sword and try to defend himself, defend Ellie …

A moment passed and, shockingly, Danny found himself still standing, still alive. He turned, and his mouth fell open.

'*Steve?*' he blurted out in delighted disbelief.

Of all the things, in all the world he had ever expected to

see, even after the events of the last few days ... after the faerie monstrosities and the living darkness clouds and the empty universes the last thing on that list was the sight of his best friend, looking like an extra from Westeros, bloodstained and with his arm around Carman's throat.

'Ellie said you were–'

'Tossed through a house and then pushed at high-speed out of a moving car?' Steve finished. He winked. 'All in a night's work for Big Balls McGee, Danny.' Then, following a significant growl from beside him, 'Ably assisted by these huge hairy bastards.'

'Wily?' Danny said, astonished once again. 'Is that you?'

The massive wolf inclined his head. 'Morrigan,' he said gravely. 'It is good to see you again.'

'You learned to talk properly,' Danny observed.

'For a start,' Wily replied.

'You! You shielded this human's approach from me, didn't you? You're shielding him right now,' Carman accused Wily. 'Traitorous dogs ... !'

'Wolves,' Wily corrected her calmly.

'Steve, you're alive!' Ellie was beaming. She looked as though she wanted to hug him, if it wasn't for the slight matter of Carman blocking her way.

'Where's your da?' Steve asked, and just like that, Danny's euphoria was sucked away.

'He didn't make it,' Danny said, after a long pause, in which the only sound was the soft, insistent sound of Carman's mocking laughter.

'I'm sorry,' Steve said, his levity gone now too. His arm

tightened, and Carman's laughter abruptly ceased. He seemed about to say something else, but looked as if he couldn't quite figure out what it should be. Instead, his eyes flicked to the man standing alongside Danny and Ellie. He frowned, and Danny expected him to ask the obvious question, but he didn't. He kept on staring, and then his jaw dropped.

'Ach, you're fuckin' *shittin*' me,' he said eventually.

'It's really him,' Ellie nodded, confirming the unspoken question.

'Jesus Christ,' Steve said softly, glancing at the other wolf, who was a whisker smaller than Wily but no less fearsome-looking. 'So that's what you meant,' he said, and before Danny could ask, Steve nodded to Luke. 'All right, big lad?'

'You're Steve,' Luke replied.

Steve looked quite pleased. 'Remember yer Uncle Steve?'

'I've watched you. You came to my father's house to drink beer and smoke drugs and try to convince him he was better off before I came along.'

Not for the first time in the last few moments, Steve seemed to be at a loss for words. He looked from adult Luke to Danny, to Ellie, and back to Danny again. Carman, still in his grasp, still being curiously placid, was beginning to smile, a grin so wolfish that Wily would have been hard-pressed to match it.

'Aye, well. You watched *In The Night Garden* and thought it was fuckin' mint, so there's none of us perfect here,' Steve shot back.

'Luke,' Danny said, finally daring to take his eyes off Carman to turn to his son, spreading his hands in what he hoped was a calming gesture. 'That doesn't matter now. All that matters is we figure out some way to put things back the way they–'

'You had sex with my mother,' Luke said, still addressing Steve.

– *were.*

The word died on Danny's lips as the breath died in his throat. His heart thudded in his chest. He turned back to Steve, and saw that his friend wasn't looking at him at all, he was looking at Ellie, and Ellie wasn't looking at anyone, she was staring at the impossible grass beneath their feet in this impossible clearing on this impossible slice of unreality.

Carman closed her eyes. Her lips moved silently. Wily's head raised and he sniffed the air. 'She's calling to them!' he said urgently.

The wind began to pick up inside the world of the stone circle. It whipped Ellie's hair around her face and she lifted her hand to brush it away, but still couldn't meet what she knew would be Danny's searching gaze. Murmurs began to sound from the periphery of the standing stones, cacklings and rustlings made by approaching creatures. Wily and Larka began to pace agitatedly, growling at the source of the noises, moving their great heads this way and that.

'They're coming!' Wily said again. 'Morrigan, you must do something!'

'Steve!' Larka pleaded.

Their words fell on deaf ears. The four humans only had eyes for one another, and they seemed to have quite forgotten about the witch-goddess in their midst.

'Did you?' Danny asked Steve. Tiny sparks of pitch-black energy were crackling from his feet upward, as if he were a lightning rod for an upside-down world. The air began to taste heavy and metallic, a taint Danny would have remembered from his visions as the fingerprint of heavy concentrations of potential magical energy; if he had been thinking clearly at that precise moment. He wasn't.

Steve licked his lips. Since waking up from that parallel existence he'd lived for a few days, after realising what he'd done while living that other life, he had known this conversation was coming. He began his defence.

'It was crazy, it wasn't real. It was a spell, it was bizarro world, a parallel universe, call it whatever *Star Trek* load of oul balls you want!' he said. 'None of us, Danny, including you, were who we really were! Far as I knew, Ellie and I had been together for years! We had a kid together, for fuck's sake!'

Danny's attention was now on Ellie. 'You and him?'

Wily and Larka were running around the group now, bounding in huge leaps, passing over each other to create a constantly patrolled perimeter. Shadows were forming at the spaces between the four great pillars of stone, but there were sources of light in the darkness. The glint of glowing eyes, of teeth. Carman's lips were still moving. The fingers of black energy around Danny's legs had climbed as far as his waist now.

Luke watched all of this unfold without moving a muscle, but he had the expression of someone eager to see how this would end.

'Yeah,' Ellie nodded, drawing up to full height. 'So nothing happened between you and Maggie, Danny? Because if you've noticed, I haven't asked.'

'Guess now I know why,' Danny replied. Ellie blanched at that.

'She is manipulating you!' Larka screamed at them. Leaving Wily to guard the perimeter, she had tried to get closer to Steve, to Danny, to Carman herself, only to find she was unable to come within ten feet of the tightly-grouped bunch. Parked impotently at an invisible border, all she could do was try desperately to attract their attention before it was too late. Carman's lips were moving so quickly as to be a blur. The energy around Danny was now at shoulder height – a twilight cape swirling faster and faster.

'Here they come!' Wily called.

Faeries. Monsters. A moving wall of them, all shapes and sizes, came pouring from between the stones, converging from all sides on the group at its epicentre. Larka gave up on trying to distract the humans and went back to her leader's side as the faerie army rolled and bounded and lumbered and slimed toward them.

'I had hopes,' Larka said, turning to look at Wily. 'Hopes for us. I have never hoped before, for anything. I liked that feeling.'

'I know,' Wily replied, dipping his head in apology. 'I'm sorry.'

The energy had fully enveloped Danny now. His eyes burned with black, endless fire. Steve and Ellie found their mouths could move but no sound could emerge from them. Carman extricated herself from Steve's grasp and he could make no attempt to recapture her.

She moved to Danny. He ignored her.

'Perhaps I underestimated you,' she told him, in a low voice.

'Perhaps you, after all, are the one I should have given my attention to. Your whole life you've wanted to be something more. You've been held back by people like these,' she indicated Ellie and Steve with a contemptuous flick of her head, 'for far too long. Demonstrate your power.'

She extended a hand and the silver Sword Danny had discarded when refusing to fight his son rose into her grasp. She held it out to him.

The faerie hordes had reached Wily and Larka, who threw themselves into the melee without hesitation, biting and snapping, leaping against creatures that defied description – things that were little more than fangs in the blackness, hunger in the mist. Larka howled as the crest of the faerie wave swallowed her.

Danny took the Sword from Carman's hand. He stared down at it then at his son. Luke nodded, knowing what his father was about to do, readying himself.

'Do it,' Luke said.

Danny called on everything he'd learned. Every ounce of power, every scrap of will he possessed, he took it and he gathered it up inside him. Every betrayal he had suffered, every disappointment, every regret, all of the rage and the hatred. Every time he had felt inadequate, felt like a failure, every time he had burned inside at how things had come to this or how helpless he had felt when they had.

All of these things he took into himself.

All of them he discarded.

The darkness exploded from him, drained into the ground around him as though he had pulled some invisible plug. In its place, light. At first diffuse, an ephemeral heartbeat of illumination, but with every pulse it grew stronger.

Bleeding, dying, bitten by a hundred different mouths, half-consumed by the soulless emptiness of the creatures swarming around them, Wily and Larka felt the light wash over them and felt the creatures weaken, then vanish, as it did.

'What are you *doing?*' Carman screamed in frustration. She lashed out at Danny, and her blow, which looked powerful enough to have split an elephant, was caught mid-downstroke.

'What you asked him to,' Luke told her. 'He's demonstrating his power,' and with a shove he pushed his one-time *Mitéra* away, sending her tumbling end-over-end away from them.

When she rose, all pretence of humanity, of subtlety had fled from her. She dropped her palms to the surface and all of the darkness that had tried to claim Danny as its own abandoned him and redirected itself into her, through her.

Carman grew.

Larka realised she could move. Her wounds throbbed numbly, as if from a distance, somewhere faint and warm. She got to her feet and discovered Wily was doing the same, blinking in the newfound light rising into the air above the Morrigan. His attention was on them, which seemed a remarkable thing, seeing as how the most appalling thing imaginable was rising into existence behind him.

It had too many heads, too many everythings – every persona, human and otherwise, Carman had adopted over the few millennia of her existence. Its stomach, swollen and distended in some grotesque parody of pregnancy, irised open and closed like some great mouth, displaying circular parasitic ranks of teeth, as if offering a return to a womb forged in Hell itself.

'Get them clear,' Danny called to the two wolves, indicating the petrified figures of Ellie and Steve. Whether frozen through fear or some supernatural means, it didn't matter – both were completely immobile, mouths agape, staring in horror-struck terror at the monster unfolding before them.

'Move them!' another voice said, trying to shake Larka into action. It was Luke, standing at Danny's side, weapon ready. Two halves of the same whole. Father and son met each other's eyes for a moment, as the wolves Danny had freed finally sprang into action and, with a gentleness that belied their savage countenance, picked Ellie and Steve up in their jaws and carried them off, back through the standing stone circle. Once between the stones they vanished entirely from Danny's view. He exhaled.

Now he and Luke were alone before the still-unfolding Carman-monster. She was thirty feet tall. Now forty. Centuries of waiting and brooding and biding her time were being unleashed in one awesome display of power. Carman was lost to the magical spasms that wracked her body, drawing each ripple of dark power from the twilit world she inhabited. Danny saw the shades of some of her more nightmarish creations spiral back through the standing stones, screaming as they went, their life-forces absorbed into the central mass of their mother.

By now she defied description, a Lovecraftian deity made flesh. If you tried to look at her bloated body as a whole, you could persuade yourself you were looking at a multi-limbed, elastic, wyrm-woman hybrid. Try to focus in on any specific part of her, however, and the mind would shy away, yelping.

When she spoke, from the thousand orifices that dotted her diseased, disgusting body, she did not bother with things as mundane as sound waves. Her words were acid, etching themselves indelibly into the fragile nooks of the mind.

No match. No match for me.

Luke screamed in pain as his black sword, a gift from his *Mitéra*, dissolved in his hands, its individual particles whipped in the winds and were sucked back into Carman's still-growing mass. He was defenceless.

The growing stopped. She loomed over them. Even with the Sword of Nuada, even with all that he had learned, Danny felt as though he were about to try and stab a mountain to death.

I am all of my children. I am thousands. I am legion. What hope do you two have?

'You'd think,' a new voice said mildly, 'from way up there, she'd at least be able to count.'

That voice ...

'Daddy?' Danny said, as if a small child once again.

Tony Morrigan, holding a silver Sword of his own, looked proudly at his son and his grandson. 'Would you look at you two lads,' he said softly, gesturing to Luke in particular. 'I knew it when you were wee. You've the look of my da about ye.'

Who brought you back? The creature raged above them, its anger radiating so strongly through the psychic channels it was using to communicate that it caused Danny and Luke to stagger, almost to fall. The skies darkened and cracked. The four monoliths shook. *Who?*

'Dunno about that. I think the wee fella must take after his ma,' another new voice sounded. Dazed both from the psychic assaults from the Carman-monstrosity and from the reappearance of his dead father, it was all Danny could do to redirect his attention towards Luke.

Beside him was another impossible ally. Another silver Sword.

'Da?' Tony Morrigan said softly.

'Son,' James Morrigan returned. He looked exactly as he'd looked the night he died, not a day older – making him look of a similar age to Tony. He appraised the scene going on around him. 'Call this a fuckin' afterlife, do yis?' he said evenly.

'Granda?' Danny said faintly.

Upon seeing this latest arrival, Tony Morrigan did what Danny had been tempted to do himself. He ran forward and embraced his father fiercely.

THIS ENDS NOW!

'Look out!' Danny cried. He tried desperately to shove the others aside before Carman's grotesque bulk could smash down upon them.

'No.'

The word was spoken softly, yet it reached the ears of all four Morrigans standing there. On Carman, though, that single word seemed to have a more dramatic effect - the seemingly inexorable collapse of her demonic form on top of them was arrested, suddenly, completely. There was an ear-splitting *crack*, a smell of ozone and burned flesh and, somehow, that hideous bloated mass was repulsed, its attack blunted.

Smoke curled from Carman in great belching clouds. Her scream of pain and hatred resounded in their minds, increasing in intensity until Danny felt his grip on reality narrow and contract into a pinpoint of consciousness. He was blacking out, his mind squeezed to a pulp by the pressure exerted on it.

'No, I don't think so.'

As the voice spoke again, he felt the pressure ease off, and a presence he hadn't felt in some time settled back into a corner of his mind and curled up there like a dog settling itself by a fire.

Four Morrigans became five.

'Well,' the Morrigan – the original version, the Mk1, triple goddess, ex-crow – remarked briskly as she took in the scene around her. 'What's the craic, lads?'

'Who in the name of fuck's *this* meant to be?' Tony said.

'Tony!' James snapped, rebuking his middle-aged son for his language.

'The Morrigan,' Danny and Luke said, in unison.

'Well. It's about fuckin' time too,' Tony said.

'You brought us back,' James said.

'Yes. Brought you back and armed you for this battle,' she said, gesturing to the silver Swords they all carried, save Luke. She nodded in Luke's direction and a silver Sword appeared in his waiting grip. This time, perhaps because he was attuned for it, Danny felt a slight tug on his own copy of the Sword, as though it were being diluted to create the copies.

'She's been working with Carman,' Luke said. 'She brought this about. They hatched this plan together.'

Danny felt as though he'd been kicked in the chest. He recoiled from her presence inside his head, and felt her recoil at the same moment.

'You just love blurting this stuff out, don't you?' the Morrigan said, addressing Luke.

'Is it true?' Danny managed to ask.

She didn't bother denying it. Behind her, the Carman-thing had, insofar as these things could be judged with something so hideously misshapen, righted itself after its unexpected setback and was moving toward them once more. Whether weakened by the Morrigan's initial attack or whether the Morrigan was doing something to time itself, the huge creature's approach seemed a mite more ponderous than before.

'You were given what you thought you wanted, and you discovered you didn't want it. Not at the price you'd have to pay. The same thing has happened to me. I'm sorry for what I've done but there's no time,' she said, directing her words at Danny. 'We're all going to die unless you all trust me, completely. Yes or no?'

Danny realised, to his somewhat lightheaded horror, that his artificially-aged teenage son, dead father and dead grandfather were all staring at him, waiting to follow his lead.

'It's you,' Tony said gently.

'No,' Danny protested meekly, aware that Carman was coming in for another go and that this time the element of surprise was not on their side, 'I'm not the one in the prophecy. Luke is.'

'Ach,' the Morrigan said, and Danny only dazedly noticed that she was talking like a Belfast native now. 'Prophecy. What a load of oul balls.'

'Son,' Tony told him in a rush. 'You're the one. Forget about prophecies and witches and all that. Luke's your wee son and he's in danger.'

'But–' Danny began, indicating the brick shithouse that was baby Luke.

'*So?*' Tony shot back with such forcefulness it made Danny start. 'You're his *da*. Protect him. That's what you're *for.*'

Yet again, it was all about choices. He'd longed to be the master of his own destiny, to feel like he was in control. Hell, he'd bitched about it. And now, four generations of his family – and that wasn't including the Morrigan, who added on a couple of hundred more – had placed him in complete control, and all he could think was, *I don't want it. I can't handle it.*

So?

That '*So?*' was the key to it all, Danny suddenly realised. He hadn't wanted to have a child so young; he hadn't handled the responsibility that well. He didn't want to face this monster now, he didn't want to lead, and be responsible for the fate of his loved ones.

But, *So?*

Life did these things, life short-changed you and stacked the deck and delighted in throwing its faeces in your face like a demented chimp. What did it really fucking *matter* what you wanted or what you'd received before this present moment in time? What really mattered was what you did right now, what you kept doing.

What mattered was the bottles you kept making and the pints you kept missing, the friends you kept by your side through it all, and the commitment to a little bundle of skin and sore gums who had no idea you were doing it all for him, but who loved you anyway because you were his daddy, and his whole world, and you were awesome, and you owed it to him to try to stay that fuckin' way for as long as possible … or at least until he saw you dancing at a family wedding.

'You're *how* old?' James was asking Luke during Danny's latest revelation.

'Long story,' Tony interjected quickly.

'What the fuck're they *feedin'* kids these days?' James whistled.

Danny squared his shoulders and faced the beast, ready to–

DIE!

Carman's scream was no longer being blocked out. Something – the closest analogy would have been a tentacle, if tentacles were thirty feet long and as thick as a small car – lashed out at the group with enough force to send every one of them sprawling end-over-end, arse over shite, backwards. Danny landed next to his Granda Morrigan in a heap, and only the prospect of imminent attack and gruesome demise made him hurry to untangle himself. He helped his granda get to his feet.

'Fuck this for a game of darts, son,' James wheezed as Danny pulled him up. 'Aren't ghosts meant to be insubstantial?'

There wasn't time to reply. Much as her darling son had done when activating the Network, Carman had thrown out the book on Gloating Super Villain Etiquette. She wasn't interested in taunts, or a good old *mwahaha-let-me-explain-my-plan-and-oops-also-my-weakness* monologue. She was using her ludicrous size and weight advantage to try and wipe out her opponents as quickly and as messily as possible.

Take control. The words sounded in the four men's minds, planted there by the Morrigan. Each of them swung their silver Swords like never before, in powerful and graceful arcs, and the Swords themselves glinted with inner light as they sliced through gargantuan tentacles, chopped into grotesque excesses of flesh. Black ichor gooped out from under Carman's mottled, pallid skin.

Screaming like banshees, the five Morrigans charged.

Danny, Tony and James acquitted themselves admirably, but they were mere amateurs compared to Luke and the Morrigan. Those two fought like legends made flesh. Danny caught sight of his son once or twice as he leapt and ducked and dove in his desperate attempts to keep himself alive, unflattened and undevoured.

Luke was leaping twice as high, moving faster than the rest of them, almost keeping pace with the Morrigan herself, who was more or less single-handedly keeping them all alive. He had time to marvel that, in his brief, if intense, one-on-one duel with Luke he had been able to hold his own for any length of time at all.

You know why. Because even then, even when he thought he despised you, he was holding back. He knew. Even here, even now in the madness of the melee, the Morrigan still spoke to him.

Roars of pain, both audible and psychic, ripped through the standing stone circle. Great disembodied pieces of that horrific body flapped on the grass. Carman's central mass was noticeably smaller now, her attacks less deliberate and measured, more frenzied and desperate.

We can win this! Danny thought, the first flicker of hope he had felt since the battle began.

No, the Morrigan's voice came back instantly. *Not like this. She's about to—*

Another roar, this one entirely on the psychic plane, so powerful that all of them were knocked flat on their arses. Danny rolled as he impacted, steeling himself for Carman to press her advantage. No attack came. As he got to his feet, he saw that Carman had retreated into the centre of the circle. Her monstrous visage, leaking blood in copious quantities, had withdrawn into itself.

'What's she doing?' James hollered into the sudden storm-intensity winds that had sprung up. He had planted his silver Sword in the earth and was using it to brace himself. Danny, struggling to keep his balance, did the same.

Watch.

The winds were all heading in Carman's direction, as though she were the centre of the vortex. At first Danny thought this was a new style of attack – that she was trying to suck them towards her where she could finish them off – but then he saw what she was really targeting.

More faeries tumbled into the circle. They were all shapes and sizes, all screaming. Just as she'd done before, she was drawing her own creations back into herself, leeching their essences, using every faerie soul she consumed to regenerate her own wounded form a little more and leaving them hollowed-out husks. The reduced bulk that had given him hope had swollen back to its former levels.

Carman didn't stop. The faeries kept coming, screeching in their death throes as they went.

Danny felt himself despair.

Look, Danny, came the Morrigan's voice. *Look what she's using!*

He looked around, his arms on fire from the effort of holding on to the Sword still anchored to the earth. For a few seconds he wondered what the hell he was supposed to be looking for and how much longer he could keep his gaze fixed on the carnage – in myths, people had been turned to stone for looking at things a hundred times less terrifying than this – and then, that great carcass shifted, and he saw it.

The Dagda's Cauldron.

Objects placed in the Cauldron were resurrected; at least they were once upon a time, until Carman had perverted the magic behind it, turned the Cauldron into the birthing chamber for her species of horrors. Now, it must be serving as her power source, her regeneration battery.

When she's done regenerating, it will vanish again, the Morrigan told him. She was standing about six feet to his right, her long hair whipping out in front of her. He was reminded of the first time he'd seen her physical form, on that beach long ago, when he'd been reduced to a bumbling idiot by how beautiful she was, how imposing. She was no less so now. Danny noticed for the first time that she was unarmed, wielding no sword. Unlike her male descendants she was showing no signs of strain against the vortex, she seemed in no danger of being sucked into Carman's hungry mouth.

How do we kill her? he asked her.

She looked over at him and smiled. It was a tired smile on that beautiful, ancient face, one that displayed every single one of those thousands of years she had existed.

Kill her? Here, in this place? I'm not sure you can, Danny. I'm not sure anyone can. She was born on far-off shores. She is of Greece, not Ireland. She has never felt at home anywhere; that is her strength, and her weakness. She belongs to this world and to yours, to both and to neither.

He could barely stand now. It was chaos. Tentacles whipped around, snatching at arms and legs, waiting to flick them unawares into that black hole of a mouth. They were trapped in the funnel of a tornado with a Kraken at its centre.

Tell me what to do, he begged her.

I don't need to. You will know, Danny. You will know when the time comes. Love will form your choice. I only hope you make better choices than I did.

And at that, she began to run, faster than any human could hope to match, straight for Carman. Some part of that monster registered the tasty morsel it was about to swallow whole and a rumble of expectancy and desire made the monoliths tremble.

The Morrigan leapt gracefully into the air, over and under tentacles that *snicked* out in an attempt to snag her and prevent her escape. Escape was not her plan, anyway. She dove, straight into the heart of the beast, and just before it closed around her and enveloped her, she thought of Mag Tuired and the glories of battle and slaughter. She was able to reach into the monstrosity and pull something out, throw it clear.

This done, the Morrigan's mind turned from thoughts of war. She thought of the washerwoman in the pool, dunking her little sons under the surface, and her handsome husband walking toward her with her baby in his arms. A moment of perfect happiness. She held that moment close.

Then, she was eaten whole.

The little universe they inhabited paused for a fraction of a heartbeat. Somehow in that deathly still, Danny had time to register his connection to the Morrigan change, as a sense of powerful contentment radiated from her. Impossibly, he could have sworn that in the midst of the madness, he saw the image of a little girl, her eyes closed and her chest rising and falling gently as she slept.

Then, all was white light, and noise, and the sensation of being knocked backward even more powerfully than they had been pulled forward.

Carman exulted in her triumph. She revelled at the glorious stupidity of the sacrifice of her greatest enemy, a hollow gesture of desperation, a ...

'Lose something?' Danny said, free hand resting easily on the rim of the Dagda's Cauldron.

Carman's triumph flipped to outrage in the blink of an eye. Danny staggered under the fresh psychic assault – she threw everything she had at him and, despite all of his training and his heritage, his defences simply weren't going to be enough.

Another hand fell on the rim of the Cauldron. He felt the pressure in his mind ease, and thought for a second that the Morrigan, had somehow been belched back into existence.

'Dad?' the owner of the hand said.

His vision cleared. It was Luke who had spoken. Danny nodded gratefully at his son to let him know he was okay. Tony and James joined them at the Cauldron. They were still alive. All of them, still alive, thanks to the Morrigan's sacrifice. He tried to put the Morrigan's words out of his mind. Surely with the Cauldron at their mercy, they had the power to end this, here and now? All he had to do was–

Stop. Don't. It was Carman, but not with her former, withering power. She had even ceased her approach, hanging back. To his astonishment, her fully monstrous form began to fold in on itself – flesh rolling into flesh with a noise he would try to forget for the rest of his life – until she stood before the four men in her human guise once more.

'Can we talk?' she said.

There was a long and slightly disbelieving pause by way of response.

'I think I speak for us all,' Luke replied, garnering looks of surprise from his older companions as he spoke, 'when I say, *fuck no.*'

Danny grinned. As one, all four men raised the Swords. Normally he would have despaired of chopping a metal cauldron to death with swords, but he knew – they all knew – that this was different. When they plunged those Swords into the cauldron's interior, it would be their *intent* that would get the job done, not the physical act itself, and the Dagda's Cauldron would be no more.

'Wait!' Carman said desperately, taking another half-step forward. From this distance, they could see her skin rippling. Danny wondered if she really *had* folded herself back up from

Cthulhu-sized proportions to human, or whether she'd simply fooled their brains into *thinking* she had. He realised he didn't want to know.

'Destroying the Cauldron won't kill me,' she said.

His initial thought was to dismiss it as desperate ravings, but Danny thought of the message the Morrigan had given him. Carman could not be killed in the Otherworld. She belonged to both worlds, and to neither. *Whatever the fuck that means.*

'She's right,' Luke said. At the looks he got from the others, he shrugged. 'I know how she works. The Cauldron is channelling her powers, but it's only the amplifier, not the source. Destroying it will weaken her, but it won't kill her.'

'Do rightly,' Danny said, raising his Sword again.

'Think about this!' she begged them. 'Think about what's been done to Ireland tonight. Think about how many people have died. This Cauldron can bring them back – can bring them all back,' and now she was looking at only Danny. 'Including your father.'

'I'm here now,' Tony pointed out.

'Within this circle, yes,' Carman shot back. 'You have the Morrigan to thank for that. She's gone. Outside this circle, if Ireland goes back to the human world, you won't go with it. You can't. But with *me* on your side, you can go back. Everyone who died when I brought Ireland to Otherworld … I could bring them back.'

'You'd swear an oath?' Luke asked.

Her eyes flashed as she looked at the young man she had once hoped to be her ace in the hole. 'You know about–'

'I know more than you think, *Mitéra*,' Luke said.

'Oath?' Danny asked.

'Magical rules for magical creatures. She swears an oath and she's bound to carry it out,' Luke explained.

Danny felt elation wash over him. If they could get Carman to tie herself up in knots she could never undo, she would never pose a threat. He could use the powers she possessed to finally do some fucking good.

'Makes sense,' James nodded. 'Magic's full of that stuff. Why they're so big on tricksters. Half the battle's working out the get-out clauses in the contracts. Explains why all lawyers are proper bastards.'

'You think I should do this?' Danny asked him. He noted that Carman had made no promises about what would happen to James.

James snorted. 'Jesus, no!' he said. 'Only reason she's here now is people have had the chance to kill her before and haven't taken it. Don't make the same mistake, Danny.'

'It won't just be your father you'll lose,' Carman pressed on, again addressing Danny directly. 'All of those years your son has lived with me? Destroy that Cauldron, and they'll be taken from him.'

'I don't want them,' Luke returned hotly. 'Not the way you gave them to me. Here, alone? With only the bad memories you allowed me to see, over and over? You can have those years back. I *never* wanted them.'

'We don't ever get all that we want. The process is called *living*,'

Carman snapped, reminding Danny uncomfortably of his own 'So?' revelation of not long before. 'Take my word for it, Danny, a human body, even one with Luke's unique heritage, can't cope with losing nearly twenty years in an *instant*,' and she snapped her fingers with a sound like a rifle shot. 'You'll get your precious baby son back, Danny. Whether you want him back alive – that's your choice.'

Danny felt like screaming. Was this what the Morrigan had meant, about choice?

'Leave me my Cauldron intact and I'll return you and your family to your world,' she went on, her voice silken. It was astonishing to think only moments before she had assumed a form that made Godzilla look like the Cookie Monster.

'You'd put things back the way they were?' Danny asked. Hadn't this been what he'd been hoping for since he'd held his father's body in his arms. A reset button? A do-over? An 'and then he woke up and it was all a dream' ending, to *all* of this madness?

'Danny?' Tony said warningly.

'This is a mistake, son,' James echoed.

Carman just shook her head. 'No. No going back. Our two worlds wouldn't be as separate as they were before. After all,' she went on, very reasonably, her talking-to-children intonation making her sound like a primary school teacher. 'There's got to be something in it for me, hasn't there?'

He thought of Ellie, somewhere outside the circle, probably trying to get back inside. She wouldn't be able to. The only reason they had both been allowed in previously was to allow the showdown between himself and Luke that Carman had engineered.

What would he tell her, if he took the chance to destroy the Cauldron, if he succeeded in trapping Carman in the Otherworld forever, and if in doing so …

He looked at his son, the living anachronism. There was no terror on Luke's face, despite what was being talked about. For a moment, just a moment, Danny saw, not the magically aged adult, but the little boy he had picked up and tickled a thousand times over this past year. The baby who had fallen asleep on him during midnight feeds at least twice a week; that weight of his little head that he'd missed so while in parallel-Belfast with his shiny, empty new life.

'You made a deal,' he told his father. 'You made a deal, for me.' Tony nodded. He could hardly deny it. 'Did you regret it?' Danny asked him. 'Making that deal? Even when the day came, and you had to walk away from me? Would you have gone back, if you could have, erased the first ten years we had?'

'No,' Tony admitted. 'Not for a second.'

'This is what life is,' Carman said harshly. 'No clean endings. Sorry to say, the evil witch doesn't get vanquished and go quietly into the night. Life is making deals. Life is making the best of what we get.'

'You're right,' Danny said.

'Then we're agreed,' Carman said, trying and failing to keep the salacious edge of pleasure from her voice as she spoke.

'No,' Danny said.

That brought her up short. The human-skin she was wearing

232

rippled more forcefully this time, and wondered if she were to throw her true form at them at this reduced distance, would he even have time to destroy the Cauldron before she annihilated them?

'No?'

'No,' he repeated. 'I don't accept your terms. What you're offering is not enough. But,' and he exhaled, knowing what he was about to say would likely define every second of the rest of his life, not to mention those of countless others, 'I'm willing to talk.'

She narrowed her eyes. He increased his grip on the Sword, prepared to bring it down on his side of the Cauldron, saw his three companions do the same. The moment passed and she began to laugh, clapping her hands admiringly.

'You do your kin proud, Danny,' she said. 'Talk, then. What else would you ask of me?'

The Ultimate Boon

'I can't get through!' Steve said, for the hundredth time. He gathered himself and charged once again at the nearest gap between the standing stones, screaming a war cry and swinging the flail in his right hand–

Ellie winced at the *dooooofff* noise that followed shortly thereafter as Steve was knocked onto his back. She knelt beside him and saw that he was breathing heavily, face red with exertion.

'We're not getting back in, Steve,' she said.

'I'm not giving up,' he replied, and got back to his feet. He paced along the circumference of the circle, pressing experimentally here and there, probing. The invisible barrier remained solid wherever he tried. With a cry of frustration he swung the flail against it, causing a brief emission of blue-tinted sparks to erupt as if two electrical fields had collided, but no other effect.

'Your efforts are admirable,' Wily told him, 'but fruitless. It is not the witch keeping us from returning.'

'What's he talkin' about?'

'Danny,' Ellie said. She was oddly, insanely, calm. 'Danny's the one keeping us out. Probably doesn't even realise it, like, but he is.'

'Danny's keeping us out?' Steve scoffed. 'Why the fuck would he do that?'

'He's protecting us, Steve.'

'Safe!' Steve spluttered. 'Did'ja see that thing in there? How safe's he?'

She put her hand on his shoulder. He almost recoiled, but caught himself just in time. 'Steve, he knows,' she said.

'I *know* he knows,' Steve mumbled miserably.

'He took it well, I thought.'

'Yeah, well, as we said – alternate universe and all that shit. Plus he'd been living with Maggie as you said, and he'd probably been regularly throwin' the lad into–' and he caught Ellie's *very* meaningful look at this point and did just about the neatest conversational three-point-turn in the history of oral discourse. 'Anyway, yeah. I have to help him. He could be gettin' hurt in there, Ellie.'

'He isn't.'

'How d'you know?'

'I just do. He can handle it, Steve. He wanted to keep us–'

With a roar that shook the street, a fleet of jeeps and trucks appeared on the scene. Personnel transports, the size of which they'd never seen, full of army grunts – more and more of them disembarking with each passing second. Two military helicopters crested into view over the top of the nearby courthouse.

Steve, Ellie and the two wolves found themselves encircled by a ring of steel, ranks of soldiers dropping to a crouching position, guns trained on their positions. The wolves placed themselves between the guns and the humans, their bodies crouched, ears flattened, teeth bared.

'DO NOT MOVE,' a voice boomed from above. 'ANY ATTEMPT TO ESCAPE OR TO ATTACK AND WE WILL OPEN FIRE.'

'—safe,' Ellie finished.

FORMER SITE OF LECARROW, COUNTY ROSCOMMON, NOW

'I can see it! I can see it!'

Tom Beckett craned his neck to look in the direction the bus driver was pointing. They had formed a little community here, when all of them felt as though they had driven for long enough to put that nightmarish vertical wall of suspended sea far behind them. Horns had been blared and hand signals exchanged and the little convoy had come to a halt.

The fact that the phones still worked seemed the one thing that was keeping them all from completely falling apart. Families were in contact, some for so long that batteries were running low and a sort of bonding event had grown up around the scavenging and sharing of mobile phone car chargers.

They'd all crowded round on the bus and watched the TV, which not only still worked but was still picking up channel signatures effortlessly. Rolling news channels had finally found a topic worthy of rolling news, although the fantastical nature of events still didn't seem to vary their content from a succession of people saying, 'Er, from what we can tell' in five hundred and

236

forty seven different ways.

Some of the convoy had even appeared *on* the news using FaceTime, or whatever videocalling equivalent their smartphones possessed, to give live updates to the world. Tom had already overheard one businessman brokering a book deal.

A couple of hours ago they'd received the order, not only from the government officials and UN representatives various people had managed to contact, but also loud and clear from the rolling news coverage, that they were to head to Lecarrow in County Roscommon, or where it had once stood at any rate. The vast majority of their vehicles possessed satnavs so they would be able to navigate there without much of an issue – could even travel as the crow flies since the roads and byways the satnavs were recommending now no longer existed.

Lecarrow had been chosen because it was deemed to be the geographical centre of Ireland, the furthest point away from the sea. If the barrier should break and the waters rush in, it would buy them a little extra time.

Besides, they were not the only ones. Other ships had tried to dock. Other planes had tried to land. The news channels had claimed eight hundred people were now heading toward Lecarrow from all directions.

Those eight hundred, Tom included, were now the most famous people on planet Earth. The complete disappearance of Ireland's landmass was the biggest news story in human history and, with the interconnectedness of the planet, there was barely a person alive on Earth who didn't know about it.

Tom wondered about that. He liked to think of himself as a

man of reason – he hadn't gone to Mass since he was eleven years old and he didn't hold much truck with the paranormal. He regularly watched Brian Cox documentaries and, though they mainly featured the professor walking moodily up a mountainside, he had even understood some of the science. Yet as much as he racked his brains, there just didn't seem to be a rational explanation for something that could not only neatly excise a landmass from the planet *but leave the seas suspended around it.*

The scientists on the news were giving it a go, of course; talking about exotic matter and strangelets and quantum tunnelling, but the religious nuts almost seemed more plausible than they did. The consensus seemed to be that Ireland had either been Raptured to some form of Heaven for the unwavering faith of its flock, or cast into one Hell or another for the unwavering blasphemy of its sinners.

I know which one my money's on, Tom thought.

They'd arrived not twenty minutes before at Lecarrow, after only one stop so the bus could take on an extra passenger whose van had run out of fuel. There had been some people there already, more of the lost and stranded, waving to them as they arrived in a circle of headlights on the endless plain.

The bus driver was right. Above their heads, they could see a blinking light move across the sky. A faint roar of engines carried across the air. Everyone began jumping and embracing one another. Their rescue had indeed arrived and, thanks to the miracle of technology the whole world would watch every impossible minute of it.

For the first time in a long time, humankind would begin to really *believe* that there were bigger things out there than themselves.

LITOCHORO, GREECE, NOW

The mountain began to awaken.

BELFAST / OTHERWORLD, NOW

'You need to release whatever hold you have on the human world,' Danny told Carman.

She looked at him, through him. Carman's eyes didn't stop for mere physical obstacles. She could have made Superman's eyes water.

'Just so I understand you, Danny, you're asking me to release my hold?' she asked.

Danny thought about it. He had to be careful not to give her something she could use during these negotiations, a slip of the tongue she could exploit and pervert. Carman had brought nothing but disaster to his world and he failed to see what unfortunate consequence could arise from her control being taken away.

'Yes,' he said, feeling like he was growing into this leadership thing after all. 'Let it go. Now.'

Carman bowed her head. 'Consider it granted,' she said.

*

Tom's phone blared. Everyone with a working mobile who wasn't currently engaged in a call negotiating image rights or talking to hysterical relatives suddenly found their phones ringing, all at once.

The rescue plane was coming in, a huge barnswallower of a military beast, landing about a mile away. The noise was unreal – the ground shook as the giant wheels of the craft touched down. He saw little point in answering a call he wasn't going to be able to hear, so he let the phone ring even as he watched others in little refugee group try in vain to scream loud enough to be heard, or cup their hands around their ears to block out the din.

The bus doors opened. One of the passengers, a girl in her early twenties, sprinted out. Arms and legs pumping, she ran until she stood in front of the motley group of onlookers who'd gathered to witness the plane's landing.

She screamed and hollered and gesticulated but thanks to the noise from the plane's engines, still roaring from its descent, he could hear nothing. Tom's phone vibrated in his hand. It was a text from his sister.

Go, was all it said.

'… out! Go! We have to go, right now! Now!' the girl's voice finally could be heard as the plane's engines wound down a little more, and Tom, and the rest, heard it.

Not all of the noise was coming from the plane. Not all of the rumbling underfoot was coming from it either. The winds were picking up around them, whipping cruelly. The taste of the sea was upon them, the tang of salt.

For a heartbeat the world seemed to pause, everyone trapped in a paralysis of horror as the realisation of what was thundering toward them from all sides sank in. And then–

There was only running, and the throttling of engines. Tom processed the next few minutes in flashes. He seemed already to be drowning, not in water but in terror. When his mind was able to come up for air, he saw time moving incrementally around him. He got into his car. The shaking underfoot was growing stronger. The plane's engines, not getting the time to idle down, were already powering up again, setting the world afire with noise. The cars beside him were roaring past – it was less than a mile to the transport but no one wanted to waste a second.

He could see men in military uniforms, shouting, as he exited his car, knowing that this was the final time he would see it. Had he been able to think, he would have realised that the shouting men were doing so because some of his fellow refugees, in unthinking hysteria, had driven their own vehicles in front of the transport before getting out, blocking the plane's takeoff route.

The Ulsterbus was waved right on, the transport's ramp lowered so it could drive straight up. It went past Tom with inches to spare, knocking him over with a rush of air at its passing. Hands were upon him, men pulling him up, shouting instructions. He was shepherded to seating, told something about buckling in, and straps were shoved at him. There seemed to be some sort of high-volume debate about whether the bus passengers should come out or stay inside. With numb fingers he tried to fasten the buckles.

A shot rang out.

There was a second or two of relative quiet after the shot, albeit with the plane's usual roar continuing to *thudthudthud-thrumm*, but Tom was already becoming accustomed to that and was now picking out other sounds. An elderly couple were deposited beside him, with what looked like a family of four, filling his row of seats. There was a little girl of about seven who was screaming in panic, constantly screaming and thrashing, preventing her mother from buckling her inside. The father slapped the girl across the face.

Another shot rang out at the same time. Tom could see the father's face contorted in wretched guilt. For a moment it had sounded as though his slap had been performed with incredible force. The girl was strapped in and the father met Tom's eyes for a split-second.

They began to move. Tom had never felt such relief, capped a nanosecond later by frustration. They were moving too slowly, far too slowly. He and the rest of the passengers screamed and hollered and begged and cursed, but the damn plane was still ambling along as though it hadn't a care in the world.

The plane's entry ramp began to close. Craning his head around over the seating, Tom could see there were people still out there, still driving. They weren't waiting any longer. That could only mean–

A great force shoved them all backward into their chairs. Those passengers with lung capacity left for fresh screams let loose. He feared the worst, expected to see water crashing in through the entry, but when none came he realised that the plane had hit the gas in a hurry.

Above the rumble of the plane's engines, a deeper roar was now impossible to ignore.

Outside, blessedly out of Tom's capacity to see but in full terrified view of the plane's pilots, the Atlantic Ocean was approaching from the west and curving around to the south, the Irish and North Seas from the east and north. Lecarrow had been chosen wisely, but its centrality also meant that, when the water eventually reached it, it would do so from every direction at once.

Three unstoppable mega-tsunami were about to obliterate the final tiny remnant of the Irish bedrock.

From observation aircraft, from satellite footage, the world watched as the rescue plane desperately increased its speed, until finally the nose of the great beast pointed upward, and the plane climbed as fast as its pilot dared into the dawn skies where Ireland had once stood.

Seconds later, the waters finally met; first two, then three incredible forces acting upon one another. A mighty torrent of water shot vertically into the air, thousands of tons of sea arcing many hundreds of feet upwards and missing the rising plane by a whisker, as though a final attempt to prevent their escape.

The seas roiled and swirled, seethed and spun into a furious maelstrom, a moving liquid scar, the mobile tombstone of all that was left of Ireland.

*

Four generations of Morrigan men stood together. Emotions were running high. The air was thick with unspoken pride and tacit sadness. There was only one way to deal with this smorgasbord of sentiment.

'So they've still not won the title?' James Morrigan said incredulously.

Danny shook his head. 'Nah. Had a decent Cup run a few years back, like.'

'Bunch o' overpaid prima donnas, the lot of them,' Tony said.

Luke was following this conversation as best he could. 'Sport?' he offered. This was met with grunts of approval from his father, grandfather and great-grandfather, as though he had contributed something of grave import.

'You should come back,' Tony said, into the long and awkward pause that followed. He was addressing his father. 'We'd head to a game. Take the young fellas.'

'I can't,' James said quietly.

'We've got her by the balls,' Tony protested, gesturing to the centre of the stone circle and to Carman, currently embroiled in a complicated ritual to bring something forth from the Cauldron's depths. 'Look what she's doin' for Ellie! Danny could tell her to bring you back properly too!'

'Son,' James said, setting his hand on Tony's shoulder, 'you're missing the point. I don't want to go back, even if I could. What am I goin' back to? I've been dead for donkeys years. Who would I live with? What would I do with my time?'

'I miss you, Da,' Tony said wretchedly, 'Danny never even

got the chance to know ye. Wee ...' and he had the good grace to hesitate here as 'Wee' Luke, currently towering over them all, reacted to his name with a cheery wave, 'Luke as well.'

James glanced at each in turn. 'I think me and the lads here understand each other pretty well. Son, I'm at peace. Your mummy's at peace. I'd tell you more but I'm pretty sure it's against somebody's rules, somewhere. Someday you'll know.'

'It's not fair,' Tony said, sounding almost childlike himself.

'I know. Ach, c'mere, my big son. C'mere to me.'

Father and son embraced, one last time. Tony had no words, and if he had, he could not have formed them. When they parted, James gathered Danny and Luke into a hug so manly that if it had lasted a second longer they would have spontaneously grown beards. He told them how proud he was of them both.

Then, he was simply gone.

'Da?' Danny said. 'Are you okay?'

'Should we talk about sport to mask our emotions?' Luke whispered urgently. Danny waved away the comment.

'I'm fine,' Tony said, his voice hoarse. He cleared his throat. ' Are we getting the fuck out of this circle, or what? Away from *her*?'

'Yeah. Yeah, Dad. Grotbags over there is gonna do what we asked her for Ellie and then we're gone.'

'Good,' his father nodded. 'I'm tired, son. I think when we get out of here I'm going to go home. Make sure your ma's okay, know what I mean?'

But I need you, Danny wanted to say. *You're the expert. You're the calm one. I have no idea what I'm going to do next.* He said none of those things. During the battle with Carman they had looked to him to lead, and he had. He was exhausted and terrified and he knew if he begged his da to reconsider and come with him Tony would do so, because that was what parents did.

'Away on home then,' Danny said. 'Get the pipe and slippers out, ya oul ballix. Make sure my ma does that ironing I sent her over an all.'

Tony smiled.

'Sport,' Luke said, and they couldn't have agreed more.

*

Stepping forward into the spotlights of the encircling armed forces, staring down the barrels of guns, it was Steve spoke for them all.

'Where the fuck have you cunts been?' he demanded.

Ellie couldn't help but grin.

'Hiding down the bottom of my garden when I was a kid and scarin' the shit out of me as I walked past, oh aye!' Steve carried on, seemingly completely oblivious to the array of lethal weaponry now trained unerringly on his head. 'Fuckin' faerie army of bastards invades the fuckin' place and starts eatin' people left right and centre and none of you dickheads can be found! Did you see what happened in the city centre, aye? When we kicked the cunts out of the streets? That was *us* done that! No help from any of yous fuckin' twats!'

'I REPEAT,' the voice over the loudspeaker began again.

'Ach don't give me that "I REPEAT", ordering people about, fuckin' army *shite!*' Steve said. 'You've lost the right to be all high and mighty! Now answer my fuckin' question; where *were* yis?'

Larka padded forward, only a step or two. Guns swung in her direction. She was now level with Ellie. 'You need only say the word,' she said, so softly Ellie knew only she would hear it.

'Well?' Steve was saying.

'Stand down,' a non-loudspeaker voice said from amongst the newcomers. A man emerged from the ranks; an officer, if Ellie was any judge (and Christ knew she was no expert). He glanced around at his troops with annoyance. 'Put the fucking guns down now!' he barked, and the barrels drooped. He walked to Steve and proffered a hand so quickly that Steve shook it almost by default.

'Brigadier Derek Hughes. I'm …,' he looked back at the array of force behind him and Ellie saw embarrassment on his face, 'well, I'm in charge of what you see here, and pretty much of everything else we've got here, at least in the North.'

'Steven Anderson,' said Steve, with the air of a dog who's chased a car and now, having caught it, has fuck-all clue what to do with it. 'I'm, um …' and he trailed off, waving behind him helplessly to take in Ellie, Wily and Larka.

Wily stepped up. 'He is a friend of the Morrigan and of the Named, and can readily speak for both.'

The brigadier's ruddy complexion went white. Some of the guns behind him snapped up again as Wily's words were heard. Steve saw the brigadier go for his own sidearm and then catch himself with a visible effort. Composed, he turned and motioned for his men to lower their guns, which they did. Eventually.

'I'll keep this brief,' the brigadier said, his voice low and his gaze fixing itself on Steve as though he were an anchor to some form of reality. 'You were quite right to ask about our whereabouts. In our defence, however, our bases seemed to be targeted as a matter of priority, and defending them proved somewhat of a challenge.'

A haunted look on the man's face hinted that he was, in the fine British military tradition, understating things magnificently here. 'A challenge?' Steve pressed.

'He is referring to their guns. They do not function here. In fact, they have not functioned since the worlds began to Merge,' Wily said.

The brigadier flinched as if physically struck.

'The guns don't work?' Steve said, disbelieving. 'Then what the fuck's all this for?' he indicated the show of force, the array of weaponry that had been pointed at them.

'Intel on the ground said this was their home office, so to speak,' the Brigadier replied. 'When the biggest building in the country falls over and doesn't make a sound, and then this,' he indicated the mega-Stonehenge of the monoliths forming the stone circle, 'springs up in its place, it doesn't take Sherlock Holmes to figure out that's where we need to be. We didn't know,' and he looked to Wily, 'if they knew about the guns or not. A grand entrance seemed a risk worth taking.'

'You were bluffing,' Ellie said.

'Is the short way of saying it, yes,' the man sighed. He looked again to Wily. 'I've had help from the others like you,' he told the wolf. 'At the Lisburn barracks. We were about to be overrun. I ... I've never seen anything quite like it. Not sure I really believed what I was seeing until you, um,' and he flushed as he tried to say the words, 'spoke up. As it were. Er. Yes. You have my thanks.'

'I am told your men fought well with what they had to hand,' Wily replied, inclining his head, one soldier to another.

A man broke ranks to approach the brigadier. 'I've got Stormont back on, Brigadier,' and he paused whilst his superior officer let loose with a stream of invective so chock-full of expletives that even Steve and Ellie, Belfast born and bred, were taken aback. 'They're wanting an update, and they're demanding we return.'

'What am I supposed to tell them?' asked the old army man, suddenly powerless. 'When this went down, they were locked in some late-evening session in the Assembly. I've got seventy-two of the country's most senior politicians trapped in a room surrounded by what's left of the rest of my men. They're convinced this is some sort of major terrorist attack. And since some of them believe some of the others *are* terrorists ... well,' he sighed deeply and pressed his hands to his temple. 'It's not an easy situation.'

'How about tellin' them to away and fuck themselves?' Steve spat. 'There's people have had their entire families ripped apart in front of them tonight. This isn't about politics. We're being invaded.'

The brigadier looked at him almost pityingly. 'Take it from a soldier, son. Being invaded is just about as political as you can get.'

Wily and Larka looked up suddenly, their ears pricked. Steve could have sworn he saw Ellie react in a similar way only a quarter-second or so behind the wolves.

'Step back,' Ellie told him.

'Wh–'

'The circle. Something's coming out,' Larka said urgently. She nudged Steve with her head, softly but insistently. If he'd been thinking straight he might have been touched by the gesture of concern.

Ellie grabbed his shoulder. 'Do you really want to be standing there if Carman is the first thing to roll out?' she hissed and, not giving him time to answer, promptly dragged him backwards. From this distance, they could see the slight shimmer in the air from the barrier separating the world inside the stones from the Merged world outside them.

Yet for all her trepidation, Ellie couldn't shake the feeling of hope surging inside her. When they'd been dragged outside the circle by the wolves, a move that had almost certainly saved their lives, she'd reacted just as Steve had at first – banging on the barrier, trying desperately to get back in, until her energies had been expended and she'd been forced to take a breath.

And when she had, she'd heard it. Faint, far too faint to make out discernible words, but there was something in her mind, something that tasted like Danny, if thoughts could be said to have a taste. Of course, Danny's synaesthesia had always made strange connections like that, hadn't it? She'd never understood it but had, at times, been secretly quite envious, and not just when he was able to rattle off thirty-digit numbers for fun.

Though she couldn't make out the words, she could sense the tone. It was calm. Hopeful. Those same emotions had permeated through to Ellie herself.

So it was that when the barrier came down, when the figures within walked free, Ellie was not surprised to find that her first emotion was delight, not horror. There was Danny and there, beside him, was Luke. Both of them still alive, *thank God, thank God, thank God.*

The third figure to emerge, looking a little unsteady on his feet, was Tony Morrigan. As she watched, frozen to the spot with astonishment, Danny's formerly very dead dad caught sight of her and smiled fondly. He exchanged words and hugs with Danny and Luke, and then moved off purposefully toward the soldiers encircling them. She started to track him, to call out, and then the final figure emerged from the circle.

'Ellie!'

'*Daddy!*' she shrieked.

Father and daughter collided, embracing each other, tears already falling. Sobs of happy disbelief wracked her. She trembled from head to toe, hardly daring to let go.

'You died,' she kept saying. 'You died. You were dead. You *died*. I saw you. They killed you and you died. You're *dead* ... and now you're alive, you're alive, you're alive, you're ALIVE!' and she half-staggered with the enormity of it, only for Danny and Luke to appear as if by magic at her sides, propping up an arm each as she gabbled. 'So this, all of this, it *is* a dream. It's a dream …' now anxiety shot through her and she squeezed her father's hand hard enough to make him yelp in pain, as if she were daring him not to be real. 'Or I'm dead now. Am I? Am I dead? Are we all dead?'

'Relax,' Danny soothed her. 'None of us are dead …' and he paused. 'Not here.' He gathered himself, took a deep breath, and for the first time noticed the assembled ranks of army forces surrounding the stone circle. He looked to Ellie and a corner of his mouth tugged upward. 'I can't leave you alone for a minute, can I?' he said.

Ellie gave him a *who, me?* look. 'What happened to your sword?' she said, noticing for the first time that he was no longer wielding the weapon he'd used to such dazzling effect at the top of Lircom Tower.

A shadow fell across his face. 'All part of the deal,' he said, and eyed Ellie's father significantly. 'She needs it for what comes next.'

'She needs it? Who needs it?' Ellie asked.

'Carman,' Danny admitted, and stepped backward involuntarily. It turned out to be a fairly wise move.

'*Carman?* What the fuck d'you mean, Carman? She's not dead? You were supposed to … What the fuck d'you mean, she needs the sword? She kidnapped my son and turned him into He-Man for fuck's sake! And you! You let her keep the fucking magic fucking sword that caused all this shit in the fucking first place?'

'Ellie,' Danny said, placing his hands on her shoulders and slowly bringing his forehead to rest against hers. 'Ellie, please, I had to make a deal. Your da coming back is part of it, so is mine.'

'She's gonna do it all again,' she said, feeling her chest tighten and the panic begin to rise. She couldn't go through all of this a second time.

'No,' Danny shook his head. 'She's promised to send it back up.'

'Up? Up where?'

'Long story. I'll explain, promise.'

'Might wanna start with that. The army ones are in touch with Stormont,' she said.

Danny made a face. Suddenly, monstrous faeries, collapsing buildings and fights to the death with glowing swords didn't seem so bad. He felt like he'd been summoned to the headmaster's office.

'Brigadier seems decent enough,' Ellie said. 'Go talk to him.'

There it was again, the absurdity of being looked to as some sort of figurehead or spokesperson during all this madness. Squeezing Ellie's arm, and giving her a too-brief kiss that hopefully conveyed an urgent sense of *more to follow*, Danny walked over to meet the brigadier. Ellie turned towards her son, standing there beside her, all grown up.

'So,' Luke said. He cleared his throat. 'I–'

He got no further, caught up in his mother's arms. Initial awkwardness melted to acceptance, and the young man who Danny had personally witnessed performing the sort of feats that would have caused Hercules to go green with envy hugged his fully foot-and-a-half-shorter mother.

When she pulled away, she had to blink away tears. 'I'm sorry,' she said. 'I didn't mean to. It's just that,' and she craned her neck back a little more, 'you're my baby boy.'

'*Muuuuuummmmmmmm*,' Luke squirmed, looking significantly at Wily and Larka, who were watching all of this with equal parts interest and amusement, it seemed.

'Strange,' was all Larka said.

'What?' Wily asked her.

'The gifts the Morrigan gave us – the emotions, the perspective, the soul. It's all so new to me.'

'To all of us,' Wily said.

'Seeing this woman, how she acts with her child, is causing me to feel something in response.'

'Maybe you're broody,' Ellie suggested offhand.

'Broody?'

'I believe she means you may want children of your own,' Wily explained.

'Ah,' Larka considered this.

'Of course,' Wily went on, 'that cannot be what you are actually–'

'No, she is correct,' Larka said calmly.

'*What?*' Wily said. 'But we used to consume our young!'

Larka considered this, too. 'That was then,' she said. 'This is now.'

Ellie watched all of this, aglow, forgetting for a moment the army and the faeries and all of that nonsense, and basking in the wonder of having her son back (albeit slightly taller) and her father back (much less dead). She watched Danny, deep in conversation with the brigadier, pointing this way and that. He seemed barely recognisable from the perpetually-unsure of himself young man who had muddled his way through premature parenthood, and yet – he sensed her eyes on him, and smiled over at her before returning to conversation – in so many ways he was still the same, still her Danny.

My Danny. She took a second to let that sink in. Had she ever really considered him hers before? She had fancied him, she had desired him (obviously), and she had been willing to make a go of a life together with him. It was probably, if she was honest, for Luke's sake more than hers. Living with him, going through the sleepless nights and the money troubles, she felt like a headless swan most of the time – frantic activity going on under the surface, fuck-all left above it.

Having been shown the glimpse of a life without Danny, however fleeting, had clarified things. It was tough to know whether you were happy when you had nothing to contextualise that happiness against, bar her parents' relationship, and that would have been like using the Manson compound as a template for opening a Bed & Breakfast. It wasn't as if she could drop into other people's houses and see them in their daily grinds. Soap operas pretended to show that, but they didn't. They couldn't.

What they showed was life distilled and distorted into a thirty-second clip that you were then supposed to take on faith represented weeks, months, years. *Any idiot can sit through thirty seconds*, Ellie thought. *Try staying awake for fourteen hours with a sick screaming baby, feeling despair open up beneath you like a living thing, and then trying to figure out if you're 'happy', whatever that even means.*

More than anything, she just wanted to be home. To close her front door and be in her own house with Danny and Luke, and just sit and do stupid things. Make a coffee. Watch TV. Close the curtains and put the heat on for a bath. Do all those silly little things that felt like fuck-all at the time, but were actually the key Lego bricks in the playset of life.

There was a commotion from behind her.

'Holy shit!' someone exclaimed. It sounded like Steve. Her heart sank. What now?

She turned, reaching for Luke, absurdly wanting to draw him close and protect him, despite the fact he was some sort of mystical ninja Jedi or something. She didn't care. Anything or anyone went near her six-foot and change baby boy and she'd fuckin' cream 'em.

It wasn't what she anticipated, or feared. In fact, it was pretty much the last thing she'd expected to see. 'Oh!' Ellie squeaked.

'Mum?' Luke asked.

'Um. Well. One of the wolves, has an itch. And the other wolf. Um, the other one. Yes. The other one's trying to scratch it.'

Wily and Larka were engaged in a visceral and completely unashamed display of vigorous wolf-sex.

Her hand reached out and, with no small amount of difficulty, she managed to physically turn Luke's body around so he was facing the other way. They were joined a second later by Steve, also with his back to the X-rated lupine action. Within moments an awkward line of people had formed, shuffling their feet and trying *very* hard to pretend that they couldn't hear the howling going on behind them. Even the soldiers ringing their position seemed to have found something immensely fascinating going on around their own navels.

'It looks like …' Luke said.

'Wily's found Larka's itch. Yes,' Ellie cut him off. 'Yes, and Larka is ever so pleased and grateful,' she risked a quick glance behind her. Her eyes boggled. Her head whipped around again. She cleared her throat. 'My mistake. It hasn't gone just yet,' she said.

'I thought they were having sex,' Luke said, puzzled.

Steve had abandoned all pretence of diplomacy. 'Somebody get a fucking bucket of cold water,' he called. He paused. 'Better make it a big one.'

IRELAND / OTHERWORLD, NOW

It was time for the Sword of Nuada to perform its greatest feat.

Across Ireland, at the moment the shimmering veil separating the world inside the standing stones had come down, those who had lost their lives in the chaos that had ensued hours before – through accidents created by the panic, or at the claws or teeth of Carman's children – all of them found themselves reconstituted, whole and healthy.

They rejoiced. They made their way back to their homes, to their loved ones, and there were hundreds, thousands of joyous – if slightly stunned – reunions, filled with tears and with dazed happiness. Those resurrected gave thanks, thinking their return a miracle.

Many of those who returned, though – on realising that

Ireland was still cut off from the rest of the world, marooned in its own little cosmos – had seen enough death and craziness this night to go a little wild themselves. Revellers, mostly the younger of the recently revived, littered the streets, convinced they were experiencing some sort of mass afterlife. And hey, it was still dark outside and it should have been dawn hours ago, but there was plenty of drink and plenty of the opposite sex, and a lot of people seemed in a good mood, so all in all it could have been worse.

Plus, the giant talking wolves that were padding along the highways and byways quite unconcernedly kind of added to the unworldly feel. Some, of course, were mistaken for the monsters that had rampaged earlier and were made the target of attacks. However, it's difficult to disagree with a talking wolf when it's got you pinned to the ground and it's asking you in a *very* nice voice to please stop throwing rocks at it.

PARLIAMENT BUILDINGS, STORMONT, BELFAST / OTHERWORLD, NOW

Steve had been to Stormont only once before, as a schoolboy on a field trip. He remembered the long driveway leading to that huge white building. In the crimson light of the moon, seemingly hanging only a stone's throw above them in the Belfast skies, Stormont seemed almost pinkish in its hue.

Thankfully, the presence of Brigadier Hughes at the head of their little convoy of army vehicles and massively oversized wolves smoothed their passage through the military ring that surrounded the grounds. Despite the fact that, as soon as things had gone to hell, every gun had refused to fire, all of the soldiers and police officers Steve saw were still packing, still carrying. For comfort, he supposed, if for nothing else.

As they climbed the hill up to the big house, he took a moment from his vantage point on Larka's shoulders to glance back over the Belfast skyline. Smoke rose and fires raged from multiple sources. The huge monoliths where Lircom Tower had once stood were as much of a landmark as the skyscraper had been, and more – they dominated Belfast effortlessly, not only with their size but with their sheer incongruity.

Wily, Larka and two other wolves had made the journey with them. On Danny's instructions, Wily told the rest of the Named to spread themselves through the city, protecting its inhabitants, ensuring that the faeries reabsorbed into Carman's bloated mass during the showdown did not reappear.

After a minimum of raised eyebrows and voices, the newcomers and their wolves were allowed into the building itself and then directed to the Assembly chamber. Steve was prepared to meet those he'd seen regularly on the news, but he was taken aback by the smell. The place reeked of sweat and fear.

Danny stepped forward. To Steve's mild surprise, but to Danny's credit, he kept his hand firmly attached to Ellie's, pulling her beside him so they could face the political leaders together. To complete the family line up was Luke – right there alongside his mother and father. Ellie had hold of his hand whenever she could and Steve was ready to wager that nothing short of a chainsaw or a crowbar could have separated the mother and son given what they'd been through.

'There's been no contact with the outside world,' the brigadier admitted. 'Christ knows we've tried. From the moment we were taken here we've been squawking with every piece of communications equipment we have. Nothing.'

'And yet so long as you're dialling somewhere in Ireland, the phones work perfectly,' one of the assembled politicians said. He sounded like a man defeated.

'Thanks to Lircom. The Network they used is built on ley lines – like magical isobars on a weather map – and it amplified them massively. Don't ask me how,' Danny added quickly, anticipating the question, 'but it did.'

'Are you saying we should stop using phones?'

'I don't think it's necessary,' Danny said and looked at Ellie. She squeezed his hand; this was it. 'I've spoken to their leader, Carman. She's ...' and he floundered, trying to think of a way to describe her that didn't include a string of his more usual forms of speech. He needed to sound as professional as he could to these people.

'She's a witch-demigoddess from the Greek pantheon,' Luke spoke up.

Danny cleared his throat. His son was making a real career out of helpful interjections. 'Yes. There was a confrontation. I made it clear that I could weaken her significantly, and had her agree to, well, a cease-fire I suppose you could call it. Certain conditions will have to be met ... on both sides.'

There was a long stretch of silence at this, then, all at once, everybody started to talk, to demand, to shout over one another.

Danny simply stood there, his face impassive. He wasn't going to try and shout over this riotous cacophony. Thankfully, he didn't have to.

'Silence!' Wily thundered.

It beat the hell out of banging a gavel, that was for sure.

Danny laid his hand on the wolf's head as a gesture of thanks. 'I get it,' he said. 'Who am I to come in here and *blah blah blah*. I get it. That's why I'm not dictating anything. You'll see what I mean if you let me finish.'

More silence. Satisfied with this small victory, Danny pressed on. 'I had the chance to stop all this craziness, and I took it. The way these fuckers work, if you have them by the balls, you can get them to swear an oath and they're bound to carry it out. So here it is. The good news – anyone who died tonight is being brought back.'

'Back? What do you mean, back? From the *dead?*' a woman called from among the crowd.

Danny nodded. 'I know how it sounds, but after what we've all seen–'

'This is satanism. This is the Devil's work, pure and simple,' the woman declared, elbowing her way to the front of the throng. She stared at Danny, vibrating with rage and indignation. 'I refuse to allow anyone to be denied access to the Lord's country, or for them to be brought back as a vessel for evil. What happened tonight is judgement from the Lord' – and she had to raise her voice now, to be heard over a growing rumbling of discontent from her peers (and, Steve noted, a few rumblings of approval) – 'a final judgement on the wickedness and the depravity of our society.'

Larka spoke up then, in a deceptively soft whisper that nonetheless commanded attention. 'Children killed before their mothers are now coming back to life. You would have this stop?'

'Children killed by creatures like you!' the woman screamed. 'Demon spawn!'

On and on it raged. Steve took a seat and let the accusations fly across the room like knives. Once he saw Wily look at Danny questioningly and Danny shake his head.

'Ireland isn't going to be separated from the rest of the world any more,' Danny said at last, trying to quell the rabble. 'Carman has agreed to send Ireland back up to our world, away from hers. And some of us with it.'

Some of us. Steve looked at his friend and he knew instantly what that meant.

'Anybody who's been brought back, will have to stay here. It's something to do with magic. Down here … this place, it runs on it. Up there, if you die, you stay dead. Down here, it's possible to be brought back, but it means you can't leave. Carman's promised never to come back to the surface world – *our* world – and that her people won't bother those left behind in *her* world. She'll create,' he shrugged, 'a *copy* of Ireland for them to live in.'

'This is your victory?' the accusation came back instantly. Danny didn't know who spoke; it scarcely mattered. 'You'll have children abandoned and alone–'

'No,' Danny said. 'The people brought back have to be left behind, that's true. But others will have a choice. They can stay, if they wish, with the ones left behind.'

'And how will this Carman know what people have chosen?'

I will know.

Everyone in the room, everyone in the city, everyone all over Ireland, heard her as the words appeared fully-formed in their minds. Over six million people – from those who were cowering in fear in their homes, to those trying desperately to escape; from the people celebrating their resurrections, to those who, by some miracle, had slept through everything – all stopped what they were doing to listen.

Attention, people of Ireland.

I will be brief. What you so arrogantly regarded as 'your' island has been moved somewhere ... different, somewhere much more interesting. By now I would imagine most of you are aware of this. Many of you will have met my children. Many of you will have died at their hands. All of you who have, have been returned to life. You have the Morrigan to thank for this. If it were up to me, you would have stayed dead ... at least for a while. Corpses do not make good sport.

At the Morrigan's insistence, I will shortly arrange for 'your' island to be returned to your awful, colourless human world.

However.

Those of you who have been returned from the dead ... you, I'm afraid, cannot return. Your deaths were not make-believe. They were quite real. To have you returned to life requires magic. Strong magic. Your human world cannot support this. You have turned your back on magic. If you were returned, you would be dead on arrival, and that, I'm afraid, would be a best-case scenario. So in an act of mercy, I will permit you to remain here. Alive.

I will retain this semblance of the land you knew. You can keep your homes, but your new world will be quite different to the one you remember.

There will be no sunlight here.

It does not agree with me, or with my children, and in time I will have more children. I know that, for reasons best known to yourselves, humanity is quite fond of sunlight, so this may be quite a jolt for you at first. But in time, who knows? You humans are adaptable creatures.

Here, now, we come to the crux of the matter.

Those of you who were NOT brought back from the dead … I have watched your world for many centuries. You are so in love with the illusion of choice your leaders provide you, that you play along with the theatre show they give you, even though you know that no matter what X you put in what box the same decisions will be made. I must admit it really is quite brilliant.

Well, here is a real, genuine choice for you to consider.

I can send you back.

Or, you can volunteer to stay.

For some of you – the lucky ones, you'll term yourselves – this will be an easy choice. Perhaps nobody you care about was resurrected. Go back to your world. Rejoice. Spend your time debating which celebrity ice-skates better than which other celebrity.

For most of you – a choice lies before you. Leave your loved ones behind and go home, or stay here with them in this brave new world. When the time comes, and you will know when that is, the choice you have made in your heart will define whether you stay or go, and I will respect that choice.

So please, feel free to lie to your loved ones. Feel free to tell them you will stay with them when you know you are about to abandon them. They will soon know the truth of your decision.

The vote will take place in one hour. Voting booths will be provided *inside of your little human souls, so I imagine electoral turnout will be quite high.*

When her words had faded, and the shouting and the recriminations had recommenced, Danny gathered Ellie and Luke and asked Wily to take them home. The brigadier smoothed their departure with a nod. Danny shook the man's hand and meant it.

They moved swiftly through the highways and byways of the city. Here and there, people moved through the streets, cars screeched by. Danny guessed families were assembling themselves before the hour was up. He held Ellie close. There was no conversation between the three of them – there seemed little worth saying.

Ellie sagged with relief when Wily deposited them outside the familiar shape of their little house. She was less pleased, however, when Danny finally spoke.

'What d'you mean, you're *going*?' she demanded. 'Going *where*, Danny?'

He told her.

'Go,' she reassured him. They kissed. He and Wily were gone an instant later.

BELFAST / OTHERWORLD, NOW

Larka had gone with him without a word of protest. They flew along the darkened roads of Belfast, the she-wolf's massive hind-legs eating up the streets like they were nothing. For the first few minutes, they travelled in silence, and then he could stand it no longer.

'Why did you save me, Larka?' Steve asked her.

The wolf didn't slow one iota as she replied. 'We had a debt to repay to the Morrigan.'

'I'm not a stupid fella,' Steve said, suddenly hot with anger.

It was a few seconds before the reply came. 'No,' Larka admitted. 'I apologise.'

'You came lookin' for me. You were sent to find me. To save me,' he said. It had been itching the back of his mind. He had been a crumpled heap by the side of a road. The odds of anyone finding him in time were laughable, and yet Larka had been there to save him.

'Steve … please, let me explain. There's so much about magic you don't understand,' Larka said, abruptly changing the direction of the conversation. 'Try to remember – I am not human, was not born from a mother's womb. I sprang fully-formed from a magic cauldron, willed into existence by an evil witch.'

That brought him up short. He'd been so wrapped up in his own pain he'd never considered the origins of these strange, noble creatures that had saved him, and thousands like him, over the past few hours. He didn't know what to say, but Larka wasn't about to wait him for speak anyway. 'None of us, none of my people, can survive in what you would call sunlight,' she said.

His lips moved as he worked this out. 'You're vampire wolves?'

A guttural rumble shook Larka's body and he realised she was laughing. 'No,' she said. 'Your blood is quite safe from my appetites, Steven Anderson.'

'Fuck-all wrong with my blood,' he sniffed regally, enjoying the feeling of paternal pride at hearing Larka make her first joke. 'So if you're not vampires, why can't you take sunlight?'

'Because magic is a negotiation. When Carman spawned us, it was to act as soldiers in her war against the Tuatha, who were themselves powerful magicians. She wanted a powerful caste of warriors. The Tuatha wanted to stop her. The two opposing forces struggled, and eventually a compromise was reached; a mighty race of wolves, but who had to keep to the shadows.'

'Okay,' Steve said, with as much of a *get to the point* edge to his voice as he dared.

'When Danny imparted his humanity to us, it was a … blueprint, if you like, with which we could create our own identities. We received his philosophies, his empathies. His priorities.'

Steve waited for more, but none was forthcoming. 'Wait,' he said, 'by priorities …'

'I was not born from a womb, but I now consider myself alive. You were not born from the same womb as he, but you are a brother to him,' Larka said quietly.

To the eternal horror of every scrap of machismo he still fancied himself to possess, Steve wept to hear the words spoken aloud.

'We fulfilled our debt to him by protecting the humans, but the best and swiftest of us were sent to protect those most precious to him. Unfortunately some – his father and Ellie – were hidden from us, shielded by Carman and her sons' influence. You, we could sense. We could locate. I was sent for you. And from that moment to this, it has been an honour to protect you, to know you, to come to call you friend as he does.'

'How did you know where to take me?' Steve said, eventually, when he trusted himself to speak again. Larka had brought him back to Belgravia Avenue. There, sitting shivering on the doorstep, was Maggie.

The wolf merely gazed at him with those incredible eyes as he dismounted. He nodded and, on an impulse, leaned in and hugged her, great armfuls of soft wolf-coat, warm against his touch. 'Thank you,' he said.

Larka padded away as Steve walked towards Maggie. She had witnessed the embrace. 'Should I be worried?' she said, forcing a smile.

He went to shrug off his coat to put around her shoulders, before thinking better of it. Holding up a *wait a sec* finger, he bounded into the den of iniquity to retrieve a thick purple throw from the living room settee. He settled it over them both and sat down beside her. She snuggled closer to him, put her head on his shoulder, and for a moment or two they just sat there, quiet in the light of the red moon.

Well. Here goes.

'I have to stay,' he said.

'I know.'

'I was hoping you would …' and he couldn't even bring himself to finish.

'You were right,' she said. Her head still hadn't moved from his shoulder. He'd missed that weight, he realised.

'Right about what?'

'The baby,' she said.

He said the words he never thought he would. 'No, I wasn't.

The wee glimpse of the other life told me that, Maggie. I woulda made a shit da. I wasn't ready. You could see that; I couldn't. You were trying to be grown-up about it and I–'

'Steve, listen to me for a second, please. Don't talk, just let me finish. Something went wrong,' she said. He realised she was crying and his throat closed over so nothing else would escape. 'Post-operative infection, they called it. Used to be really common but now,' and she laughed, shortly, bitterly, 'now it's really rare because they're done properly. Probably if I lived in America I coulda sued the balls outta the lot of them, but I didn't have the cheek, Steve. I didn't have the *cheek* to complain of being robbed of kids when I'd …' she drew a shuddering breath and moved closer to him, unable to continue.

Cry. For the love of fuck, cry. Steve's mind was screaming at him. Not a few minutes previously he had been blubbing like a child and now … now, he just sat there holding Maggie and the tears wouldn't come. What was he supposed to say? What was he supposed to feel?

She pulled away from him, shrugged off the purple throw and got to her feet, all in one smooth motion. 'I'm going back,' she said, tear-tracks gleaming in the ochre glow from the skies above, 'I'm sorry, Steve.'

He got up, pursued her as she walked away. 'Maggie, wait!' he said. 'I don't care about having kids. It doesn't matter!'

She kissed him, unexpectedly, passionately. He returned it. When the kiss broke he could see from her expression that she wasn't doing this to be cruel.

'Yes it does,' she said. 'You'll make a great da, and you know it.

You have the best heart of anyone I have ever met, and I love you for it. I won't let myself be with someone who's going to look at me and see the kids he'll never have. Neither of us deserves that, Steve.'

'So you're going to leave me, here? In this world?' he said.

'I can't stay.' She shook her head, wriggling free of his grasp. 'I can't, Steve. I can't do this.'

Before he could say anything else, she was gone.

BELGRAVIA AVENUE, BELFAST / OTHERWORLD, NOW

He was sitting on the front step, as Danny had known he would be. Larka was there too. Dismounting, Danny patted Wily's flank and the two wolves retreated to a discreet distance. Danny sat down beside his oldest friend, the light from the front porch throwing their shadows onto the street.

'You were gone by the time I looked for you,' Danny said.

'I asked Larka to go. I didn't want to stay there,' Steve replied. He looked over at Danny and smiled weakly. 'I don't have much time left.'

'But you weren't dead. Carman didn't have to bring you back,' Danny said. 'I don't understand–'

'Carman didn't. Larka did,' Steve said. 'Before we came to the circle, I was dying. She saved me. I knew there was something more to it, I just … I never guessed it would be this.'

'I had to be brought back too,' Danny said. 'I was ripped apart, Steve. Limb from limb. They threw me in that fuckin' Cauldron–'

Steve barked a mirthless laugh. 'Bit different for you, isn't it mucker?' he said. 'You're the Morrigan. You're special. The way your da tells it, no one brought you back; you brought yourself back. So I don't think all this *election* shite applies to you.'

Those words, *you're special*, could have been dripping with bitter sarcasm – Danny almost wished they had been – but there wasn't a trace of it to be found.

'Well if I've got powers, maybe I can use them,' Danny said, desperately. 'I can bring you with me. I can, I don't know, I can bring you up there myself. If it takes,' he inhaled, still forcing down the sense of embarrassment at even saying it, 'magic to make it work up there, maybe I can provide it. Fuck's sake, it's worth a try!'

Steve smiled faintly. 'Think you can provide enough for my ma and da too, lad? And my sister?'

Danny closed his eyes. 'They were …?'

'Brought back? Yep. Them faerie cunts really did a fuckin' number on the city. Nice of them to leave the phone lines workin' though,' and Steve held up his mobile. 'I finally caught up with my text messages. Just off the phone there with my da before you showed up, in fact. Most of my family was done in and brought back,' and he let out a long breath, 'Which, I mean, if it wasn't for you they'd have *stayed* dead. That cunt said as much when she put those fuckin' words in all of our heads. So, Jesus, I owe ya, lad. Practically everyone on this fuckin' island owes ya.'

At some point, Steve had started to cry. Danny sat there helplessly.

'I'm sorry,' Steve said. 'I'm sorry about Ellie, man. I'm sorry I–'

Danny cut him off with a hug. Years of friendship went into that hug – years of meaning more to each other than almost anyone else ever had, or likely ever would.

'Maggie's not staying,' Steve said, when the hug ended.

Danny said nothing.

'D'you remember the day you left here? To move in with Ellie?'

'Course.'

'I wanted what you had. I was so jealous of you. And there was you, mopin' about, face trippin' ye. I wanted to give ye such a good slap.'

'I'd have deserved it.'

'I wonder what I'd have been like. As a da,' Steve went on. He didn't seem to be talking to Danny so much now as to the world, trying to fill up the silence of the city.

Danny didn't tell him that the hug they'd shared had filled in the gaps, whether he'd wanted it to or not. He knew. He knew about Maggie's abortion, and everything else. He knew the depth of his best friend's pain. What he didn't know was what the hell he could do about it, and it was killing him. Tears stung his eyes.

'Same as me,' Danny said. 'Fuckin' clueless. Terrified. Fumbling about in the dark hoping you're getting it right.'

'You talking about *being* a da or how you *became* a da?'

'Sir,' laughed Danny. 'I am in awe.'

He studied his oldest friend. Something had happened to Steve over the course of this insane night; he had a new sureness about him. It suited him down to the ground.

'Anyway,' Steve said, making a conscious effort to move on. 'If the situation in Belfast is any guide, near half of Ireland is going nowhere, and that's not including the volunteers. So it's not like we're gonna be on our own down here, is it.'

A shadow fell across them.

'No,' Larka said firmly. 'You won't be alone.'

'I'm sorry,' Wily apologised. 'She insisted on coming over. Relentlessly.'

'What will it be like?' Danny asked the leader of the wolves, as Steve placed his hand gratefully on Larka's pelt and patted her and she, in turn, settled one of her paws down on his shoulder with deceptive grace. 'Down here, I mean. What will it be like for the ones left behind?'

There was only flint-hardness on Wily's face. 'Difficult,' was all he said.

NOWHERE

It's over, Mother. You lost.

Dian's words hung in the empty, shapeless infinity that persisted inside the Dagda's Cauldron. He had come here, been drawn here, as he often was when he was without body. He knew Carman's essence was here also, squatting in the void; he could feel the weight of her presence warping the non-space around him.

Now who's sulking?

He had done as she had asked; leapt into the body of his own son, brought about the death of Tony Morrigan, and in so doing, acted as the catalyst for Danny Morrigan's part in the Merging.

He had seen the look on the elder Morrigan's face as the thin blade of the letter opener had ended his life, the betrayal. It had been sweet, for a moment.

Now, Dermot was gone. His little boy, lost.

Why did I listen to you? he sent the bitter words into the nothingness.

It was hard for emptiness – by definition lacking in colour – to darken, but darken it did, as Carman's presence made itself known, surrounding him from every side. He did not try to withdraw. There was little point, and he lacked the energy. Oblivion – if she could provide it – would have been welcomed.

I have lost nothing. Danny surprised me, true. I respect him for that.

He got you to swear an oath, Dian reminded her. *You cannot break it. You'll stay down here forever. So you have some human subjects to toy with. You'll tire of them, just as you tired of your own children. You're a monster, Mother. You claim to want only Ireland, but the truth is, you wanted Greece and you weren't powerful enough to take it. You thought you could come to a lesser Pantheon and assume control, gain worshippers, and come back to Grecian shores as the Milesians came here – at the head of a conquering army. I knew it then and I know it now.*

You are courageous indeed, agoráki mou, *to speak to me in such a way.*

I have nothing left to lose, was his reply.

Something parted in the nothing. A tiny little spark in the centre of Carman's bloated mass. He recognised the shape of it immediately. *Dermot!*

She closed herself over the spark of Dermot's life-essence once more. *I brought everyone else back,* she said. *Did you really imagine I wouldn't do the same for family? Admittedly, he took a little more work. He was at – I believe the term is 'Ground Zero'. Thankfully, he has his father's heritage. Lack of a physical body will be no issue for him.*

Let him go! Dian screamed, and threw what he had against her. It was like trying to take on a mountain. Her coils wrapped tighter around Dermot's fragile essence, the ethereal equivalent of strangulation.

You were right, she said airily. *The oath is an issue. I need it removed. Danny must be motivated to seek my assistance.* Tighter and tighter she squeezed. The little spark flickered, a whisper of a flame in this endless black.

Make your old Mitéra proud. Play the villain one last time.

GRIFFIN STREET, BELFAST / OTHERWORLD, NOW

Should he even be here? He'd been asking himself that question at least once every few seconds in the time it had taken to cross Belfast and come here. How tempting it had been to simply wait it out, and then discover what the future held.

No. He owed her more than that.

Drawing a deep breath, Tony Morrigan opened his front door.

'Linda?' he called.

No reply. He tried to quell the anxiety rising in him as he called her name, over and over. He'd tried to phone her several times, of course, so had Danny, but neither of them had received a response.

He found her in the kitchen, lit by candlelight and by the glow of a cigarette she was holding in her mouth. Judging by the ashtray, she'd been sitting there for some time, and had been through a few packs. For a heartbeat he thought she had died and that her body had remained propped up in some grotesque pose, but no; as he watched, she raised the cigarette to her lips. He hadn't seen her smoke in years. She'd given up when they'd been trying, without success, to conceive – before he'd made the deal that had finally given them Danny.

'Love!' he said, throwing his arms around her. 'You had us all worried to death! Why haven't you answered your ph–'

Crack.

His cheek smarted from the slap and he stepped back in shock and disbelief. She'd dropped the cigarette, the light on her face now seemingly coming from the simmering fury in her eyes.

'Hurts, doesn't it?' she snapped. 'Losing contact? Goin' out yer head with worry?'

'You decided now was a good time to get even for me leaving you?' Tony said, not quite able to believe what he was hearing. 'Have you fuckin' seen what's going on out there?'

She sat down, trembling. 'Seen?' she echoed. 'I don't know what I've seen. I have memories … memories that don't make a bit of sense, not one bit. Grandsons that came and went, and one minute they're called Luke and one minute something else. I'm losing it. Then tonight – things coming out the fuckin' ground, the dead coming back to life, that *voice* in my head–'

The phone rang and Linda had risen to pick it up before Tony could ask her to ignore it. They had so little time left.

'Hello?' she said, before shaking her head, and putting the phone back down.

'Listen to me,' Tony told his wife. '*Listen* to me, Linda. You're not going crazy, do you hear me? I know the last few days have been crazy, but, well, there are things going on that you don't understand–'

Something entered his stomach. Something incredibly, shockingly cold. He gasped at how cold it was, and how *familiar* the sensation was.

Tony met his wife's eyes. That light of fury lit them still, even as she pushed the kitchen knife further into his stomach.

'Try me,' Dian said.

REGENT STREET, BELFAST / OTHERWORLD, NOW

Ellie was making herself a cup of coffee. Her son was in the living room; she knew because she had checked he was in there six times since the kettle had started to boil.

It was the best feeling in the world.

Her phone rang. She frowned in surprise at the caller ID. 'Maggie? You okay?'

'I said goodbye to Steve.'

'Mum told Dad the same thing,' Ellie said. He had called her to tell her so. She hadn't even had time to process what that meant. She had watched him die in front of her, and now he had been brought back … only to be taken away again. Unless she 'voted' to stay down here with him; but then what would happen to Danny and Luke? Her father had forbidden her from doing so anyway, had made her promise. It was all too much to process. Hence, coffee.

Maggie was silent. 'How'd he take it?' she said eventually.

Ellie sighed. This conversation was tiring her out and it was only twenty seconds old. 'How do you *think* he fuckin' took it?' she replied.

'Some of us just aren't strong enough,' Maggie said.

'Or that some people give up on themselves too early.'

'Meaning?' Maggie's voice was clipped with annoyance. Ellie felt her patience shed another few pounds.

'Meaning that Mum's decision didn't come as a huge surprise to me, and I don't imagine it did to Dad either, although that's not going to help him feel any better right away. Those two weren't in love, Maggie. Oh they *might* have been, once, but all I can ever remember is this attitude from them both that they'd "outgrown" love or something. That oul "ach wise up" sort of attitude when it came to it. Like love is a fucking coal seam that can run out once you've mined it too much. That's a load of shit.'

'So what is it? Big dramatic sacrifices? Pain? How's that fair?'

Ellie actually laughed. 'My mistake,' she said. 'I thought you were in love with Steve, and so you were going through hell or something.'

'I *am* going through hell!' Maggie spat angrily.

Ellie spoke into the phone very slowly, as if she were talking to a complete moron. 'Then what the fuck are you asking if it's *fair* for?'

Letting that sink in, Ellie calmed herself down with some effort and spoke a little more gently, but only a little. 'Love isn't *fair*, Maggie. It's hard fucking work and it's long nights. It's arguments, it's passion, it's lying there watching soaps on a rainy Tuesday night and being content doing it. But it never has to be *fair*. If you'd any brains in your pretty, selfish little head you'd realise that. You know what? Steve deserves better than you.'

And with that, Ellie hung up.

GRIFFIN STREET, BELFAST / OTHERWORLD, NOW

Light rushed toward him.

Tony coughed, violently, over and over again. There were spots of blood in his hands when he brought them away from his face, but when he patted his stomach urgently, he could feel no wound. His wife. Linda. Linda had *stabbed* him. Linda, who was standing over him now.

'Drop of Gaviscon?' she asked him.

Tony scrambled away from her, getting to his feet as quickly as he could. This only made Linda roar with laughter. She was still holding the kitchen knife she'd stabbed him with, and it dripped with blood – *his* blood – as it rocked in her grip.

'You *killed* me,' Tony said, as though saying it would make it any easier to contemplate.

'I did,' she said, and the face he'd loved all these years contorted in savage pleasure.

He felt as though he were about to throw up, as though his stomach, currently healing from this most recent fatal puncture, was about to heave.

'I thought it might jog your memory,' she went on. 'Not often you get to kill someone twice in the one night.'

'What?' he choked.

Her eyes seemed to glitter in the light of the single candle on the table. She looked less than human ...

'When I heard you'd been brought back, I knew you'd come here, to her. It was just a question of getting the timing right.'

Tony gaped. 'You ... you're not Linda?'

His wife made a growling noise of impatience that was not native to her own larynx. 'Quick on the uptake, aren't you? Think back, Tony. You and your darling daddy, a few decades ago ... your first big-boy mission.'

'*Dian?*'

'In the flesh,' Dian responded, bowing with Linda's body. 'Well, in the flesh you and your father have forced me to resort to, at any rate.'

'You? *You're* the reason Dermot killed me?'

Dian advanced on him, knife gleaming. 'No, Tony,' he said. 'What you did to me is the reason Dermot killed you. I was merely the push he required.'

'Dermot would never–'

'Tell yourself that if it helps,' Dian shrugged.

'GET OUT OF MY WIFE!' Tony roared.

Dian giggled. 'That sounds a little rude, don't you think?' he said, and started running his, Linda's, hands all over her body. 'So *nice* inside your wife, Tony. She's still in here, you see. That's why I wanted to live inside brain-dead people, can you remember that, you little prick? Brain-dead people are gone. No-one cohabiting. But when I jump from human to human – they're in here. Mind to mind. It's so ... *intimate*. I can see every thought, every memory, your wife ever had. And when I flick my finger across them,' he shivered with pleasure, 'ohhh, your honeymoon. Tony, you stud.'

Almost blind with anger, Tony's hands balled into fists. 'I'll kill you,' he said hoarsely. 'I'll fucking kill you. I swear I will ...'

Dian laughed again. 'Ah, but you won't! How can you? Kill me by killing Linda? Go ahead!'

'Nobody dies down here. She'd come back. Just like I did.'

Dian inclined his head thoughtfully. 'That she would,' he allowed. 'That she would, at that. But, and correct me if I'm wrong here, wouldn't her coming back entail her having to stay down here? Forever?'

'She'd be with me.'

'Agreed! She would!' Dian hopped up and down delightedly. 'And *that's* what you came over here to find out, wasn't it? Whether she would agree to stay down here with you! Her answer to my mother's little dilemma!'

There was no point in denying it. Tony looked away. Never in his life had he felt so helpless as he did now.

'So it's a win-win!' Dian wasn't finished. He stepped forward in a quick movement and, before Tony could even react, he had tossed the knife casually upward in a short arc. Tony's hand shot out instinctively and he caught it. Dian spread his arms wide and shut his eyes.

'So?' he said. 'Come on then, Tony. I'm waiting.'

Seconds passed. Dian opened one of Linda's eyes in an overly exaggerated manner so he could peer in apparent confusion at the man standing well within knife range.

'Something wrong?'

'I can't,' Tony hissed.

'Why ever not?'

'I'd never be sure it was her choice,' Tony said, every word dragged from him.

Dian blew out a long breath that was almost post-orgasmic, savouring every moment of this. 'Aye, there's the rub,' he agreed with mock gravitas. 'Chase me from inside your wife and keep her down here, never knowing whether she'd actually have *wanted* to remain here with you.'

'She would,' Tony said, weakly.

'Then, please, by all means,' and Dian resumed his former position of surrender. 'Go ahead and strike, if you're so confident of that. Of course, speaking as someone who's sharing her thoughts right now, I can tell you with complete authority that, given the choice between staying with you and going back to the real world, where she would see her son and grandson again, she wouldn't pause for a single *second*, Tony. Not a single second. But then … I could be lying, I suppose.'

The phone began to ring. Dian looked over at it, and Tony saw an expression of concern pass over his wife's face. Something about the phone ringing was unsettling the deity. Reaching down, Dian yanked the phone cable from the wall, and the ringing died immediately.

'Where were we?' Dian asked, but his voice lacked the sadistic relish of a few seconds before.

Tony's mobile rang.

'*No!*' Dian cried, lunging forward.

Tony looked at the caller ID, and he understood. He answered the call–

– and he *screamed*.

With care, Dian laid the man he'd stabbed only moments before onto his back and stroked his brow. 'Sssh,' he soothed as Tony's body began to convulse. 'It's always hardest the first time. Find the senses, and use them; they'll bring the rest along.'

The convulsions gradually decreased in severity, but Tony's face was beginning to darken and purple in hue.

'Breathe,' Dian said. 'You must remember to breathe.'

Tony's body shuddered as he drew in a huge, gasping breath. His heart thudded in his chest. Sweat poured from him. He looked up with red-rimmed eyes into the face of Linda Morrigan and the ancient entity occupying her.

'Da?' he said.

Dian cradled his head. 'Yes,' he said, grateful tears spilling down his face. 'Yes Dermot, it's Daddy.'

REGENT STREET, BELFAST / OTHERWORLD, NOW

'Look after your mother,' Michael Quinn's voice sounded throughout the living room, as Ellie, Danny and Luke assembled around the phone.

'I will,' Ellie promised, in a small voice. 'I'm your Steady Ellie.'

'You were always much more than that,' he told her quietly. 'I'm sorry. Sorry I couldn't see what you had. Danny is a good man. I thought he was a waste of space. An utter moron. Completely beneath you.'

'You're on speakerphone and I'm standing *right here*,' Danny pointed out.

'I was wrong,' Michael continued, ignoring the interruption. 'He's a good man.'

Their time was almost up. Like pressure in the air signalling an approaching storm, Danny could feel the build-up of power that was going to regurgitate Ireland back to reality like a late-night drunken kebab.

He thought of Steve, of his father. It was now likely that he'd never see them again. He put his hand in his pocket, felt the weight of that incongruously functional mobile phone inside and, for a brief moment, considered calling them. He dismissed the idea almost straight away – he had said his goodbyes insofar as he ever could. He simply couldn't face the thought of more pain.

'What will you do? Down here?' he asked Michael.

'The way I see it,' Michael said, an audible shrug in his voice, 'there are going to be thousands, maybe hundreds of thousands of people down here who are gonna have to deal with a whole new world, whole new way of living. Someone's gotta lead them. Someone's gotta take charge.'

'And,' Danny started, dismissing his original thought and opting for a more diplomatic response, 'you think that might be you?'

'Me? Take *that* job? Not a chance in hell,' Michael admitted. 'But someone's going to have to work behind the scenes for the poor bastard who does end up taking it.'

With a final goodbye, he was gone.

There were only minutes left now, Danny knew, so they sat, as a family, for a few moments. He had his arm around Ellie while their son sat on the armchair opposite. Danny couldn't resist, he had to ask. 'Do you remember?' he asked Luke.

'Remember?'

'What it was like. Being a baby. Being *our* baby. I mean, it was only a few days ago.'

'It's ...' Luke shook his head. 'Some of it I remember. It's impossible to describe. It's like I still exist, but I've been sort of scattered. Dispersed. Most of the time the world is this *huge* place, filled with giant people and it's just feelings, sensations. When I'm like this, when I'm older, feelings and emotions are kind of diet versions of themselves – muted. Babies aren't like that. When you're big, you think, "I'm hungry, I'm thirsty. Fine, I'll get something to eat or drink." When you're a baby, it's like, "Oh my God, the hunger! Must. Have. Food! Why don't I have some food right now? What's going on?" And then there's–' and he coloured suddenly.

'Yeah,' Danny said, 'you used to piddle on me all the time when I was changing you, you little shit.'

'It wasn't deliberate,' Luke said weakly.

'Forget about it. I'm just glad Ellie isn't breastfeeding you anymore.'

'AWWWDADNOOOO!'

'DANNY!' Ellie reached across and punched him, hard, in the upper arm, so hard Danny tasted elderberries and smelt Wednesday. He shook his head; he'd almost forgotten the comforting strangeness of synaesthesia. He couldn't help but laugh, though, and after a few seconds Ellie and Luke joined him. What the fuck else could you do?

'Um. Can I ask you both something?' Luke said. He sounded excited.

'Anything,' Danny replied.

'Can I … can I say a swear word?' their Thor-esque son asked, fairly vibrating with illicit thrills at the mere thought of it.

'No you fuckin' can't,' Danny tutted.

'Luke Christopher Morrigan!' Ellie said, shaking her head. She glanced over at Danny. 'I dunno where we get him from, swear to fuck.'

'But …'

'Fuckin' disgrace. Imagine wanting to say a bad word in front of his mummy and daddy.'

'But …'

'Although,' Danny mused, winking at Ellie. 'He has missed fuck knows how many birthday and Christmas presents …'

'Ma? Da?' Luke said, getting to his feet. He sounded panicked. Ellie was by her son's side in an instant, Danny only a fraction of a second behind her, all joviality forgotten.

'What's wrong?'

'I feel … strange,' Luke said.

He was growing younger before their eyes.

Now around sixteen and approaching fifteen fast, Luke looked like someone who'd borrowed a warrior's costume two sizes too big for him for Halloween. His parents stood with him as his frame continued to shrink, and despite the extreme changes his body was having to withstand, Luke actually smiled.

'You're gonna be our wee baby again,' Ellie said.

'You're smiling,' Danny said, with some small measure of astonishment.

Luke, now twelve, going on eleven and accelerating, looked up at his parents with wonder. 'Why wouldn't I be?' he said.

Those words, enough to bring tears to his eyes, were the last Danny heard Luke say before the change fully overtook him. Without quite being conscious of doing it, Danny scooped Luke into his arms, and saw the light of experience and knowledge in his eyes flicker and dim, replaced by the unmistakable gleam of innocence.

Together, he and Ellie held their son tight.

GRIFFIN STREET, BELFAST / OTHERWORLD, NOW

'Why are you doing this, Dad?' Dermot said in Tony Morrigan's voice.

'For you,' Dian answered through Linda. 'For what was done to us.'

'Not by him. Not by Tony.'

'He stood by and watched.'

'He followed his father just as you followed your mother. He's not to blame.'

'You were the one who killed him first,' Dian pointed out mirthlessly.

'You forced me to.'

'Did I?'

Did he? Tony asked his oldest friend. He was ... not trapped, exactly, inside his own body. When he'd answered the phone, Dermot had flooded into him, overloaded and overwhelmed him, but it had been more out of blind panic than malice. Dian's instructions on how to access Tony's senses had calmed things down considerably. Tony had sensed – buried somewhere within that clumsy assault – that Dermot was *asking his permission* to do what he was doing.

He'd given it.

I hope so, Dermot's soul replied. *I'm sorry, Tony.*

Tony thought back to that night, the long drive into the country. His father had been so sure he was in the right, and his father had been a good man. The best man he'd ever known. Unfortunately, that didn't mean good men didn't sometimes do bad things. It was just that sort of world.

'Don't hate them,' Dermot begged. 'You can't claim to be different from the rest of our people and then hate all humans equally for one mistake. You were a good man *and* a good father. I loved you. Don't become this.'

Hearing this, Dian's face grew pinched with pain. 'You don't understand,' he replied. 'There's one more job I have to do.'

'Then let Tony come up too. Let him be with his wife.'

Dian didn't reply for a moment. 'I can't,' he said finally. 'I can't, even if I wanted to. Once I go up, I'll let her go. I … I promise. I won't hurt her, or any of them.'

'Then let her stay! Let it be Linda's choice. Go hitch a ride in some other body if you need to.'

'There's no *time!*' Dian cried desperately and grabbed Tony's hand. 'Come with me,' he said, and tried to pull Dermot out *through* Tony and into Linda.

Tony and Dermot screamed through one mouth at the horrific sensation, watching in horror as Linda's flesh began to smoke.

'Come with me!' Dian said again.

'Let go! You're killing her!' the words came from both Tony and Dermot.

'I won't lose you again!'

Together they lashed out, knocking Linda's hand away – her skin stopped smouldering almost immediately.

'You can't,' Dermot sobbed. 'She can't take us both, Dad. You'll kill her. I won't let you do that. For Christ's sake just let her *talk*. Please. Let her talk to her husband.'

A violent shudder rippled through Linda's body and she fell to her knees, sucking in deep, gasping breaths. Dermot stepped aside inside Tony's mind, allowing his friend full control. Tony was at his wife's side in seconds.

'Linda?'

She was shivering as he held her. 'He's ... he's still inside me. But he's lettin' me talk.'

'Don't,' Tony said, feeling the sting of tears, knowing from the pressure in the air that they didn't have much longer. 'Don't speak if it hurts.'

'I have to,' Linda said urgently. 'I know what he knows. I know why you left us,' and despite everything, she managed to smile at him, a smile he hadn't seen properly in years. 'I know the truth.'

He smiled through his tears as a weight he'd been carrying for over a decade finally lifted from his shoulders. 'I'm glad,' he said softly.

'I want to stay,' she said. 'I want to stay with you. When we vote, he thinks he can fool her – make his mother believe that I want to go back.'

He kissed her then, kissed his wife of almost-thirty years. When he finally pulled apart, he looked deep into her eyes and said the most difficult words he'd ever had to say.

'Do it,' he told the spark of Dian within her. 'Fool Carman. Make sure my wife gets back. If there's any good left in you, *please.*'

'Tony, *no!*' Linda sobbed, horrified. 'No! I want to stay!'

'DO IT!' he screamed, and the magical pressure finally reached its peak and the permanent twilight outside turned to light – bright, searing light that burst in through the windows and blurred the vision no matter how hard you tried to look away.

IRELAND / OTHERWORLD, NOW

White light burst from the centre of the standing stones and rolled across Ireland. It tumbled across the lanes and byways of the nation, so slowly in places that many had the fortune – or the misfortune, depending on their perspective – to watch it approach, knowing that their lives would change irrevocably when it hit.

There was time, then, in many places, for last words and last goodbyes and last lies – final words of cold comfort for lovers about to be torn apart. Relationships were ultimately defined in the illumination of that approaching truth, for the light did as

Carman promised it would; it looked into the souls of those it hit and it got things right every single time.

Almost.

In a terraced house in Belfast, Tony Morrigan found himself embracing thin air. He allowed himself time for one utterance of 'thank you' before the tears overcame him.

The Master of Two Worlds

'To begin, let me sum up the events of the last twelve hours,' the President addressed those sitting around the table as well as the faces on video screens. 'Last night, at 10.12 p.m. local time, the landmass of Ireland vanished off the face of the Earth, leaving behind only bedrock. Some sort of intangible barrier held back the seas around the island. Early this morning that barrier vanished, and the seas returned to fill the void. At 6.12 a.m. Ireland reappeared in its entirety. Immense water displacement from the instantaneous return of the Irish landmass has caused tsunamis which have devastated the Isle of Man, the western coast of the United Kingdom, the north-western and western coasts of France and the northern coast of Spain. Cities on the Eastern seaboard of the United States are being evacuated – we're expecting a twenty foot-high, three hundred mile-long tsunami to impact New York within the hour.'

No one spoke.

'In addition,' the President continued, 'around three hours ago, the town of Litochoro in Greece began to experience seismic disturbances which have since spread to the surrounding area.

Contact with Litochoro was lost ninety-seven minutes ago. Satellite imagery of the area has confirmed that a massive landslide has swallowed the entire town. The source of this landslide, and of the seismic disturbances, is the mountain behind Litochoro. Put simply, the mountain is growing. It's already risen in height by nine hundred metres. If it continues to rise, in a few hours time it will overtake Mont Blanc as the highest mountain in Europe.'

He paused.

'The mountain's name is Olympus,' he said.

REGENT STREET, BELFAST ABOVE, NOW

'Once again,' the news anchorman repeated, 'the helpline number for those of you with friends and family left behind is displayed on the bottom of the screen. Advice from the government is to stay in your homes, at least for the moment. A state of emergency has been declared. And once again, please do *not* try to travel to ports or airports to leave the country. All travel outside Ireland has been suspended. Anyone attempting to leave the country, even to go offshore, may be ...' and he hesitated, as if not quite believing what he was saying himself, 'fired upon.'

'Jesus,' Ellie said softly. She and Danny were sitting together on their small settee. 'They've quarantined us.'

'Could be worse,' Danny said softly.

As if sensing the increase in tension, Luke mumbled something in his sleep. His arms and legs jerked once or twice and he moaned softly. Ellie shushed and soothed him until his breathing returned to normal. She looked at Danny and saw he was watching his son sleep, his expression unreadable.

'What's going to happen?' she said, speaking more quietly now.

Danny mulled it over. 'Dunno. What do they usually do in films? Send in teams dressed in big yellow suits to kill ET?'

'I didn't mean to the country,' she snapped. 'I meant *us*. I mean, we're back, but … everything's changed. *Everything*. My da … your da … Steve …'

'I don't know,' Danny answered, when he felt able. 'I don't think anyone up here knows how this works. That's probably what's scaring the shit out of them the most.'

'Not just them. What's to stop her, Danny? What's to stop her from trying again? What's to stop her taking Luke again?' Ellie said, hugging her child fiercely. Even the thought of it made her sweat, made her tremble.

'She swore some magical oath or somethin'. Fuck, I dunno, Ellie,' Danny said, annoyed at the questions but mostly annoyed because Ellie was entirely correct. 'According to Luke and the Wolves, she can't fuck about with breaking oaths.'

'You really think we're safe?'

'Put it this way, what *else* can happen?' he replied.

WASHINGTON DC, NOW

Tom Beckett had just finished giving his evidence. He had talked of falling into the abyss and finding himself alive. He'd spoken of the long drive to the centre of Ireland, and the scramble onto the plane to avoid the onrushing Atlantic Ocean.

He told the assembled crowd of the visions he had received, of the psychic messages he had picked up on. When he had tasted the bedrock of Ireland, he said, they had come to him and spoken to him and told him Ireland was only the beginning, that soon it would spread beyond those shores.

Europe and America would be the next to fall, he said. First they would vanish from the world and, when they came back, the people within would have come back wrong. Whoever this force was that was doing this to Ireland, he said, it hated humanity and it would not stop.

Through all of this, Tom screamed and screamed inside his own head, as the entity occupying his brain *sssssh'd* him repeatedly and told him it was almost over. He was half-telling the truth about one thing – the last time he had spoken to his girlfriend, she *had* sounded different … and then something had passed through that phone and into him, and now here he was.

If you knew how, a mind could be made to behave in any way you wished. It could also be set to self-destruct. Dian did this as he prepared to flee Tom's body. When the first of the onrushing medics touched him, he began a journey from body to body that took him from medics to aides to officials and to his final destination as he prepared to complete his mother's task.

One more job.

'May God have mercy on us,' the President said, in a voice that was not quite his own.

*

'Can I get anyone a wee cuppa tea?'

'Ma!' Danny scolded, half-rising out of his seat. 'You're meant to be resting!'

He'd insisted his mother come to stay with them for a while. When he'd found her, she had been beside herself with grief, stunned beyond comprehension by the loss of her husband. It had taken Danny long hours to talk her around, to make her see that what his da had done hadn't been another act of abandonment, but of love.

'Resting?' Linda Morrigan snorted. 'Aye right. Resting. The whole world's gone mad, son. I don't think anyone's gonna be *resting* for a while yet.'

She stroked Luke's cheek and smiled down at the sleeping baby still cradled in Ellie's arms. 'I wish I could have seen him. All grown up. Wee heartbreaker.'

'You will,' Ellie promised, but she made no move to release her son. Danny was beginning to suspect that Luke would be around eleven before his mother let him go, and he didn't really blame Ellie for feeling that way. She had needed a toilet break two hours ago and Danny all but had to sign a permission slip to hold Luke while she'd gone.

'Your granda won't let anything happen to you, little one,' Linda whispered, before her voice wavered. Wiping her eyes, she muttered something about tea and padded out to the kitchen, avoiding gazes as she went.

Giving Ellie a semi-smile of support, Danny suppressed an urge to howl with frustration. He felt *ridiculous* just sitting here, on the sofa, watching television, especially after the frenetic chaos of the last few days. The entire country – the entire *world* – was going through complete upheaval and he could think of no way to help.

But what, exactly, could he do? Sure, he'd made his wee speeches in Stormont that night, but he'd been in no rush to supply them with his name and address. He'd counted on the huge wolves at his side to stamp his authority, and somehow that had worked.

Only one person from that night knew who he was. He had told the brigadier his name, even gave him his address, before leaving to chase down Steve on Wily's back. He had done so on the proviso that the officer share it with no-one.

Okay, the name *Morrigan* had been name-checked in Carman's psychic broadcast to the entire population so his last name might attract a little attention, but whilst it was a fairly unusual surname he could easily shrug it off as coincidence.

He thought back to ancient Ireland, to the reactions of the villagers when they'd discovered the Morrigan's Tuatha heritage, to the tragic events that had followed. Would things be so different now? Were people, when you got down to it, really more advanced now than they'd been then in terms of dealing with things they didn't understand?

He doubted it. No, it was best for Ellie, and especially for Luke, that he continue to exist under the radar. That was why he had made the brigadier swear he would tell no one, unless there was no other option. They had shaken hands and Danny had used his newfound gifts to probe the brigadier's mind and confirm that he was trustworthy.

His thoughts kept drifting back to his father, and to Steve. Left behind in a strange world, a twilit facsimile of Ireland, with only the Named as allies against Carman's hordes? Granted, Carman had consumed most of her creatures when assuming her final monstrous form, but how long before she was able to use the Cauldron to produce more? Ellie was right; what *was* to stop her from trying again?

BELFAST BELOW, NOW

The city was dark, but it was far from silent.

Tony knew its streets better than most; he had roamed them from his early teens, tailing his father on some mission or other. Later, after James' death, he had taken on the responsibility himself, lied to his wife and son, told them he was working on mapping the country when in fact it was more like patrolling fields and city streets alike for murmurs of faerie activity.

He was fond of the old place, despite itself. He had noticed down the years that native Belfastians, indeed natives of Northern Ireland itself, needed little encouragement to launch into a long and impassioned stream of invective about the state of the place. Any self-respecting Norn Ironlander could readily give you their top twenty-five reasons the place was pure shite.

And yet, should they hear or see or sense so much as a syllable of unearned criticism from 'an outsider', they'd close ranks. Gazes would steel, brows would furrow, and voices would drop an octave or two – though in the case of Belfast males, they had a pretty high starting bar on that front.

It's a shithole, but it's our shithole, seemed to be the sentiment.

All of which was lovely in a Hallmark sort of way, he reflected, but it in no way explained why the inhabitants had been hell-bent on knocking the melt out of each other since time immemorial.

'Balls,' he said.

There were, he estimated, about sixty or seventy of them. He had been drawn to the racket they'd made, without even consciously realising it. Males, mostly. Young, in the main. Roughly equally matched on each side, with only a set of massive balls between them – the huge wire-frame spherical urban sculpture that had been officially named *Rise* for about seventeen seconds and had been always and forever 'The Balls on the Falls' thereafter.

Like everything else in Ireland, it had been copied down to the smallest detail. But this was not the world they'd left behind. It had been twenty-four hours since the white light, but he knew that only by consulting his watch. The skies had not changed. No dawn had broken. The night had remained, the dull crimson hue from the blood-red moon the only natural illumination.

A wee bit up the road, the police had cordoned off one of the shopping centres. He was fairly sure they were rushing to do the same to as many others as they could. Their motivation was obvious – to protect the supplies within. Whether they were protecting them for the greater good in an effort to ration them, or simply to fence them off for their own use was, for the moment, rather less obvious.

They were effectively in their own self-contained universe. The old social order was hopelessly obsolete. The trouble was, the old universe that supposedly *had* social order had still resulted in groups of young fellas like this gathering to lift lumps out of each other.

Of course, he could always let them have at it, he reasoned. After all, there was no permanent death here, as had been made perfectly clear – that was the whole reason he and these luckless lads were trapped here in the first place. He could stand back, get a comfortable seat, and wait for the first stone to hurtle through the air or the first dig to be swung. They'd surely get bored eventually when they realised even doing their worst wouldn't do anything permanent.

And yet …

'All right lads,' he called out, walking to the front of the nearest group, immediately identifying the chief agitator. The one on the 'other' side he gestured over to and something, some dormant ability of command he hadn't called on properly for years, prompted the youth to trot over. Capitalising on this tenuous momentum, Tony nabbed the head honcho nearest him and before he could protest, escorted him into the no-man's land between the two groups.

Time to wing it.

'Somebody lookin' to start something?' Tony began.

'Prob'ly *them* fuckin' Orange cunts,' said the first, theatrically stabbing an accusatory finger at his opponent. He did this so exaggeratedly and with such limb elasticity that he would have had a fine career as a ballerina. Tony decided to keep this observation to himself.

'Aye fuck! I'll knock your fuckin' cun–'

'Sure 'mon then, 'mon ta fuck then!' roared the would-be ballerina, arms and legs akimbo, and moved to strike.

Tony moved, and he was nothing if not economical. As the two young men attempted to rush each other headlong, he reached, pulled, twisted and swept and before either quite knew what had happened, they found themselves none too gently deposited on the ground beside each another.

The real skill, which was sadly lost on them, was that Tony had done this so quickly and efficiently that the watching crowds on either side never even saw anything untoward transpire.

He sat quickly down as both were still recovering, and before they could react he reached out with his thumbs and found the pressure point on each boy's ankle.

'Laugh,' he said.

'Y'fuckin' *wha*?' one managed to gasp.

'Laugh,' Tony said again. Even with his speed, the crowds were growing restless. 'Laugh, or I'll pop your ankles like fuckin' corks out of a bottle,' and he increased the pressure before lessening it again.

'Ha ha,' they intoned.

Another brief increase of pressure. 'Funnier,' Tony ordered.

From somewhere deep within, both boys found their inner Olivier, and produced a series of guffaws that caused the crowds to cease their uncertain advance. Confusion was reigning, but he still didn't have much time.

'Now let's have a chat,' he said cheerily. 'What seems to be the problem? And for a wee geg, let's try to form our responses without the inclusion of the following words – Taig, Prod, Orange, Fenian, cunt, bastard … oh, what the fuck, let's just say all swear words are banned, aye?'

A long, contemplative silence. Tony could see their lips moving with conscious effort.

'I …' the ballerina began cautiously. 'I came down here cos every fu– … every *one* knows that this,' and he waved a hand to indicate the cosmos in general, such as it was, 'is some sort of Brit doomsday plan.'

'My holeeeeowww!'

Tony relaxed his thumbs and waited for the expressions of pain to subside once more. 'I believe you had the floor?' he said brightly. 'Would you like to rebut?'

'We didn't do this! Sure now yous have got what yous always wanted!'

'Fer fucks sake–' Tony said.

'Oh aye he's allowed to swear,' muttered one boy to another.

While this three-way conversation went on, one onlooking hothead decided he had waited long enough. He'd been holding a half-brick for so long his arm was starting to get tired. He drew in a breath to scream.

'Drop it, son,' a quiet voice sounded from behind him. 'On your big toe, preferably, but the ground'll do. Just you stand there and wait.'

'Who the fuck d'you think yer talkin' to – *oh holy fuck!*'

The impromptu peace conference concluded not long

thereafter without serious incident. The two leaders waved their crowds over and slowly, slowly, they drifted into the middle, underneath those incongruous skeletal testes, and with much shuffling of feet and avoiding of eyes and exchanging of not strictly legal cigarettes and other combustibles, the tension began to ebb away.

A shadow fell across Tony. He glanced up … and up.

'Holy Jesus, you're a big fella,' he whistled.

'Good work there.'

Tony nodded to the prone body of the would-be half-brick chucker, currently spread-eagled on the tarmac, very deeply unconscious. 'That you?' he asked.

'You're welcome.'

'There's always a critic,' Tony tutted. 'He okay?'

'Sleeping.'

'Suppose even if he wasn't, he'd have come back.'

'He may hope that works on his balls too.'

Tony laughed.

'How'd you get them not to kill each other?'

'I found some common ground between them, Dermot.'

Wind whistled through the dark city. There was only the hubbub of adolescent conversation and the shine of mobile phone screens, as another precious few percentage points of battery charge were sacrificed.

'It's the eyes,' Tony said quietly, by way of explanation. 'I'd know them eyes anywhere.'

'When the light hit and the power went out it hit the hospitals, too,' Dermot said. 'The coma patients on ventilators died.'

'Died? Here?'

'At first,' Dermot admitted. 'When they came back, they didn't need the respirators but most of them were still more or less empty shells. This,' he indicated his body, 'was Paulie. He's been brain dead for eighteen months. There isn't a lot of him left in here,' and he tapped his head. 'But there was enough. Enough to say *yes* when I asked for his permission.'

'How'd you find me?'

'Family heritage. I'm growing into it.'

'*Why'd* you find me?'

'Your da killed mine, Tony. Your family ruined my whole childhood.'

'Yeah. Well. You killed me.'

'Crybaby.'

'Fuckpot.'

Tony regarded his old friend and comrade, unwelcome memories of the night he and his da had made the fateful trip to Dermot Quinn's childhood home resurfacing. How different would everything have turned out, he wondered, if he'd been able to make his own da see sense that night?

He doubted he would ever forget the feeling of the letter opener's blade entering his body, or of looking into Dermot's eyes, filled with hate, as he pushed it deeper. Yes, the man had been possessed by a faerie whose specialist subject was instilling murderous rage. Yes, Dermot had helped him – or at least tried to – when he'd been forced to say goodbye to Linda. He knew all of this, but could he ever really forgive a man capable of murder? Could he ever stop seeing his friend's face, contorted in hate?

It was then he noticed that, during all of his musing, the now-merged group of lads were trying their damndest to toilet paper the Balls on the Falls.

'You know what their common ground was?' he asked Dermot as they watched.

'Terrible aim?'

'I told one to run away home to his ma and he burst into tears,' Tony went on. 'The other fella, I expected him to have a complete field day with that, and next thing you know, he starts bawlin' too. And I realised, when the worlds split, their mas didn't stay with them, das either. Some of them said they would, and then Carman's election came and went. These lads – near all of them, I'll bet ye – found themselves on their own down here. That was yesterday. And what else did they know, but troopin' down here and flinging a few stones?'

'There'll be more than these lads need looking after, Tony. This whole city, this whole country, island ... it's busting to the gills with terrified people, hurting like fuck at being left behind. Somebody's gonna need to step up.'

Tony simply nodded.

'We made a good team a long time ago, didn't we?' Dermot asked.

'That we did, mucker. That we did.'

'Fancy getting the band back together?'

'Band?' Tony snorted. 'Two people's more a duet, wouldn't you say?'

'How about five?' came another voice from behind them.

Tony turned to see Steve and the two Named, Larka and Wily.

Steve was just about holding it together, Tony could tell that at a glance. He nodded to the wolves and shook Steve's hand. The young man surprised him by coming in for a full-on hug, which Tony returned.

'How'd you find me?'

It was Wily who spoke up.'The Morrigans enjoy our protection. Now, and always.'

'What are we supposed to do down here?' Steve asked Tony, his voice hoarse.

Tony looked to Dermot, nodding almost imperceptibly. He did the same to the wolves, and fancied he received the same in return.

'Like the man said,' Tony stated firmly,'we step up.'

PARLIAMENT BUILDINGS, STORMONT,
BELFAST BELOW, NOW

Whether through luck or judgment, for good or for ill, there were not many politicians who had either been forced to stay behind or who had elected to.

What little remained of their number had gone to Stormont – where else could they go? – a great white expanse set against crimson skies and surrounded by the darkness of the trees that lined the mile-long driveway.

Dire as their situation was, the debate that resounded across the candlelit assembly chamber was strangely cordial. There seemed little point in bluff or bluster, in point-scoring or one-upmanship. No one was even sure they had a country left to govern, much less how to govern it.

Outside the big house, three security guards – two men and one woman – stood watch. In many ways, the debate they were holding amongst themselves mirrored the debate going on inside the assembly chamber.

'What are we doing here?'

'Our jobs.'

'Jobs? And who's going to pay our wages?'

'I have a family to feed. I have children. I could go ... I should go.'

'Go where?'

'I don't know. To a supermarket.'

'There's no power.'

'Tins and all that shit will be grand for a while yet.'

'And pay with what?'

'Who's paying?'

Silence.

'So this is it. This is how we're going to live now.'

'What other way is there? We've no power. No electricity. The guns don't work.'

'And the sun is never coming up.'

'Ach, the fuck with this,' the older man moved off the steps he'd been sitting on. 'I have to go. I've kids. They're sitting in the dark around candles and I'm sitting here guarding twenty stupid fuckers with no more power than I have. World's changed. Whatever old life we had, it's gone. *Gone*. We need to–'

'Ssssh,' said the woman.

'Don't you *ssssh* me,' the man bristled.

'Look.'

They looked in the direction the woman was pointing. At the beginning of the driveway, one mile distant, a pair of lamp-posts, positioned on either side of the drive, were sputtering and flickering into dim life. At this distance, they were no bigger than fireflies, but they were the most beautiful sight any of them had ever seen.

The second pair of lamp-posts began to illuminate.

The third.

'Something's coming,' the woman said, matter-of-factly. 'They're bringing the power with them.'

'We'd better tell them,' said the younger man, and he ran off inside to do just that.

The two left behind looked at each other, and then back at the steady progression of the lights, a line of illumination growing longer and longer, heading straight towards the big house on top of the hill, its inhabitants … and its guards.

'What is it?' the older man croaked. 'I can't see. Can you see?'

'I can see,' the woman replied, still maddeningly calm. 'It's a woman.'

'Alone?'

'Yes.'

'Get her inside,' the older man said. 'She's out there on her own. She must be terrified.'

His colleague shook her head. 'No,' she said quietly. 'No, I don't think she is.'

*

Luke was showing little in the way of ill effects. He was his old baby self, so far as Danny and Ellie could make out – same genial little personality, same capacity for loud squeals of excitement prompted by not a great deal. Same uncanny accuracy with urine.

Admittedly, however, there were some small differences.

'He's not going over,' Ellie said. She was sitting in their bedroom in a chair beside the cot. The bed, fully three feet from the cot, had been quickly deemed as being much too far away, hence the evolution of the cot-chair. Ellie, knowing that Luke was unlikely to sleep with his mummy's face looming over him, had ensured she was out of his line of sight, but it wasn't helping.

Danny sighed. Gar-gah the ex-hippo was already in there. They'd wound the mobile fifteen times. It was approaching 1 a.m. Police and media helicopters whirled overhead, as they had for the past day and a half. He had a *bastard* headache.

'Do it,' he said.

And so, seconds later, the first strains of Metallica's 'Enter Sandman' began to filter through into the bedroom.

Luke's limbs splayed. Gar-gah was callously discarded, impacting the back wall of the cot with a moist *splaf* and slowly sliding down in a sodden heap. Luke's breathing increased; his little chest rising and falling, his head jerking from side to side, tiny little feet beating the mattress in what, if you were inclined to believe such things, would be more or less perfect time with the thumping bassline.

They'd discovered the effects of this song quite by accident earlier this afternoon. As she always did in times of stress, Ellie had turned to loud and angry rock music. Luke, still in her arms at the time, had lain there peacefully enough throughout most of her selections. For this song, though ...

Danny glanced across at Ellie. He knew she was as tired as he was, but she gave him a wan grin and even managed to make the universal symbol of rock with her fingers, which made him laugh silently and reach out to touch her hand.

He glanced back into the cot. Luke Morrigan, the Chosen One, all of eight months old, was drifting peacefully off to sleep as if the song pounding through the room was 'Brahms' Lullaby'.

His little eyes finally closed, his chest rose and fell steadily, deeply. Danny reached out and touched his son's cheek. There seemed little point in wondering what was going on in there. He wasn't even sure he wanted to know. It was enough that he was able to reach out, that his son had been returned to him. He'd paid a price for that, a price so high it terrified him even to think of it.

A price he'd pay again in a heartbeat.

Ellie switched off the song, slightly disturbed that her son found so much comfort in lyrics about watching for things in the darkness, and sleeping lightly for fear they would come for you in the night.

'Never thought I'd fuckin' miss "The Wheels on the Bus",' she muttered.

*

The command was given. The keys were turned. The button pressed.

One more job.

Wonder of wonders, Ellie was asleep beside him. Danny shifted, causing her to stir slightly and mumble something incoherent, before she resettled. He lay there, beside her in their bed, just taking a moment. Just one moment. It wasn't too much to ask for, after all he'd been through. On trips through time and through dimensions, in seeing his father's past and Ireland's ancient history and meeting mythic washerwomen and creating entire universes, this was what he'd fought for, wasn't it? The right to *not* be doing those things.

The strangeness of it all ate away at him. For hours he'd been unable to decide why he felt so strange, and then a few hours ago he'd come to something of an epiphany. It was because things were *continuing*. In the back of his mind, he'd been expecting end credits to roll, the word 'Fin' to appear. The events he'd been through were so outlandish, so shattering, that for real life ever to return seemed one miracle too far. And yet if real life, if nappies and bedtime rituals and worries about paying for oil never returned, what the fuck had it all been *for*?

He couldn't stop thinking about Steve, about his father. Mired down there, in a dark reflection of this world – a partitioned shadow of Ireland that ran on magic and where death was only a momentary inconvenience. Would he ever see them again?

The bedroom television was on in the background, volume turned down to a fraction above mute. The murmur of voices used to always help Luke get to sleep. Danny was just grateful that Ellie had finally relaxed enough to get some sleep of her own.

'What about us?' she had asked him, before she had gone to sleep.

'Us?'

'Everything we've been through. I feel like I'm supposed to cuddle up to you and give you some sort of speech about how I've realised how you and I are meant to be together and how nothing's ever going to change that. Then we kiss and everything's fine, forever.'

He kissed the top of her head. 'I love you,' he said. 'All I know, all I can say for absolute certain is that I remember – when things *changed* – I remember how *wrong* it felt to feel someone else's head on me, lying where you are right now. I know that's not some grand speech that makes everything okay, but–'

She shook her head. 'You eejit,' she said softly. 'It kinda does. I love you too.'

Those had been the last words she had uttered before sleep had claimed her, and that had been almost three hours ago now.

There was a knock at the front door. Loud, insistent.

Amazingly, given her jumpiness and overprotective mania, Ellie still had not stirred. Luke likewise remained flat out. But it wasn't going to be possible to just lie there and ignore it and, c'mon, what evil faerie worth its salt was going to knock on the front door?

Gently, he extricated himself from the duvet and, stepping carefully so as not to disturb his sleeping girlfriend and son, quickly pulled on jeans, trainers and a T shirt. If it *was* a faerie demon, fuckin' sure he wasn't going to face it *au naturel* or wearing a fluffy blue Eeyore robe.

It wasn't a faerie.

'Danny,' Brigadier Hughes said. If Danny thought the man had looked haggard when they'd first met – cut off from the rest of the human race and armed with non-functioning guns – it was nothing compared to how he looked now.

'Brigadier? What's wrong?'

'They don't understand what's happening here! When we told them what we'd seen it only made things worse! Olympus …'

Well, here it was. Danny had known the other shoe would drop sometime; he just hadn't expected it to be this soon. 'What's happening?' he asked.

After the Otherworld and the Dagda's Cauldron, Lircom Tower and the battle with Carman, whatever the man had to tell him couldn't possibly be that bad.

*

From launch silos across America and Russia, the missiles emerged, trailing fire into the skies. Calculations had established that it would take two hundred and seventeen warheads with a five-megaton yield to effectively carpet-bomb the surface area of Ireland into a radioactive quagmire from which nothing would grow for thousands of years.

England and France had, not surprisingly, raised a few issues with this approach but the response from the rest of the world was swift.

It was the only way to be sure.

IRELAND BELOW, NOW

'Hello,' Carman said. Her face was being broadcast on all TV channels, her voice simulcast on all radio frequencies. Every television and radio in the land had switched itself on to tune itself in. She was sitting, not on a faerie throne, not in a standing stone circle, but in a place they all recognised. She was in Stormont, in a room of wood panels and blue carpets. She was looking particularly human. She wore no otherworldly attire, merely a modest gold circlet around her head and what looked like a very businesswoman-esque light green jacket.

She was sitting in the speaker's chair.

As if to acknowledge her appearance and setting, she smiled disarmingly into the camera. 'I realise this method of communication is a little different to the one I used before,' she said, inclining her head with a slight grimace, almost as if she were acknowledging an error on her part. 'Well, what can I say? I'm learning. And I have a lot to learn.'

Her expression hardened slightly, but only slightly. 'We all do,' she said. 'Like it or not – and I'm sure, for all of you watching me out there, it's *not* – you're my guests down here. Some of you chose this. Most of you didn't. All of you will be wondering just what exactly you're in for. I'll admit that, until recently, things didn't look too bright, did they? Our worlds are so different. Yours runs on technology, on electricity. Mine has none of these things.'

She smiled. 'You're probably wondering how you're watching me now if I'm telling you electricity doesn't exist down here. The reason is because your technology, your televisions, your fridges, your iPods, every little gadget you've come to surround yourself with over the last hundred years or so – I have reconfigured them to run on something else, an alternative source of power. Magic. This world runs on magic,' she smiled.

'I'd hazard a guess that until very recently, most of you would have been convinced magic was fiction. Now you know better. But what you know is only the beginning. Where you came from the magic has been running out, winding down. Up there, it's almost gone. But down here, well, down here, you'll see that things are *quite* different. Magic is unlike anything you know. It's more than a source of power. It's clean. It's' – she paused, but only for half a heartbeat, a pause easy to miss – 'limitless. I'm not only piping it into your homes, so you can use it to power all of the things you've grown dependent upon. I'm giving it to *you*. All of you. I'm giving you all *back* something that was taken from you hundreds of years before any of you were even born. Something you all miss terribly, without even knowing what it is, without even knowing why.'

Hearing her words, in homes all over the country, Carman's new subjects, over one million souls strong, sensed that if there was to be a *but* anywhere in this speech, it was imminent. Hands tightened around other hands, or gripped chairs. Children were clutched. No-one could look away from those eyes, those perpetually calm and never-blinking eyes staring back at them from their televisions.

Never one to disappoint, Carman told them exactly what she wanted in return.

'Your leaders,' she said, and the camera panned around to take in the assembled ranks of politicians, all sitting emotionlessly, 'have been wise. They have asked me to assume responsibility for the well-being of all the souls on this island. You once prayed to a distant and unfeeling God who never answered those prayers. All I ask is that once a day, you pray to a goddess who will never fail to.'

BELGRAVIA AVENUE, BELFAST BELOW, NOW

The transmission ended.

'Is she takin' the piss?' Steve said. '*Pray* to her?'

Wily's voice was emotionless. 'Look around you, Steve. She's brought back electricity. Light. Methods of communication.'

Despite his best attempts not to, Steve thought of that moment inside the standing stone circle when Carman had changed from woman-shaped and humanoid to something so far beyond his worst fears he suspected – hoped – that it would take his nightmares a while to catch up.

'She runs on belief. She's powered by worship,' Wily said. 'Before long, she'll have more power than she's ever had.'

''To do what?' Tony wondered aloud. 'She swore an oath to stay away from the surface world, an oath she can't break no matter how much power she gets.'

'The oath cannot be broken,' Wily said. 'But it can be withdrawn. Only by the same person who made her swear it in the first place.'

'Danny?' Tony shook his head. 'Why the hell would Danny *ever* do that?'

LIRCOM TOWER, BELFAST ABOVE, NOW

The doors to Dother's office at the top of the (still very much in existence) Lircom Tower were thrown open with such force that they shattered.

'Do come in,' Dother, sitting at his desk, said mildly.

'Surprised to see you back here, *boss*,' Danny said. 'Thought you'd had enough of it all?'

'Oh, I have,' Dother replied.

'Then what are you doing here?'

'One last job,' the man formerly known as Mr Black replied. He was looking at Danny in a way the younger man couldn't quite decipher. Gone was the malice and the hunger. In its place was something that could almost be mistaken for desperation. He had the nagging feeling Dother was trying to communicate with him without speaking aloud. The pity was, he hadn't time for games.

'Where's the Sword?' Danny said. 'She promised she'd send it back. I'm betting she was stupid enough to send it right here.'

Dother pursed his lips and shrugged. 'Yeah,' he agreed readily, and reached under the desk, hefting and sliding an object across the ornate surface. 'Nail on the head there.'

'The fuck is *this* meant to be?'

'This,' Dother said, indicating the charred, burnt-out sliver of metal, 'is the Silver Sword of Nuada. Well, what's left of it. You juiced it up nicely once upon a time, but resurrecting all those people, splitting a landmass in two and throwing the original back through a portal ... well, it takes its toll.'

Danny lifted the remnants of the once nigh-omnipotent relic. Dother wasn't lying, he could have sensed it if he was. He discarded the ruin of the Sword with disgust. So much for *that* part of the plan.

'After all this, our own people are gonna blow us all to fuck?' Danny said. Ellie was right behind him, baby Luke bundled up in her arms.

'So you've heard? The news leaked moments ago,' Dother said, pointing to himself casually with a thumb. 'Can't think who may have released it to the masses. Twitter is abuzz with horror. Rest assured I'm unfollowing several world leaders in protest.'

With a flick of his arms, Danny sent the ornate desk tumbling end-over-end until it crashed against the thick glass of the windows of the Lircom Tower penthouse. He grabbed his former CEO by the lapels of his expensive suit, so that his feet no longer touched the ground and strode purposefully to the windows he had just weakened.

'If you're asking for a pay rise,' Dother remarked, 'I fear you may have left it a little late.'

'Do *not* fuck me about,' Danny said. 'I didn't go through hell over the last few days with the family Faerie just so we could all come back up here and be nuked. Stop it.'

As he spoke, he pushed Dother against the glass. The cracks in the windows spread from the pressure exerted by Dother's body.

'I'm open to suggestions,' Dother managed.

Danny stretched out his hand and Dother's phone leapt through the air and dropped neatly into his palm.

'Get yer ma on the phone. Now,' Danny said. 'We need to talk.'

BELGRAVIA AVENUE, BELFAST BELOW, NOW

In Tony Morrigan, Steve knew he'd found someone else who had experienced every single toe of the kick in the balls the last few days had been.

After Carman's television address, they had debated long into the night about what their next move would be. Steve had contributed, at first, but more and more he'd found himself lapsing into silence. Now, he was just staring blankly out of the window.

It was too much to take in. He'd lost his best friend, lost his entire way of life. In the course of that crazy night when Belfast had gone to hell, when he'd charged around with Larka like some sort of knight on wolfback, it had been … well, it had been fucking terrifying, but he'd felt energised, like he was *part* of something, making a difference. Killing those things and protecting Maggie – well, it was proper caveman stuff, wasn't it? A far cry from clocking in for a nine to five job, slaving over a hot network setup for some faceless small business.

The clarity he'd felt at being the knight had been swept away. The monsters were gone. The closest thing to them were the Named, and he feared what would happen if they turned – though considering the way the humans down here were treating them, he'd be hard pressed to blame the wolves if they did. Travelling here to Tony's house earlier, Wily and Larka had been the subject of much abuse. The wolves were the only plainly otherworldly creatures now in sight, despite the fact that, if not for their heroics …

But that was the rub, wasn't it?

His actions, those of the wolves, they'd made no difference. At least, not to the people trapped down here. Those who the Named had saved from death had escaped, allowed to live in Ireland Above. Those who had been killed before the Named could intervene had been forced to stick around, to live in this perpetual darkness and seeing a horde of talking wolves stalking the crimson streets of Belfast at one in the afternoon did little to improve their outlook, whether the televisions were working again or not.

Apathy was overwhelming him. He could feel it rising up from his bones to choke his spirit, and yet he could think of nothing to spur him into fighting it off.

You have your family to take care of, he told himself. But did he? If death wasn't even possible here, what looking after would they require, exactly?

He could see the future stretching out before him. It was filled with two kinds of people – those who would cower in their homes, too old or too young or too timid to understand what kind of world they'd found themselves in; and the other sort, the ones who would adapt in all the wrong ways to this place.

How were they supposed to save people? Three humans and a group of talking wolves, versus an ancient and incredibly powerful witch who already, it seemed, had a fair portion of the country's governing machinery behind her.

How were they supposed to save people who didn't need saving? If Carman was trying to win some sort of popularity contest here in order to power her magic, she wasn't likely to start breeding her hellish minions and sending them to the four corners of the country to terrorise people. And even if she *did*, he'd witnessed first hand that anyone killed would simply spring back to life again.

Worst of all, how were they meant to save people who didn't *want* saving?

His phone rang. He started in surprise and fished it from his back pocket.

As he looked at the name displayed, his fingers became as dextrous as oven mitts, and the phone slipped from his grasp, clattering to the floor.

PARLIAMENT BUILDINGS, STORMONT,
BELFAST BELOW, NOW

She had an aide now. He wasn't a giant spider like Dother's had been, but she could fix that. The little man didn't have a spidery look about him. He was more of a rat …

He scurried over to her, holding her mobile. 'First Minister,' he gabbled excitedly, 'it's him.'

She waved for everyone to leave the assembly chambers. 'Danny,' she purred. 'I had a feeling you'd be calling ...'

'You broke the oath.'

'I did no such thing,' Carman replied, indignant. 'This decision has been taken by *your* world's leaders, Danny. Shocking lack of humanity. As the leader of a sovereign nation, you can rest assured I shall be sending a strongly worded email.'

'You expect me to believe you didn't cause this?' Danny said.

'I expect you to remember that the clock is ticking. We can stand here and debate who's lying to whom but I have a feeling your side of this call's about to experience some transmission issues. Unless you plan to learn how to saddle a giant cockroach and buy some three-legged trousers, I suggest you be a dear and have my son set up a – what are they called, rat? Oh yes – a videoconference, won't you?'

Danny reeled off a number to Dother and a large LCD screen slid down from the ceiling, like something off a Bond film. If Danny had had time, he'd have been jealous. Carman's image appeared on the screen.

'How am I even able to talk to you, let alone see you? You said we couldn't breach the gap between you and us anymore,' Danny said.

'No,' Carman replied. Danny saw, with a sinking heart, that she was currently sitting in the assembly chambers in Stormont looking like she owned the fucking place, 'I didn't say we *couldn't*, Danny. I just said I *wouldn't* as part of our agreement,' and she flashed him a dazzling smile that seemed to have too many teeth, far too many teeth. 'But that *is* what we're here to discuss, isn't it? Dother, be a good boy and show him how precarious his situation is. I know you can.'

Dother worked more controls, pausing to look at Danny once again. There it was, a flicker, a gleam, some intangible fragment of a message that Danny was supposed to be picking up on, gone as quickly as it had appeared. As he worked with the screen, a video feed appeared in the corner of the conference call.

'Missile trajectories,' Carman said.

'Fuckin' hairy Christ,' Danny breathed. There were dozens of the things, all heading for Ireland. 'Stop them. *Stop them!*'

Carman shrugged. 'That power lies within me, but, as someone wise once said, if you're good at something, never do it for free.'

He looked at Ellie, and saw his own growing suspicion mirrored on her face. He turned to face the video screen.

'What do you want?'

'What does any self-respecting goddess want?' she replied, leaning forward. She was staring directly at Luke, her eyes glittering. 'Sacrifice.'

BELFAST BELOW, NOW

Larka had brought him here as quickly as she could. Steve dismounted and nodded to her in gratitude, as he always did. She returned the gesture, but did not move to follow him, for which he was grateful.

She was there already, leaning on the railings and looking out across the Lagan. Her hair was whipping in the cold wind, and Steve noticed that there was no scent of the sea in the air – perhaps because, beyond the shores of Ireland, no true sea now existed. He didn't know and right now, he didn't really care.

'Maggie?' he said softly, when he had reached her.

She didn't turn. Her phone, he saw, was still in her hands. He saw her pocket it and, unsure how to proceed, unsure whether he should embrace her in case she reacted badly for some reason, he settled for standing beside her at the river's edge, the Lagan Weir footbridge immediately to their right.

He couldn't stop himself from looking at her, mostly to reassure himself that this wasn't some hideous prank Carman was pulling. It wasn't. He couldn't stop the fingers of his left hand from covering the fingers of her right. He intertwined them with hers. She made no effort to stop him.

'Maggie?' he tried again.

Her make up was streaked and her eyes were red. She had the look of someone who was cried out. She still didn't look at him, staring ahead to some point at the head of Belfast harbour.

'I thought,' he began, and had to gather himself. 'I thought you'd gone.'

'I wanted to,' she whispered.

Not enough, you didn't, he thought. He said nothing, content for now just to hold her hand.

324

'This place …' she said, shivering, finally tearing her gaze away from the watery horizon, which presumably now led to nowhere. 'It's awful. It's horrible. It terrifies me. I didn't think in a million years that I'd want to stay in a place like this.'

'Then why did you?'

She turned. Instead of the love he'd hoped to see, there was hardness and anger on her face. 'For *you*,' she said. 'I stayed for *you*, Steve. I've got no family here. I've left everything behind. *Everyone*. To be with you.'

There were a thousand different responses to that, but in the end, Steve went for the simplest, and, without doubt, the most heartfelt. 'Thank you.'

'I must … I must want this. Us. Right? Otherwise I would have gone, right?'

'You're stronger than you think you are,' he told her.

'How can we make this work? Here?'

'I don't know.'

'What will we do? How will we live?'

'I think,' he said carefully, in the instant before he kissed her, 'this is where we find out.'

LIRCOM TOWER, BELFAST ABOVE, NOW

'Away and fuck yourself.'

'Send him to me, Danny. My mistake before was taking him from you. This time, you'll send him back to his loving *Mitéra*. Oh, and in addition you'll forfeit any and all agreements for me to stay away from those lovely sunlit lands up above, but I expect you already knew that.'

'Hi,' Ellie broke in suddenly, stepping in front of Danny to address Carman directly. 'Remember me? I was the one who punched your ugly oul cunting face across this room. Give you Luke? You ever come near my baby again I'll make before look like a *picnic in the fuckin' park*, do you get me?'

Carman shrugged. 'As you wish. I hear Boots has a 3 for 2 on Ambre Solaire. I suggest you go there now. Avoid the rush.'

'I'd think about this if I were you,' Dother said mildly. He addressed Danny directly, eye-to-eye, and Danny was overpowered with synaesthesia – sensations flooded him with every word Dother spoke, one in particular, over and over again. 'Sending your child below is better than having him end up as radioactive dust when those missiles hit in … four minutes from now. And there's the small matter of the millions of others about to be obliterated.'

Purple. Purple. Purple. The colour was flashing in every word Dother spoke. It was Ellie's colour, Ellie's taste, the sensation that had brought him around in the bizarro-Belfast; it was his echo-location of truth, his epicentre of rightness, and right now it was coming off Dother in droves.

Danny wanted to vomit. He wanted to scream. He wanted to put his fist through every faerie, every fucking *person* in the world. Looking at Ellie now, as she held her sleeping baby close, he saw she was going through the same hell. How was anyone supposed to make a choice like this?

Giving Luke away, however much their hands were twisted behind their backs, was still giving him away. Considering what they'd both gone through to get him back, he knew sacrificing their child would destroy him and inevitably destroy Ellie.

He had an impossible choice to make, and he had four minutes to make it.

Larka returned to Steve's house alone.

'How did it go?' Wily asked her, when Tony and Dermot were out of earshot.

'The boy has his purpose back.'

'Larka, I understand your connection with the boy …'

'He must never know,' the she-wolf said, flattening herself and growling at Wily, ready to launch herself despite his height and weight advantage.

Wily made the proper gesture of submission. 'You think she will honestly come to believe that deep down this is what she wanted? To stay here?'

'How will she know otherwise?' Larka countered defensively. 'In keeping her here, I acted out of kindness. Without her, he would have lost all hope.'

'Their entire relationship will be based on a lie. She was not prepared to sacrifice everything to be with him.'

'So what?' Larka countered hotly. 'Why should *anyone* have to make that choice, let alone a human? Carman delights in playing to their concept of what true love is – some grand sacrificial gesture – and those who are not prepared to accept it are left to think of themselves as weak. I do not think that is love.'

'You're right,' Wily replied evenly. 'It may not be love. But it may be human.'

Larka sighed. 'How do we know? We were such simple creatures before the Morrigan changed us. Now we have emotions and feelings. How will we live? As wolves pretending to be human, or as humans who look like wolves?'

Wily nuzzled her. 'We will live as we wish to,' he said firmly. 'We are the Named, and nothing will–'

'I'm pregnant,' she broke in.

'Oh, *balls*.'

LIRCOM TOWER, BELFAST ABOVE, NOW

'Portal,' Carman said and, with that one word, a crack appeared in the world directly between the video wall and where Danny and Ellie stood, a crack through which he could see the assembly office in Stormont and Carman herself, standing not ten feet away. Slowly, with an evil smile spreading across her face, she spread her arms wide as though expecting to receive a present.

'I can't,' Ellie sobbed. She turned away from Danny, as though fearing he was about to lunge for her, or for their son. He burned to see the movement, the sudden flaring of distrust, because he knew it too would be heavenly for Carman to witness.

'I can't, I can't, I CAN'T! I WON'T EVER!' she screamed, and somehow the baby slept on, even as every remaining window in that magically rebuilt penthouse office blew outward, glass shattering. Shock passed over Ellie's face as she realised she was the source of the explosion.

'There's that family heri–' Carman began, and then coughed. Just once. She recovered herself, patting her chest, a momentary look of puzzlement on her face.

Despite Ellie's distress, Danny found his attention inexorably drawn to Dother. The man, or whatever approximation of a man he was, remained seated. Tastes flooded Danny's mouth, smells assaulted his nostrils. Phantom sounds rang through his ears. It was nothing short of a full-scale assault on the senses, but it was not done to confuse or to obfuscate, he knew that now. It was a message.

Purple. The colour of trust.

Trust me, Dother was telling Danny.

He flashed back to storming back into the office. *One last job*, Dother had said. Danny had assumed Dother meant one final task to be performed for his mother. What if he hadn't?

The sword, hollow and useless, shrivelled. Carman standing near the portal's edge, reaching forward eagerly to retake his son, ravenous for his power. He saw her cough again, lose her concentration for a moment, and in that instant Dother's placid expression wavered and the sensory tsunami he was sending Danny's way increased a hundredfold.

And Danny understood what he had to do.

You will know, Danny. You will know when the time comes. The Morrigan's final words, before she had been swallowed whole by Carman. *Love will form your choice.*

'Make your choice, Danny,' Carman said.

In the end, it all came down to this.

'I'm sorry,' he told Ellie, and he held out his hand toward her.

'What are – NO!' she said, and she felt her arms and legs freeze in place, just they had in the stone circle the first time they'd faced off against Carman together. Danny was doing this, he was holding her securely in place.

He took the sleeping baby from her paralysed grip. Ellie screamed and cursed and called him all the bastards and the fuckers of the day, promising and pleading and sobbing.

'I'm sorry,' he said again, and he took their son away from her. As soon as Luke was in his arms his eyes opened and he began to wail. The sound of it cut through Danny. He had never seen his son act like this. The baby thrashed and screamed and threw out his arms to get back to Ellie, and all she could do was scream in response.

Danny turned away from Ellie, toward Carman. He moved toward the portal at a run, extending his arms to thrust Luke through the crack and into the waiting arms of Carman who rushed forward from the other side.

She stopped, another cough wracking through her body. Confused, she raised a hand to her mouth and, as Danny watched, she pulled something from her mouth, something long and black.

And feathered.

She belongs to this world and to yours, to both and to neither …

'NOW!' Danny called.

Mid-stride, he turned and threw Luke back to Ellie like a rugby player passing the ball. He used all the abilities he had to ensure the baby had a smooth passage through the air before dropping into Ellie's outstretched arms once more. Coming out of her paralysis, Ellie clutched her son to her with a grip no earthly power could have shifted. Mother and baby crumpled into a ball.

Erupting from his seat like something out of legend, Dother threw the Sword end-over-end.

Danny reached through the portal, as a large and satisfied crow stuck its big ugly head out of Carman's horrified mouth. 'Haven't got all fucking day!' it said in a familiar female voice.

With his right hand, without looking, Danny caught the Sword of Nuada. The crow leapt from Carman's mouth and plunged forward, merging with the blackened ruin of the Sword. Becoming the Sword. Silver light erupted across the length of the blade.

With his left hand, he pulled Carman halfway through the portal, halfway between our world and theirs, halfway between the realms of magic and science, and he looked her straight in the eyes as he said, 'I choose *this*.'

With that, he drove the Sword hilt-deep right through her black heart, a stroke that began in our world, passed through the nether space between and ended in the Otherworld she called her own.

NOWHERE

Danny found himself back in the whitespace between spaces, the blank canvas from which he had created a universe. Here, after being ripped apart by Carman's faeries and tossed into the Dagda's cauldron, left alone for a time beyond time, he had come to terms with his abilities, but not before the solitude had almost driven him mad.

He was not alone here now.

'WHAT DID YOU DO TO ME?' Carman thundered, a lumbering black mass lunging toward him, still with the Sword thrust through her.

The elevator cable of creation snapped.

In a featureless white nothing, it should have been impossible to feel a sensation of falling, and yet Danny felt as though he were plummeting, accelerating beyond the speed of light. He was aware that Carman was also falling, but he was too busy trying to stop screaming to care.

There was no *splat* of impact. In fact he couldn't quite pinpoint when the falling sensation ended, only that the endless whiteness had given way to a landscape infinitely worse, a tapestry of red. The heat more than oppressive, eighteen notches above unbearable. It was a living thing, worming its way through his body and searing him. Sulphur stung his eyes until they were next to useless, and even using his synaesthesia to change the nature of things couldn't fully clear the effect – whether it was because he wasn't powerful enough, or because he couldn't focus his talents, he wasn't sure. He was even less sure that he *wanted* to see properly.

'Carman of Athens …' a voice from the depths rumbled. His first instinct was to look for its source. Thankfully, his mind intervened and prevented him.

The witch-queen was begging, fumbling, repeating, 'My Lord,' over and over.

'Welcome home,' the voice said.

She was gone from beside him. If he had strained, he may have heard a sound that was halfway between a splinter and a splash. He didn't strain.

There was something in front of him. The voice's owner had risen from below. Danny couldn't look away. Even with his synaesthesia firing, he could only discern parts of the whole. His eyes wouldn't close, no matter how hard he tried. Nothing was working anymore. He felt like a full stop that had found itself staring at *War and Peace*.

'You …' the voice said, and even hearing the word almost drove Danny out of his mind. This was it. He was about to die at the whim of this awakening behemoth.

But before that unmentionable beast could utter another sound, something cool wrapped around his hand and pulled, and he felt a sensation of rising that was every bit the equal of the falling he'd just experienced.

'Trust me when I tell you this,' the Morrigan said, glorious in her goddess guise once more. 'Do *not* look down.'

WASHINGTON DC, NOW

Those assembled in the room watched the computer track the progress of the airburst nuclear warheads, designed to detonate a quarter-mile above ground level for maximum dispersal, as they arced into the Earth's atmosphere and then descended.

Olympus was still rising. It was now the highest mountain outside the Himalayas. The seismic shift caused by its elevation was devastating the Greek lowlands, causing a tsunami to race across the relatively narrow expanse of the Mediterranean and smash into North Africa.

A massive super storm was raging at the rising summit of the impossible mountain. From space, the size and colour of the storm front looked like something lifted from the atmosphere of Jupiter or Saturn, entirely out of place on planet Earth. Gargantuan flashes of lightning peppered the storm, illuminating its ferocity from within, lancing out and connecting earth and heaven in massive river deltas written in pure light.

'Impact in thirty seconds.'

LIRCOM TOWER, BELFAST ABOVE, NOW

Danny burst through the door onto the roof of Lircom Tower. Above their heads, streaking across the skies, they could see it; a tiny contrail of white about to become an annihilation blast that would wipe the city clean of all life.

Not if the goddess beside him had anything to do with it. The Morrigan was restored, tall and shining, beautiful and invincible. The Sword was gone – she *was* the weapon now, he knew. She seemed to pulse, a silver heartbeat reverberating through her, from her.

Time seemed to slow and shrink until all that he could see was the goddess and the white streak descending from the heavens. Nothing else.

'Thank you,' he told her, knowing this was it. 'You brought me through hell.'

'Hades, to be precise,' she corrected him, smiling. 'Thank *you*,

Danny. It had been a few thousand years since I'd been human and I had forgotten what it really meant. Then you showed up and you were human enough for the both of us.'

'What happened to her? To Carman?' Danny asked.

The Morrigan smiled, not pleasantly. 'She got her wish. She finally got noticed.'

'Is this really it?' he asked her. 'Is this how it all ends?'

She nodded towards the warhead falling in bullet-time. 'Remember when Carman said the power lay within her to stop them?' she said, and tapped herself on the chest. 'She was talking about me. I can do this. After all …' and she smiled and bared her teeth proudly, addressing the whole world, 'I *am* the Goddess of fucking War.'

'You can stop nukes?' Danny said, hardly daring to hope.

'What is magic but turning one thing into another?' she said. 'When they explode, when their power is released, I will change it. Destruction will become creation. You'll see, Danny. I promise.'

'Simple as that?' he said.

She shook her head. 'No, not quite. Converting this much raw energy … I don't know what it will do to me. I'll probably be scattered beyond even my people's ability to regenerate. But who knows? Perhaps this will be a new beginning for me as well. I believe … I believe I could use one,' and she kissed him, on the cheek.

'Follow your heart, Danny Morrigan,' she told him. 'Don't take the long way around.'

She changed her shape to that of a bird for the last time, if you could call the dragon-sized, jet-black magnificent creature hovering there something as mundane as a bird. He knew at that moment, for the first time, he was seeing her as she would have appeared on the battlefield in her prime. The omen of victory.

'Go as the crow flies,' she said.

With that, she took off like a bullet in an unerringly straight line toward the falling missiles. There was a flash as the nearest warhead detonated, and a blindingly brilliant tendril of nuclear fire was birthed into the world.

THE FUTURE

The little girl woke up, just for an instant. 'Oh,' was all she said, and her eyes closed once more.

'She knows,' her mother said.

LIRCOM TOWER, BELFAST ABOVE, NOW

Danny risked opening his eyes. When he'd felt that incredible flash of light wash over him, bright enough that he could see his very bones through his skin, he'd expected to feel the wave of heat and the crushing kiss of oblivion. Neither had materialised. Belfast was still standing – bathed in glorious, undiluted light.

The blast had been frozen. A second sun, suspended high in the skies above Belfast, was blazing with ferocious intensity. Toward the horizon, in every direction, he could see a third, a fourth, a fifth – a suspended daisy-chain of obviated oblivion, a string of nuclear pearls.

Doomsday had been aborted.

*

It was the same all over Ireland.

The warheads detonated successfully, every single one of the two hundred and seventeen launched achieved nuclear fission reaction a quarter-mile above ground level.

A nanosecond after detonation, in the light of the blinding flash produced on detonation, every single one of those explosions was frozen in place, pinned to the sky like a butterfly in a collector's album.

Every one of the country's incredulous population found themselves bathed under a string of blinding flares of light popping in the skies above, as though the Milky Way had turned into a camera lens and was taking a photo of all of existence, with Ireland as its flashbulb.

And how it *shone*.

The flares did not fade away. Two hundred and seventeen suns now burned in Ireland's skies. It looked like Tatooine's wet dream. All over, people emerged from their homes, blinking in disbelief. The light should have fried them in place a hundred times over, cast nothing but human-shaped shadows onto a ruined ground. Blast waves should have knocked over buildings like matchsticks and seared mountainsides and valleys clean.

None of that happened.

The light from above felt warm, and it was hard to stare at those sources of light, much as one could not stare directly at the sun, but that was it. That was all.

On the roof of Lircom Tower, Danny Morrigan sat down on the hard concrete and did something he hadn't done since he was a small boy.

He prayed his thanks.

LIRCOM TOWER, BELFAST ABOVE, TWO WEEKS PD (POST DETONATION)

Danny looked into the sea of camera lenses and microphones, shielding his eyes from the camera flashes. He was a spokesperson. Time to start acting like one.

'My name is Danny Morrigan, Director of Communications at Lircom. Thank you all for coming along. I'm sure you must all be grateful for a news story, God knows it's been kind of quiet out there.'

A slight ripple of laughter passed through the throng. The past fortnight had been anything but quiet. The highest mountain on the planet now belonged to Greece, not to Tibet. The seismic upheavals that had accompanied this shift had had devastating consequences for the entire eastern Mediterranean, although – and nobody quite knew how – human casualties had been spectacularly low.

Prayers had been answered.

Satellites trying to peer through the lightning storm surrounding the summit had been swatted from orbit by targeted electrical bursts, directed – some were muttering the word *thrown* – with pinpoint accuracy.

The complete nuclear annihilation of Ireland had been averted. A second wave of missiles had, of course, immediately been triggered but these missiles never got beyond their launch pads. Mysterious, unstoppable system failures were plaguing every weapon of mass destruction on planet Earth.

HARRISON STREET, BELFAST BELOW, TWO WEEKS PD

In a huge and empty house on one of the poshest roads in Belfast, a house they'd laid claim to ten days previously and which they were starting to furnish, Steve lay with Maggie in a post-coital tangle of arms and legs.

Though they were already pressed together, Maggie cuddled herself closer and Steve moved his limbs slightly to allow her to do so. It was dark outside, as it always was in this world, but in his heart, all he felt was a contentment that he hadn't felt in so long.

Maggie was quiet. The sex had been good and the orgasm had made her feel something other than despair. Now, afterward, she could feel the darkness outside pressing inward once more.

The loneliness, the knowledge that she was shut off from the rest of the world, everything she'd ever known, reached out, and the only thing she could think of to do was to worm closer to Steve's sweat-soaked skin.

I wanted this, she thought. *I stayed here. I must have wanted this.*

It was warm in bed and the bedroom was brightly lit, but in her heart, all she felt was cold and empty.

LIRCOM TOWER, BELFAST ABOVE, TWO WEEKS PD

'Lircom will be able to use our state of the art communications network to do something unprecedented. Something the whole of this island is crying out for.'

Danny paused. Dother was watching from the sidelines.

'We're going to give people here the ability, through the phones, through text messages, through the Internet even, to get back in touch with the loved ones they lost.'

He licked his lips, knowing what he was about to say would change the world all over again. 'We can bridge the gap between the Ireland Above and the Ireland Below. We will work to bring them both back together.'

The rest of his speech was drowned out completely by the uproar that ensued.

REGENT STREET, BELFAST ABOVE, TWO WEEKS PD

'Here comes the big aeroplane!'

'Pbbbbt,' said Luke, blowing a disgusted raspberry.

'Here it comes!'

'Pbbt!'

Another globule of baby muck came dribbling out of his mouth. He fixed Danny with a look and then chuckled delightedly at his own wit, grabbing for the food pot and his own ear simultaneously.

'Fuck the big aeroplane?' Danny said.

Luke laughed. Danny plucked him from the high chair in one motion and deposited him flat on his back on the sofa and proceeded to tickle his belly until the baby was gasping for air from laughing. After that he was dropped into his *Doctor Who* walker and he was off, happily pinballing around the living room and hitting the buttons to make Dalek noises, much to his apparent confusion.

Watching him, Danny had to fight the urge to pluck him out and gather him back up. Working with Dother these past few weeks had not been easy. He had been at great pains to point out that he had helped Danny considerably. His depth of knowledge and his power made him an impossible ally to refuse, particularly if Danny ever wanted to get in contact with his father and Steve again. Carman may have been able to open portals with a wave of her hand, but Danny was nowhere near that league, and if Dother was, he wasn't telling.

Telling Ellie that he had taken a job working with the man who had run her father through with a sword had been … an experience.

It was more than that, though.

In the stone circle, when she'd charged at Carman in the throes of a berserker rage, Danny had pinned her with his mind. The move had probably saved her life, but she'd made him promise never to do that to her again. He'd broken that promise in Dother's office.

Danny went into the kitchen to find Ellie there, with her

scented washing-up liquid out from under the sink. She wasn't actually doing the dishes, of course, she was doing the puzzle word in *Take A Break*, but she had all the equipment ready, and that was the main thing.

He kissed her and felt it again, that half-second of hesitation.

'I'm sorry,' he said for the hundredth time.

'You don't need to keep saying that.'

'Yes I do,' he sighed. 'Ellie, it was all an act. You know that. I hadn't time to explain anything and even if I had, there's a chance she could have read both of our minds. I realised what it meant, what I had to do, and I had about two nanoseconds to make a decision and I made it. I'd *never* hurt Luke. I'd *never* give him up. Never.'

'When she remade the world for us, you had given him up.'

'That wasn't *my* wish, remember?' he said pointedly.

'Neither was having him in the first place.'

'No,' he admitted. 'But it wasn't yours, either. When we were in that stone circle and Carman showed us our past, I was ashamed of myself – not for the thoughts I'd had back then, but because I'd never really taken the time to think what it was like for *you*. You were going to look after Luke no matter what choice I made and you stood to sacrifice just as much as me, and yet I was one acting like a spoiled dick.'

'I thought you were building up the courage to leave me,' Ellie said quietly. 'When you left for work that day, the day it all began, I needed to know. I was going to ask you–'

Danny kissed her then, impulsively, out of a sudden need. She didn't turn away and there was no hesitation in the kiss this time, but when it broke she looked up at him, still troubled.

'I won't–'

'Shut up,' she said, not unkindly. 'Don't say what'll never happen, Danny. If the past few days have shown anything it's that nothing can be ruled out. I can't promise anything any more than you can, so please don't.'

'No,' he shook his head. 'You're wrong, Ellie. I love Luke, and I'm in love with you. I know both of those things are true right at this moment. I know I want to stay with you. I know making things work with you took effort and will continue to take effort, but it doesn't *feel* like work. But if it ever does, and I can't promise it won't …' he took a deep breath. 'I promise to *try*, Ellie. I promise I'll never just walk away.'

He thought of a hundred other things to say and a hundred other questions he could ask, but he dismissed them all and held her close, knowing he'd made the right choice.

'So much has happened,' she said. 'Part of me wishes we could just …'

'Hit a big reset button and go back to before?'

'Yes,' she admitted. 'I mean, how are we supposed to process any of this? *Magic is real?* Not only that but the world *knows* it is. There's been so much damage – Ireland and Greece shut off from the rest of Europe, no-one knows what's happening in India and Norway and Australia. It's like it's a whole different world now. We've seen our son all grown up and now he's a baby again and you, me, him … all of us are caught up in this in ways I don't fully understand and I'm not even sure I want to. I don't know what sort of world this is any more and I'm scared of what that means for *me*, Danny. Not to be selfish about it or anything, but what does it mean for *us* and for ...' she waved into the living room where Luke was, from the sounds of it, busily trying to EX-TER-MIN-ATE one of their walls.

'Do you love me?' he asked her, and then shook his head as he saw her start to mull it over. 'No, no, no. Don't think about it, just answer the question with the first answer that pops into your head.'

There was a pause.

'Well?' he said, sounding slightly worried.

She laughed. 'Well I had all that time you were talking about saying the first thing that pops into my head to think about it. So it's not really gonna work any more, is it?'

With a tiny amount of trial and a frankly ridiculous amount of error, Luke had emerged from the living room in his walker. He bumped into his old nemesis the kitchen baby-gate and squealed at it by way of greeting before beginning to plot its fiery destruction.

'True,' Danny allowed, inclining his head at her. 'If only there was another question you wouldn't have had time to think about.'

'Yeah, well,' Ellie said, putting down her magazine and picking up a pie-encrusted pot to begin washing the dishes. 'There–'

Crash.

'–isn't,' she finished, staring down at the ring in Danny's outstretched hand. She jumped into his arms and they danced around their tiny kitchen – a room so small you couldn't have swung a crow in it.

Luke's little head bobbed up and down, once. Then, too low for Mummy and Daddy to hear, he gurgled, 'Uck meee!'

It *could* have just been random baby noises, and not some vestige of his adult self, some spark of intelligence and destiny pinging around in there behind those tiny, mad, baby eyes.

It probably was. Almost certainly.

When Ellie and he finally separated, Danny pressed against her and asked her in a low, seductive voice what they should do now. With a smile that ran a shiver up his spine, she bit her lip and huskily replied that Luke was still awake, but that there *was* something that he could do in the meantime …

*

A rumbling sound began to build, from distant murmur to thundering rattle. With a *whip-crack*, a bolt was drawn back. Several groaning creaks signified the stop-start opening of a reluctant door.

Danny Morrigan, creator of universes, slayer of witch-goddesses, saviour of a nation, reversed into the back alley, dragging the wheelie bin behind him. As it rocked dangerously from side to side while Ellie watched smugly from the kitchen, Danny raised a middle finger in salute to his future wife. She blew him a kiss.

It was almost midnight, but the skies above blazed with light from over two hundred miniature suns. The alley, once a scene of darkness and squat shapes promising scuttling terrors, was brightly lit. For one absurd moment, Danny wanted to burst into song. His baby boy was back. His girlfriend – no, his *fiancée* – was the most amazing woman on the planet. The air was warm. Myths and legends were real. The world was full of magic–

'Would you ever *fuck the fuck away off* bringin' that cunting bin out!' a voice cried out. Danny looked up to see the Fat Controller screaming at him from his back window. 'Fuckin' big rattlin' bastard! How am I s'posed to fuckin' sleep, eh? Them bastardin' things in the fuckin' sky?'

'Fuckin' blackout curtains my hole!' another voice drifted from a few doors down. 'Fuckin' twelve quid down the chute!'

'I LOVE THIS TOWN!' Danny cried out, and then bolted for his back door as large objects began to rain down on him.

The Future

The child awoke, her mother and father beside her. She reached for them and they placed a hand each upon her shoulders, calming her as the Origin slowly unwound from her cerebral cortex.

'Welcome back, smelly head,' Steve said softly.

'You're a smelly head,' she told him, and stuck her tongue out. Clearing her head with a quick shake, she sat up, propping her pillows behind her. Her parents seemed to sense she needed time to process, time to breathe.

'Danny did it,' she said. 'He and Dother. They worked together.'

'Yes,' Maggie nodded. 'At the start it was just phone calls and video, but eventually they were able to open portals between Ireland Above and Ireland Below.'

The child made a face. 'Pffffew, "Ireland Below". I *hate* that name. When did they change it?'

'To Ériu? Not long after you were born.'

'Ériu. I used to love that name,' the child said. 'Now I'm not so sure,' and she could see her mummy and daddy trying not to laugh at this.

'It was his idea.'

'Uncle Danny?'

'Mmm. He seemed to think it was something she would have wanted.'

'The Morrigan,' the child said.

'Yes. Personally I think he just didn't want his name attached to it in case it was shit ...' she added, somewhat under her breath.

'And after the portals, that's when people started to flip?'

'They realised they didn't need portals to step through. They could just will themselves to move from one world to the other. Even the ones left behind originally.'

'Like you and Daddy?'

'Like me and Daddy.'

'But not the wolves?'

'No, not the wolves. They couldn't take the sunlight. But they didn't mind. Ériu was theirs, for them and their children ...' and the mother's voice was weary in a bemused way. 'Their many, many, *many* children.'

'Like Rascal and Bosco?' the child said. Maggie *harrumphed* indignantly.

'Yes, like them two wee ...' she said, remembering the state of her living room rug after it had been pissed on and mated with last time they'd cub-sat. 'Like them, yes.'

'They did a wee-wee on our rug didn't they, Mummy?' the child said earnestly.

'Yes, love. Yes they did.'

The child giggled, but not for as long or as hard as once she might have. There were other questions to ask. 'Mummy, I saw you tell Daddy you couldn't ever have babies,' she said.

The room temperature plummeted as Steve panicked. The child sighed, and raised it back up herself, casting him the sort of look only little girls can truly master.

Steve grimaced. 'Sorry.'

'I'm sorry, love,' said Maggie. 'It's part of the Origin. That's why we weren't sure if you were old enough.'

'So if you couldn't have babies, where did I come from?' the child asked.

Steve and Maggie looked at one another for a long time. Eventually it was her daddy who spoke. 'You were a gift,' he said. 'When magic came back, dangerous and wonderful and all that, it made things possible again. All of the love me and your mummy felt for one another, it became a person. It became you.'

'I was ... born?'

Maggie laughed. 'Yes!' she said. 'God, yes, you were born! Thirty-seven hours of agonising labour can attest to that. Back in them days we hadn't quite figured out magical epidurals.'

The child breathed a sigh of relief. So many other questions swirled around in her head but, to her astonishment, a yawn that could only be described as epic decided to work itself to the surface.

'God, it's half past two in the fucking morning!' Maggie said, no longer caring about watching her language in front of her child. 'Get to sleep. You've had the entire Origin story, young lady, two or three years before you're supposed to hear it as well. Want to know what happened next? Fuckin' going to sleep happened next!'

The little girl tutted in disappointment. 'I need to pee,' she said instantly.

Maggie frowned for a second. 'There,' she said, producing a handful of rose petals from a curled fist, the former contents of her daughter's bladder.

'Teach me to do that! Teach me to do that!'

'Not tonight,' Steve said gently. He tucked her in securely, took her hand, took her mother's hand … and flipped.

The light streaming in from outside died as, in a heartbeat, they travelled from Ireland to Ériu, as easily as moving from one idea to the next – because after all, what was Ériu if not an idea of a place?

'Listen,' Maggie said, raising a finger. Distantly, a wolf howled in the night. 'See? Keeping you safe. Keeping us all safe.'

'I know, Mummy,' the little girl said. She was fighting sleep now, to her eternal chagrin. She tried to sit up and was gently encouraged to abandon the attempt.

'So, what did you think of it?' Steve asked her.

'Magical,' she said.

'Because of all the faeries and the magic? Because of the witch and the wolves?'

She smiled. 'I'd forgotten about them.'

'My wee woman,' her daddy said softly, 'I am so proud of you. Now come on, time for sleep.'

But their daughter was already gone, sometime between 'so proud' and 'come on'. Not the sleep of the story bubble – true, deep sleep had claimed her. Given all that she had witnessed, it was not outlandish to expect her to sleep for a day or two. Schools were understanding where the Origin was involved.

'Goodnight, Regan,' Steve whispered, and kissed her lightly

on the forehead.

There were scrabbling noises from the roof above. Maggie opened the bedroom window, leaning out to glance upward. 'If you have to roost up there could you at least not try to shite all down the fuckin' windows!'

They moved into their own bedroom and Steve went to shut the curtains, exchanging a respectful nod with Larka, currently camped out in their front garden, Rascal and Bosco two little shadows curled up beside her. He kissed Maggie. 'Honour guard all present and correct.'

'Roof's covered in crows,' Maggie said. 'As per fuckin' usual.'

They got under the covers together, cuddled, kissed. It hadn't been easy these past years. Maggie could still remember the feeling of emptiness that had terrified her that first night she and Steve had spent together after the worlds had separated. Despite the magic and the monsters now loose upon the world, real life was never a fairy tale. Sometimes, though, it got close enough not to matter.

'We're the parents of the reborn Goddess of War,' she said. 'What's that make us?'

Steve grinned. 'Haven't you been listening all this time, love?' he said. 'It makes us fuckin' *legends*.'

THE END

Acknowledgements

As ever, massive thanks to everyone at Blackstaff, particularly the awesome Michelle and the frankly worryingly (albeit loveably) bonkers Stuart.

This trilogy simply would not have happened without the support and belief of people like Jo Sayer at Last Passage, my gorgeous wife Kath (yup, made an honest woman out of her) and my two boys, Laurence and Adam.

Coming soon, by the way – so Laurence informs me! – is *Folk'd Off*, the fourth book in the series, written by him. I've even read the first few pages, and honestly, there was just something in my eye. Ahem.

Hanging out with Danny and Ellie and Steve has been so much fun and I'm grateful and privileged that others have enjoyed it too.

THE FIRST INSTALMENT IN THE
BRILLIANT *FOLK'D* TRILOGY

eBook
EPUB ISBN 978-0-85640-239-5
KINDLE ISBN 978-0-85640-240-1

Paperback
ISBN 978-0-85640-918-9

www.blackstaffpress.com

THE SECOND INSTALMENT IN THE
EXCITING *FOLK'D* TRILOGY

eBook

EPUB ISBN 978-0-85640-543-3
KINDLE ISBN 978-0-85640-555-6

Paperback
ISBN 978-0-85640-922-6

www.blackstaffpress.com